COLLEGE TOWN

Doug Vinson and June Vinson

ISBN: 0692918078
ISBN 13: 9780692918074
Library of Congress Control Number: 2017910907
Legacy Publications, Newnan, GA

PROLOGUE

"The South – where the past is always present."

William Faulkner

"Memory...Strange that the mind will forget so much of what only this moment has passed, and yet hold clear and bright the memory of what happened years ago, of men and women long since dead... There is no fence nor hedge around time that is gone. You can go back and have what you like of it, if you can remember... Men like my father cannot die. They are with me still, real in memory as they were in flesh. Loving and beloved forever."

Huw Morgan from the 1937 Academy Award winning film *"How Green Was My Valley."*

PREFACE

I t may not have been Camelot, but our Southern college town during the '60s and '70s was mighty close.

"College Town" is a true labor of love. June and I wanted to write something that captured "the way we were." Our story is *your* story – about *your* college years, "the best four years of your life," set in one of the greatest college towns in the country. Although the plot and some of the characters are fictitious, most of the intriguing tales in the following pages are true or based on actual people and events. The book's a lively beach read, chock-full of great memories and humor.

Caricatures of college days like "Animal House" certainly have an element of truth, but they don't tell the *whole* story. Our book is an authentic, yet lighthearted look at those college years from an "average" guy from a "normal" family who grew up in the shadow of the university.

We Baby Boomers grew up in a world that's long gone. One with traditional families and real neighborhoods. As youngsters, we played outdoors, rode our bikes for hours and cooked up great adventures. And in the summer, after mowing the lawn, it was back to baseball with the neighborhood kids or an afternoon at the local pool. Our dreams flourished in that environment. We really believed we could be astronauts or big league ballplayers – the sky was the limit.

Our imaginations were stronger and more vivid than any 3D or virtual reality gadgets of today. But now, even in the slower moving South, we don't take much time for reflection in our Instant Grits and Instagram world – and that's unfortunate.

Later, we headed off to college and faced sweeping changes that shaped us, tested us and ushered in a new era. It was a turbulent time. And, here in Athens, The University of Georgia and the town are so intertwined that new ideas and different viewpoints always kept your mind percolating. And when you throw in fabulous football, a vibrant music scene and tons of Southern charm, you'll understand why Athens is the quintessential college town.

But how *good* were the "Good Ole Days?" Weren't there glaring examples of social injustice at home and conflicts abroad? Sure there were – and those things should be and have been analyzed in dozens of books and movies. But it's refreshing to remember "the rest of the story" and enjoy an amusing book that takes you back to your moment in time.

If you're only focusing on the warts and the wrongs of those years, you may miss the forest for the trees. You risk forgetting the good times, the positives, and the beautiful. Sometimes we should just look back and laugh, ponder a thing or two, and embrace the good without trying to digest another weighty PBS documentary. In the end, true, heartfelt, collective memories are what bind us together as a community and a nation.

So what's so special about this place? College towns are known for their mix of intriguing characters and Athens was bursting at the seams with them. They were just as much a part of the town as the stadium and the old drug store and our engaging narrative connects you with the best of them.

Every UGA Dawg has his day... so many memories... a quiet walk across old North campus in spring, a chili dawg at the Varsity, dorm buddies, cramming all night for exams, hoping to meet "The One" and (trying to get rid of the *wrong* one), going to incredible concerts at the Coliseum or Legion Field and great parties *every* weekend. Changing your major three times, *plus* trying to figure out what you were going to do with your life before "senior panic" set in. And who can forget the smell of fresh cut turf from the football fields or hearing the Redcoat Marching Band practice when fall rolled around?

You only have to mention a familiar phrase, or hear an old song to get you drifting back. *Can it really be that long ago? No way.* As the cliché goes, nostalgia "isn't what it used to be." Looking at the past through rose colored glasses or now through 2.5 readers... (*By the way dear, where did I put those things...? They're around here somewhere.*) can get a little fuzzy. But come back with us "and remember when."

"College Town" is a "love story" recalling a unique time and a wonderful place. Camelot? Well, King Arthur may have said it best, "In short, there's simply not, a more congenial spot..."

TABLE OF CONTENTS

Cover design by Britt Schaefer
Back cover photo by Gordon Haws

THE YELLOW BRICK ROAD

W ill could barely breathe. His body was slammed into the plate glass doors so fast that his feet dangled a few inches off the concrete floor. He couldn't move a muscle. All those stories of stampede riots at soccer matches or wild concerts flashed through his mind. He imagined the headline in the local paper. "UGA student sustains serious injuries – crushed at Elton John concert." The odds of a couple of broken ribs and maybe a ruptured spleen were increasing. But why did he have to be crushed by these two hefty nerds reeking of Boone's Farm wine and B.O and not those gorgeous girls to his right?

What would James Bond do? Cool and debonair were out – for goodness sakes – it took all he had just to inhale and exhale. He hung in suspended animation for what seemed like an eternity.

Finally, the campus police waded through the masses and pushed back the sea wave surge that penned Will and other eager fans to the glass doors ringing the Stegemen Coliseum. Restoring a semblance of order, they at long last opened the doors to the arena.

Will stumbled into the lobby, slowly emerging from his sardine can position as he desperately clung to his front row press pass. He was covering the much anticipated "Yellow Brick Road" tour of England's "Mad Man Across the Water" for the student newspaper. Thrilled to be in one piece, he settled into his seat.

Elton John pounced on his gaudy grand piano, masterfully moving over the keys, and belted out the lyrics for over two hours.

The crowd roared with the opening notes and knew the words of every hit by heart, from the silly to the sublime. They sung and swayed right along with each song.

"Saturday! Saturday! Saturday night's all right! (Nobody had to tell UGA students that Saturday night was all right. They demonstrated that every weekend!) The ecstatic fans yelled out the phrase over and over and danced in the aisles on the ground floor level as Elton egged them on.

Tonight, everything was simply marvelous. One hit after another, performed with tremendous passion and style.

The roadies and stage hands earned every penny they were paid. The lights, the music – not to mention the album quality sound for each song blasting through huge pyramids of speakers – all combined to transform the massive concrete cavern (built for basketball, agricultural shows, and commencements) into a pulsating audio and visual extravaganza, immersing the audience in the experience.

Students knew instinctively that graduation day would roll around all too fast and once they were handed their diplomas and walked off that stage they'd be saying goodbye to the "Yellow Brick Road" and to one of the greatest college towns in the nation. Then, shedding their comfortable cocoon, they'd venture into the dreaded real world. So tonight they were "grabbing all the gusto they could get."

Being squashed like a bug was a small price to pay for a priceless night of memories.

Athens was a place everyone loved...and no one wanted to leave. What's not to love? A quaint Southern town that's home to a major university. But to Will, it was simply home. Not many young folks give much thought to their old home town... familiarity gets in the way. But now that he was older, he understood what everyone else already knew – the true charm of this amazing place. He realized more than ever that this vibrant college town was part of him and he'd always be part of it.

Will worked into the morning hours to capture the fabulous concert as best he could. After all, this music was the backdrop of his college years and one day would evoke a flood of great memories. He tucked the papers in a folder to turn in to his editor.

The crisp, sun-kissed morning was one of those magnificent gifts of October. The oppressive heat and humidity of August had given way to the beauty and magic of fall. Will drove through the narrow streets of Athens, along Milledge

Avenue where majestic antebellum homes lined the road. Lush lawns, stately columns and porches with rows of rocking chairs conjured up images of Southern hospitality and heritage. Sororities and fraternities had claimed many for their own and breathed new life into the old mansions. Students overflowed sidewalks and bus stops. And everyone felt "Forever Young."

Traveling down Broad Street, Will passed by a cluster of eclectic eateries filled with outdoor diners savoring the beauty of the season. At one table, a pair of "young scholars" talked intently, pausing only to sip their drinks. Probably a couple of intellectuals (real or imagined) grappling with some profound issue of the day.

In a few minutes he turned by the student center where all kinds of people stirred up interest in the free speech area. The Hari Krishnas chanted away in long white robes next to a dozen or so shaggy-haired demonstrators who marched around with signs protesting another misdeed of "the Establishment." Athens was full of fascinating folks and ideas all within a few square miles – it kept an aspiring feature writer spinning with story possibilities.

Will Andrews was thoroughly stricken with the blight to write. It was the early '70s and he was now in his junior year in the University of Georgia's School of Journalism. And as a writer for The Red and Black, Will was definitely in his element and out to make the most of it.

Will's editor took the folder and got straight to business. "OK. Ready for print?"

"Yeah, and, man, it was great. You shoulda been there."

Sue interrupted, "Good enough. But there's a lot more to cover around here. I'm gonna give you a couple of short ones. Write up the next student government meeting. Then by Friday, do something on the rising costs of textbooks." Her rapid fire instructions didn't give Will a chance to say much.

Sue was no nonsense. Her short cropped hair and nondescript clothes mirrored her obsession with efficiency. But the hard driving overachiever also possessed an uncanny instinct for a good story.

"OK. Sure thing."

Obviously the talking time was over. Will realized he was starving and had just enough time to meet up with the guys for a snack.

The Guys

Ed and Ronnie secured their usual table at the Memorial Grill and a few minutes later, John arrived – looking a bit grim, even for a Monday. These were *the guys*; and they'd all been friends since first grade at Barrow School.

"OK, home game with Clemson this week, all in?" Ed said.

"Wouldn't miss it," John answered.

Will turned to Ronnie. "What about you? Pledge duties?"

"Have to pass. Bunch of alums are throwin' a big tailgate, can't give up all that food."

Ronnie never missed a good time. He employed his charm and good looks to do pretty much what he wanted. His Lacoste shirt hugged his chiseled body, showing off bulging muscles developed from years of high school football. He was only halfway listening to the conversation because his attention was clearly elsewhere. The young hunk was totally into the ladies passing by. He sat back and checked them out, basking in waves of inviting smiles that came his way.

"That's three of us and the usual tagalongs. Will, how 'bout gettin' there early and stake out our spot?" said Ed.

"Sure."

John was unusually quiet.

"You all right, man?" Ed asked

"Yeah, I guess, barely making it in algebra," John slumped even further down in his chair.

Ronnie shook his head. "Man, my Dad would kill me if I failed a class. What'll your parents do?

"Who knows, they're pretty out of it," said John, "They don't really care."

All the other guys had grown up in fairly solid homes, but John's family struggled. His dad worked long shifts at the textile mill, trying his best to make ends meet. John's real passion was music. He loved playing an old guitar he'd acquired for a few dollars at a yard sale. The oldest of several brothers and sisters, he'd essentially raised himself – except for the neighborhood.

Back then, everyone had real neighborhoods and families actually knew each other. During their younger days, the moms looked out for John and made enough ham sandwiches on white Sunbeam bread to share with him and any hungry kid who showed up at their screen door.

Youngsters rode their bikes around the tree-lined streets and did this very novel activity – *they went outdoors to play* – where all kinds of marvelous adventures awaited – especially for those with a lively imagination.

They'd race down the steep hill on Gran Ellen Drive to Memorial Park and on languid summer days, the kids cooled off in the creek and chased crawdads and salamanders. Later, the chill of winter brought its own season of fun. No one thinks about winter sports in Georgia, but the guys enjoyed some unique Southern-style sledding. They'd pull out an old piece of cardboard as their make-shift sled and head to their favorite hill. To the uninitiated, it was quite peculiar, but sliding down a super slick bank of dried kudzu made for a very fun afternoon.

On other days, the woods turned into a battleground - full of barricades, barbed wire and danger at every turn. The gallant marauders hurled pinecone grenades and dirt clog missiles in fierce combat. But when the tide of battle turned, it was time to escape. They zigzagged their way to safety through briars and bramble, slid under logs and scrambled over fallen oaks. Swinging on a sturdy vine, they crossed the creek and, one by one, crash landed on the bank, declaring another victory.

The grumbling of empty stomachs signaled it was time to end the day's exploits. They rushed home just in time for supper and popped through the side door, ready for the kitchen strip down and bath. With a covering of dirt from head to toe and assorted debris stuck in their hair, they looked like kids auditioning for a Tide commercial. Finally, the bath water washed away all the marks of a terrific day.

The four friends shared a history. But by far the strongest bond among them was forged on the field where they played – the old sandlot field. Others saw it as weed-infested wasteland behind the water reservoir tank – between Milledge Terrace and Lumpkin. But for the guys, it was their Sanford Stadium. The sheer fun and camaraderie from those football and baseball games was hard to convey to an outsider. The turf was a delicate blend of weeds, briars, and a few stumps jutting out of rock hard red Georgia clay. But they leveled it and raked it and loved what they'd created. No sign up sheets, no meddlesome adults, no expensive uniforms.

The all-star athletes just showed up in their worn Levi jeans, Keds and white T shirts and played until they were all played out. Crushed cans and pieces of ripped up boxes marked the out of bounds and goal lines. Intense competition went on for hours... fueled by high octane sweet tea, Kool-aid, and warm water from the garden hose. After a full day, the best place for a post-game celebration was Add Drugstore. They rode their bikes to Five Points and forked over 10 cents at the counter for a Coke or an ice cream cone. One of the young athletes turned poet said it best, "The field where we played, that's where memories were made."

Chance Romance
Will had been around long enough to know that geology 101 (or *rocks for jocks*) was the best way for a liberal arts guy to meet his science requirement. And the *best* way to get *back* to the journalism building was hopping on a bus, one of those gleaming goliaths that so impressively negotiates the narrow streets of Athens. UGA boasts that it has the biggest fleet of campus buses in the country and they really do run like clockwork.

Everybody has their bus stories – some quite memorable. "There's nothing new under the sun" is very true in life and even more so in cross campus travels. And mass transit mishaps are no respecter of persons – you missed the bus to your final exam that's *way* across campus and there's no way to make it on foot. When you jump onboard and spill your backpack all over creation – it is, of course, during a torrential rain. And probably worst of all, the same obnoxious rider sits next to you every day on the 8 am zombie run down Milledge Avenue.

It was pretty much the same routine everyday – the swish of air brakes, the smell of diesel fumes – the scramble for the doors – carefully edging to the front of the line with backpacks jostling. Then standing wall-to-wall with several others clinging precariously to a steel pole with one hand while you wolf down a bite to eat. Or maybe you just ride alone with your own thoughts, bouncing to the herky-jerky movements of the bus while the driver tries to avoid jaywalking students.

"Please step up... and move away from the doors... step up... and *MOVE away from the doors!...*"

Drivers had different ways of complimenting the experience. Some tolerated the students with indifferent silence, others got to know you – engaging passengers with an exuberant "Hi honey, how ya doing!"

Today, Will plopped down for his usual ride when a beautiful young girl squeezed in right beside him – mainly because no other seat was available.

Could it be? Like those mysterious, random encounters in old movies – a chance romance. It happens, right? Will cleared his throat and tried to think of something suave to say, but before he could flaunt his coolness, the vision of loveliness started talking. And talking and talking some more – non-stop. And everything was *cute* – the ubiquitous word she used to describe *everything* – people, articles of clothing, things that happened. Then he got a full de-briefing on how her day was going, and her friends, the soap opera she followed, problems with her beaus, her cat's digestive issues, favorite hobbies, and where she got those shoes. She paused only long enough to take a breath, apparently to avoid asphyxiation. With her litany of news briefs out of the way, she went on to focus on her crowning achievement – winning the Miss Honeysuckle pageant back home. Her syrupy, sing-song voice droned on and by the time the ride ended, Will realized he never got to say a *single* word. But he did nod a lot.

Of course, the real tragedy, from Will's perspective, was that there was no time for him to talk about himself. She'd missed how clever he was and hearing him brag about an exaggerated athletic feat or two.

Alas…she got off at the Brumby stop. "Wailll it wasss *SO* nice talkin' to you! I really enjoyed *our* conversation. You have yeurself a real nice day now*! Bye Bye!*"

So much for a chance romance…

Game Day on the Tracks
Saturday rolled around again.

The guys weren't always prepared for class, but getting ready for game day was an altogether different matter.

This week, Clemson dared to take on the Dawgs and everyone expected to glory in another solid "whupping."

10

The friends headed to their favorite seats, but they were not in the stadium. They made their way up the hill to the ever popular railroad tracks that overlooked Sanford Stadium. This untamed territory was a great place to see the game, and with its mishmash of rowdy fans; it was also an experience in itself.

The guys proudly counted themselves among the railroad regulars, devoted Dawg fans, second to none in zeal. They sat and slid on the hard baked clay in the scorching sun and chilly winds. The crowd pressed in and quickly filled up the site making folks work hard to keep their footing and avoid the peril of a downhill dive.

Everyone knew the unwritten code of this revered ground, so they made sure to secure their place early. Blankets and coolers filled the hill claiming territory. Many die-hard fans even camped out the night before to stake out their favorite spot. They unwittingly employed the strategy of an old general who said, "The object is to get there the firstis with the mostest." (Who said you can't learn something *practical* from a history class?)

But when the red and silver buses pulled up, everyone jumped to their feet. Cheers reached a fevered pitch as the Georgia team, decked out in jerseys, helmets in hand, filed by and took the steps down to the war zone. Nothing pumped them up more for battle than the outpouring of unbridled passion from this crowd. (Some players even said they wished they could stay up on the tracks "and party with the best of 'em.")

The renowned Coach Erk Russell loved the track fans. "Oh I know they do some crazy things – like turning over opponent's buses – but they do stamp out Kudzu and love the Dawgs almost as much as I do. When you get off the bus to their cheers, it's impossible not to be inspired. They choke me up."

The assortment of fans was a great melting pot. A family reunion. A miniature Woodstock. Freaks and Greeks, pretty petite picnickers, dorm buddies. Sometimes several generations gathered in their same area year after year.

"Express yourself," declared the song. So they did - American flags, fraternity flags and signs of all kinds flapped proudly in the breeze for thousands to see. The guys waved their own spray-painted renderings on bedsheets and cardboard all urging UGA to victory.

Game time finally came. Texas A&M may have had their famous "12ᵗʰ man in the stands" with cadets in full uniform cheering the Aggies on. But the Dawgs had their own unmatched fans - the track people who implored their heroes on to gridiron glory. No bleachers, people just stood and whooped and hollered until victory was declared. The rambunctious crowd on the hill also provided a very entertaining sideshow for those inside the stadium. But paying patrons were also quick to admit their envy as they watched the folks up there revel in their freedom from all the rules and regs of ticketed seats.

The authorities were smart enough not to venture into this enclave but fans always enforced a couple of rules of their own. First, no one from the opposing side was to set foot there. Any violators were promptly turned back by a barrage of colorful insults and the threat of a crushed beer can or two landing on their heads. And if, on occasion, a territorial dispute arose, they settled it among themselves – and it usually had something to do with the exchange of a beverage.

Game or no game, the trains kept rolling. Besides the "Midnight Train to Georgia," an afternoon Norfolk Southern regularly rambled down the rails. The conductor announced its arrival with a huge horn blast (which folks claimed was "louder than an obnoxious Tech fan") that triggered a mad rush to get out of the way.

Folks headed to lower ground for safety and Ed described the result as "a live demonstration of the philosophical slippery slope argument – a human landslide." The domino effect was especially in full force if some well lubricated fans were more wobbly than usual.

The guys looked around for John who was known to be accident prone. Everyone was relieved that he'd successfully dodged the iron horse. But with all his scrambling, he inadvertently planted his foot right into a lady's potato salad and leveled an entire family. The guys quickly helped everyone to their feet and dusted John off. All in all, it was a great day.

Oh sure, the safety issues of this unconventional seating arrangement were often debated. City officials, UGA and the railroad barons went round and round in discussions.

But after many a game day spent up on the tracks, the guys all agreed that luxuriating in the President's box couldn't compare to the sheer joy of being one of the faithful fans on the hill.

Will struggled with his usual morning malaise. The thought of sitting through a day of classes after the exciting events of the weekend was downright dismaying.

The victory over Clemson was still on his mind and made it tough to face another day of lectures. But he was paying good money for this education so at least he had to show up for class. When he finally roused himself and threw on some clothes, one comforting thought hit him. His first class wasn't a dud but taught by a prof who was very much worth listening to.

If anyone could awaken a sleep-walking student, it was Dr. McDuffie. In his mid-30s, he appeared even younger. Nothing nerdy about this guy: good-looking with a full crop of brown wavy hair and a rugged build. He'd come to Athens a couple of years ago with a Ph.D. from the prestigious media program at Columbia University. First impressions may have left folks underestimating his intellect, but when he spoke it didn't take long to realize his depth of knowledge on a wide range of issues. Everyone admired his remarkable blend of idealism and common sense. The course was "Media and Society"...sounds boring, but the man who taught it made it anything but.

Dr. Mac was just the spark students needed to ignite their thinking. The guy was high energy and his infectious enthusiasm kept everyone tuned into the topic at hand.

The prof wrapped up his insightful analysis of the Pentagon Papers incident. Several months ago The New York Times published information obtained from classified documents at the Defense Department on the Vietnam War. It dominated the headlines, stirring great concern among doves and hawks alike. Vietnam had divided the country for years, but now people on both sides of the issue were upset that such high level military discussions were so publically exposed. What's more, the documents clearly showed the serious doubts of top military brass about involving the U.S. to begin with. It was interesting stuff, especially as the dynamic Dr. Mac laid it out. Students appreciated how he handled tough topics objectively and resisted coloring them with his own progressive political views.

Dr. Mac summarized the heart of the issue. "What this comes down to is the tension between the public's right to know verses national security. So journalists have to make hard decisions on how to handle sensitive information."

THE CLASSIC CITY

Will had all he could take of his last class which had degenerated into more preaching than teaching from the overwrought Dr. Hall. The "amen corner" comprised of the professor's protégées on the front row just added to his frustration. One fueled the other until most students realized that the actual course content had been totally abandoned somewhere along the way. As a prominent faculty member, Dr. Peter Hall took an extra measure of digressional liberties – rehashing his own pet views in "Journalism – Special Topics."

But on paper, the prof's credentials were impressive – Ivy League undergrad, Ph.D. from a prominent university in the Northeast and several published papers on cutting edge issues. An aloof man, in his late 30s, he usually wore a tattered corduroy jacket and earth shoes. He openly scoffed at the traditions and ways of Southern culture causing folks to speculate why he'd come to Georgia in the first place. Turned out he'd skipped a tour in the Peace Corps to come help enlighten the South. One Athens's citizen was convinced that the professor had formed his view of the state by "watching too many episodes of 'Hee Haw.'" When Dr. Hall arrived, he made sure to position himself on, not *one* requisite committee, but *three* and quickly made use of his newfound influence.

Will and Ed were more than happy to break for lunch and venture off campus for a change of scenery and food. Will thought some fresh air and a visit downtown might clear his head. They rambled up a couple of blocks on Broad, past the old Varsity and couldn't resist stopping at one of their favorite haunts, Barnett's Newsstand on College Street. Out on the sidewalk, racks of newspapers and magazines were strategically placed to lure passersbys in to browse and buy a couple of items. The heart pine boards creaked as the two walked in and promptly side-stepped a portly gentleman purchasing his favorite box of cigars. The newsstand was a cozy place with well-worn counters and floors giving the store a very familiar and comfortable feel.

Will didn't know where to start as he stood before a large array of publications. But Ed knew – he automatically reached for the New York Times, checking out the latest column by James Reston.

"Will, listen to this," he read, "'All politics are based on the indifference of the majority.' Makes you wonder if that's how Nixon got elected in the first place, and here we are, in this Watergate mess."

"Yeah, that says it. I think Reston's on to something."

Ed was deep in thought, looking intently at the newspaper. "This guy really knows what's happenin'. Man, can he nail the issues."

Will offered an "uh, huh," but wasn't really paying attention as he zeroed in on his own brand of writing. He thumbed through the Atlanta Journal for Lewis Grizzard's latest column then interrupted his friend's musings with a chuckle. Ed looked up.

"OK, time for some insight from my guy." He read, "I'm the only person in the history of Moreland, Ga. to ever be on the New York Times Best Seller list. I'm the only person from Moreland, Ga. who ever *heard* of the NY Times Best Seller list." Ed laughed but clearly was somewhere else.

A thoughtful and serious sort, Ed was genuinely concerned about national events and politics. Through his hard work, he'd earned a position as a regular columnist on The Red and Black and also served as scholarship chair for his fraternity. Heading back to campus, they passed numerous specialty shops and eateries and watched motorists jockeying for an elusive parking spot. Some businesses were old and established with deep ties to the community, others were new and trendy.

Dodging traffic, they crossed Broad Street, the main thoroughfare in the city that borders the university. Leaving behind the bustling downtown you enter The University of Georgia. Sunlight sifting through clusters of beautiful magnolia and oak trees cast deep shadows over old North Campus bordered by an elegant wrought iron fence built, at the time, to keep neighboring cows from roaming in. This pastoral enclave was the original college well over 200 years ago.

And there in front of you is the Arch – faithfully marking the entrance to campus. The iconic forged iron structure had evoked admiration and pride from students across generations. The steps are now uneven and worn down more on the outside of the Arch because of a long-standing tradition that students aren't allowed to walk *through* it until they graduate. And back a few decades ago, if folks got careless, there was the "Vigilance Committee" made up of upper classmen who stepped in and administered a good paddling to non-compliers.

The three pillars of the Arch are patterned after the state seal. Each pillar represents one of the founding principles of UGA: "Wisdom, Justice and Moderation." But many would argue that students got their real mission statement from the incomparable soul group, The Tams –*"Be Young! Be Foolish! Be Happy!"*

Walking among the historic buildings and stately lampposts, Will's friend grew even quieter. Ed was already contemplating his next column, spurred on by the words of Mr. Reston.

Tailgating

This Saturday, whatever plans Will had for the game were scratched when Sue assigned him to cover the "most creative tailgate" competition. But what's to complain about? Nobody had to twist his arm to write about something he'd loved all his life – the hallowed tradition of tailgating.

Fans flooded the grounds and parking lots around Sanford Stadium – the countdown to the game was on. The spirited fans knew exactly how to prime themselves for kickoff. Pre-game hours were filled with lots of good eating and drinking and cavorting. And today, UGA folks ratcheted up their efforts and barred no expense. And the conditions were perfect.

Fall was simply spectacular in Athens. A stunning array of glorious autumn leaves adorned the hills in brilliant color. Overhead hung a cloudless sky that was the perfect hue of blue.

All the old familiar sights and sounds that welcome a Bulldawg home hit Will as he neared the site – fans hollerin' "Go Daaawgs!," non-stop chatter and clouds of smoke from the grills mixed with whiffs of beer, cigarettes and cigars. All around, radios were cued up to the incomparable voice of Larry Munson giving his pre-game rundown – others blasted hit after hit. It was clear that the Bulldawgs had come to party.

Strolling through tailgate territory was like stepping into another dimension... RVs, campers, gleaming red and black pick-ups and endless cars sporting their UGA flags all squeezed into the beloved grounds – it was a great scene. Everywhere you looked, there were coolers and more coolers. Tailgates were down and loaded with a vast treasure trove of the very best in Southern cuisine. Some laid out their delectable dishes on fine linens; others threw down the time honored picnic blanket and piled on heaping portions of grilled hot dogs, burgers and all the fixins. The last course was the best. Will feasted his eyes on homemade desserts good enough to grace your grandmother's table for Sunday dinner.

Will loved meandering through the sea of red and black. Friends embraced old friends and raised cups, toasting the team and the hopes of another big season – everyone was caught up in a time warp of euphoria that eclipsed the hum-drum of everyday life.

"Will! Right here, man!" Ronnie motioned him over and introduced Will to his pledge brothers. *These freshmen look so young,* he thought. Ronnie had finally made it to UGA after getting his grades up at community college, so it was time to celebrate.

"Hey man the party's on. We're just gettin' started!" Ronnie announced.

"Take it easy, man, it's only 11:30." Will tapped a nearby pledge on the arm, "Keep an eye on him for me, will ya?"

The pledge nodded dutifully. He was apparently used to taking orders.

The Greeks were well represented at any UGA game. Dressed in their finery, they were an unmistakable part of the landscape. The gentlemen donned designer shirts and ties for the occasion. And then there were the ladies. A week's worth of preparation definitely paid off. Heads turned as they made their Saturday afternoon debut in stunning outfits.

Later, at half-time, they'd introduce some former football stars on the 50 yard line. Then honor members of the Panhellenic Council, representing the sororities on campus, for raising a record breaking amount for Special Olympics this year. And for the finale, the contest winner would be announced. Word was, to no one's surprise, the SAE moms apparently took it hands down. Without question, nobody tailgated like Southern moms especially those with Greek pedigree themselves. Years of practice from their own SEC college days clearly showed in the lavish display of heirloom tablecloths topped with all manner of fine crystal and china. Centerpieces of silver champagne buckets, freshly polished by the pledges, featured exquisite arrangements with dozens of white roses and magnolia leaves. Will and the photographer tiptoed around the elegant tableau that could have easily made the cover of Southern Living.

Will spotted a friend from high school at yet another sumptuous spread. About 40 people were eating and drinking it up at a long table decked out with all things *Bulldawg.* The guests were a who's who of former athletes and big money football supporters. Tom Marshall was a nice guy, usually sort of quiet, probably because his flamboyant dad was always the center of attention. Jack Marshall slapped Will on the back and turned on the charm.

"Will, great to meet you! Journalism? Got to be fascinating. Need more good men in the business." With a hand on the young man's shoulder, he guided Will to the table. "Come on, help yourself. Food's here and drinks over there. Go for it!"

Will thanked him and dug right in. Marshall was one of those guys who instantly made you feel like he was your very best friend.

Marshall was a prominent UGA alum who'd been an outstanding cornerback and all SEC two years. Since then, he'd enjoyed a promising career as an investment guy at a leading brokerage firm in town. Then a couple of years ago, he struck out on his own, going great guns ever since. Alums and townsfolk flocked to befriend the man who was famous for throwing the best parties around.

The accomplished Bulldawg was as "a lover of life" and filled his free time with exotic vacations and challenging hobbies – kayaking, rock climbing and his latest classic car.

As he puffed on his long cigar, he described, in great detail, his '61 Jaguar XKE roadster to Will.

"Will, my man, come by my office next week. We'll take the Jag out. Just hearing about it doesn't do it justice, you gotta experience it."

"Sure. OK, that'd be great."

As he left, Mr. Marshall blew out a big puff of smoke. "Now I mean it, hear? If I don't see you by Friday, I might just hunt you down."

Girls on the Gridiron
Will couldn't get thoughts of the Jaguar out of his mind. He'd often spotted it around town but never knew who it belonged to. Classes were done for the day so it was time to check it out up close.

Mr. Marshall's secretary called into his office. "He'll be with you shortly," she said. Will sank comfortably into the plush leather couch and looked over the walls that were covered with photos of Mr. Marshall's travels and adventures and numerous plaques honoring his professional achievements. And of course, the largest picture captured the young, dashing man decked out in his UGA uniform. *What an impressive guy – and so friendly.*

Marshall bounded out of his office, "Will, my man, your timing is perfect. Breaking for a late lunch. You hungry?"

"Yeah. I can eat."

" It'll be a busy afternoon. The stock market's all jittery, so into the close, it gives a guy like me a chance to get in and out and back in again, making some serious money. All right then. She's out back, you ready to ride?"

Will followed through the back door. "Sure thing."

And there it was, the dazzling 1961 Jaguar XKE in gleaming British racing green with tan leather interior. Will jumped into the passenger seat.

They drove a few blocks, well over the speed limit, and swung into a parking lot marked by a gargantuan red V. In his red jacket and signature hat, the Varsity server bellowed out the familiar… "Whadaya have?, Whadaya have?"… and in a few minutes, brought them their chili dogs, onion rings and frosted orange drinks. Mr. Marshall picked up the tab.

He continued to talk and Will took in every detail about the luxurious automobile – the history, the specs – that marvelous engine – that *nobody* could keep tuned. But what did it matter? When the long sleek hood was crowned with the majestic chrome plated Jaguar, ready to pounce and devour any competition.

Will hadn't known Mr. Marshall for long, yet they chatted non-stop. After cars, it was football; last Saturday's game was never far from the mind of any serious fan. The town overflowed with self-proclaimed coaches, so Will and Mr. Marshall got to it. They scrutinized the game, rehashing all the "should ofs" and "if onlys."

"Where you headed now? More classes?"

"No, meetin' some friends on the intramural fields."

"OK, then, I'll just swing over there and drop you off."

Ronnie had jumped at the chance to coach one of the sorority intramural football teams and today, his End Zone Angels went up against the Silver Bullets. It was a great way to meet more ladies and he checked off a pledge duty as well. His usual assistant couldn't make it, so he asked his old friend to help out. An easy decision for Will, as he envisioned a field full of females awaiting him. Confident in his above average athleticism, it was time to make some good impressions – show 'em how it's done.

With several games starting on the fields off College Station Road, Will looked through the crowd and finally found Ronnie going over last minute strategy with his team. Will was all smiles as he checked out the ladies who looked so demure in their pastel lettered jerseys, politely waiting for kick-off. This was shaping up to be a very promising afternoon – the girls were sure to need some really *good* coaching.

But as soon as the ball was in the air, the Angels came out roaring. Their quarterback had a great arm, throwing one completion after the other putting them up by two touchdowns in short order.

Will had his hands full trying to keep the special teams straight – 13 to 14 confused players ran around the field in all directions. He corralled the extras back to the sidelines and the game continued.

He'd assumed the girls were just out for a fun time – but soon realized he was dead wrong. Tempers flared on both sides as the game deteriorated into more of a brawl. The Angels were out to *crush* the competition.

Ronnie called out play after play, then looked at Will, "Pretty impressive, eh, coach? This team knows how to ramp up the pressure." He shouted back to his players, "Enough squealing! Get in there and block!"

Will winced at the dirty play and was sure someone was going to get hurt. "Man, don't the refs call 'em on those penalties?"

Ronnie laughed, shaking his head, "That's the fun of it, relax – besides, you couldn't stop 'em if you tried."

Will paced the sidelines nervously. He always enjoyed an intense game but this one had a lot more drama than he'd bargained for.

Ronnie made a slight attempt at comforting him, "Hey, don't worry, we haven't had any real injuries yet."

One of the girls next to Will leaned in. "Not so sure about that. You shoulda been here last week."

"Yeah?"

"Sent a girl to the ER – the blood was awful."

"You're kiddin' me!"

Ronnie quickly chimed in, "C'mon. It's all minor stuff – gashes, a few stitches. No broken bones or nothing, well maybe a finger once."

The girl looked at Will, raising her eyebrows, "I thought this would be so much fun but I watched a few minutes and said *no way*! I'll just stand back here and cheer – where it's safe. There's a lot goin' on out there that you can't even see – and it's not pretty." She took a step back and melted into the crowd.

Maybe she was right. With all the pushing and shoving, it was definitely rough on the field. A sharp whack to the nose sent a girl to her knees. About then, Will figured out what was going on when he noticed spots of blood here and there – those lovely manicured nails had a dual purpose and could stop a play in no time. Amid the subterfuge, the ref tried his best to sort out what all the crying was about. Meanwhile those who were most culpable just stood there smiling innocently.

As the Bullets marched down the field, a piercing screech got everyone's attention. One of the Angels, turned devilish, yanked the ball carrier's hair. It worked – she fumbled and the Angels took possession.

Only one rusher poised any real threat to Will's quarterback, relentlessly storming the backfield on every play. The Angels had had enough of her. The next play was a blur as they were determined "to neutralize her." They succeeded and stopped her cold. She let out the most unearthly wail and grabbed her arm. All eyes were on the injured girl as teammates escorted her off the field. Will rushed over to help and couldn't believe what he saw – *bite marks!* Baffled and horrified, he couldn't remember any playbook that called for *biting* as an offensive measure. The Angel's right guard had indeed stopped the rusher – not with a block – but with a formidable set of molars.

The play resumed and on the crucial third down, the Angels threw a long spiral down field to a wide open receiver, putting them only a yard from the goal line. But the exasperated ref threw a flag and called another penalty, "illegal use of hands!" Will mumbled," Yeah, sure but how'd you miss *illegal use of teeth*"?

It was goal to goal and to seal the win, the Angels steamrolled in for a fourth touchdown.

The ruckus finally stopped when someone called a time out. Both teams huddled. The Bullets motioned the ref over and agreed to call the game as it stood. They'd been battered enough. Final score 28-0.

Will got the picture. If a sorority found it hard to compete in service awards or pageants or academics, they may as well bring out the claws on the intramural fields.

Ronnie was exuberant. He'd coached his team to another questionable victory.

Then Will's angst evaporated as he noticed one of the cheerleaders, a real beauty, looking right at him. To his amazement, she kept gazing at him with an inviting smile. Will was not about to miss this opportunity so he went over and struck up a conversation with Amy. They sat on the grass and chatted long after the others had gone and the field stood empty.

The Protest
It was another Friday night before a home game and the whole town was in party mode. Will and his buddies headed downtown where the music scene beckoned. After a group huddle, Ed and Judy decided on a great little local band where the cover charge was reasonable.

Judy was a reporter for The Red and Black – a dependable, down-home girl who was easy to be with.

"So what you got coming out this week? "Will asked.

Judy sighed, "OK. How's this for boring? Proposed addition to East campus parking lot and the City Council's latest attempt to tighten noise control. Good luck with that."

"Well, somebody's got to cover that stuff and you're good at it," Ed said.

"Thanks, *I guess.*" She turned to Will, not missing a chance to tease him. "Not everyone gets to write about tailgates and partying."

They walked along College Street and passed the old Palace Theater. Will smiled. "Ed! Remember?"

"Oh, yeah."

"That's where we met Raquel."

Judy rolled her eyes, "I know. If I've heard this story once, I've heard it a hundred times!"

Will ignored her – he couldn't resist.

The guys were 12 and had looked forward to the dinosaur movie for weeks. "One Million B.C." – in Technicolor.

Over the years, they'd acquired an impressive collection of plastic toy replicas of the prehistoric creatures and had read most of the books at the library on the subject.

But a few minutes into the movie, the terrifying T. Rex was suddenly bumped from top billing when Raquel Welch made her entrance as a free-spirited cave woman in a skimpy, fur bikini. John spilled his Milk Duds all over the floor. Ed got busy wiping down his glasses. At that moment, the guy's interest in paleontology suddenly began to pale. Watching the leading lady on the big screen proved much more captivating than dinosaurs attacking each other.

And a couple of days later, Will packed up his beloved collection in shoeboxes and shoved them under his bed. (The poor creatures, who'd once roamed freely on the living room rug, now faced a second extinction.)

Raquel may have only had a handful of lines in the movie, but to the guys, it was an Oscar worthy performance.

These days, a lot of guys gravitated to a more caveman lifestyle – throwing off the shackles of social convention – at least in their own unkempt rooms. Not surprisingly, thousands of posters of Raquel, in her famous fur bikini, adorned the living quarters of modern male cave dwellers on campuses across America – and UGA was no exception.

Judy chimed in. "OK, I get it. I remember reading Rousseau. So I'm hangin' out with a couple of 'noble savage' types."

"Something like that," Will said. "This is what the hippies are all about. Right? Keepin' it simple. Back to nature. Maybe they're on to something."

Judy was more than ready to wrap this up and move on to another topic. "So you think you're gonna go around clubbing each other, hunt wild beasts, throw bones over your shoulder and *then* get some babe to marry you?"

"I wouldn't put it *exactly* like that," Will said.

"Well, Rousseau may have been enlightened, but you two remind me more of Fred Flintstone and Barney."

Judy kept a lot on her plate. Besides the paper and a full class load, she was a resident assistant for freshmen girls at Brumby Hall. The guys had coaxed her away from her duties for an evening of fun, something she found little time for.

Turns out, Judy wasn't the only one who needed a night out. For the past few days, Ed had been on quite a rollercoaster. First, his parents dropped the bombshell that after 25 years of marriage, it was over. Ed never saw it coming – everything seemed so normal. But his dad had already moved into an apartment while Mom remained in the family home, for now. They said they just couldn't endure the pretense of another holiday together so both were determined to get on with the divorce. But the thorny financial settlement was another matter.

Later, Ed got some unexpected good news. A prime internship at the Washington Post had popped up and Dr. Mac encouraged him to go for it. This was a big deal, the kind of thing Ed had dreamed about for years. The prof had already pitched him as a strong candidate to a friend who was an editor there.

The concert provided a reprieve from their work and worries.

"That was fantastic – kinda like that Lynyrd Skynyrd concert awhile back," Judy said.

"Yeah, they were great," Ed agreed.

But then the carefree evening changed.

As they turned the corner on the edge of campus they saw that a large mob had taken over the street and sidewalks. The three edged closer to the action and saw lots of signs advocating legalization of marijuana. Apparently the rally had been going all day. The friends listened to a couple of speeches and noticed that quite a few protestors were older. (Like most university towns, Athens had its share of recycled hippies and hangers-on – students who found it difficult to accept graduation and get a job.)

Amid the melee, they caught a glimpse of Simon. Will immediately recognized his familiar voice from Dr. Hall's class and watched as Simon led the crowd with his chants.

Simon was from a prosperous Atlanta family. His dad was a vice president at a large bank and had invested a small fortune in his son's education at one of the city's finest prep schools. But Simon had little use for conventions and high society; instead he preferred hanging out in the hippie district on 14th Street. And that's where he "found himself." (It was also very convenient – you didn't have to travel all the way to San Francisco to put a flower in your hair and make a statement.) Simon wasn't just messing around; he was a true believer who sought to enlighten the masses with his impassioned prose in the radical paper, The Great Speckled Bird. And after a hard day of expounding on the ills of the status quo, Simon spent hours discoursing with like-minded visionaries in coffee houses and head shops. Zealous, sold out and bright – radical leaders recognized him as one to groom for even greater things.

But his dad was none too pleased when his son turned down offers from the likes of Oberlin and William and Mary, and of all the plebian things, enrolled in a public university. Little did Dad know it was only the beginning. Simon was "out to change the world" and UGA's journalism school fit his mission. No more preppy living and country clubbing for him. As soon as he arrived on campus, he jettisoned the trappings of his affluent upbringing – except for his dad's high limit credit card – and adopted a more "earthy" existence. (Deodorant went too –although no one was quite sure why it made the hit list.)

In addition to sincere activists, college rallies always attracted a few loonies and "professional" protestors who gravitated to these events like moths to light and were all too ready to push the boundaries and cause some trouble – and that's exactly what happened.

Things heated up. Demonstrators screamed and shoved, prompting anxious police to move in tighter and brandish batons.

Then someone threw a bottle hitting a student in the chest. Another bottle smashed a window and shards flew, cutting bystanders. The police pressed forward to prevent an all-out riot, but the show of force wasn't helping. Protestors ratcheted up the rhetoric as they cursed and screamed at the "oppressive pigs."

Finally, another unit arrived and their threat to use tear gas caused the mob to back down and weigh their options. University officials and a police negotiator seized the moment to reason with demonstrators and eventually the police pulled back a few steps, but things still remained dicey.

A major sticking point was that no one knew for sure who'd flared up the disturbance – most observers said that the police had over-reacted.

Law enforcement had handled a few protests in this college town from time to time. But sometimes peace demonstrations had ironically turned violent. But this was Broad Street, and not Haight Ashbury. Local cops and liberal hippies found it challenging to experience "harmony and understanding," Age of Aquarius or not.

The three friends stood back at a safe distance but still had a clear view of what was going on. Just then, Will watched a familiar figure in jeans push his way through the mob and jump up on one of the concrete planters. The man gestured to the crowd to quiet down and began talking to the protestors. It was Dr. Mac.

They couldn't make out all he said, but he definitely got everyone's attention. The mob listened and gradually calmed down. Some left and those who stayed began to just mill around and talk among themselves. Dr. Mac hung out and continued to listen to everyone's viewpoint and encourage civil conversation.

"Judy, I think you've got another story," Will said.

They all took a deep breath, realizing it could have ended much differently.

"Yeah, that was a close call. I'm just glad we weren't *part* of the story."

Maybe it was the full moon because the disturbing events of the night weren't yet over.

A frantic girl ran towards them, pleading for help. "Over there." She pointed back to campus. " He came outta nowhere and tried to grab me." "Who?" "He came outta the bushes. Some guy. I was on the sidewalk." She just stood there, staring back at the campus. "Are you hurt?" Judy asked. "No, don't think so." She tried to talk but was out of breath. "It happened so fast."

Judy put her arm around the trembling girl's shoulders and eventually calmed her enough to get the facts straight.

"I was just walking over here to see what was goin' on. Then he lunged at me. I fought and yelled. A couple of guys came up. I guess from between those buildings. When he saw them, he let me go and took off."

Ed and Will walked Judy and the frightened girl back to Brumby. There hadn't been any crime around campus in a good while so the incident was very alarming.

Judy found the girl's RA. They both stood by her as she recounted the harrowing incident to campus police.

Will made it to his feature writing class just as Mr. Reynolds adjusted his bow tie and called roll. The man was a delightful combination of experienced newsman, Southern gentleman and classic professor type. He brought a wealth of hard earned experience as a reporter and editor to the classroom and still loved teaching as much as ever. Now with graying hair, the fatherly professor encouraged and coached many a struggling student.

Standing behind the wooden lectern, he put down the roll book and began one of his inspiring talks on life and journalism:

"Ladies and gentlemen, in your writing careers remember this – if you stay on a steady diet of hard news, you run the risk of ending up with a jaded outlook. Cynicism will creep into everything you write. Let's think about this." He stepped closer to the students. "H. L. Mencken, the noted Baltimore journalist, said: 'A cynic is a person who knows the *price* of everything and the *value* of nothing.' "

As he continued along this vein in his melodious Southern voice, Will witnessed an awakening occur right before his eyes. Many of the budding Pulitzer Prize winners emerged from their normal mental drifting and dreaming. They were actually listening – soaking it in. They weren't the most mature bunch, but they still realized that there was a lot to learn from this wise mentor.

Ed whispered, "Here it comes, a little Grizzard." He knew Will was a big fan.

Lewis Grizzard, the nationally syndicated columnist for The Atlanta Journal, often cited Mr. Reynolds as his most influential teacher. The professor was very fond of his former student, and in turn, used many of his anecdotes to emphasize a point.

He concluded his lecture. "In your own reporting take note of what Grizzard used to say when he made a mistake at the Journal, 'The public more often than not will forgive mistakes, but it will not forgive trying to wiggle and weasel out of one.'" With a wry smile, he added, "And by the way, I can assure you that when Lewis sat in this very classroom, he made his share of mistakes – so you're in good company."

The professor peered over his half-glasses. "And finally, in the coming weeks you'll develop a good eye for human interest profiles. And remember, you're giving someone a voice to tell *their* story. Everyone likes a good story, so go out and find one that resonates with your readers."

Will felt like he was speaking only to him.

BETWEEN THE HEDGES

A my had put about as much preparation into her outfit as the coaches had put into this week's game and it showed. She was absolutely regal in her black dress with just the right splashes of red and her long, dark hair flowing over her shoulders.

The two had spent a lot of time together the past couple of weeks and it was safe to say that Will was smitten. For a long time he'd hoped to find someone and here she was.

Today, they were going in style to the Tennessee game. Mr. Marshall had given Will tickets to some of the best seats in the house, close-up on the 50 yard line.

Tens of thousands of UGA sons and daughters faithfully made the pilgrimage to Sanford Stadium year after year. The couple knew they were *home* when they were greeted by The Redcoat Marching Band as they entered the stadium – brass swaying in sync to the drums – thundering out "Glory,

Glory to Old Georgia." Everyone was swept up in the soul stirring pageantry that is fall and football in the South.

The couple settled into their seats next to Tom Marshall and his date and if first impressions proved true, it'd be a great afternoon. Will gazed at the stately hedges that fans hold so dear and breathed in the aroma of freshly mowed turf from the field. Then he leaned over to whisper in Amy's ear and caught the fragrance of her Chanel # 5. For a minute, it was hard to tell which scent was more intoxicating.

Fans poured in and filled the stadium. Everyone cheered as the mascot, "Uga," took his place on the field. But the English bulldog was much more than a mascot; he was a celebrity in his own right. On Saturdays, his "stylists" groomed and dressed him up in his game day jersey and spiked collar. Then off he went to the stadium, parading through the streets of Athens in all his wrinkled furry glory and finally escorted to his air-conditioned doghouse on the sidelines.

In route, admirers cheered the panting mound of fur and pressed in close to get their picture with him. But unfortunately, the dog is a delicate breed and Uga spent a good bit of time *benched*, suffering more ailments and injuries than most players. Whenever word got out that he was sidelined, get well cards stacked up from all over the state. After the bulldog had given his all, Uga was immortalized alongside the others who'd gone before him in the prominent mausoleum on the southwest end of the stadium.

In 1956, Savannah attorney, Frank W. (Sonny) Seiler, brought his English bulldog to the season's opening game. Coach Wally Butts took one look at the noble beast and asked if he'd serve as mascot. Apparently the first Uga barked a "yes" and ever since then, Seiler has been breeding generations one of the most recognized mascots in college sports.

Another Sonny arrived – Sonny Butler and his wife took their seats in the Marshall block. Will had met Sonny a time or two and certainly knew who he was – a friend of Mr. Marshall's and an up and coming football booster. The man brought a fanatical zeal to the booster business along with big donations.

The Athens's native loved UGA even though he'd never been a student there. Right after high school, he and his brother started a construction company. Sonny could build most anything and his brother managed the business side. As Athens and the university hit a huge growth spurt, the two made money hand over fist. No one loved the Dawgs more than Sonny, so it was only natural that a good amount of his new found wealth flowed into the football program. The alliance also meant that he had the right connections to get the best contracts. And so it went. Everyone was happy and prospering.

Regardless of Sonny's intense loyalty, he remained under the watchful eye of long time booster, Ben Fowler. From a well-to-do Athens's family, the former placekicker's ties to UGA were as strong as any.

Fowler was highly respected especially for his impeccable integrity. And as much as he loved winning, he also made sure the program stayed above board in complying with all NCAA standards. If anyone was tempted to compromise, Fowler was there – like the all-seeing school teacher who stepped in to keep everyone in line. Most folks appreciated his vigilance and had read the stories about other schools that'd paid dearly for their transgressions.

Fowler was in his mid-50's and had seen plenty of *Sonny's* before – the ones full of fire but light in the thinking department.

Sonny dismissed Fowler's caution and felt that he torpedoed recruiting. "In college ball, you gotta take the gloves off to get somewhere. Everybody bends the rules. The trick is being smart about it and not gettin' caught."

But the elder booster knew other teams that had followed Sonny's shenanigans – and they got somewhere, all right – suspended, titles revoked, the whole nine yards. Of course, he did appreciate Sonny's dedication, but he wasn't about to let *anyone* do *anything* to taint UGA's program.

In spite of being on a short leash, what Sonny loved best was being part of the program's "inner circle." The athletic staff listened to him and even called him "Coach." That sealed it. To Sonny that was the most coveted title a man could have.

Amy looked around, taking it all in. "Wow, these are incredible seats. This is great!"

Directly in front of them, one of UGA's most famous fans unofficially led the cheering. Every game day, the bald man painted an elaborate Bulldawg on his head. During any televised game, the cameras always caught him. As loyal a fan as any, he hadn't missed a game in years. And as sure as the sun rose over Sanford Stadium – there he was, fully adorned and rarin' to go.

Amy was taken back for a minute and then laughed. "Look at that head!"

"I've never seen him up close," Will said, "How long do you think it took to paint all that?"

"I can't even imagine," said Amy.

The moment arrived. The Dawgs charged through the huge banner inside the goal post and fans instantly jumped to their feet, cheering wildly. You'd think from all the deafening noise that you'd missed the game entirely and victory had already been declared.

Despite a reputation for rowdiness, most UGA fans were usually well behaved and courteous. You could certainly spend an afternoon with more ill-mannered SEC fans, but they will remain unnamed here. But on occasion, you found yourself surrounded by a collection of characters and a rabid Dawg or two.

Will glanced around as he braced for kick-off and that's exactly what he saw. Several diehard enthusiasts dressed in outlandish outfits more appropriate for Halloween or "Laugh In." No sooner was the ball moving, than a couple of guys with their faces painted up started the running commentary, dissecting every single play and yelling out choice remarks to the ref. (Unfortunately they didn't add the mouth guard to their game day ensemble.) Fans just rolled their eyes and hoped for laryngitis to set in soon.

A couple of rows back was the *Jack in the Box* type – up and down and up and down on every play – screaming and spilling popcorn and peanuts on everyone around them.

The game lived up to everyone's expectations. The second quarter see-sawed back and forth with both teams making great plays. The Dawgs had a terrific goal line stand then ran a dazzling kick-off return to score. "Touchdown, Georgia!" Fans went crazy as one dramatic play followed another but they still trailed 14 -7 at the half. After laboring against a tough Tennessee team, the players were more than ready to get to the locker room.

Fans had their own halftime rituals and it usually involved standing in long lines at concession stands and bathrooms. Afterwards, everyone balanced drinks as they scrambled and squeezed past one another getting back to their seats. The second half began. Amy did her part, cheering play after play. Then it happened. Behind them, an excited fan dumped his entire oversized cup of bourbon and Coke all over her, drenching Amy from head to toe.

Will stood, horrified. "Oh my gosh, I'm so sorry."

Then his attention turned to the culprit. "What a jerk!"

Amy composed herself and grabbed his arm. "No, Will. Don't ... It'll just make it worse. It was just an accident."

Everyone nearby offered Amy their napkins and condolences. The man apologized profusely and handed her a $20 for dry cleaning. Then justice was served as his "genteel wife" very eloquently let him have it – for all to hear. The dramatic tirade she served up was extra entertainment for anyone within earshot who couldn't help but laugh as she went on and on berating him.

Sonny, oblivious to everything but the game, continued with his famous Bulldawg bark while his wife sat by silently. At this point, even Amy found it all amusing.

Everyone turned their attention back to the gridiron. Fans screamed as the Dawgs drove relentlessly down the field for 65 yards and very late in the fourth quarter tied it 21-all. Finally, on third and eight at the Tennessee 10 yard line, the Dawgs got in formation. The clock was running – three minutes left. The pressure weighed heavily on the Vols defense. Horace King, a Clarke Central High man, broke loose on the outside thanks to great blocks by Davis and McKenzie. The tailback shook off Volunteers and leapt into the end zone. Everybody went absolutely berserk.

After the kick-off, a rattled Tennessee quarterback fumbled on the first play from scrimmage. Georgia recovered. Everyone leapt to their feet and all but fell over high-fiving anyone within reach. At this point, an unhinged Sonny repeatedly thrashed a man's back with a program, but the stranger hardly noticed. Someone behind Will held his shoulders in a vice-like grip until Andy Johnson, the Dawgs' star All American quarterback and hometown hero, kept the ball on an option play for a touchdown to sweeten the win. The crowd couldn't be contained and the *Woof! Woof! Woofs* went on and on. Coach Vince Dooley had done it again; his Dawgs had seized another victory *Between the Hedges.*

Sticky and hoarse from hollerin', the couple weaved through the mob of revelers, hand in hand, until they at last reached the East Campus exit and made the mile long trek to Will's car. And later, they'd realize that sometimes mishaps make the most amusing memories.

Dooley's Dawgs

The phenomenal football team wowing the capacity crowds in Sanford Stadium week after week didn't develop overnight, but was the result of Coach Vince Dooley's hard work.

When the 31-year-old Dooley, arrived in Athens in 1964 and signed his coaching contract for $12,500 a year, he was the youngest head football coach in the nation.

Two other Auburn War Eagles also flew the coup that year and landed in the Classic City. The first person to join the Dawgs was Auburn coach Joel Eaves who became UGA's Athletic Director – and within a month Eaves hired

Dooley who in turn brought along another young coach, Erk Russell, to head up the Dawgs' defense.

Dooley hit the ground running and, with his analytic mind and discipline honed as a Marine officer, he began building a stellar program. But he knew the job, that he'd accepted from a phone booth in Newnan, Ga, was baptism by fire and he told his wife not to unpack just yet. His first game was against the mighty Crimson Tide and its legendary leader, Coach Bear Bryant. If that wasn't daunting enough, they faced Joe Namath, Bama's dynamite quarterback. They beat up on the Dawgs 31-3.

But with Dooley at the helm, the team went on to win seven games that first season, making it the first winning season for the Dawgs in a decade. Dooley's first five teams had winning records (1964-1968), beat Tech five times and brought two SEC championships to Athens.

Vince and Barbara and his young family were also winners in the Athens community. The affable coach with his reserved but steely demeanor made friends in town and anywhere he traveled on the recruiting trail.

It was tough for college coaches to handle the pressure cooker job when they lived in a fishbowl, but Dooley passed the test with flying colors and, year after year, chalked up big wins.

Fans came to look forward to a bonus treat – sure to happen at any nail-biting moment of a tense game. Caught up in a pivotal play, the coach briefly abandoned his reserve, threw off his headphones and broke into the "The Dooley Shuffle."

Not to be confused with the Twist or Watusi, the "Shuffle" was Vince's spirited sprint downfield, alongside his ball carrier – doing his best to cajole the player into the end zone.

It was great entertainment – watching the head coach "bust a move" worthy of James Brown and wreak havoc on the sidelines, bobbing and weaving between TV cables and water boys.

He dashed by anxious trainers, making a run full of strange contortions – arms and legs twisting around like a pro bowler right after he releases the ball and coaxes it down the alley for a strike.

Dooley's antics provided colorful fodder for TV commentators. They noted with great amusement how out of character it was for the methodical ex-Marine to abandon restraint and express such passion...But then again – it's Georgia football!

Sportswriters and fans also liked to tease Dooley about heaping such extravagant praise on upcoming opponents during radio and TV interviews. "I don't know how we can walk out on the same field with those boys. There's talent at every position. And you can bet their coaches will have 'em primed and ready for Saturday... If we don't hustle and play our very best, it'll be a long day for us." And to conclude, he was known to get a bit philosophical and note, "To err is human, to forgive is divine, but to forgive a football coach is unheard of."

It was the same David vs Goliath script every week – whether or not their opponent was from the formidable top 10 with the four horsemen of the Apocalypse in their backfield OR some obscure college team of blind hobbits who hadn't won a game since the pigskin was invented. But

Dawg fans were perfectly happy with Dooley's poor mouthing because more often than not, they won. It was classic *under promise, over deliver.*

Dooley cared passionately about winning, but he also cared about his players. He enforced standards, worked hard, and earned the respect of his players – who became known far and wide as *Dooley's Dawgs.*

Dooley's Dilemma

"That's the thing about sports. Once people can play together, they see they can live together... Coaches should build men first and football players second."

> Eddie Robinson, legendary
> Grambling football coach

Eventually, Dooley had a couple of lackluster seasons and readily admitted that he should shoulder much of the blame for the team's uneven performance and lack of intensity on the field. He talked to lots of people and determined that part of the problem was underlying racial tensions.

For young boys growing up in the projects, not far from the stadium, the best part of the week was their pickup games, especially on Saturdays when they heard the roar of the crowd from Sanford Stadium. The guys loved the game and *knew* they were good. But unless things changed, they'd never have a shot at making the college team.

But sometimes dreams do come true. Horace King came first, then Richard Appleby, Chuck Kinnebrew, Clarence Pope and Larry West – three of whom were former Clarke Central High stars. Dooley broke ground and coached UGA's first black players.

A few years back, Athens High School and Burney Harris High School merged to form Clarke Central High School – one fully integrated school. It was something that needed to be done. For the most part, students got along OK, but it was a mixed bag for sure. Tensions and misunderstandings lingered. Educators, community leaders and students selected from each school had planned and talked and planned and talked and held endless committee meetings "to facilitate the necessary transition and maintain quality education for all students." But both schools ended up losing years of their heritage and honored traditions. The Athens High Trojans and the Burney Harris Yellow Jackets became the Clarke Central Gladiators (Gladiators historically are more often associated with Rome not Athens, but that's the kinda thing you get when an institutional committee comes up with a compromise).

You have witnessed a transition. You have seen utter alteration change to dislike, dislike became tolerance and tolerance to acceptance.

You have seen groups of people who used to denounce each other to the point of violence begin to work side by side in a degree of peace.

We begin this year with leftover fragments of the past. In short, we still could not get used to the idea of being together.
We slowly began to feel as one. The groundwork had been laid and we had something to build on.

1972 Gladius Yearbook staff

But in the spring of '71, tensions came to a head and a fight broke out. The crowd of students grew larger and started acting more like a mob. Before the situation spiraled out of control, Assistant Principal Charles Allen (formerly the principal of Burney Harris) stepped up and proved to be the right man for that very volatile moment. He led the way in calming a group of highly agitated students.

"It has been a year of tradition and change; of excitement and boredom; of harmony and hostility; of all and of nothing.
For the Seniors is has been three years of turmoil and dissatisfaction, for we have witnessed something unique. We have seen old traditions ended and new one begun. We lost the spirit we thrived on in the past and found education to be mere necessity instead of a pleasure.
The idealistic theory of consolidation and true togetherness seemed only a "pipe dream," for we fought it with all we had. But after fighting for so long, we have begun to care – a little.
Now as we start to accept the new and commit the old to memory, we see another change coming, and the institution

that was brought together to be one will again be divided. Remember that we are the only ones who experienced the arrival of the Clarke Central that we know today, and we will soon see its departure.

No one else will ever know what it was really like – from first to last. We were the youngest class of one tradition that died and are now the oldest class of another."

Fae Epting, Yearbook editor

When Dooley took stock of his team's troubles, he decided that he'd placed too much emphasis on rigid rules and discipline and that players needed a forum to talk things out. During a tense team meeting, players poured out their pent-up feelings and concerns. It wasn't exactly a "Kum Ba Ya" experience, but still a new measure of respect and understanding emerged and Dooley quickly capitalized on it to build unity.

"From now on we're not gonna have white players and black players, we just gonna have football players," said Dooley.

"Being prejudice is something I just can't see,"

Ray Charles.

And things were changing at the university as well. Eventually, a Black Student Union was organized and a Black Studies program began. And the first black fraternities and sororities opened chapters at UGA in the late '60s and early '70s.

But there was still more work to be done. Most civics leaders urged every one "to take the high road" and get along, but visceral feelings of being misunderstood persisted on both sides. Although sincere black and white leaders worked for harmony, it was often the news media from out of state who tried to stir the pot. The ones who didn't know grits from gravy and had already made up their minds "about those backwards, cousin-marrying racists." Then throw in a few grandstanding politicians and professional agitators and things really heated up.

The greatest strides between blacks and whites during that time were made by individuals working together and learning to understand one another – and the best success stories came from people simply developing friendships and common bonds through activities like team sports, music, or the church – it was something that politicians and government officials didn't pay enough attention to.

Throughout all of this, there was plenty of discussion going on at "Hot Corner." At the intersection of Washington and Hull Streets downtown, Hot Corner was an early center of successful, entrepreneurial black commerce. The Morton Theatre at 195 W. Washington St. was one of the oldest surviving vaudeville theatres built, owned, and operated by an African American, Monroe Bowers "Pink" Morton. In its heyday, the theatre hosted famous entertainers like Cab Calloway, Duke Ellington, Louie Armstrong and Bessie Smith.

Will was friends with some of the old black men that hung around the neighborhood barbershop near Hot Corner.

One day Reuben invited Will to hang out for coffee.

"I know you're hearing a lot of stuff over there at the university, but if you really wanna understand what folks are thinkin' about all this race stuff, you should pull up a chair and listen to the regulars that come in. Might do you some good," Rueben said.

"Sure, I'll do that."

Will settled into a cane chair and listened to opinions percolate around the room from the regular armchair philosophers who'd lived a lot and seen a lot. The men stopped by the shop to sit awhile, have some coffee and then work on "solving the world's problems."

"Like anything worthwhile it takes time and effort and hangin' in there. But some of us feel like that's all we've been doin' is *waitin'!* Waitin' for things to get better; and we're tired of waitin'."

"Attitudes and prejudices don't just change overnight."

"Yeah, it's like our preacher says 'each one reach one.' If you just get to know folks one on one and try to see things from the other fella's viewpoint, then you can make real progress."

"Like Dr. King said we're supposed to judge folks by 'the content of their character – not the color of their skin' – that should cut both ways."

"But I don't feel like folks are really listenin' to us. They're just pretendin'."

Mr. Edwards, the elder statesman of the group, got up and poured everyone another round of coffee.

"Yeah, but when somebody's robbed, the cops come straight over to our part of town to find him."

"And I know places I can't go without gettin' *the look*."

"Hold on, hold on. Time out. Everybody can't talk at the same time. Charles, you haven't said much, but you look like somethin's on your mind."

"I'll tell ya what really gets me. Seems like it's always innocent bystanders that get hurt when tempers flare and people start spoutin' off in the heat of the moment."

"We need more Dean Tates – he did real good helpin' Charlyane Hunter out when integration started at the university back in '61."

"And I'm gettin' sick and tired of these professional protestors – they're all mouth. I've seen 'em – they're the ones who wouldn't think of doin' a day's worth of work in a soup kitchen, but boy do they talk and carry on."

"Reuben, you gonna do any work today or just keep jawbonin'? I need a shave and a cut." Reuben got his scissors, but kept talking. "What we need is to be represented. All those folks in office come from the same rich neighborhoods."

"But the government can only do so much – no point waiten' for 'em. It's gotta come from folks' hearts. And that only happens when the Lord gets ahold of a man and sets him free. That's what I'm talkin' about."

"Yeah, that's it Emery. Don't go puttin' lipstick on a pig."

"There's some guys breakin' through. Like Number 42, Jackie Robinson did, and what's that new tennis guy's name?"

"Arthur Ashe," Will said.

"Yeah, he's for real."

The Odd Couple
After Will left the barber shop, he drove down College Station Road and noticed something strange in the horse

pasture – some sort of small white creature following a mature mare. He'd seen it before, but now he had to check it out.

He pulled into the vet school parking lot and found Dr. Paul Hoffman of the large animal clinic. "I know they're an odd couple – the little goat and the horse. But it works." He described Tinker Bell as "the school's resident psychiatrist and comforter."

Dr. Hoffman explained that the unusual relationship developed when the young quarter horse came to the clinic with a head injury that blinded her and made her extremely irritable. The vets tried various remedies to no avail, then they remembered that horses have a herding instinct and enjoy companionship. They'll often establish a buddy relationship with any animal that happens to be around. The staff wondered what would happen if they introduced the blind horse to an orphan goat they'd raised.

"As soon as they put the two out to pasture together, they struck up an immediate friendship and became inseparable," Hoffman said." Her little friend relaxed the horse and gave her a sense of security."

Tinker Bell came by her name when the staff hung an old Christmas bell around her neck so the mare could follow the sound and always stay close.

When the mare was sent off for breeding, Tinker Bell got a new assignment, 20- year-old "Grandma." In her old age, Grandma had gotten into the habit of cowering all alone in a corner of the pasture. Another friendship developed. The two shared the same stall and at night you can see them together – Grandma lying on the hay with the goat on her back, nibbling her ears.

Will's eyes hadn't fooled him. Yes, it was an *odd couple* – the horse and a goat. Which begs the question –*If God's four-footed creatures, who are so distinctly different, can get along – why can't his two-footed creatures live together in peace and harmony?*

━≺┤┼⊁━

Safe to say that not everyone on campus was pondering social issues but just trying to find the next party.

And the girls had found one, but now it was late and time to call it a night. It'd been great time, trying out a new club and discovering a fresh group of cute guys and things really got rolling once they'd ditched a bouncer who kept coming on to them. The guy was a real nuisance and downright creepy when they thought about it. Something about him was a little off.

The young lady squinted. Headlights from behind almost blinded her. For several blocks, the car stuck to her bumper at every turn until she finally gunned it through a yellow light and got away.

They all looked around frantically, hoping the car wouldn't reappear. In a few minutes the carload of girls were very relieved that everything seemed back to normal.

All they'd seen was the light. It'd been too bright to make out the driver or even the make of the car, besides none of the ladies were in the best shape to notice details.

The girls did realize the need to report it, though, and police hoped it was the break they needed to find the assailant from the protest incident. But after checking out all the club employees, they were still at a dead-end.

It's Greek to Me

Every town brags about the merits of their municipality. There's nothing wrong with good ole fashioned Chamber of Commerce boosterism; it's universal. And the movers and shakers of Athens – the Classic City, as it is known – were no exception. References and allusions to Athens abounded throughout the campus and town reflecting "The Glory that was Greece." For one thing, dozens of buildings and homes in the community paid homage to the classical roots in their architecture.

Paramount to the tradition was the stately classical design of the 1832 UGA Chapel built to replicate a formal Greek Temple, complete with imposing Corinthian columns. True to form the oldest student group on campus was the Demosthenian Society which was dedicated to oratory and debate. The second oldest group was a spinoff from the Demosthenians, the Phi Kappa Society also dedicated to classical debate and writing. And of course, the Greek social chapters with their annual Spring Greek Week featuring "Olympic-like" events such as chariot races hauling beer kegs and toga-clad athletes doing three-legged races. The contests required Herculean strength, the daring of Ulysses and the mental acumen of Aristotle – and then the festivities were topped off by a myriad of parties.

Athens didn't have a "Dionysus Tavern" paying tribute to the Greek god of wine. But the Classic City Package Store did have its loyal patrons who adhered to a slightly altered Socrates adage: *From*: "The unexamined life is not worth living..." *To*: "The undrunken beer in a red solo cup should never be wasted." (In the original charter for UGA the college was supposed to be located in the small hamlet of

Watkinsville, but founders feared that the nefarious Eagle Tavern there would corrupt young students so the college ended up in Athens – a safe distance from the lure of the fermented grape – or so they thought at the time.)

But there was one Athenian who didn't ascribe to Socrates admonition and had no qualms about "corrupting the youth of Athens." Bubber was the proprietor of Bubber's Bait Shop. As Lewis Gizzard said in one of his columns, "Bubber didn't sell much bait but he sold a ton of beer to a couple of generations of students and alumni." The scruffy, ragtag brick building on Broad Street, across from the projects, was a regular rendezvous for thirsty patrons of all walks of life and all ages – particularly those underage. Gizzard told of walking in on his 21st birthday and announcing that he was there to buy his first legal six-pack. Bubber handed it to him and said, "This one's on me."

The dimly lit gravel parking lot was a continual revolving door of customers preparing for weekend festivities.

An Athens's native of humble beginnings – the genuinely affable owner had built his business one customer at a time. You never forgot Bubber's one of a kind demeanor especially when he talked – a very prominent speech impediment made him sound like Willie Nelson gargling.

In a feature in the local paper, someone nailed it: "The two most popular people in Athens among the students of UGA are Dooley and Bubber."

Other businesses joined in aligning themselves with the mantle of Greek culture by naming their services the Classic City Cleaners, Classic City Car Wash etc…

The high school also got in on the act and embraced the storied Greek warrior spirit by christening the athletic teams at Athens High School – the Trojans. Naturally, Southern football coaches spent more time working with the boys on the gridiron than elucidating the finer points of "The Iliad" and "The Odyssey" which explains why the sports team had a fierce warrior image even though the Trojans were of course from Troy – not Athens. *But hey, as long as you had a winning team galvanizing the school and town under the magical Friday night lights... What did it matter?*

It certainly didn't matter in 1969 when The Athens High Trojans went to the state play-offs. Fran Tarkington, the Minnesota Vikings star QB and former UGA QB and hometown hero made a "surprise" phone call during a frenzied pep rally. Via a live hookup, he led the cheering and implored the team to grab the state title from those Valdosta Wildcats who'd held onto it way too long. (Unlike the Hollywood sports movies, the Trojans lost. But it was an epic battle down to the last dramatic play.)

So what would happen if you combined a modern day fire-breathing, good ole boy football coach and classic Greek athletes playing under "Friday night torches" in the shadow of Mt. Olympus?

But let's not get the chariot before the horse – so to speak. First, you've got to have an awe inspiring warrior name for the team. Think back to our roots – ancient Athens – "The Athens Stoics"? *Can't really see fans jumpin' to their feet yellin' their lungs out for the Stoics.*

Let's see ...there were artists, playwrights, poets – AND of course world famous philosophers. Eureka! Hit pay dirt! "The Fightin' Philosophers." Fits like a Corinthian column.

"First and 10 let's think about it and debate it again!" won't strike terror into the hearts of opponents, but hey we'll be outsmartin' 'em so much – the other team won't know what hit 'em.

"All right boys, huddle up – I mean, let's gather in a concentric circle and discuss dialectically our game strategy."

"Think boys! Think! Like the Athenians of old – we're gonna do a whole truckload of cogitatin', ponderin', and thinkin'! Thinkin' all the time… 'bout big things, little things! Thinkin' on the field and off the field. Use your noggins – don't be like old Ignoramus – you *know* what happened to him when he messed up at the Battle of Thermometer. That was one heck of a fight!"

"Ugh, Coach don't you mean Thermopylae?"

"Course, son – just seein' if you're listenin'."

"And remember – all those Stoics on the other team got nothin' on you guys. Ya'll done run endless laps and done drills, with no water or salt tablets – 'cause that's the sorta thing we thrive on. Common sense has no place in football – it's all guts and glory – that's how you ascend to the playoffs on Mt Olympus!

"Here's a rundown on the injuries: Achilles is out again with his heel. Demosthenes's jaw is busted and Euclid's shoulder is all triangulated.

"But we're in good shape with a whole Pantheon of Players – a dadgummed full orb of 'em! Oblivious and Obnoxious in the backfield, Ostentatious receiving, and our All Greek offensive line – Superfluous, Obsequious, Ignominious, Miscellaneous and Obstreperous – and Preposterous starting at quarterback!

"Remember, I done ya'll right last night at the banquet – I let the Epicureans gorge themselves on some good eatin', but there better be no partyin' "like its 20 A.D." – or I'll have you runnin' a marathon bright and early.

"I'm tellin' you...It's your time, boys, Remember where we were last year? In last place and now look at us! After the losses and all the adversity we had early in the season, we've gone from the outhouse to the big house – from the Acrapolous to the Acropolis – so let's go out there and get us a victory!"

Mr. Reynolds arrived early as usual and found Herman in the hallway – he always enjoyed catching up with him.

Herman's job was to keep the Journalism/Psych building in tip-top shape – no small feat considering the hundreds of students who filed in and out of the classrooms every day. The good natured janitor had been at it for 35 years and retirement was coming up.

His years of hard work had kept the tall man lean and fit but also accounted for his gray hair and arthritic knees. One look at Herman's broad smile and you knew that he was a people person. His list of friends seemed endless – starting at his Baptist church where he'd served as a deacon for 22 years.

Mr. Reynolds and Herman had known each other for a long time and shared a very genuine fondness and respect for each another.

"Good morning, Herman. How are you?"

He answered with his customary reply. "Oh fine. Just thankin' God for life. How 'bout you?"

"Very well. Had my son home this weekend. Enjoyed every minute of it."

"I know what you mean."

"And how's your family?" Mr. Reynolds asked.

"Doin' just fine."

"I've kept my eye out for Carl, how does he like being a college man?"

He leaned against his cleaning cart and beamed. "He's taken to it like a fish to water. Even comes by to see his ole granddad now and then."

Mr. Reynolds stood with his usual near perfect posture and looked very dapper in his sweater vest and tie. He removed his glasses, pulled a handkerchief from his pocket and methodically cleaned them as he thought about Carl. He remembered all that Herman had told him about his grandson through the years – an outstanding student who'd never let his ball playing get in the way of his studies.

"That's wonderful. He's a smart guy with a good head on his shoulders. He's one who'll excel, I'm sure," said Mr. Reynolds. "We all want the best for our kids and grandkids. That never changes, no matter how old they are."

Herman agreed. "And the more education they get, the better. Makes me think of somethin' I just read: 'The mind once enlightened cannot become dark again.' Thomas Paine said that."

Herman was a self-educated man and a life-long learner. And, of course, he was in the right place for it. His many professor friends kept him supplied with all kinds of books. He could recite a quote from one of the greats at the drop of a hat – not in a showy way, it just naturally flowed from his lively mind.

"Thomas Paine, eh? That's a good one. I'll pass it on to my students today."

Will had endured another one of Dr. Hall's classes and looked up to see Ed sprinting down the long hallway.

"You gettin' all your stuff in to the Post?" Will asked.

He caught his breath. "Yeah, just dropped the academic verification form by Dr. Hall's office. Said he'd take care of it. Transcripts, writing samples, all sent. That's about it. Guess it's just time to wait."

"Double check everything. This is huge," Will said.

"I know."

Herman turned the corner. A chat with the older gentleman always did Will good. Herman often encouraged him with his positive outlook, especially on days when he felt the pressures of his studies and was just generally trying to make sense out of life. Will volunteered to cover his retirement celebration for the paper. He wanted to make sure it was done right.

"You're about to be a man of leisure."

"Well mostly, don't think it's really sunk in yet. But I'm sure gonna miss everybody. Got lots of friends here."

"And you're just about to see just how many you *do* have. Everybody I've talked to's comin' to your party. They may have to move it to the coliseum to hold 'em all."

Herman chuckled.

"So what you gonna do now? Any plans?"

"I don't need no plans. My wife, she's got all the plans. I've seen her makin' long lists. Think I'll fix up the garden first, got my stack of books – and me and the grandkids do a good bit of fishin'. There'll be plenty to do."

"Sounds good. Now you have some quotes ready for the paper. I know you've seen a lot in these 35 years."

Herman's smile vanished. "Sure have and by the way, you know what's worrying Mr. Reynolds?"

"No, not really."

"He hadn't said anything, but I can tell. He's not himself. There's always things brewin' 'round here, now more than ever. And let's face it, not everybody's a gentleman like he is. You gotta know who to trust – just the way it is."

HAVIN' A PARTY

I t had been too long. There hadn't been a prank, well a *good* prank on campus in a while. Everyone was too busy with other things. But to be fair, the prank world hadn't been completely dormant; there'd been a couple worthy of honorable mention.

The traditional standby, though done and redone, with a few twists and variations, never failed to offer an abundance of hilarity – a good, old-fashioned snipe hunt. This unique form of Southern hospitality was particularly fun if played on an unsuspecting student from above the Mason-Dixon Line. The victims didn't know what hit 'em when good ole boys yanked them out of bed in the middle of a humid night and carried them down a long dirt road. The forest was said to be particularly thick with the elusive creatures "around this time of year," they were told. But having seen some of the critters their friends mounted on the walls of their lake cabins, snipes didn't seem so very farfetched.

Of course, fraternity pledges were regularly sent out to count the innumerable cobblestones on the steep hill on Finley Street, all the way up to the tree that owns itself. Years ago, legend has it that old Professor Jackson loved the old oak so much that he deeded the tree its own eight square foot portion of land and a sizeable inheritance for its perpetual care. Later on, an arborist determined that the tree was dying from within – "heart rot", subsequently, the beloved oak crashed to the ground during the night of October 9, 1942. The good ladies of the Junior League came to the rescue by cultivating a sapling which they re-planted and named "The Son of the Tree that Owns Itself."

Forty years later, calamity struck once again when the offspring of the tree was beset by a virulent slime. The UGA Ag Dept. sprung into action and brought the dying patient back from the brink. And now the storied, sixty foot oak still resides over its lawful domain on the corner of Finely and Dearing.

Some of the best pranks involved retrieving (or *stealing*, as those more prudish chose to call it) various types of women's undergarments with raids on the girl's dorms – the old panty raid. The latest effort was when some guys secured the largest bra they could find to serve as a parachute. The payload was a dozen chicken eggs. The students, undoubtedly thinking of Cape Canaveral and inspired by the triumphs of our nation's space program, launched the eggs from the roof of Russell Dorm. Accounts differed widely as to the success of the endeavor, but witnesses at "ground control" said that the chute deployed spectacularly.

The heady achievement sparked yet another idea. What fun it would be to "go live" and enlist one of the small monkeys from the Memorial Park zoo for the next ride. Then a rare moment of reason cut through the giddiness. They realized they weren't Georgia Tech engineers and it was probably not a good idea to entrust calculating a safe rate of descent to a bunch of mischievous guys, thus a hapless little chimp was spared.

Now everyone knew it was high time for a really *good* prank, so the man to pin your hopes on for this kind of thing was Ronnie – and he was already cooking one up.

TK Hardy's was the site – a hot spot for hanging out at the south end of the old train station. In the university's earliest years, burgeoning young scholars disembarked from the train, took a carriage or wagon up the hill, through town to their dorm – known as the Old College building where they lodged for $5 per month.

The depot had evolved into a bar. TK Hardy's served up drinks and other fare and the proprietors were well versed in prying UGA students away from their studies - 50 cent drinks on slower weeknights and "zoo night" on Wednesdays. Then there was a $10 night, all you could drink – but with one caveat – the tippler could imbibe in the eye of the dog without limit until he just *had* to use the restroom. Some enterprising fellows found a way to circumvent the stipulation by going to the back deck and discretely emptying their bladders through the wooden railing, taking care to avoid splinters. This practice also enhanced the meaning of "local watering hole."

This home-spun tradition was the perfect set-up for a prank on one unsuspecting Harold Sherman. Sherman was a wallflower; there was just no other way to say it. He was intelligent, but also a bumbling hypochondriac and a complete teetotaler but he loved orange juice because it "stimulated neurons in his brain" and helped mitigate acne. During high school, the guys at Clarke Central had never been mean to him, but he just wasn't one of those people on their social radar. But now Harold was dealing with college guys who loved to play pranks and generally embarrass each other.

Ronnie concocted a doozie with the help of his pledge brothers.

To keep Ronnie out of the dean's dawghouse, Dad hired Harold to tutor his son. And for the tutor's birthday, Ronnie treated him to an all-expense paid birthday dinner plus unlimited orange juice. Harold was pleased that his student had extended such a nice gesture of gratitude, so he arrived right on time in his short sleeve white shirt with his glasses case and three Bic pens hanging out of his pocket. His jacked up powder blue polyester pants completed his ensemble and the two settled into a table on the deck where his host invited him to order the works – it was on him.

In no time at all, Harold was munching on a double cheese burger with fries *and* onion rings. Let the good times roll.

Ronnie beamed. "Glad you're enjoying it, Harold. And now let's have a drink or two; it's your birthday, man, so it's all the orange juice you want."

Of course, this time it wasn't just Florida's pure and natural, Ronnie was slipping generous portions of Smirnoff vodka into each glass. The easily disguised alcohol was having its effect on the unsuspecting scholar.

Harold slurred his words and swayed from side to side. "I had no idea that excessive amounts of Vitamin C could trigger a *re-action of this mag...magnitude.*" Then he said, "Excuse me, gentlemen, I have got to urinate...I mean really bad."

Ronnie led a shaky Harold to the rail and he relieved himself sufficiently enough to put out a small brush fire, knocking over a huge potted fern in the process. He also managed to get his poly pants caught on an errant nail and when he yanked it to free himself; he ripped a pants leg to mid-thigh. But at this point, it didn't even faze him.

Then after another round or two, Harold transformed from his Mr. Spock persona to a dancing maniac. He drummed his fingers to the beat of every song, but that wasn't enough for him. "Born to be Wild" came on and out came the party animal. He jumped to the dance floor, singing the words, "*Get your motor runnin'! Headin' for the highway...like a true nature's child, we were born, born to be wild....*" After his unusual, yet stellar moves to Steppenwolf, a small crowd gathered, prodding him on.

The next song up was "Love Train" and Harold grabbed onto a plump young lady in a tank top that was overflowing and cut-offs that should have remained bell bottoms. The two star-crossed dance partners got a few other inebriated bystanders into a tipsy conga line and they shimmied their way around the deck a couple of times. After a few more trips on the dance floor, even Ronnie realized it was time to break up the group and get Harold home before things got totally out of hand. Besides, Ronnie was worn out from laughing so hard and he just couldn't take anymore.

The guys escorted the life of the party to the Waffle House for some coffee to sober him up. Finally, they knew Harold was OK when he ignored the jukebox and went on about his physics project. But during the short ride back to the dorm, he did belt out a couple more verses of "Born to be Wild." It must have been all that Vitamin C.

And among the pranksters, the night was forever known as "Sherman's March to Pee."

Huddleston

> *"The germ of the best patriotism is the love a man has for the home he inhabits, for the soil he tills, for the trees that give him shade, and the hills that stand in his pathway."*

Henry W. Grady

It was a great day for cruising in the country. Amy had invited Will along for a trip home so they took the lightly traveled two lane highway to Huddleston, Ga.

Since the Dawgs were playing Kentucky up in Lexington it made it a little less painful to give up a weekend in Athens. Fans who didn't take the journey north showed their allegiance back home and for Amy's clan that meant a huge Bulldawg BBQ and almost everyone in town was invited.

Huddleston was a small hamlet in the heart of farming and cotton country. The couple left the hills of Athens, drove through several small rural towns and eventually came to land so flat land that it stretched all the way to the horizon. Vast expanses of farmland full of low crops, crowned with white appeared in all directions.

The pleasant drive was interrupted when it suddenly came out of nowhere. Buzzing overhead, it shook the car so fiercely that Will tightened his grip on the wheel to keep from veering off the road. About then, the single engine plane swooped directly overhead with a guttural roar and made another pass over the crops.

Amy threw her head back and laughed. "It's just a crop duster...guess we're used to it."

Will let out a sigh of relief, "Oh...yeah...hey, I bet that's a fun job...ever been up in one?"

"A couple of times...it was great...he's a friend of Dad's and owns the business."

They watched the plane in the distance and Will marveled at the precision it took to fly so low and spray the crops row by row.

Their trip seemed short as the two laughed and found more than enough to talk about. They went on about the usual things – happenings on campus, music, the antics and drama of their friends. Then the talk was more about themselves – things they liked and things they'd done. Will explained his work on the paper and Amy talked excitedly about her sorority's involvement in the Big Brother, Big Sister program and all the strong relationships that had developed. Amy appreciated Will who seemed different than the typical college guy – more grounded than most – and he always showed her respect. Besides, the guy was easygoing and had a great sense of humor.

As they approached the outskirts of Huddleston, one tall building emerged from the level terrain. Amy described the cotton gin and how a hometown fellow had built the thriving business from the ground up, making his fortune

in processing and brokering cotton. Many said that his success was due to a special charm bestowed upon him – he
had the distinction of being a Double Dawg, with both an
undergrad and a law degree from UGA. Times were good,
at least in that sector of the economy. Double digit inflation
had shot cotton prices up dramatically and locals enjoyed
the payoff of a commodity boon that was in full swing.

No sooner had they opened the car doors, than Amy's
mom and dad rushed out of the house to meet them.
Whatever they'd been doing that late afternoon, they were
never far from the front window, glancing out to the driveway, eager for the sight of their daughter returning home. It
was the same for empty nesters everywhere whose children
had grown up all too quickly and left home.

Her parents ushered them into the dining room for a
wonderful home cooked dinner. Amy had brought home
her share of suitors so her parents relaxed with the young
fellow and figured he was likely just another friend.

Much of the talk centered on Saturday which was shaping up to be the day of the real festivities. Amy's extended
family was a large clan, so the rundown of guests was mind
boggling to Will who was from a small family...one brother
and two cousins he only knew from a Christmas card each
year. After a good effort at trying to remember a few names
and their place on the family tree, he gave up, hoping he
could wing it with some small talk.

The next day they came in droves carrying lawn chairs,
blankets and the most delicious dishes imaginable. They
didn't have to travel far, Amy's home was on something of a
family compound with an uncle next door and cousins who
lived within earshot.

Everyone was warm and welcoming – there's just nothing like Southern hospitality. The genuineness of these "salt of the earth" folks was refreshing especially after enduring some of those elite types at the university who take themselves all too seriously.

A flurry of activity over took the lawn. Will was amazed that everyone knew what to do as they pitched in and made preparations. The neighbors worked in exact tandem with each other as they had so many times before and the event came together splendidly.

From talking to friends who'd grown up in small towns, Will knew there was another side to things – an unspoken caste system still held. At the top, were the blue-blooded, landed gentry. Most were benevolent and community minded, but everyone clearly knew their place on the social ladder and it was nearly impossible to climb out of the class you were born into. Ever polite and mannerly, they still held tightly to their time-honored status, but it didn't take long to pick up on the resentment of everyday folk whose place in the community seemed all very preordained.

All the right ingredients were coming together for a great day: a crowd of people, plenty of food and the Dawgs playing football. So the merriment began. The barbeque itself generated the most excitement – it wasn't ordinary take-out from a local joint but a slow-roasted pig in the ground. The evening before, the men had built the fire just so with well-seasoned pecan wood and cooked the choice porker for hours. Forfeiting sleep for a higher cause, the men enjoyed these times together as they carefully tended the guest of honor and swapped tales. As a final touch, the main course simmered in a secret sauce producing the tastiest BBQ this side of the Mason Dixon line.

Several of the aunts now *tended to* Will.

"You just help yor..self. You simply must have a big helpin' of the sweet potato casserole. There's a top layer of shugared pecans *and* anotha layer of marshmallows. Now you're probably used to one *or* the other. But we don't think anyone should be forced to make such a horrid choice...so we do both, turns out simply divine."

"Land sakes don't be shy now...a young fella like you needs mor' than that...Fill that plate up!"

"Now, we can't let you pass up Sarah's cornbread – it's *melt in your mouth wonderful*. She's famous for it. Part of the secret is her hand-me-down cast iron skillet. Why, that thing's survived three generations...and a brush with General Sherman!"

Will took their advice but politely passed up the colorful congealed salad topped with globs of mayo. It was a dish that never failed to show up at any potluck or funeral, yet he wondered who actually ate it.

After supper, darkness crept over the lawn and the cool night air drove the women inside to the warmth of the house. The ladies systematically cleaned up what was left of the delicious spread still visiting and talking without skipping a beat as they migrated indoors.

The menfolk stayed outside at their favorite spot – a cluster of chairs around a fire pit with a radio tuned up to the game. The coolness didn't bother them. The fire was going nicely and they put on their UGA sweatshirts and parkas – most from past birthdays, bestowed upon them by relatives who knew that anything *Bulldawg* made the best gifts.

The initial welcome was great, but it soon wore off as Will realized that, when it came down to it, he was obviously an outsider with this tight knit group. Being a people person, he could usually find a common bond with just about anybody. But now he was struggling as he looked around uneasily and found himself alone. Then Amy appeared. On the high deck, the fading evening light highlighted her beauty as the breeze gently caught her soft dress and flowing hair. She waved and smiled at Will. One look at her and a second slice of a delectable coconut cream pie fortified Will to carry on. He knew his football and, with a few quips and comments, made small inroads with the men.

It was clear that one particular uncle was the patriarch and he set the tone for the group. Uncle Roy eyed Will cautiously. The man had his issues. It was hard sending a son to Vietnam. But it was even harder seeing him return home so physically and emotionally scarred only to be met by the scoffs and jeers of anti-war protestors. A WW II vet himself, Uncle Roy held an unwavering belief that it was a sacred duty for any able-bodied man to serve his country. He couldn't shake his bitterness.

The uncle's suspicions peaked when he learned of Will's upbringing in Athens, "with all those university radicals." But after a while, the two began to chat. Will asked him more about his life and the man slowly opened up. He mainly talked about his son. Will listened. It'd been a long time since anyone had done that – especially on this tender subject. Most people were just tired of hearing about it. Besides, what more could be said? But the pain was still there and as he stared into the fire; he told Will all about it. Uncle Roy had a lot bottled up inside. Will felt sorry for the man and also knew that he'd just barely missed the draft himself. That troubled young man could've easily been him.

The two sat quietly for a few minutes, watching the flames dance. Then somehow they got to talking about Hank Williams, Sr. When Will described his front row seat at a Hank Williams tribute concert, an excited Uncle Roy moved his chair closer and talked almost without taking a breath.

"Now, you mean they'd do that? Play Hank in Athens?"

"Sold out. Standing room only."

"And what'd it sound like?" He threw sticks in the fire and the sparks flew up.

"I tell you, if you closed your eyes, you'd swear it was him."

Uncle Roy slapped his knee. "Dang dog it...wish I'd been there, 'Hey Good Lookin',' used to sing that to my wife."

"Know somethin'?" Will said, "I'm So Lonesome I Could Cry" is just about the saddest song I ever heard."

The patriarch slowly shook his head. "Sure is. Makes a grown man wanna cry like a baby. Don't make 'em like Hank anymore."

And on they went, talking about the merits of one song after the other – quoting lines – and wrapping it up with a solemn recounting of the singer's tragic death on New Years, 1953. Only 29 years old, he died in the backseat of a Cadillac, in a remote West Virginia town in route to his next concert.

Will had made an unlikely friend that evening. The men followed Uncle Roy's lead and, at least for the time being, he was one of the guys.

Eventually everyone called it a night and Will and Amy were left alone, cuddling by the fire.

"Soul Man"

He finally found her. A slightly used red convertible MG Midget. And at a fair price – $995. It met most of his criteria: foreign, cool and sporty – and supposedly it ran well. Since the country was still in the middle of an Arab oil embargo, getting decent gas mileage was a big plus. Sure the gas guzzling muscle cars were awesome and fun – the GTOs, 442s and Camaros. But throwing money down a thirsty gas tank didn't fit Will's limited budget.

He jumped at Mr. Marshall's offer to come along for the final look. It was great to have an experienced car guy check it out – who was also a smooth-talking negotiator.

The two met nearby to drive the short distance together and go over more details. "Sounds like this could be it, but just take it slow, don't show emotion, stay cool," Mr. Marshall said.

" OK, but I just hope it works out. Haven't seen one quite like it and I've been lookin' for a while now."

"Sure, but you can't let *him* know that."

"You know what? You remind me a lot of myself when I was young."

Will looked at him. "Really?"

"Yep. You're interested in all kinds of things. And I've been thinkin'. You and Tom should do more stuff together. Bet you'd hit it off. He could use a friend like you. Round out his people skills."

"Sure, Tom's a great guy."

"He's kinda serious, smart though, doing real good in his finance classes. But he needs to loosen up."

"Uh, huh."

"Yeah, I'm plannin' for him to work with me someday. But clients go for the more outgoing type. They like to mix business with fun."

As they walked up to the vehicle, Will tried to keep Marshall's advice in mind and resisted the urge to gush over the diamond in the rough.

Mr. Marshall stood there with his hands in his pockets, carefully examining the car. Will was afraid that something was wrong. Then Mr. Marshall finally spoke. "Ya know, I had one of these a few years back. Brings back lots of memories."

Will fidgeted, eagerly waiting for Mr. Marshall's verdict. "I've looked at a lot of cars, and I'm sold on this one. I mean if you think it's a good deal."

"Yeaaaah…." Mr. Marshall strolled around it. "The great thing about the Midget – it gives you a real feel for the road."

Getting on to the business at hand, Will said, "I know it needs a little work, even the guy admits it's time for a brake job, a fuel pump, and obviously a new top."

"That shouldn't be so bad. You know the Doster brothers, right?" said Mr. Marshall.

"Oh sure."

The five Doster brothers down on Pulaski Street were a car guy's best friend. They could fix anything – eventually – by mixing and matching new parts with a few of their vintage items from their own special *inventory* of wrecks and cast-offs scattered among the kudzu on the hill behind their garage. All the brothers held advanced degrees in the

School of Hard Knocks and years of experience working on all kinds of car.

Yeah, there were five brothers working five days a week under one roof – peacefully. They repaired foreign cars and each had his own specialty. Horace and Harvey handled the Volkswagens. Don and Charlie took care of the rest – from Mercedes to Porsches and even an occasional Rolls Royce. Charlie tackled transmissions and Bobby ran the paint and body shop. Don was the engine wizard and he'd tear into one with his massive arms, tweaking and torqueing this and that like a pathologist doing an autopsy. He'd cajoled many a sick manifold or clogged carburetor back to life through diligent detective work and colorful cussing.

In 1965, the brothers found a small garage and adjoining storage shed on two and a half acres of land so hilly that no developer wanted it. They opened up their garage and the customers came.

The clientele at Doster Brothers was as diverse as the brothers themselves. On any given day, you'd see a college student, wearing ragged jeans and a grim expression, pushing in an ancient VW that'd just died on the road – right next to one of Athens's high society matrons asking Don why her brand new Mercedes was acting up. The town's leading businessmen brought their ailing top of the line foreign imports to them because they knew they'd be treated right.

A small green poster over the water cooler summarized their business philosophy: "If we can't fix it – nobody can – destroy it."

After a test drive, Mr. Marshall talked more with the owner and gleaned key details about maintenance history and such while throwing in a little small talk as well. The seller let his guard down, obviously enjoying the banter with a fellow car enthusiast. Little did he know that he was slowly but surely being disarmed by the master wheeler-dealer.

Mr. Marshall stepped next to Will, cocked his head near his and whispered, "You got yourself a good deal, Will, my man. Take it." During the process, the amount dropped from the asking price to $900 even. The seller was very happy with the sale and now believed the two had done *him* a big favor by taking the car off his hands.

Will thanked his friend and roared off in his very own MG Midget. A few miles down the road, the radio went out. But not for long. Bouncing over the railroad tracks jiggled the wires just enough to get WRFC to kick in again and besides, in just a couple of weeks he'd get the eight track player installed.

Will procured his new wheels just in time for Saturday night. Now he and Amy could go in style to her sorority's Fall Formal.

The two had some good times together, but the relationship was not without its highs and lows. Some days, she seemed restless and distant so he hoped tonight would fire up the romance.

Will spent the day polishing up the Midget and smiled as he thought back to his first dance and Patsy. The Episcopal Church was on to something when they decided to corral the junior high kids in the fellowship hall with plenty of chaperones and sponsor a dance.

The boys stood like suspects in a police line-up against a long wall, shuffling their feet and occasionally mumbling to each other. The girls milled around in clusters on the opposite wall, chatting excitedly and throwing furtive smiles to the guys.

But when the moment came, you had to muster all your courage to cross that vast no-man's land in the center of the room with all eyes watching. Then to everyone's relief, a chaperone finally dimmed the lights and the dance got going.

Patsy was the lovely girl next door who'd propelled Will's casual interest in the opposite sex to full blown "puppy love." This was his big chance and he was coming off pretty cool in a nice pair of bell bottoms, a new Alpaca sweater and an unavoidable scent of High Karate which he'd applied liberally.

With the first guitar riff of "My Girl," he headed straight to Patsy. They danced. Will couldn't get over how soft her hands felt – even softer than his worn baseball glove.

Usually it's the girls who don't wash their sweater for a week, but this time it was Will. When he got home, he tucked it in his dresser to keep the lingering scent of Patsy's perfume as long as he could.

Patsy grew lovelier with each year. She became her sorority's Philanthropy Chair, always made the Dean's List, and was dating a football star. She probably never thought twice about that night, but Will always remembered.

But he was just a kid back then and now it's the real thing. He cleaned himself up and in suit and tie, picked up Amy. She was dazzling. As they walked down the sidewalk, he waited for her reaction to his prized possession. His spirits sank when all she said was: "Is *that* it?"

"Well, yeah. It's an MG. Pretty cool, huh?"

"Um, it's kinda small," she said.

Well, it's a sports car."

She hesitated, "Oh...well I guess it's cute."

Cute...But maybe cute is good.

Off they went into the starry night. Amy didn't say much. Will became more aware of the car's flaws and hoped she didn't notice the duct tape securing the side mirror. He was also getting worried about the way he'd rigged up the passenger seat. It was really worn so to keep the springs from popping through, he'd stuck a thick biology textbook under it – just a temporary fix.

The old mansion, outside of Athens, was ablaze with lights and music flowed out into the darkness. As they parked, Will was blown away. Seemed he'd chosen a spot in the unofficial luxury car section. He loved the MG, but now it was up against a customized Austin Heely to the right, then a beautiful Mercedes 230SL and just ahead were two immaculate Corvettes – no scratches or duct tape to be found. Those rich Buckhead boys were out in full force tonight.

Then Ronnie pulled up in his super cool Trans Am, a rugged guy in his rugged car. As they all walked up to the mansion, Ronnie took the opportunity to check out Amy – she was beautiful and that's all it took to get some serious flirting going.

The Motown band was one of the coolest around and they did what they do best – got the party started. Everyone was swept up in the moment – the pulsating beat "lifting" the crowd "higher and higher."

"Now I want everybody...I mean everybody – that means you two *bodies* standing over there to...yeah...come on up and let's get it goin'. Let's get it right...tonight! Come on everybody – right up here with your lady. We're gonna have a great time!"

Will felt like he was losing *his lady*. Amy flitted around the room, talking to everyone. She didn't miss a soul and worked the room like a seasoned politician running for re-election.

With her blitz over, Will spotted her over in a corner chatting with Ronnie as the band leader yelled out – "Now ya'll *know* how to do it. And I wanna see some shimmin' and shaggin'! We're 'bout to get it goin' for real!"

With a subtle hand motion to the horns and the stomp of a foot, the band launched into "Do You Like Good Music?"

At that, Will grabbed Amy's hand and, along with everyone else, flocked to the front like it was the California Gold Rush – swinging and swaying to the music and shouting the words back, right on cue.

"There we go now...I'm seein' some real party people in action now...All right...let's do the whole thing again! This time, come on UGA...I want you to really let loose!"

The lead vocalist wiped his brow and told the partiers "Hey, yeah – that's pretty good...you got it...But I can't hear ya that good...You know we've been doin' these parties for a long, long time and we love 'em! But I'm gettin' a little hard of hearin'. So I need some *volume* from ya'll...It's time to turn it up now!"

"Yeah, *that's it*...gettin' in the groove...all right! You know you can cut loose here cause we're waaaaay out in the country...and I think...I said *I think*...we're about to raise the roof on this old place and they're 'bout to hear us way down on Milledge. That's it, UGA!...*Nobody* does it like Georgia Bulldawgs!"

The band ripped through one great song after another, covering all the classic Motown party hits – from "Hold On I'm Comin'" to Otis's "Love Man."

"I was... I was just wonderin' if we have any *soul men* in here in this establishment tonight! If we do...I wanna *SEE IT* with my eyes and *FEEL IT* in my heart... Right here on the dance floor... Ya'll know good and well what I'm talkin' about...I wanna see some movin' and groovin' with your lady and ALL ya'll singin' ...sing it back to me...You know it."

Yes siiiir!

Comin' to you... on a dusty road...

Good lovin'....

Got a truck load...

I'm a soul man!

"You're a soul man! *How "bout it now!"*

"*I'm a soul man!*

The band wrapped up an incredible party with one last throw down – *Shout!* – compliments of the Isley Brothers. (And it was just the kind of awesome night you'd expect on the yellow brick road.)

Amy's mood had taken a noticeable turn to the positive after a slow dance with Ronnie. She was completely different on the way home and talked nonstop about bits of gossip she'd picked up and questions about Ronnie's date.

Even with all the chatter, Will felt like she wasn't really talking to him – just talking period. Then right before they said goodnight, she wrapped up her ramblings in a manner worthy of Scarlett O'Hara, "I sure do love a great party."

It was a week night with nothing much going on. A good night to catch up on some sleep.

But about three in the morning, screaming sirens jarred Will awake.

Several fire trucks roared through the streets and he had to know what was going on. He jogged along a couple of blocks until he saw the men converging on a towering freshman dorm.

By now, everyone was used to fire drills so they automatically lined up like sedated zombies, filing out of the building onto the lawn. No one was happy about leaving snug beds and standing in the chilly night air. The ladies shivered in an assortment of sweats, fuzzy slippers and PJs sporting oversized cartoon characters. Some with a head full of those big pink foam curlers. Not exactly "the look" they were known for.

But smoke bellowing from the top floor of Brumby Hall made it clear that this wasn't a drill. Anxious onlookers watched firefighters burst into the building in full gear. Frantic students searched for friends and asked the big question – *is everybody out?*

It took almost an hour for the smoke to clear. After going floor to floor, they determined that the blaze had broken out in a top floor storage area. Apparently, enterprising students deemed it a good place to host a small gathering. Turned out that 18-year-olds, pot, beer and cigarettes don't always mix well.

Everyone cheered the news that all students were accounted for and applauded the crew as they finished up their work.

When the last truck pulled away and students were back in their rooms, it was finally time to sleep – except for a

select few who decided it would be great fun to memorial-
ize the event with its own soundtrack. Groggy students were
jolted yet again by Jim Morrison's voice booming through
the halls, "C'mon Baby Light My Fire."

But soon a campus cruiser pulled up to the front door
and put an end to the night's drama.

⇒⊦⊦⇐

With everyone caught up in the mania of football, it was
harder and harder for writers to satisfy the insatiable appe-
tite of fans for all kinds of stats, predictions, and interesting
back stories.

Just when it looked like the well had run dry, Will found
another source to tap. He reached into the rich history of
UGA football and pulled out a nugget.

Like most Athenians, he knew the story of Clegg Starks.
But before finishing his final draft, he had to talk to Herman
because no one could tell the story quite like he could.

But today, Herman wasn't in much of a mood to chat
and seemed a little down. But with some gentle coaxing,
Will got him talking.

"You OK, Herman?" Will wondered if his arthritis was
acting up. The constant physical demands of the job had
become too much for him.

"They're things I just don't understand. We got lots of
decent people around here and mostly always have, but I
just can't stand to see nice folks mistreated. You shoulda
seen that young girl comin' outta Dr. Hall's office. All torn
up and cryin' her eyes out. Broke my heart."

"Oh, man."

"I hear things. They say she's a good student. And I can't imagine she did anything deservin' that. Word is he's not treatin' her fair, has it in for her."

"Yeah, people say he's got a long black list and when you're on it, you better look out," Will said.

"It's just a shame. And you'd be disgusted at the way he talks to Mr. Reynolds. Loud and mean, right out here in front of students and everybody."

"Really?"

"There was a time when folks showed respect to anybody older. Makes me wonder what the world's comin' to."

"I guess in a place this size there's bound to be a jerk or two," Will said.

Herman just shook his head.

Will knew that if anything could brighten him up, it was some good ole football lore. "Hey, guess what? I get to write up the old Clegg story for the paper. You gotta tell it again, so I get it right."

Herman managed a weak smile now. "Oh yeah, that's a great one." And he started in. "Now anybody who knows anything about this place remembers President Barrow – that's who Barrow school's named after.

In the '20s, President David C Barrow, who students affectionately called Uncle Dave, resided in a house on campus along with his live-in cook and her son.

Herman got a gleam in his eye. "And the cook's son was some kinda athlete. A big fella, with long, lean arms. He could pick up a basketball with one hand and hold five baseballs in one hand. Nothin' but muscle and those huge hands were just made to handle a football. So livin' right there close to Herty Field, he'd go over all the time and watch the teams practice. He was kind of a fixture. Finally, the baseball coaches put him to work, doin' odd jobs. And when he got older, they made him a trainer for the football team. So he grew up hangin' 'round the athletic field – just naturally learnin', watchin' and throwin'. He'd throw the football for hours and got to where he'd throw the thing clear down the field, I mean the whole 100 yards."

"Herman, tell me the truth. Is that story exaggerated? "Will asked.

"No way, it's all true, on my life. So anyway, coaches told him to use that strong arm on a baseball and see if he could make it to the minor leagues. Well, he did. He pitched fast balls in the old Negro League for a while and even beat Satchel Paige who was the most famous of all the pitchers back then. That happened at an All-Star game in Charleston."

"Wow, I'd forgotten that," Will said.

"Yeah, and lots of folks thought he'd make it to the ma-jors one day, but he got tired of the bus travelin' and came back to his old job at the athletic department. Sometimes they'd bring him out at halftime and he'd throw his *long* passes for show. The crowd loved it."

By the time he got to the Coach Stegeman part, the jani-tor was really on a roll, totally caught up in telling the tale.

"Clegg traveled with the team and when they went up North to play tough schools like Yale, Harvard, all them – Coach Stegeman liked to play a trick on the sportswriters there.

As a matter of course, local writers liked to interview visiting coaches and ask if they had any players they needed to particularly keep an eye on. Stegeman talked about his team, the upcoming game and how "honored they were to be invited."

"He was stallin' and teasin' 'em along and then he'd nonchalantly say, 'You fellas ever seen a guy throw the ball a hundred yards? Well, we got one,'" Herman said.

The writers scoffed in disbelief. They knew that Southerners were prone to embellishment and would snag you with a tall tale while totally mesmerizing you with their charm.

"They hadn't figured out that the coach and Clegg were in cahoots. So they thought they'd be smart and turn the tables, put bets on and shake some money out of 'em."

Herman finally stopped laughing long enough to finish. "So old Coach Stegeman put up some money, then got Clegg on the field. He'd warm up, throw some short passes, nothin' special. The guys watched – lookin' pretty smug and ready to pocket their winnings. Then he let loose. Clegg did his crazy sideways wind-up, and threw the ball clear to the end zone. A full one hundred yards."

The onlookers took it all in with a gawking disbelief that quickly turned to fearful astonishment. They scratched their heads, wondering how they could have missed this guy and so underestimated their opponent. After a sleepless night and lots of antacids, they took the field the next day and there was no Clegg suited up – just a guy with remarkable hands, helping out on the sidelines.

"Man, what a story. But all that bettin'?" Will said. "Good thing the NCAA wasn't around yet."

"You know that's right, there wouldn't be an old 'Clegg and Stege Act' to tell about."

Will had exactly what he needed to finish the piece and Herman got his mind off the likes of Dr. Hall for a while.

FUTURE SHOCK

Campus life was a round the clock, caffeine-fueled ad-venture. With so many things to do, where do you start? Endless social events, sports, music, the arts and maybe even some academics. Will, for one, enjoyed all of it and didn't want to miss a thing.

Even though most of his thoughts for the past few weeks had revolved around Amy, he'd looked forward to hearing a bestselling author tonight whose book, "Future Shock," was making a big splash in the national media and on the talk show circuit.

Will and Ed were both covering the event for the paper but from different angles. The columnist would critique the talk while Will would get student comments and opinions – a "man on the street" kind of thing.

That was the plan. But first Will met Amy for lunch.

"Hey there. You sure look fabulous in that outfit."

"Oh, thanks," She sat down in the booth, hardly looking at him.

Will had hoped for a more enthusiastic reaction. Then again, she knew full well how good looking she was and had plenty of people telling her so. But it wasn't just anybody noticing – *it was him* and Will thought that should have meant something.

"So you went to the fire, uh?"

"Yeah, it really scared everybody till they knew no one was hurt."

"So who started it? Amy asked.

"Nobody knows. Probably some crazy freshmen."

Amy sighed. "A fire. A weird guy hidin' in the bushes. What's goin' on?"

"I dunno. It's a big campus, sometimes things happen. But you're being careful, right?"

"Yeah, we go out in groups and that kind of thing."

Amy quickly left her worries and got back to the business at hand. "*So* my friend, Jill, said she heard that Beth – you remember her from intramurals – was going out with Ken Tolbert."

Will hesitated. "No, haven't heard that." Will thought, 'W*ho cares?* Besides on this campus you'd need an elaborate bracket system to keep up with who's going out with who in a given week.

"I just thought you'd know since Ken went to your high school."

"Yeah, I guess I know who he is, maybe a class behind me. Say, how 'bout tonight? Let's go hear this guy, he wrote "Future Shock.""

"Don't think so. A bunch of us are hangin' out at the house tonight. We spent yesterday getting started on the Toys for Tots drive, so tonight's girl's night."

Will realized that was that. He'd hoped they could be together tonight and go out for pizza afterwards.

"And what about the band party this weekend? Did you talk to Ronnie about us all going together?" Amy asked.

"Uh, haven't seen him lately. Didn't think it was important."

"Well, I just think it would make it more fun."

Will left feeling confused.

Students overflowed the Memorial Hall ballroom, some out of interest, most for extra credit. Alvin Toffler, the "futurologist" took the podium and warned of new things to come and how our society was transforming faster than ever before – an avalanche of change was upon us.

"Future Shock," he said, "is the shattering stress and disorientation that occurs when people experience too much change in too short a time." Scanning the audience Will saw that many were listening and suspending thoughts of romance and good times to ponder the implications of these trends on their lives.

Toffler had "student cred." He was an editor for Fortune magazine and known for his writings about the digital and communication revolution and changes in technology. He'd coined the phrase "information overload," describing a society undergoing an enormous structural change that overwhelms people.

The young audience could identify. Even now, they'd felt another seismic change rumbling through universities since the '60s. Students were caught in a clash of cultures. In classrooms, the pressure was on not only to master various subjects, but to navigate around ideological landmines.

It hadn't always been this way. Until the past decade, established principles of education had been universally accepted. The foundations were laid over 300 years ago when Colonial clergymen chartered New England colleges to carry on the tradition of European liberal education.

In 1785, Yale educated Abraham Baldwin founded UGA and since its inception, UGA has been a tale of Yale. Under the direction of Georgia's governor, the noted scholar and signer of the United States Constitution also served as the college's first president and adapted Yale's classic curriculum to Georgia's first public university – in fact, the first land grant university in the nation. In keeping with prevailing beliefs, Baldwin believed that the main purpose of education was to "build character" based on the tenets of the Christian faith.

So deep roots of the time-tested classical standards that had shaped the best New England colleges extended to UGA. The consensus on this view of education was so strong that from 1819-1899 six university presidents were ministers as well as outstanding educators.

Another Yale professor, Josiah Meigs, became the second president of the university and continued strengthening its ties to the Ivy League school. In 1807, he built the first permanent structure on campus, Old College, as a replica of Yale's Connecticut Hall.

Many professors still held to more traditional thinking and saw their impact on students and society as part of a continuum, believing their efforts would bear fruit over time. But vacant faculty positions were rapidly filling with more activist professors whose mission was to enlist students in a fight for immediate social and political change.

And tonight, carefree students heard forecasts of more sweeping changes that made them stop and think about *their* future. Subconscious worries surfaced. They wondered what their "brave new world" would look like and how they'd fit in.

By the early '70s, the "flower children" had lost most of their bloom. The turmoil of the '60s had disrupted the status quo but mainly left people bewildered by it all. Students felt adrift as they wandered into a new decade that was yet to be defined. Even though violent protests had subsided, the debate over Vietnam wasn't over. In fact, no one could even agree on whether to call it a "war" or a "conflict."

In May 1970, a different kind of tragedy hit home. At Kent State University, four students were killed by the Ohio National Guard during an anti-war protest. Outrage over the May 4th incident spread and about 1,500 agitated UGA students filled the streets of Athens, demanding that the university president condemn the Kent State killings. Word traveled fast. The crowd swelled and moved to Brumby Hall, then to the Academic Building, culminating in 3,000 protestors flooding the president's lawn on Prince Avenue. The stand-off between protestors and administration tottered near the tipping point of violence and went on for four days, closing the university for two.

Officials labored long and hard to reach a mutual understanding, but one clear voice stood out above the tumult and led the way to a resolution. As the beloved dean of students, William Tate had earned the respect of everyone on campus for decades and it was nothing new for him to be in the middle of a messy situation. Dean Tate was one of a kind – the grandfather you always wished you had and a delightful combination of James Stewart and Sheriff Andy of Mayberry.

He got right down to business. Determined to reach a fair agreement, the aging dean put on some love beads, flashed a peace sign and sat cross-legged on the lawn in the middle of the chaos. After hours of listening and reasoning with protest leaders, one asked him. "Dean, we're going to be here all night. Are you staying too?"

Tate said, "Well, when you send out for breakfast, make mine two over light with toast."

His winsomeness and sharp negotiating skills deterred a near calamity during the largest, most disruptive demonstration ever held on campus.

But there was more to come. Later in 1971, the SDS, Students for a Democratic Society, formed a small, but very active UGA chapter. Infamous for firebombing ROTC buildings at major universities, they vowed to abolish ROTC. Even though UGA had survived four other minor incidents in previous years, this time the damage was again minimal, with only one Molitov cocktail shattering a window. Administrators met with the group and UGA's program carried on as usual.

The large 1970 protest had been a high water moment for UGA's anti-war groups. The missteps in Vietnam still stung for many and now a handful of students led by Simon decided it was time for a do-over. Although their numbers had dwindled, protestors were still determined to rev up antiwar sentiment. Demonstrators came out again and demanded an end to ROTC. Simon had convinced them that the memory of the legendary event would draw the masses and strike a real blow. But this time, hardly anyone paid attention and the small gathering went largely unnoticed.

Simon was upset that all his planning and protesting that day was for naught. But at least he'd be heard in the story he'd write for The Red and Black. Unfortunately, he didn't bother to mention he was reporting on the very event that he'd helped to organize – an obvious conflict of interest.

The two ladies wanted to *talk* – that couldn't be good. Sue had summoned Will in for an afternoon meeting. He didn't have a story due, so he wondered what they had to discuss. Then Amy called and asked him to "just come by." His mind raced back and forth, what was all this *talking* going to be about? *Maybe it's something good...could be...* He allowed himself a bit of hope.

He sat in Sue's office, across from her, and tuned in to her every gesture. Propping her elbows on her desk, she got right to the point. "OK, Will, we need to talk about your last piece. It needed a complete overhaul, extensive editing."

Will tried to remember the article in more detail. "Really? What was wrong?"

"A lot, which meant it took way too much of my time to correct it. Typos, spelling, even basic grammar mistakes."

Will sat thinking for a minute.

"I *can* say the content was good, your usual flair, but it was way too raw and unpolished."

Not at all sure how to respond, he mumbled, "I'm sorry. I'll be more careful."

Her expression never changed. "Now you're fully aware of the fast pace of publishing a paper this size. And no one, including me, has time for extra work. So this simply can't happen again."

Will remembered how hurriedly he'd cranked out the article. The past couple of weeks had been full of parties, dates, and football – and now he had a girlfriend to share it all with it.

She wrapped it up. "Will, you have real talent, but it's up to you to develop it. Do the work."

Sue's day was not going well at all. Despite her tough exterior, she really got no pleasure in confronting people – besides, it was just one more thing to wedge into an already full schedule.

She tried to refocus on the final changes to tomorrow's edition when Judy appeared in her doorway. The look on her face made it clear that it wasn't something that could wait. She handed Sue a paper, addressed to Judy by name. In an almost illegible scrawl, it read: "I'm gona give you somethin' to rite about. You can't look out for all them dorm girls."

Sue starred at the note. "Where on earth did this come from?"

"Came in the mail, just now. I guess he knows my name from the article, but it's the part about the dorm that really scares me."

Will walked up to Amy's door. She led him to the parlor of the sorority house and the first thing he noticed was the absence of her smile.

Amy sat down in a chair, which left Will the loveseat – all to himself.

"I don't want to go out anymore."

Will just sat there, dumbfounded.

"We're just not headed in the same direction. I think we want different things."

He was still speechless.

"I'm not sure what you're going to do with your career and I want more out of life."

About all he found to say was "OK." As he left, she slammed the antique door behind him hard enough to rattle the delicate glass panes…a rattling that also shook him to the core.

Will drove around – to no place in particular and allowed himself to sink into self-pity – finally ending up at Memorial Park. He stopped the car and sat alone trying to sort it all out.

Apparently she wanted something he couldn't give her. She was out to secure a certain lifestyle and needed a different guy to make that happen, but he'd let himself fall for her anyway – and this hurt – but he also felt pretty stupid.

The alarm jarred Will from a fitful sleep, he'd totally forgotten it was Saturday. He got to the food bank late, but in such a muddled state of mind, showing up at all was an accomplishment. Dr. Mac immediately knew something was wrong, "Will, you OK?"

"Yeah, fine." To avoid conversation, he jumped in with the others, pulling cans out of boxes.

There was plenty to do. The group sorted stacks and stacks of cans and boxed foods, organizing the items on shelves. Dr. Mac did more than talk persuasively about correcting social ills – he lived out his convictions. All the work he did out in the community dispelled any accusation that he was just an ivory tower intellectual. The man was a sincere progressive.

The prof had mobilized dozens of volunteers and with the respect he'd earned from students and townsfolk alike, a record number of donations flowed in. Ed's fraternity had also contributed in a big way by taking on the project as their local philanthropic work.

The Thanksgiving food drive was shaping up to be the best in their history.

The Old Drug Store
Will wasn't really himself and was just going through the motions. Ed and John had extended a reasonable amount of sympathy over the break up – for guys. Although they didn't talk about it much, they had made good efforts to rescue him from the times he was tempted to sit around and mope.

After class, Ed suggested they get some ice cream – good for any ailment of body or soul, he believed, so they trudged up the long hill on Lumpkin to Five Points.

"So how ya doin'?" Ed asked.

"Oh, I'm fine. I mean, it was all strange and I can't understand why she dumped me like that, so quick. All of a sudden she decided I was a big loser. But deep down, I kinda knew we weren't right for each other."

"I can see that," Ed said.

"Yeah, I mean she was great and all, but now I see it a little different. I had some doubts but just didn't face 'em."

Will turned the conversation to Ed now. "And how 'bout you? It's gotta be weird with your parents splittin' up."

Ed looked straight ahead as they walked. "Yeah that's exactly it – weird. And pretty confusing. It's changed everything, too. Now Dad says not to count on the same amount of money for school. He doesn't know and is givin' me a heads up, in case I need to get a job or somethin'."

"Oh, man."

They continued along in silence a couple minutes, then Will asked," so what's goin' on with your internship?"

"Good – I think. Just waitin' for Dr. Hall to send that form. They say they've gotten everything else."

"It all sounds great. Man, you've been hittin' it out of the park with your columns. Even guys who don't read the paper have been checkin' it out."

Ed's weekly column for The Red and Black had picked up lots of followers the past few weeks and stirred considerable comment with his piece on "Future Shock." He had a knack for explaining current trends and distilling real life implications from them. And before that, he'd done a short series on issues that students were into based on a little informal polling in parking lots. Surveying bumper stickers was a novel approach and catchy in itself. The process yielded six hot topics: "Give a Hoot, Don't Pollute." "Surf Naked." "Think Globally, Act Locally." "Flower Power." "Impeach Nixon." And everyone's favorite – "Alfred E. Newman for President."

"Thanks, man. It's hard not to think about working for the Post. And the stipend would be a huge help, especially if Dad cuts my money. If I'm here next fall, I'll have to move out of the frat house and find something dirt cheap."

"Hey, what's the latest on this stalker guy?" Will asked.

"Last I heard, they've got a general description of him, but not enough for a sketch. Late 20's, sandy hair, tall, thin."

Will shook his head. "Well, that narrows it down. Only a couple of hundred guys look like that."

"But they have a car, too. Gray Ford Pinto."

Most students were taking the warnings to heart and exercising more caution. Rarely did a female venture out alone at night and they made sure to travel in groups. Mace had become a big seller and law enforcement stepped up patrols. Shift change briefings at the precincts always led with – *he has to be caught before he hurts someone.*

Hodgson's was a dose of hometown comfort. Their generous scoops of ice cream – only 15 cents each – brightened anybody's day for sure.

The pharmacy was the epitome of the classic corner drug store – except it was not on a corner, but located at one of the central hubs of Athens just up from campus. Five

Points was the convergence of five narrow streets creating carnival bumper car like congestion.

And besides ice cream, if you timed it right, you could catch the show that the Coke delivery guys put on when they restocked stores. The twin brothers, born with dwarfism, exhibited amazing strength for their size as they heaved heavy cases of Coca-Cola on to hand trucks that were about as tall as they were and effortlessly wielded them around with split second precision. It was as impressive as watching a polished military drill team in action. Then, not missing a beat, they'd speed off in their bright red Coke truck, criss-crossing town and making sure that if anyone missed "the pause that refreshes" – it was their own fault.

The guys waited for some space to open up at the counter. Serving up drinks and cones, perky young workers handled fountain orders along with at least one eager pharmacy student trying to get in some practical experience. Besides student help, the same familiar people worked in the store year after year and they probably knew your name.

If you needed something for that wicked bug that always floored you during exam week, you knew the pharmacist would give you the right elixir for your malady. Sometimes they'd even mix up concoctions with that mortar and pestle thing while they patiently answered your questions and allayed your fears.

Nestled off to the side was "Coach Castronis's Corner." Will and Ed ordered up their ice cream and browsed the vintage Bulldawg memorabilia. Coach Mike Castronis was a Renaissance man in UGA athletics. A remarkable player and coach for many years, he started out in the '40s as an offensive lineman (all 175 lbs of him) and was All-American in 1945.

Back in those days, faculty members filled any job that was needed, so Castronis juggled coaching other varsity teams along with football and also managed to teach three decades worth of P.E. classes. And when administrators were desperate, they turned to him to head up the cheerleading squad. He readily accepted, but was quick to admit that he didn't know "a megaphone from a pompom."

Many fondly remember the coach from his Y days. As director of the YMCA's summer camps in the North Georgia mountains, he made an indelible mark in building character in hundreds of Athens boys.

An avid fitness buff, he loved running and personified his coaching adage: "It's not the size of the dog – it's the size of the fight in the dog that counts."

The small, tanned Greek man (with his bow legs looking like parenthesis) regularly running the Five Points streets was a familiar sight in this college town. Hodgson's was one of his hangouts, a pit stop; folks found him there after his final stretch up Lumpkin Street and it didn't take much to get him going about his football days, particularly the war years. He'd tell you about the 1944 season when most of his teammates were off fighting and about playing with Hall of Fame running back Charley Trippi.

Besides sports, Coach Castronis made another contribution to the community by having a very attractive daughter, Helen, not of Troy, but of Athens, duly noted by the young men in town.

Will and Ed waited on the sidewalk to cross the busy intersection. When the traffic came to a halt, a familiar Trans Am pulled up to the light. Ronnie looked over and waved – and so did his lovely passenger – Amy.

Ed was shocked and didn't know what to say. Any lingering doubts Will may have had about their relationship were answered at that moment. She'd had her strategy from the intramural game on – and now it was clear – all the angling for the couples to go out together and the flirting added up to one conniving young lady.

Coach Mrvos
Next day, the guys were very curious about Simon's take on the protest. They made sure to pick up a copy of The Red and Black and had just enough time to look it over before P.E. Simon usually hovered on the edge of credible journalism and there were plenty of wagers on just when he'd go over the edge. And for anyone with big money on it, today was their lucky day.

Will read Simon's words out loud. "Although no injuries were reported, the show of force by campus police resulted in unwarranted intimidation. Protest leaders were quoted as saying that the reason the demonstration fizzled out so quickly was due to authorities "not respecting our First Amendment rights."

"Did it really happen like that?" Ed asked.

"Man, I dunno. Seems like we woulda heard something."

"But everyone I've talked to said the rally was no big deal."

"I guess we'll see. I mean if it's as bad as he reported, it won't just blow over."

Will was still sulking around. But the hurt from being dumped wasn't the only thing gnawing at him – it'd also made him question some things about himself. *What had Amy seen that he didn't?* He was hitting his stride in his field but did he really have the drive to compete in a tight job market? And where was he really headed? He realized he had more questions than answers. But for now, some good old physical exertion would surely chase the blues away. If you didn't spike a sharp endorphin release in one of Coach Mrvos's intense workouts, you best seek immediate medical attention.

The guys turned the corner on Lumpkin and walked to the old Stegemen gym as they had so many times before. The sprawling brick building was a welcomed sight.

"Hey, remember when we were kids? All those sports camps we went to here?" Ed said.

"Yeah. We had some kinda fun."

It was always the highlight of summer. A mob of eager kids quickly filled up UGA's sports classes, taught by some of the college's best coaches and grad assistants.

"Man, was it hot in there. How'd we make it?" Ed asked.

"It was brutal," Will said.

Back then, the aging gym was like a battleship boiler room. The only illusion of relief came when a couple of fans prodded along a pitiful hot breeze seeping through the top windows. This was the air conditioning system.

But for several weeks, the youngsters enjoyed all manner of sports – from archery to wrestling – you name it and even bowling downtown for 50 cents a game.

And now in their college years, the guys still made the trek to the old gym. They'd survived three grueling quarters' worth of P.E. classes under Sam Mrvos and the journalists had made it to *advanced weightlifting* – a class geared only for varsity players and P.E. majors. It'd been a humbling start for Will who could barely bench press his own weight. But this quarter, he was up to a decent 245 lbs.

The crusty coach had come up through the ranks and after playing football at the university in the early '50s, he'd served as the team's strength coach for years. The first day of his class was epic. Standing before them, he curled a 60 lb. dumbbell with *one arm*. You watched him do one rep after the other as he barked out class requirements. It got your attention. But the remarkable thing about this brusque man was his genuine excitement over the progress of average guys as much as big time athletes. A marvel at coaching and dishing out tough love, he pushed students to lift a little more each week and reach beyond their limits. And when they met a goal, he was also the first one to lead the cheerleading.

But on the other hand, if you showed up just one minute late to class, you were sure to regret it with every wearying mile you ran the next day at the crack of dawn.

Mrvos had his methods and making good use of the steep stadium steps was one of his favorites. Conquering the concrete steps leading uphill to the Chemistry Building was a rite of passage for anyone under his tutelage. The phrase that struck fear into many a student was "Now guys, we're gonna have some fun. Out to the stadium!" Both Castronis and Mrvos claimed that the steps routine *built character.*

The first time up, you went as fast as you could landing on every step. On the next set down, you skipped every other step. When you reached the bottom, it was time to turn around and run up again – backwards. Then you repeated the drill. Your legs pumped up and down like pistons in a racecar. From a distance, the class must have looked like a giant centipede on steroids pounding up and up those flights of stairs that never seemed to end. You gasped for air as your chest heaved and your legs turned to rubber. You kept looking at him – praying he'd blow that chrome whistle dangling from his neck and put an end to the torture before you collapsed on the spot. But if you stayed with the program – one day it hit you. You felt like you could ascend Mt. Olympus and light the torch.

Mrvos himself looked like he was carved straight out of the rugged western Pennsylvania coal country that was his home. When his parents emigrated from Eastern Europe, they brought along their old world work ethic and instilled it into their son. The short, burly hulk of a man had a simple philosophy – "if you fail, try again" and "hard work over time produces results *if* you hang in there."

He stuck to his mission –to make you stronger and tougher, not to hold your hand. The hardnosed mentor successfully drilled discipline and perseverance into countless students who always remembered his famous mantra, long after P.E. class – "Do all you can and then do one more!"

Drenched in sweat and surrounded by massive UGA athletes, the guys slowly trudged to the showers. The lingering, pungent odor from the old gym had once again breathed new life into them.

Will had a big term paper due and he needed to get crackin'. Ed, who had already written his paper for the "Media and Society" assignment, wisely suggested that Will harness all that energy from his work-out and put it to good use. The topic was an easy one: "TV and American Culture."

Everyone had witnessed the power of the device and remembered how it had transformed their homes. At some point, favorite shows dictated "family time."

The entire family succumbed to the magnetic draw of the glowing communal altar in their family room. And it didn't take long for it to edge out the flicker of the fireplace and conversations at dinner tables. The mind-numbing entertainment was just too tempting while Americans morphed into couch dwellers who munched junk food or ate TV dinners on TV trays.

Behind the scenes, ad folks raked in huge profits while a tiny cohort of experts debated the impact of the constant exposure to random images, banal ads and fluff programming. Would the TV generation still be able to *think*?

Educators already saw a drop in basic knowledge of high school graduates. And an increasing number couldn't have passed the citizenship test. But somehow everyone could recite ad jingles – "pop, pop, fizz fizz, oh what a relief it is" or "Bounty, the quicker picker upper" and Mr. Whipple's repeated plea – "Don't squeeze the Charmin!" Targeting kids on Saturday mornings paid off handsomely with huge sales of Duncan yo-yos, Slinkys, GI Joes and Barbies.

When the teacher wheeled the TV into the classroom, we knew we were about to witness something big. A Cape Canaveral launch or the sad news of another assassination. We'll never forget the tragic report from Dallas, TX: "We interrupt this broadcast with breaking news: President

Kennedy has been shot and taken to Parkland Hospital."
The grainy black and white image showed it all.

Who didn't look forward to the spring showing of "The
Wizard of Oz"? Or "The Wonderful World of Disney" on
Sunday nights? And with his weekly variety show, Ed Sullivan
made stars and superstars, propelling Elvis and The Beatles
to instant fame. After The Beatles's TV performance, mil-
lions went out and bought their album, "Meet the Beatles."
Athenians were no exception and waited in long lines at
Woolworth's for their chance to buy a copy.

But there's one universal truth about TV – it makes a
great study break. And not long into his paper, Will decided
on one, ordered a pizza and flipped on "The Rifleman."

The announcer's booming voice said: "The Rifleman!"
(13 shots rang out from a smoking Winchester rifle)
"Staring – Chuck Connors!" *Oh, Man. A rerun of one of my
favorites.* This was shaping up to be a very nice study break,
although it was short on the study and long on the break.

*Good ole Lucas McCain... Now there was a man's man. He
took care of business and handily dispatched the bad guys – all in
30 minutes flat.*

The man's moral compass never wavered. He was brave
and resolute – always there to help folks who were down on
their luck.

The old town marshal, who'd won the battle with the
bottle, could always depend on Lucas. Together, they'd fend
off rustlers and other riff raff, keeping the peace in their
small Western town. Will smiled as he remembered that
they'd jailed and killed that really bad hombre, "Charlie
Gordo" at least five times. He needed it though.

After a Clorox commercial and several more slices of pizza, a protracted gun battle lit up the middle of Main Street. It sure looked like the end of the road for Lucas who was badly outnumbered and wounded yet again. But the outlaws had forgotten about his modified Winchester rifle. With a special trigger, Lucas unleashed a barrage of bullets faster than they could jump in the horse trough. The Rifleman popped up and refreshed their memories, finishing off the desperados before the last commercial and credits.

Each show was packed with pearls of wisdom about life and love. Between heavy doses of law and order, Lucas kept his little boy tenderly under his wing. In one episode, the little guy fidgeted with his tie, trying to get it just right for a girl's birthday party when Lucas stepped into help. "Son, what's troublin' you?"

"Nothin'. But why does a fella get all jumpy when yer around a girl you're sweet on? It's 'bout as bad as ropin' a calf with folks watchin'."

"Well son...its cause *this* calf can rope you back!"

It was a fun trip down memory lane, but still no paper. Even Lucas McCain couldn't rescue Will from the perils of his procrastination. Looks like he'd have to rustle up some gumption, quit goofing off, and lasso a passing grade on his own.

REMEMBER WHEN...

Will's home was a modest 1940's brick house near Five Points. Living there for his first two years of college wasn't a problem since he'd saved a bundle on dorm fees which came in handy when he got his own place.

Besides, Will had been around long enough to know that he hadn't missed much in the freshman dorm. Silly pranks, sleepless nights and smells he could definitely live without. And nursing drunk freshman in the wee hours wasn't his idea of a good time.

But an occasional stroll through the dorm was like really good "people watching" or that simple pleasure of visiting a friend and nosing around their book collection. At a time when self-expression was all the rage, students proudly decorated their 12 by 18 foot living space with a customized blend of posters and mementos along with some *hard to categorize* stuff – all displayed to declare "who they *really are*."

So next to class schedules and "to do" lists were posters of Gandhi, King, Bob Dylan, Bonhoeffer and various activists and rock stars, some illuminated with black lights by the truly hip. Peace symbols said a lot on a small budget.

But back home, not much had changed. Will's parents still kept his room just the way he'd left it.

Will had fond memories of their simple home. It was a cozy and comfortable place except for a couple of "formal" rooms. Even though the front door opened to the living room, they didn't actually "live" in the living room. It was reserved for the best antiques that Will's dad had carefully refinished over the years. The room was really more of a museum than anything else. And any young boy who dared to venture into this sanctuary was hounded with dire warnings about sitting on any of the Victorian chairs or even *getting near* an inherited piece of crystal or china. It was about as risky as trespassing into the Air Force's forbidden research Area 51 in Nevada. The same was true for the "dining room" – another misnamed room, because nobody dined there – except for holidays or "special company." The family usually ate together at a small kitchen table or in the "TV room" on well-worn sofas where they watched the news or a favorite show.

In the front yard, a sprawling oak tree made it nearly impossible to grow grass. But the creeping thrift, covering the front bank near the street, made up for that, and every spring, the expanse of lavender blooms was the talk of the neighborhood. Under the tree sat an ensemble of white wrought iron chairs that had been there as long as Will could remember. But nobody actually sat there either because the rock hard seats were more ornamental than functional.

The fun part was the very back of the property which led to their sports field and was also home to Will's elaborate tree house that rivaled the "The Little Rascals" terrific hangout. It was crammed full of army surplus items for prolonged battles and crowned with a white-walled tire at the top of the large pine for a ship's crow's nest along with a trusty Sears's telescope for monitoring exploits on the high seas or spotting approaching enemy armies. Many a foe was vanquished from the rolling waves in the make-believe vessel. But if you faced overwhelming odds or a swarm of pirates and needed to beat a hasty retreat (or get to supper after the third summons from mom) – a retractable rope ladder and a steel fire pole were at your disposal. The treehouse also had an illustrious military history serving as the campaign headquarters for Gen. Patton, Eisenhower and other notables in pivotal battles over the years.

But besides the pretend stuff, you had a few real fears that haunted you. TV newsreels often showed thousands of Soviet soldiers marching past the Kremlin followed by row after row of missiles and tanks. Khrushchev was always spouting off and *who knew when he'd get really ticked off and push the button and start WWIII.*

Kids knew all about atomic radiation and fallout shelters and that the Russians could blow us up at any minute. We curled up under our wooden desks in school during safety drills – just in case of a nuclear blast. And throw in a Godzilla movie or two and it was very scary stuff.

One day, a young Will was convinced that the worst had happened. He ran through the door screaming: "Mom, the Russians! They dropped an atomic bomb somewhere! There's a huge radioactive rat in the shed! It stared at me with glowing red eyes. The hair's all burned off. It's big and ugly and moves real slow."

After a tall glass of Kool-Aid, Will's mom calmed him down and he learned that day what a good ole Georgia possum looks like.

Will stepped carefully around the tools and rakes in their make shift carport then took the steps to the kitchen. Even before he grasped the handle, his dad was already there, opening the door, eager to see his son.

Dr. Martin Andrews was approaching 60, balding with a trim gray moustache. The professor had taught history at UGA for over 30 years. He was mainly known as a very kind and selfless man, but often surprised folks with his razor sharp wit.

They all sat down at the small kitchen table together. The meal may have been made from scratch but it's not what you'd imagine. Will's mom readily admitted that she wasn't a very good cook. She'd wink and inform you that she'd been too busy *preparing* three meals a day to ever learn to *cook*. Her interests revolved around the family, academics and good reading. When it came time to write another history book, Dr. Andrews knew he could depend on her love of language and keen editing skills. Pounding each word out on stiff Royal typewriter keys in those days made the writing process a real chore. Plus there was lots of messy blue carbon paper to deal with.

Talking nonstop, his mom fluttered around in her house dress to get the meal on the table. All five feet of herself was

a bundle of nervous energy. Even with their future retirement secured by a university pension, Mrs. Andrews still fell
into a pattern of habitual worry. The couple never forgot
what it was like growing up in the Depression, so they lived
simply, saved *everything* and were thankful for what they had.

All in all, she was happy as things were, had little use for
pretense and didn't mind saying so. On one occasion, several church ladies gathered at her home for a luncheon and
a particularly stuffy matron went on about her horses – describing at great length her equestrian competitions. "I declare – I *do love* raising fine horses." To that, Mrs. Andrews
chimed in: "Well, I love raising mules. One is named Will
and the other John. They don't win any ribbons, but they do
take out the trash from time to time."

The many interests Will shared with his parents always
sparked lively conversation. But today he was a bit subdued.
Probably a girl, they thought. But in the Andrews's household, there were just some things you didn't talk about, unless it was really necessary.

Dessert signaled the time to catch up on friends and
neighbors. Will filled them in on John and Ronnie whom
they'd known since they were kids. Ed was any parent's
dream friend for a son, since he was 20 going on 40. Sad
to hear about his parent's divorce, the Andrews discussed
the growing trend of handling marital problems by simply
walking away. Something not so common in the past. Then
Will updated them on a fellow who everyone knew as a perpetual student. The professor's son was pushing 30 and
already had three unrelated degrees under his belt. And he
was starting on yet another one – *Ancient Languages.* Even
his mother, who'd spoiled him rotten, had a "hissy fit" at

the news, as Mrs. Andrews put it. Will's dad shook his head and chuckled, "My goodness, by the time *he* finishes school, *English* will be an ancient language."

Will asked about their long time neighbor, Mary Hanes Walters. As administrative assistant to the president of the university, she knew *everything* that went on. The president had relied on her heavily ever since his years as head of the Vet school. Intensely loyal and capable, she cut through non-sense like an All-American running back tearing through a defense and if you wanted anything from the top man; you had to get through the lady who was known far and wide as "Madame President."

Even with her astute outlook and measured sense of humor, Will could always make Mary Hanes laugh. But when she was serious, her piercing eyes seemed to look into your very soul. You felt compelled to confess *something – anything.*

Mary Hanes had divorced years ago, and in all the time they'd known her, she never talked about her ex-husband or why the marriage ended. Her work was her life – along with her beloved Scottish terrier and caring for her younger sister, stricken with an early onset of Parkinson's disease.

The double name is a Southern thing. It goes like this. If there's no male heir to carry on a family name, a daughter took it as her middle name. This worked for a generation or two, but then the name eventually died out and ended up engraved on a tombstone somewhere. Nevertheless, Mary Hanes did her duty and never allowed anyone to simply call her "Mary."

Mrs. Andrews had spoken to her just the other day – doing fine and thinking about retirement. Which brought up

Herman. Dr. and Mrs. Andrews would not think of missing his party and hoped to see Dean Tate there as well. Even though his days of service were over; the dean found it hard to stay away from his beloved UGA and all his old friends.

Dr. Andrews had one final question. "Have you seen Mr. Marshall recently?"

"It's been a while."

"I have a few friends switching their accounts to him. He's sure attracting the business."

"Yeah? And what about you, Dad?"

After a thoughtful pause, he said, "Well, you know I'm pretty conservative and, this close to retirement, I think I'll remain that way."

That was about the answer Will had expected and it actually made perfect sense; he rarely doubted his dad's judgement.

Heading back to his apartment, Will drove by campus and could tell that beneath the buoyant spirit of fall was a nagging sense of fear that the stalker would strike again. Police continued to sift through multiple reports of suspicious characters and screened calls as best they could. College pranks and guys *just fooling around* made their job even harder.

But law enforcement was not letting up. City and county officials opened up the coffers and paid overtime to provide the manpower needed to protect students.

Even though Will had made up his mind that he was done nursing a wounded ego, his thoughts still drifted back to Amy. He'd realized that, when all was said and done, she wasn't the girl for him. But then a song came on the radio – and that's not the way it felt.

The Charter

A sudden sadness hit Will when he noticed Herman leaving a classroom with his cart. Pretty soon there'd be no more impromptu visits with this kind man. But today, he sure could use a dose of "Herman."

"How 'bout it, Herman? Not much longer now is it?"

"Twelve days. That's it. But it don't seem real."

"What'd ya think you'll miss the most?"

"Now you're startin' to sound like a reporter or somethin'."

They both laughed.

"Is this *on* the record or *off* the record? You know I love this place. It's been a big part of my life for a long time."

"Sure has. As long as I've been alive, I guess," Will said.

Herman enjoyed ribbing anyone he was fond of. "There you go, making me feel old. I was OK till you put it like that."

Herman paused and looked away. "I was just thinkin' that I won't be here for the next Charter Day. I've worked that event for years and it's always pretty special."

Every January 27, the charter was brought out of storage from the library's special collections department and displayed before the public to commemorate the university's founding. But that had not always been the case. In fact, for years, they'd thought they'd lost the document forever. UGA had long bragged that it was the oldest state chartered university in the nation. But for a time, they had trouble proving it.

Sometime around the turn of the century, the historic document got mixed up in a pile of scrap paper that was sent to the basement of the state capitol for burning. As the janitor fed the flames, he noticed a good stiff piece of paper that he thought might be useful for "mending something." He stuffed it in his locker, figuring it may come in handy one day.

When the man retired, his successor cleaned out the locker and found the historic document sitting there taking up space. He took it upstairs to have Secretary of State, Guyton McClendon, look it over.

When McClendon recovered from the shock of finding the original charter of the university, he arranged to have it sent, under guard, to the Special Collections Department at the UGA library. And, it's been kept there securely ever since.

Top language scholars cited the opening line of the charter as one of the finest sentences ever written in the English language. And Herman agreed.

"As it is the distinguishing happiness of free governments that civil order should be the result of choice and not necessity, and the common wishes of the people become the laws of the land, their public prosperity and even existence very much depends upon suitably forming the minds and morals of their citizens."

Calls flooded into The Red and Black. A mixture of bystanders, police and university officials contacted the newspaper and pointed out errors in the ROTC story. Even a few protestors themselves told the editor that the reports of harassment by police were patently false.

The editors moved swiftly into damage control, assigning reporters to interview anyone and everyone who'd been involved in the event or witnessed it.

The managing editor brought Simon in and reviewed the statements in his story, line by line, along with checking sources for each fact.

Judy talked to several participants and onlookers and came away with a totally different picture of what occurred that day.

When the team gathered the information, the editor marked out a two hour block for everyone to meet and sort through the information. The story that emerged bore little resemblance to the one written by Simon and published by the paper.

None of the demonstrators said that they'd been threatened by police. And, as it turned out, the authorities themselves said at no time was the situation out of control. One veteran of the force stated, "It was about the calmest protest I've ever seen. Why, I've been to Sunday school picnics that were more rambunctious."

The collective view was that the rally never got going. Folks wandered around, socializing and then left. It was basically a non-event by all accounts – except Simon's.

Two main troubling facts stood out from reviewing the information...Simon was actually there, so how could he see something so differently from everyone else? And then there was the obvious conflict of interest. He covered an event that he'd organized himself.

The editor concluded that they had printed a story with an embarrassing number of inaccuracies. They immediately printed a correction and an apology and suspended Simon until further notice.

＊＝＜╬╪＞＝＊

Will realized that even though he never knew where he stood with Dr. Hall, it was a good idea to befriend the influential professor. He hung around after class and tried some small talk.

"Interesting discussion. Hey, you comin' to Herman's party?"

Dr. Hall hesitated, looking bewildered. "Well, I know I have something like that on my calendar, but off hand, I can't remember what it is."

"I think a lot of folks will show up to say goodbye to Herman. He's been here a long time and knows just about everybody," Will said.

"Herman?"

Now Will was the one bewildered, Dr. Hall didn't seem to recognize his name even though they worked in the same building every day.

"Yeah, he's the janitor here."

The large room filled with people. Herman's family, friends and church members, dressed in their Sunday best, all came out to congratulate him. Several students, lots of faculty and staff filed by and shook his hand. Everyone celebrated with a slice of cake and punch served on a table decorated with red and black balloons. Another table was piling up with gifts and cards, many stuffed with cash. Mary Hanes stood by the president as he gave Herman a gift from the university and made a few remarks. After his "official comments," commending Herman's years of service, the speaker loosened his tie and started telling stories. They'd known each other since the president's early teaching days, so he had plenty of material to draw from.

"Back then," he said, "everyone pitched in and worked together. You never knew what you'd be asked to do. One time, this old farmer rushed an injured lamb straight through the front doors of the vet school, dripping blood all over the place. I'll never forget the look on Herman's face. We got the lamb fixed up, but the mess in the hallway was another matter. When Herman and I realized we were the only ones left, we both grabbed a mop – and still made it home for a late dinner."

The president waited for the laughter to die down and went on.

"And remember the Zebra?" Herman threw his head back and laughed. "Came down from the Atlanta Zoo with a bad break in his leg. The sedative began to wear off just as we were getting him inside. Herman grabbed his hind legs and held on for all he was worth. We managed to get him on the table for surgery just before he *really* woke up."

The president went on, reliving old times. He looked Herman up and down. "You're in mighty good shape for a man your age. I believe you have old Dr. Bones to thank for that!"

Herman just shook his head. "That man never met a rock he didn't like."

"He gave you quite a workout lugging his heavy boxes around."

"Dr. Bones" was a long time anthropology professor in one of the smallest departments on campus – well for many years he *was* the department. Relegated to the basement of Baldwin Hall, the professor filled every nook and cranny with his unusual collection, but he couldn't be contained. Fossils, bones, artifacts of all kinds spilled out the back door, cluttering the parking lot and lawn. The job of *managing* the overflow fell to Herman who discreetly *relocated* the specimens.

Herman wiped tears from his eyes from laughing so hard. "I'm tellin' ya it was a sight. As much as I liked him, I sure was glad to see him retire and take his stuff with him. And now, looks like *we're* the old fossils."

The man of the hour, dressed up in coat and tie, smiled as he continued to receive a rapid succession of warm wishes and pats on the back. Then the director of environmental services commemorated Herman's hard work. "In his 35 years, he only missed a handful of days and no one can remember hearing an unkind word from him." He recounted the many times that Herman went above and beyond his duty. The group responded with affirmative nods and much applause. But Herman seemed uncomfortable being the center of attention.

Dr. Hall leaned against a wall with arms crossed, looking rather smug as he observed the merriment. It was his turn to say a few words. He pulled a piece of paper from his pocket and glanced at it. "We all appreciate Herman's long and dedicated service and we wish him the best in his retirement. As we leave this celebration, let us not tire in our efforts to improve the rights of workers everywhere in their fight for equality."

An awkward pause gave way to polite, but muted clapping. Then Herman stepped up and shook Dr. Hall's hand and thanked him. The party continued.

The guests went on reminiscing about the days when the university was more like one big family.

Then, in walked Dean Tate who attacked Herman with a huge bear hug. The two went way back.

"Oh, I know I'm retired. But I'd have to be embalmed and laid out at Bernstein's to miss this celebration. Herman's been my friend for longer than some of you been alive. He's a true Bulldawg through and through, a hard workin' man of deep faith who's lifted my eyes heavenward on many a tryin' day."

The group was all smiles and offered up robust shouts of "Amen!"

"Like I used to tell the students, don't try to be a Big Dawg, just a faithful dog. To succeed in life you gotta know your Maker, mate, and mission. And the man we're here for today is a fine example of this; he's persevered through all the ups and downs of life. Like an old friend used to say, 'Life is full of sunshine, but what you step in is called experience'. Right Herman?"

Another round of applause. The dean mingled with guests, then slapped Will on the back. "So you're a junior now? Can't believe it, why, it was just yesterday, I'd see you in your dad's office... a little fella in a scout uniform. Why, you were no bigger than nose high to a woodchuck. OK then, since you're a reporter, get goin' with that writing apparatus and let's have a story worthy of this event."

It had been a grand occasion, but sometimes things aren't ever exactly as they should be. The large room stood empty now. Herman surveyed the area and saw what needed to be done. He shed his dress coat, rolled up his sleeves and trudged to the closet. Slowly pulling out the cleaning cart one last time, he took out a large trash bag and started with the plates and cups – cleaning up the remnants of a very special day in his life.

The paper scrambled to fix their mistake and as a follow up to the paper's apology, Ed wrote a front page column about the media's responsibility to earn the public's trust.

He got to the heart of the matter in his final paragraph.

"The temptation to interject personal opinions and beliefs into our stories is only human – but we must guard against it. How can the media have any credibility if the public doesn't believe we're covering a story with fairness and accuracy? The opinion page is just that – our opinions – and that's the proper place, and the only place, to print personal views and express editorial endorsements."

Memorial Hall

"Dulce et decorum est pro patria mori."

"I … I… I am everyday people… Yeah, Yeah! I am no better and neither are you… We are the same whatever we do…

"You love me you hate me and then…you can't figure out the bag I'm in…. I … I… I am everyday people…Yeah, Yeah…"

The music thundered through the gigantic speakers pounding the eardrums of "the everyday people" wildly rocking the Memorial Hall Ballroom. The psychedelic light show synced to the sound board projected bizarre blobs of pulsating color as the gyrating musicians threw themselves into their energetic cover of Sly and the Family Stone's hit song.

After several more prolonged guitar solos – the song reached a resounding crescendo –suddenly all the stage lights went out and the singers yelled out "*War. What is it good for? Absolutely nothing! Everybody say it with me! Say it again – War. Ah!...What is it good for? Absolutely nothing!*" The light show flashed on again. The band tried to get a chant going back and forth with the Friday night partiers but only got a tepid response. The merrier makers were much more in the mood for "putting on their boogie shoes" than resurrecting a '60s protest song. Sure, everyone agreed that "war was good for nothing," but sadly the reality was far different. During our country's history, we'd been involved in various conflicts for a multitude of complicated reasons.

Will and Ed were into the scene and the good music and then took the spiral staircase up to the second floor to get a better view of the band. Climbing the stairs, Will glanced at the rotunda and saw something he'd never noticed. It looked like an inscription of some sort so he craned his neck and rotated around to read the words.

"In loyal love we set apart this house, a memorial to those lovers of peace who took arms, left home and dear ones and gave life that all men might be free."

Will was struck by the moving words and the startling contrast of the oblivious partiers and the band's attempt to throw out a bit of social commentary. He remembered that Memorial Hall had been built after WWI to honor the 47 UGA students who had died "in the war to end all wars." The tribute also prompted Will to recall a day from Mr. Edward Richardson's poetry class last spring.

Will had always enjoyed a good story – from comic books to the classics. But he'd learned from growing up in a college town that its ongoing lectures, "symposiums," and "colloquiums" by various "experts" and" scholars" give rise to the occasional wind bag with too many bats in the belfry who could wring all the joy out of Shakespeare or Cervantes in no time. And then there were a handful of profs that were just plain looney – he concluded at a young age that there was no nut like an "academia nut."

On the other hand, an excellent literature teacher can make great works come to life. And that was Mr. Richardson – who lived for words and language and storytelling. He was a bit of an odd duck though. Students said that the nervous, fidgety fellow in his ill-fitting clothes reminded them of Elmer Fudd.

But when he talked about poetry, he morphed into quite the orator. If a random phrase or verse popped into his mind, he was off to the races, eloquently discoursing on Wordsworth or Byron.

He also knew the stories behind the poems which were often more interesting than the work itself. You never knew when Mr. Richardson would interrupt himself and spontaneously gush forth with another tangential, yet compelling tale.

The old prof had a knack for tying some of his recitations to significant historical events and the current culture. And near Memorial Day, he came up with a class that was hard to forget. He cleared his throat and launched into a spirited presentation of "In Flanders Fields":

"In Flanders Fields"
In Flanders fields the poppies blow
Between the crosses, row on row,
That mark our place; and in the sky
The larks, still bravely singing, fly
Scarce heard amid the guns below.

We are the Dead. Short days ago
We lived, felt dawn, saw sunset glow,
Loved and were loved, and now we lie
In Flanders fields.

Take up our quarrel with the foe:
To you from failing hands we throw
The torch; be yours to hold it high.
If ye break faith with us who die
We shall not sleep, though poppies grow
In Flanders fields.

Mr. Richardson's stirring rendition resonated with the class. Some were moved to tears by the poignant words especially in light of the conflict in Vietnam. Every student knew someone serving in the war. And the worst was that too many families, even right here in Clarke County, had gotten the dreaded knock on the door. Before the somber, uniformed Marine even spoke, younger brothers and sisters watched their mother collapse to the floor in sheer agony. And the children were left trying to understand why their brother would never come home.

Mr. Richardson let the verses sink in, then summarized the poem's intent and told the story about the author.

"The poet served as a colonel in the Canadian medical corps and penned the poem from the trenches of Flanders Fields in the thick of heavy fighting. He wrote from the perspective of the dead; urging the living never to forget their sacrifice and to press on. Ironically, soon after surviving the savagery of trench warfare, McCrae came down with pneumonia and died in 1918.

"Interestingly enough," Mr. Richardson went on, "in 1918, UGA professor, Monia Michael, wore a poppy year round to honor fallen soldiers. She traveled to Flanders Fields and was never the same. Compelled to keep their memory alive, she brought home poppies to grow in her own garden and distributed them on Memorial Day for donations. The professor taught classes for disabled vets, continued her fund raising efforts and went on to raise millions of dollars. Monia Michael became a nationally known advocate for veterans.

Mr. Richardson concluded, "Whatever your views on our country's engagement in foreign affairs – particularly in Vietnam – you should express your opinions honestly but always with the upmost respect and deep sympathy for the terrible sufferings of those involved."

Will had gotten to know several Vietnam vets doing press releases for their group.

Even though, they were a small part of the student body, they stood out in their scruffy jeans and faded fatigue jackets emblazoned with their unit patch. They were older and more reticent, and mostly kept to themselves. Some guys moved from class to class staring blankly, looking like lost souls. Others were laser-focused on making up for lost time. Will decided to forego the rest of the concert – the travails of other people at other times overshadowed the sting of his breakup – at least for a couple of hours.

Dr. Mac had carefully followed the Simon saga with increasing dismay. He knew that the faculty should help students learn from their mistakes, so he'd discuss the matter with Dr. Hall.

"Peter, this protest story's turned into a real mess. You've talked to Simon, right?"

"We've talked."

"Well, I hope he's learned something. Stuff like this can really damage a career before it even gets started."

Dr. Hall stiffened and looked away. "Oh, I know. Everyone has an opinion on it. But we need to think about his courage and commitment. At least give him credit for that."

"Maybe. But that was lousy reporting at best. I'm sure he'll listen to you. You helped him understand what he did, right?"

"That's not really my place, Mac. You know that I don't interfere with the newspaper."

"Peter, he looks up to you! If anyone could help him, you could."

"Exactly. I'm here to support him. All he did was try to bring attention to a very important issue, besides, plenty of others have reamed him out sufficiently for getting a few details wrong."

LOCAL LEGENDS

Every November, Florida and Georgia got together and put on the Mardi Gras of college football. It was a grand event down in Jacksonville, Fla. The show-down between the perennial powerhouse teams was wedged into days of all-out partying with the weekend known as the largest outdoor cocktail party in the nation.

The epicenter may have been in Jacksonville, but shock waves rumbled through Athens as thousands of fans packed out sports bars and clustered around TVs all over town.

After a thorough debate on the best place to watch the game, the guys decided on The Fifth Quarter. The popular watering hole was packed, but they were in luck. One of John's connections managed to sneak them through the crowd and seat them at one of the very last tables.

Ed leaned back in his chair and, as the visionary among them, he suggested a plan, "Hey, next year, we need to find a way to go to Jacksonville."

John seconded the proposal, "Got to, before we graduate."

"Yeah, but have you seen the price of hotels down there?" Will said. "Man, it's astronomical, even if you could book one."

"The only way to get there is to know somebody," John said," A friend who lives there, or something."

Ed nodded, "All right guys, we gotta get this nailed down."

It was still a good two hours before the game and everyone was well-primed and busy analyzing the teams. They'd covered everything from the kicker's cleats to the offensive coach's lucky cap.

But then the pregame chatter ended and all eyes were glued to the large screen showing the national broadcast. Cameras panned UGA fans descending on the town in their red and black finery. Flags and banners were everywhere. It made a Bulldawg proud.

Finally, the coin toss. The Dawgs lined up for the kick-off and Ed yelled, "Cut the sound!" Someone quickly silenced the network commentators and cued up a radio to THE Voice of the Georgia Bulldawgs – Larry Munson. It made no difference where fans watched the game – at home, in sports bars or even in the stadium – every Bulldawg *had* to hear it from Munson, it was the *only* way to truly experience the game. He was *the man* to call the action in Georgia football.

Larry Munson had started his career in Minneapolis. For $15 a week, he'd announced the names of boxers and wrestlers. Who would have thought that the consummate Bulldawg would've come from the frozen state of Minnesota? But in 1966 he traveled south and found his true home in Athens where he endeared himself to fans far and wide and became a broadcasting legend. He and his trusty sideline analyst, Loran Smith, made a terrific combo. Munson relied on him for key updates from the field and when fans heard Munson ask – "Whatya got Loran?" – they listened up.

Tensions ran high anytime the Dawgs tangled with the Gators and Munson captured it all with his passionate play-by-play narrative. His earnest, gravelly voice, pulled you into "the picture he painted on the field."

An hour flew by. The place fell silent as the Dawgs desperately tried to stop Florida from scoring...goal to goal... Munson pleaded with the defense, "Hunker down you guys...I know I'm asking a lot you guys! But hunker it down one more time!"

The guys were still absorbed in the game as the third quarter began. Florida was ahead, but not by much. Hot dogs sat cold as everyone held their breath and watched the Dawgs set up for a nearly impossible field goal. Munson yelled, "So we'll try to kick it one thousand miles!" The ball sailed through the uprights for three critical points.

The game rocked back and forth until Georgia decisively answered another Florida touchdown. A stellar scoring drive put them up by one point with only two minutes on the clock. Munson couldn't be contained. "Our hearts – they were torn out and bleeding, we picked it up and we put it back inside! I can't believe it! Touchdown, Georgia!"

Bedlam ensued as John jumped up on a table to lead the cheering. "How 'bout them Dawgs!"

Munson called it from Florida. "The Gator Bowl is rocking...the girders are bending...look at the score!"

The hometown celebration moved into high gear. Fans were cheering and dancing on any fixture that would hold their weight. Georgia beat Florida in a nail-biter, 17 to 16.

Munson was beside himself. "I can't believe it! Do you know what's gonna happen here tonight? Up in St. Simons and Jekyll Island and all those places where all those Dawg people have got those condominiums for four days? MAN, is there gonna be some kind of celebrating tonight!"

The frivolity of football season was only a memory as the quarter wound down and the gravity of final exams set in. But Ed and Will had learned the drill and were actually in pretty good shape. Even John squeaked by in algebra. But no one had seen Ronnie in a while.

The guy juggled a lot – pledge duties, entertaining several lady friends, and endless parties. And maybe a class now and then. The brief romance with Amy had ended a couple of weeks ago, which by Ronnie's standards, was ancient history.

About then Ronnie walked up, Will hung back, eyeing him with a smirk and let Ed do the talking. The sight of Ronnie galled Will. Ed stood between them, kept up the small talk and really hoped that the guys would stay cool.

He wasn't at all in the mood for playing referee. These two claimed to be adults, so let them work it out.

"How ya been?" Ed said.

"Good. It's been a great fall, well mostly. Guess the pressures on now. Gotta pull out some grades."

"The frat really keeps you pledges busy."

"Yeah, lots of stuff goin' on."

Will stepped up, clenching his teeth. "So what about Amy?"

Ronnie stared at him blankly for a minute.

"Amy who?" He seriously didn't get it. "Oh, that Amy. I dunno, haven't seen her."

Will got in his face and exploded. "Has it ever crossed your mind that you're just a dumb, selfish jerk? All you do is use people."

Ronnie just shrugged and laughed it off. "Whoa, what's up with you, man? Oh, wait a minute; you had a thing for her... I kinda remember."

Ed stepped between them before Will slugged him. He was about as angry as Ed'd ever seen him and he didn't want anyone getting hurt.

Will took a deep breath. He knew Ronnie well enough to know that the guy didn't take much of anything seriously.

Will finally answered his question. "Yeah, guess I did."

"Whatever, dude. She's nothin' special. You're better off without her."

Will stormed off.

"I'm glad he didn't hit me. I'd hate to have to take him down."

Ed just shook his head. He was tired of the whole thing, and changed the subject.

Ronnie had his own problems – like trying to salvage an entire quarter this late in the game.

"Dude, you've crammed a lot into a couple of months."

"Yeah, it's been one party after the other. But you only go 'round once, right?"

"Sort of, but you can't trash your future. How 'bout your brother? Did you ask him for help? He knows the ropes for sure."

"Yeah, well, he's tried. I guess I blew him off."

Ronnie's older brother had the enviable status of being very cool, yet very responsible. As an officer in his fraternity, he really believed in the brotherhood stuff and took many a floundering pledge under his wing. And after working with him on the Interfraternity Council, Ed confirmed that the older brother was for real. But as hard as he tried, Ronnie refused his help time and again – determined to do it his way.

From an early age, the two brothers understood that Greek life was their destiny. Dad had been a former chapter president and was still an active alum. His sons had legacy and they were expected to make good use of it. It hadn't gone well when Ronnie failed to get into UGA as a freshman. But his brother had exceeded his father's expectations at every turn.

Ed found Will sitting on the quad with that hangdog look of dejection. He sympathized with his friend, but Will's bouts of self-pity were getting old. What really got Ed was that he halfway seemed to enjoy it, feeding the blues with a steady diet of sad songs as he drove around and moped – this called for an intervention. He channeled his inner Phil

Donahue and looked Will straight in the eye. "OK enough. Sure the whole thing was bad, but it's time to pull yourself together."

Will looked surprised.

"She just wasn't the girl you'd hoped she was, that's it, plain and simple, so move on."

Will listened.

"Ya'll didn't even go out that long. You got a lot goin' for you. People break up all the time, so get over it."

His friend was right. Will got the message.

Ed had his own worries about the internship. It was the sort of thing that could jump start his career. Last he heard, the Post was still waiting on Dr. Hall's letter. With the deadline getting closer, the delay really upset Ed. Granted profs were busy this time of year, but Ed was tired of waiting. Besides, something didn't seem right in the department. He didn't understand everything that was going on but he knew one thing – he sure didn't like Dr. Hall's dismissive attitude towards him.

Will felt good as he turned in his last article before the break. He dropped it in Sue's inbox then stopped by Judy's desk. The young lady who usually had it all together, looked like she hadn't slept in days.

"You OK?" Will asked.

"Guess so."

"You sure? You look kinda tired."

"Yeah, didn't really get any sleep last night."

"Up studyin'?"

"No, she answered, "It's one of my girls. A real melt-down. I just couldn't leave her – she wasn't in any shape to be alone."

"Yeah."

"She's pretty much made a mess of things. First time away from home and all."

Judy's job was a tough one – handling 18-year-old girls trying out a new found freedom along with all the temptations and distractions of a college town.

"Oh man...what happened?" Will asked.

"Well, she's a nice girl from a small town. Seems it always starts like this. And she met this guy right off – older, good-looking, you know. Swept her off her feet. Spent every minute together and she totally forgot about everything else, including her classes."

"Yeah."

"So she figured her fairy tale had come true and plunged into the relationship, body and soul, completely trusting this guy. I'm sure you can finish the story. He dumped her and moved on to the next one. She's totally distraught."

"That's pretty awful...what's she gonna do?"

"Oh, who knows, what can she do? She's blown her chance here, at least for now. I just hope she can pick up the pieces and start over again somewhere."

"Won't be easy," Will said.

"It's just so sad. He had a reputation and everybody tried to warn her. But she didn't want to hear it, I guess."

It had been a while since there'd been another incident on campus. Even this guy surely knew that exam time was a prime opportunity to catch people off-guard. At first, students took the warnings seriously, but as time went on, it was easy to tune them out. But he was still out there, watching.

The young woman forgot that darkness came early this time of year as she walked to her car alone. Her exams were over for the day and after one last test tomorrow, she'd be home for the break.

At this moment, sleep was the only thing on her mind until she heard footsteps close behind her and suddenly realized that there was not another soul in sight. Just before she dismissed the sound as her imagination, a strong arm grabbed her. Pressing something sharp into her neck, he dragged her sideways. "Scream and I'll kill you."

The early evening rounds put unit five of the campus police at the North lot about 6:30. All of a sudden she was blinded by headlights and knew it may have been her only chance to get away. With one last effort, she broke free. He took off and quickly vanished at the edge of the lot.

Police swarmed the area from all directions but he was gone. They searched all parked vehicles, hoping something would turn up.

The Mayflower
After his last final, Will met his Dad for lunch at one of their favorite spots – the Mayflower restaurant – a blue plate diner on Broad Street, right across from old North campus, where they'd catered to hungry Dawgs for years.

The two settled into their regular booth. Dr. Andrews wore his usual *casual* attire – a buttoned up cardigan sweater and bow tie. Shirley scurried over to take their order in her white starched uniform and industrial strength hose.

She'd served up a lot of simple southern platters during her 21-year tenure.

"Good to see ya'll."

They both decided on the special of the day which included sweet tea and the best biscuits around for sopping up gravy. Shirley remembered their favorite dessert – banana pudding.

"Yes m'am. That'll be great," Will said.

Dr. Andrews had earned the respect of his colleagues, students and his son. Although a man of few words, it was like the E.F Hutton investment commercial said, "When he talked, people listened." The kindly professor helped anyone who asked for his advice and then applied his laser-like logic in finding solutions.

The two talked about the ins and outs of Georgia football, especially the most recent game.

The Florida win still had Dr. Andrews wide-eyed with boyish excitement. "Oh my, they pulled it out again. Sure were a lot of pivotal points where it could have gone either way. I didn't think Munson could take anymore."

"Been playin' any golf?" Will asked.

"Yes, as a matter of fact, I took advantage of the good weather and played Friday afternoon."

Growing up as a Presbyterian minister's son during The Depression was tough. Especially in a poor, rural area in eastern Kentucky where the family settled after their time in Africa. There wasn't much to do there, so young Andrews fashioned his own miniature course in the yard of the manse with a few tin cans where he'd play a round or two with a couple of old wooden shafted clubs.

During his teaching years, he had no time for golf. But with kids grown, Dr. Andrews returned to the game he'd almost forgotten. The reserved scholar was certainly not the country club type so he was more than content to use his small faculty discount and play the university course, just a quick drive down Milledge Avenue extension. When Abraham Baldwin founded the college back in 1785, he chose the site along the banks of the Oconee River for the natural beauty of its gentle, forested hills. But when you walked the undulating fairways as Dr. Andrews always did – the gentle hills didn't seem so gentle.

"Last week, I played with Reynolds." His dad's mood suddenly shifted. "We got to talk some. Will, they're pushing him out."

"Why? He's one of the best. Everybody knows that."

"Of course he is, but that doesn't matter. It's all politics. Nothing but politics."

"In all my years, I've never seen such turmoil. People are making far-reaching decisions without even thinking them through. Education's always been full of fads and fashions. It's been that way as long as I can remember. But in the past, people took more care to respect what others had worked so long and hard to build. There's always room for improvement, but they weren't so quick to throw the baby out with the bath water. That's definitely changed now."

"It's Dr. Hall, isn't it?" Will asked.

"From all that I've heard, it certainly looks like it. He's like a lot of newcomers who care more about their own agendas than teaching. They're out to completely replace an established system with a very different cultural paradigm."

"Everyone knows Dr. Hall's more into playing politics than teaching," Will said.

"So I've heard. He's become a force to reckon with in the department's tenure and promotion committee. That gives him a lot of say into who stays and who goes. And that's exactly how you change the face of a university."

"Well, I guess that explains things. Mr. Reynolds hasn't been himself lately," Will said. "But I can tell you that he's a far better teacher on a bad day than most are on a good day. It's just not fair."

The Mayflower's banana pudding was the best anywhere, but neither of them was in the mood for it anymore.

Dr. Andrews wanted to leave on a happy note so he went on to tell Will about some interesting golf shots he'd made and his birdie on a challenging par four.

LeConte Hall

"Dwell on the past and you'll lose an eye. Forget the past and you'll lose both eyes."

Russian proverb

Will said goodbye to his dad and headed across campus to his car, but was restless and didn't feel like going home just yet. He lingered around old North campus and finally sat on the steps of LeConte Hall.

He'd practically grown up here, spending lots of time as a kid in his dad's office upstairs, fascinated by shelves filled with hundreds of books. He'd pull out a random one and thumb through it for pictures, but out the window the squirrels scampering on the oak tree were just too distracting. It didn't take long for the youngster to answer "The Call of the Wild" and resume his quest to catch one.

LeConte Hall was named after the two LeConte brothers. The accomplished alums had held various academic posts in the South and then headed west in 1869. They settled at the University of California (later UCLA) where John eventually became president and Joseph went on to a distinguished career as a geologist.

Large, imposing portraits of the two men hung in gold gilded frames in the lobby, lending an air of erudition and decorum to the goings on. And every fall, from their lofty vantage point, the two brothers kept a watchful eye on the new crop of students coming into *their* building in pursuit of academic endeavors.

To a little boy, the building seemed enchanted. Daunting steep stairs and high ceilings left him feeling rather dwarfed. The place had a certain feel to it – there was something special about sliding your hand along the finely polished walnut railing as you hopped down the steps.

"We Americans are the best informed people on earth as to the events of the last 24 hours, we are not the best informed as to the events of the last sixty centuries."

Will and Ariel Durant

And now that he was older, Will appreciated the pride and tradition embodied in these halls. Peering into an empty classroom, he imagined all of the significant issues and events that had been discussed here through the years. It was certainly fitting for this old building to house the history department – the place where the past was revered and studied every day.

The profs had their own stories. Older faculty members had come up through The Depression and the searing memories of those times never left them. Scraping together enough money to pay for advanced degrees usually meant hard work and grit and gave them sympathy for the travails of struggling students. But at the same time, they were savvy enough not to fall for lame excuses – plea bargaining and death bed declarations "to *really study more, next time.*"

Through the years, Will had gotten to know many of his dad's colleagues in the history department, like Dr. Johnson. A marvelous man who was an authority in Latin America history and hustled for everything he ever got. The professor came from a family of migrant sharecroppers in Texas and never forgot his roots. He always made time to chat with a wide-eyed little boy.

The resident Russian expert, Dr. Radar, was a little quirky even by academic standards. When he lectured, he blinked and bounced around like he'd downed a whole pot of coffee. But when he expounded on Russian history, in his jittery voice that wavered around like Joe Cocker's, it was clear that he knew his stuff. The professor spoke fluent Russian, traveled there extensively and became was so immersed in the culture that he even married a Russian citizen.

For a kid, wandering through their offices was like a Disney adventure. Besides the few who were beyond fastidious, most had lots of fascinating stuff scattered around. An assortment of unusual items, picked up from their travels and research – relics, curios, manuscripts and maps. (And amid his old books and papers, Will's dad still kept a button from a history conference that read: "Make History, Not Love!")

The best finds were in Dr. Jones's office. A scholar of ancient Hittite culture, he displayed a fine collection of the odd, the really old and the obscure. He'd mastered three ancient languages, yet a very practical man with a hard-scrabble life to prove it. Dr. Jones had made his own way by earning tuition money from day jobs in his steel mill town and playing the sax at night clubs.

"Every age has its own outlook. It is especially good at see-ing certain truths and especially liable to make certain mis-takes. We all therefore need the books that will correct the characteristic mistakes of our own period. And that means old books."

C.S Lewis

Will often wondered about the office that had a big picture of a stern looking man with a funny beard. The younger faculty member proudly featured a portrait of Karl Marx over his desk. It was controversial décor for sure and particularly offensive to the vets. They didn't much like being greeted by the guiding light of communism when they stopped by to talk about their classwork.

In addition to teaching full course loads year after year and handling bunches of advisees, the professors lived and died under the "publish or perish" gun. A certain amount of research had to be cranked out to bolster the prestige of the department and compete for limited funds. Most UGA men and women produced excellent scholarship that was profitable and also readable and left the trivial, esoteric stuff to others.

But the university world wasn't a utopia. Students groused about the faculty. The faculty groused about their pay. Administrators complained about the difficulties of prying more money from the state. And alums complained about game day parking. And the cycle continued.

The best professors not only possessed a wealth of knowledge but also had mastered ingenious and sometimes theatrical tricks of the trade for keeping students engaged and Dr. Williams's may have been the most entertaining.

He'd be lecturing full steam on America history and notice a sleepy student about to drift off. Dr. Williams would stop on a dime, throw the textbook down – letting the echo reverberate through the room – and then he'd unload on the laggards.

"Mr. Shaw, I apologize for waking you from your day dreaming, but I've observed that this is the fourth day in a row you've failed to bring your textbook AND you don't seem to have anything to take notes with.

"You must have *quite* a memory. *So*, since we've discussed The Monroe Doctrine for two days now, why don't you tell us the central point of the policy?"

"Uh... well...I don't suppose... it's something Coach Russell's cooked up to slow down Auburn's running game?"

At this point, Dr. Williams went through some serious head shaking and then marched to an open window where he spotted a grounds crew planting some azaleas.

"Hey Burt, how you doing? Looks great out there, but would you mind coming over for a minute?"

"Sure Doc, be right over."

"Burt, I was just telling the class that anybody who loves our country and has learned even a little bit about history knows what the Monroe Doctrine is about. Could you help me explain it to these folks?"

The grounds crew foreman gave a succinct summation of President James Monroe's belief that the Europeans had no business crossing the Atlantic and meddling in our affairs or infringing on our sovereignty. He nodded to Dr. Williams and returned to tending the azaleas.

The class was flabbergasted and collectively looked like a scalded dog with its tail tucked between its legs. For the rest of the period the only sound in the room, besides Dr. Williams's commanding voice, was the steady hum of brain cells firing and pens racing on paper as he finished his lecture.

The professor had of coursed carefully choreographed all of this with Burt beforehand. Matter of fact, they'd had been doing variations of this routine for years – but it worked every time.

THE DOGWOOD MANOR

A large diverse crowd dined every day on the best home cooking around at the stately Dogwood Manor. The devoted patrons included office clerks, students, hardworking blue collar folks and leading Athens's citizens.

Will and John worked as busboys during lunch a couple of days a week, but short on cash and with more time over the break, they signed up for extra hours. The pay wasn't much but the grub was great – and they could eat all they wanted. Will particularly enjoyed the intriguing characters that came in regularly – not to mention a faithful contingent of young ladies who received his utmost attention and the very best service.

The busboy work was a step up from his previous warehouse job at the Big Ace pants factory where he'd come face-to-face with the mind-numbing factory grind that *scared the pants off* him.

At the time, it was quite fashionable to drop in and out of the university – to "go find yourself" or "get back to nature." But for Will, the hard physical labor at Big Ace drove home all the serious talks of "getting a good education." For a high school guy, the hourly wages were just enough to buy the right clothes to fit into the right crowd – a Lacoste shirt or an alligator belt from Dick Ferguson's – and still have a little gas money for gallivanting on the weekend.

But it was a different story for some of the folks who lived in East Athens and struggled to feed a family on those wages. The majority really worked hard, pursued honorable trades and were the bedrock of the town. But the operative word for their world was "physical labor" – the kind that gives you an aching back and arthritic joints by the time you're in your 40s. No leisurely "Southern Living" moonlight and magnolias for these folks – it was a tough and gritty life. And the university may as well have been in Timbuktu; it just didn't have any place in their world. Some even resented "the university crowd" and felt like they looked down on the common man.

Yet many workers liked the routine of plodding along in a job that meant doing *exactly* the same thing day after day. It was predictable, safe and comfortable. But Will also learned the downside as he watched lines of dog-tired workers shuffle, lemming-like, to punch the time clock at the end of a very long day.

"By day I make the cars, by night I make the bars…Oh, Lord I want to go home…"

"Detroit City" Bobby Bare

The most sobering sight had to be the older women hunched over their sewing machines with clouds of lint swirling around them. They were constantly pressured to meet quotas, as hour after hour, they pulled pieces of denim fabric from huge stacks at their side to stitch together under the eye of a snarling supervisor who looked like Lurch from "The Addams Family." He marched up and down in the cavernous building barking orders – "pick up the pace" and "keep those seams straight!" As hard as they worked, they struggled to keep up. It could have been a scene from a Dickens's novel.

Big Ace, the Chicopee Mills chicken processing plant and the Timex clock factory were three of the biggest manufacturers in town. The prospect of spending your working life at one of these plants was the only real career option for many with limited education. But Will had one bright spot in the tedium of stacking heavy piles of jeans on pallets – her name was Becky. She worked part time in some sort of accounting position near the loading dock and one day she broke up with her boyfriend. With the cool guy with the candy orange-colored Corvette out of the picture, Will stepped up and snagged her for a band party at Charlie Williams. (Turned out to be one really great date – but only *one* – and then she was back to Mr. Corvette.)

Work at the Dogwood Manor was a breeze compared to Big Ace. Besides the fine food, the main attraction at Dogwood was its irrepressible proprietor – Miss Eunice Crumwell. The old spinster maître de provided heaping helpings of food, plenty of hugs, kisses and town gossip. She fluttered about like a hummingbird, greeting people at each table; all the while directing the dinning staff and, of course, *talking* nonstop.

She pranced from room to room, decked out in one of those old Southern lady outfits with matching high heel shoes that sounded like football cleats hitting the oak floors. With one hand on the lovely mahogany credenza, the venerable matron surveyed her dining dominion like General Patton surveyed his battlefield. Her booming drawl could be heard above all others.

"Ruth, Ruth! We need some *shu-ga* for the bowls on the tables."

"Dora! How you comin' on the squash casserole? Looks like we're runnin' low."

"My My …Mrs. Coleman! You've simply got to have the peach cobbler. It's mouth waterin' fabulous – hurry on now, it'll be gone before you know it."

Her hawk-like eye spotted Will who'd been attending to the dining needs of one young lady for some time.

"Will! Come on! No time for romancin' or lollygaggin'. Make yourself useful as well as ornamental! Get the judge and his group more sweet tea – when they get to yackin', they guzzle it down like a camel at an oasis."

Will hurriedly swiped down the tables in the parlor room. It was Tuesday and the Ladies Book Club meeting was at 1 pm. They'd arrive any minute.

"Will, darlin. Remember to put cushions in the chairs for the Johnson sisters. And don't seat Thelma Eddelson by that drafty window. The others said they couldn't hear a word last week because of all her sneezin' and carryin' on."

Today was a special meeting for the ladies so the staff fussed over their setting more than usual. The holiday marked the time when the group broke from reading the classics and indulged in the latest work by a local, new

Southern Gothic writer. Word was that "The Awakening of the Nightingale" was not only spellbinding, but possibly a tinge scintillating.

As the ladies filed in, Miss Crumwell greeted each one effusively.

"Ruth Malone, *Shu-ga* darling don't you look like a rose in full bloom in that hat!

"Mrs. Epting, did you get that skirt at Herry's? You *surely* are the belle of the ball."

"Constance Thredgill... So, so... glad to see you! They said you wouldn't be out and about for another week after your surgery. What you need is some real food so come on over to the buffet table and load yourself up. It'll put some color in your cheeks. Land sakes... I know about eatin' those skimpy jello dishes forced on you at that hospital. Couldn't keep a parakeet alive for a day! Why...when I had my appendix out, I was almost reduced to a bag of bones."

She broke off in mid-sentence and made a beeline over to Mrs. Amelia Nelson.

Drawing her close with a tight hug, she whispered. "You know good and well that I would be the *very last* one to say an ill word about Mrs. Tisdale's husband. BUT do you know what he did last week? I was told the whole sordid mess just yesterday. Course I'm not supposed to say anything, but *you* surely need to know since you and Mrs. Tisdale used to be so close."

Her palaver and gossip flowed like the Oconee River in a rainstorm and spread faster than an AP wire story.

Each day she unwittingly put on quite a show with her homespun shenanigans.

The Book Club kept with tradition and began the inaugural reading with a toast, given by the chairwoman: "To life, love and fine literature!" Followed by the sipping of a vintage Chardonnay from Mrs. Eddleson's wine cellar as Mrs. Malone, a retired librarian, read the first few pages aloud, in her most elegant elocution.

Meanwhile, Miss Crumwell also considered herself the "Dear Abby" of Athens and dispensed dollops of advice – even to the busboys.

Will practically knew her sermonettes by heart – particularly the one about the "shameless hussies." She feared that she was witnessing an increase of the Jezebel types – young ladies prancing around town in skimpy outfits like you'd see at some of those "Cally-fern-ya nudie camps" she'd heard about.

And she'd start – "We have so many lovely long-stem roses gracing the campus and I just hate to see those 'other types.' You're not goin' after any of them, are you now?"

"No ma'am."

Miss Crumwell was convinced that decorum and feminine virtues had been in decline since young ladies stopped attending Cotillion classes and courting on their parent's verandas.

"Now I know that you of all people have been taught *right* from *wrong.* So don't go disgracing your family, ya hear?"

"Yes, ma'am."

"All right then. See that you don't. And rub down these tables real good with that Pine-sol."

But Miss Crumwell also had another side and the two guys witnessed it firsthand. She didn't always treat her black help quite the same – at times she was downright brusque. The cooks, Dora and Hazel, had been with her for years and understood her moods and quirks. But they worked hard and it just wasn't right. Mr. Alvin, the aged dishwasher, often bore the brunt of her rants. He hung over the steel sink looking like a wrung out dishrag himself with steam from the boiling water billowing up all around him. Mr. Alvin always wore a world weary look of resignation. Sometimes it was just too much for him and he sought solace in a little bottle of cheap gin tucked away in his hip pocket. Will and John tried to lighten his mood and talk to him whenever they could, but most of the time, Mr. Alvin's gray head still drooped over the sink and he just nodded. Maybe he'd mumble a word or two or raise his hand with a weak wave...but that was it. He was a man just beaten down by life.

Will thought about Mr. Alvin and the others – their hard lives with few opportunities. Sometimes he wondered how he would have handled walking in their shoes.

The Dogwood Manor was not only entertaining but it also gave the two young men a reality check as they watched the ebb and flow of everyday life. It had a way of tempering some of the high flown theories served up at the university every day.

New Year's Eve
It was very sad that the holiday break was almost over. But then again it was sure to end with flair. Mr. Marshall was throwing his annual New Year's Eve extravaganza and Will had made the guest list. The party had been the talk of the town for years, so he was not about to miss it.

Marshall's home was very impressive as was everything else about the man. Sitting on a hill, overlooking several acres, the sprawling house had every luxurious amenity you could hope for. The four car garage was, of course, a necessity. The pool house itself was as palatial as the typical upscale home.

Guests packed out every room and were diving into the plentiful food and drink that kept coming and coming. The host served the best of everything. Will devoured a couple of plates, then made sure not to miss the room dedicated entirely to desserts, sampling as much as he could physically tolerate. Patrons kept three bartenders in constant motion at the well-stocked bar that spread across an entire wall.

Will enjoyed mingling with folks he'd known most of his life but hadn't seen in a while. It was all fun except for a tinge of sadness at the thought of being alone for another New Year's. *Would this ever change? Out of thousands of young women in this college town wasn't there someone right for him?*

About then, Mr. Marshall appeared and interrupted his thoughts. He grabbed Will tightly around the shoulders. "Will, my man, so glad you made it!"

"Yeah, me too. It's a great party. And happy New Year," Will said.

"Oh man, I can't even tell you what a happy New Year it's about to be. This year'll be unbelievable, mark my words, things are happenin'."

Will nodded.

"And by the way, I hear you do some rock climbing," Mr. Marshall added.

"Been a few times. It's great fun."

"OK then, when it warms up we're gonna plan a weekend. You, me, Tom. I got some cool gear you're gonna love."

Will agreed and then another guest commandeered the popular host.

It had been an hour or so since his dessert fling, so Will felt he could handle another round of prime rib. And apparently Sonny felt the same.

Sonny was a large man with a large presence; a bull in a china shop kind of presence. He plodded around led by his bulging abdomen – his belt slung low, straining under the heavy load. But none of the oddities of his persona bothered him in the least.

They say opposites attract and Sonny's elegant wife was his polar opposite. A tall, refined lady with fashion runway beauty and poise, she'd met Sonny while working on her senior project in public relations at UGA. Fundraising with Sonny for the athletic department led to marriage but many assumed that the young lady was mainly attracted to his wallet. The two kept busy in separate endeavors except for football socials and the children's activities. Her work in the Athens's Junior League took up much of her time as did her duties as president of one of the garden clubs in town. The couple seemed happy with the arrangement.

He slapped Will hard on the back. "There's my buddy, you and me, the game, what a day. Remember?"

"Yeah, sure. Good to see you."

Sonny was not one for social niceties so he jumped right to what he loved most. "You know what you gotta do, Will? You gotta write about our Bulldawgs. Them boys been beaten up and battered. Help the fans feel for 'em. You can bring lots of attention to the players, the program, the future and show 'em some love. Keep up the spirit. That's what you need to do."

"Guess so. But we have sports writers who cover...." Will answered.

Sonny's face turned a deep red. "Oh, dang those sports writers. They don't know nothin', they think they do, with all their analyzin'. I'm talkin' 'bout really gettin' behind 'em. Know what?" He leaned in closer. "We're gonna do it next year. Yes sir, it's our time, the national championship. I just know it."

Will nodded. " Hope so."

"Oh there's no hopin', just doin'...and your job is to keep up the fever."

His well-spoken wife rolled her eyes and corrected him. "The fervor, Sonny. You mean the fervor."

Sonny said, "Oh heck yeah! The fervor, the fever. Keep it all goin', cause there's just nothin' too good for our Bulldawgs. Now is it?"

The devout booster was famous for waxing on. Maybe not so eloquently, but endlessly for sure...in season and out of season. And especially so when he was primed with just a smidgen of alcohol which was obviously the case tonight. His disposition rose and fell on cue with the team's performance. They'd been trounced by Miami of Ohio just before Christmas in the Tangerine Bowl, so Sonny coped by hanging his hopes on the upcoming season. About then, he recognized an assistant coach and cornered him. Even in the dim party light, you could see the color drain from the man's face as he realized his predicament.

The liveliest banter came from a group gathered around Art Collier. UGA's most popular art teacher charmed guests with talks of his travels to the great museums of Europe. He cut quite a figure in his natty ascot and you felt like you were standing right beside him at the Louvre as he extolled upon "the transcendent nature of art that can capture the soul of man." Then he'd gracefully move into harrowing tales of flying a Spitfire for Her Majesty, the Queen, in WW11. It was no wonder that the Renaissance man had a waiting list for his Intro to Art class.

Will turned to a man who looked familiar, but he couldn't quite place him. He finally realized that the guy was his old junior high P.E. teacher. The coach was gray now and had put on a few extra pounds, but he'd recognize that gruff voice anywhere.

"Hey Coach, you still at Alps Road?"

"Yep. Assistant Principal. But tell me what you're doin'."

The two caught up but Will felt a bit strange talking man to man with the guy who'd ridden him unmercifully in P.E. when he was an awkward, skinny kid in 7th grade.

But there was one thing he'd never forget about the coach – the day he gave "the talk." It wasn't so much the value of the content that made it memorable, but the humor that day was epic. One afternoon in October, teachers gathered the boys and girls in their respective P.E. classes for a special session on health and hygiene and "changes to our body we need to know about." The imposing man instructed the guys to "shut up and listen." They did. Still, the boys were very disappointed about missing dodgeball and sitting in the bleachers listening to another lecture.

"OK, guys, first off, you're growin' up and becomin' a man. It's normal stuff and we're devotin' a whole class period to it so you don't get freaked out or nothin'. I got some diagrams and pictures that most of ya'll haven't seen before. Cremens! Straighten up! No more weird faces or you'll be runnin' laps. The former UGA lineman tripped over his words and looked like he'd give anything to be somewhere else.

"So what you got flowin' through your bodies is called: tes-toss-ter-on. That's what's causin' that peach fuzz on your chin and makin' your voice go up and down like a yo-yo.

"Like I was sayin', it makes you a man. Helps you throw a football far. Go huntin' all day and fight wars – things like that. Powerful stuff. And it gets you liken girls, like never before."

The coach stammered through a very rudimentary explanation of "how males and females get together" – at the right time of course. He used some diagrams and a couple of old anatomical charts.

Next came a sequence of pictures of a woman delivering a baby. Very disturbing. Nobody said a word. Just a few gasps and groans.

"So till you get married, you'll need to take a lot of cold showers, run laps, play sports. And if you come out for football, I guarantee you that Coach Gruber and I will work you so hard you'll be too worn out to get into trouble."

After a couple of words about love and marriage came an extended warning about avoiding terrible diseases "if you go about it the wrong way." All designed to scare the heck of everybody.

"Edwards, Johnson, that's enough of your snickerin'. See me after school. You're gonna be picken' up trash under the bleachers till doomsday.

"I'm gonna pass around some pictures so you'll know I'm not makin' this stuff up. That way, it'll sink into your thick skulls. I don't want none of you gettin' the 'Bluebonnet plague' before you get your driver's license. That'd be just awful. So you gotta think and use proper precautions. And if you got any questions, go talk to that lady in the counselor's office or anybody that looks like they're happy bein' married."

Will moved on and stopped to overhear a lively conversation between Mr. Marshall and a group of clients. "Now, I'm telling you, things are changing," Mr. Marshall said.

"I know for certain – there's all kinds of opportunities to make more money than you ever imagined, so let's drink to the New Year!"

They all raised their glasses and toasted the year to come.

Meanwhile, Will made his way to a corner where Tom chatted with a couple of friends.

"Hey, man." Tom shook his hand with a smile.

"Your dad sure knows how to throw a party."

"Yeah, that he does. He loves a good party. What you been up to?"

Will and Tom discussed college stuff and their plans for the future and the more he talked with Tom, the more he liked him.

Will checked out the crowd. "Tom, we may be the only sober people here."

Tom laughed. "Maybe so, but Mom's OK – keeps an eye on things. Not many designated drivers in this group – so she takes care of that."

"You really see a different side of some of Athens's finest citizens on a night like this," Will said.

"Oh, man, could I tell you some stories." Tom shook his head and laughed. "Take a look over there at the Fitzgerald brothers doing their Sam and Dave imitation."

On the makeshift stage, Will witnessed some singing and dancing like he'd never seen before…and hoped to never see again. "That's not exactly the image they project down at their Savings & Loan during the week."

"Hey, I heard John's startin' his own band," Tom said.

"That's the plan."

"Cool. Everybody says he's really good."

"Yeah. He may just make a go of it."

"Let's go hear him sometime," Tom said.

"For sure."

John had gotten himself a great guitar – a vintage Stratocaster and with it came big dreams. Even though he'd saved up all he could, he was still a little short. But it was Christmas, that wonderful time of year when good things happen. His uncle who'd come to town for the holidays sat in on one of John's impromptu performances and was so impressed that he opened up his wallet to cover the rest.

As glorious as the sunny fall days in Athens are, the wintry days are equally bleak. It was January. The rain and dreariness hadn't let up for days. With football season and the holidays over, the let down on campus was palpable. But never let it be said that Athens is a one dimensional town. There's more to this place than football and always *something* going on. As much as Will wanted to veg in his warm apartment, the guys had talked him into hearing a speaker on campus. Lots of students attended the lecture, not so much to quench their thirst for knowledge, but for the extra credit. It never hurt to add a little boost to your grade, especially if all you have to do is show up.

"What about Ronnie, is he comin'?" asked Ed.

"No, but heard he's in the clear. Made it through pledging too. Now he's a full-fledged brother," John said.

Will smirked. "Man. He had to just barely pass and I can't believe he did it on his own."

"Makes you wonder," said Ed.

Rumors of cheating in various quarters always circulated but it was hard to know what was really true.

Leaving the cold rain, the guys ducked into the softly lit chapel on old campus and were surprised to find it packed. Within a few minutes, the internationally known author began telling his compelling story.

The Viennese psychiatrist and neurologist had lost most of his family in WWII and then he'd endured three years in a concentration camp. Frankl had barely survived. Yet out of this horrific experience, he'd penned a treatise entitled, "Man's Search for Meaning." The book became required reading in social science courses around the country.

Dr. Viktor Frankl endured unimaginable pain and deprivation yet emerged with a new understanding of life. Through the deep waters of suffering, he'd uncovered a profound truth: the main drive in life is not pleasure, but discovering what is meaningful.

He concluded with an arresting statement – "Those who have a '*why*' to live, can bear with almost any '*how*.'"

Afterwards, no one was in a hurry to leave so the guys hung around on the sidewalk and talked awhile.

"Can you imagine what that man went through?" Will asked.

"I don't really know how he made it. That's about as bad as it gets.

John just stood there, shaking his head. "Man, that was heavy."

Ed gazed across the quad. "He said a lot of things worth thinking about."

The rain had passed and a chilly mist moved in, but they didn't care much – there was more they wanted to say.

In the best of friendships, there's often a shadow of lone-liness – deep down you sense you're not completely under-stood. But every now and then you have a rare moment when friends really connect. And this was one of those moments. Lifted above the mundane, they talked – seriously – and came away from the evening with much more than extra credit.

Differing views on Simon's flawed reporting only deepened divisions among faculty and students in the J school.

But for Ed, things had hit a new low. His dad's *mention* of less money had quickly materialized. Living at the frat house was now out of the question. With so much uncertainty hang-ing over him, his only option was to pack up and pile into one of the few unoccupied corners of John's house. It was the kind of place where random guys crash – a bunch of grungy art-ist types living cheaply in a rundown part of town. Space was limited, but Ed managed to claim a sofa bed in the basement.

Fallout from Watergate continued and the Washington Post was in the thick of it. Ed followed it closely and desper-ately wanted to be there.

Post reporters, Bob Woodward and Carl Bernstein, had covered a break-in at the Watergate office complex on a

Saturday in June, 1972. The target was the Democratic National Committee headquarters and five men were arrested for stealing documents from the office.

A scandal of historic proportions unfolded as the two tenacious reporters chased down clues. Their hard work paid off when Bernstein found a laundered check that tied President Nixon to the burglary.

The duo made national headlines themselves when they broke the story and released reports on the various "dirty tricks" used by Nixon's election committee. Impeachment talk abounded.

Ed was among many young journalists inspired by the panache of the Post reporters. Finally a letter arrived. The paper notified him that he'd made the final cut, but they still needed one item, perfunctory but necessary – a sign-off from his advisor verifying his academic standing.

Ed paced the floor. He knew he'd given the form to Dr. Hall weeks ago who'd assured him that he'd send it. But dealing with the temperamental Dr. Hall always made Ed uneasy. Regardless, he had to have an answer. *Hopefully, it was just buried in a pile.*

His secretary said the professor was in – that was a relief – maybe he could get this thing resolved. After a couple of deep breaths, he approached Dr. Hall's desk.

"Just wanted to check with you about the form – for the internship."

Dr. Hall didn't look up. "I believe I *told* you I'd take care of it."

"Yes sir. I'm only here because I got a notice that they still need it and the deadline's real soon."

"Do you know how many students are in this department? And they've all got deadlines." He motioned to the stack of papers on the desk. "I imagine it's here somewhere and I'll get to it, like I said."

Ed fidgeted as he tried to interpret the conversation. "Well, I'd really appreciate it. It's kinda important."

"OK, then. See you in class."

DOWNTOWN MUSIC
SCENE

Riding a wave of national popularity, Three Dog Night arrived at the Coliseum on Friday night to rock students out of their winter slump. Although the concert had sold out early, John scored the guys some tickets with his music connections.

Back in their younger days, the guys had their own mini music venue in a corner of Ed's back yard. They regularly convened in a converted workshop well away from the family residence which meant they could crank up their music to proper deafening levels.

"The Hut," as it was known, was their favorite hangout. It had all the amenities young fellows needed – a couple of bean bag chairs, a comfortable sofa and an outstanding Pioneer stereo system complete with suitcase size speakers.

The décor was perfect with Bulldawg photos and wrinkled band posters covering the wood plank walls.

The hometown boys had excelled in the "school of rock" during their younger years. Clarke Central High School was conveniently located near several Greek houses on Milledge Avenue. It didn't take long for the guys to master the finer points of crashing the best parties. They knew how to slip in under the radar, mumble something about "my brother's a member," and, week after week, party to the top bands in the Southeast.

John was the true musical aficionado among them. He'd learned to play guitar from a couple of locals and had become really good – good enough to put his own band together. The chemistry was just right. John was so adept at mimicking the riffs and runs from the likes of Clapton, Richards and Peter Townsend that the band cranked out very credible covers of top 40 hits. They also threw in a few original numbers that showcased John's lead guitar prowess.

To the surprise of many, Athens actually had noise ordinances which were sometimes enforced when citizens complained about students "playing all that crazy music so loud." So finding a place to practice was no easy task until they drove out to a cousin's farm near Winterville and found an old building that was the perfect spot. It became their own "Muscle Shoals." Before long, they were playing open mike nights at downtown clubs and gaining a loyal following with regular gigs at The Rendezvous and Your Mother's Moustache.

Ever since the old days at "The Hut," the friends knew the right place to shop to build their album collection. The best little record store around was down on Jackson Street, Ort's Oldies.

The term "living legend" is tossed about all too casually, especially in a town full of characters, yet most thought that Athens's native, William Orten Carlton was just that. He was Athens's walking talking musical encyclopedia and jukebox. Ort was "Jeopardy" on steroids for all things pertaining to the history of rock n roll. (And as the cliché goes, he'd forgotten more on the subject than most devotees claimed they knew.)

The bachelor, Ort, looked the part – like he dressed each day with much more interesting things on his mind than matching colors or fashion. He'd started out as a DJ on a number of local stations and became a local celebrity before opening his off-beat music store. The joint was always jumping with musicians, students, faculty, and townsfolk. And in the middle of this mosh pit would be the bearded Ort – holding forth in his trademark baritone voice discoursing on musical minutia and multitasking as he dug through thousands of records he'd personally collected. The bounty was meticulously organized in old wooden fruit cart bins containing hits and near misses of rock's royalty and lesser luminaries. Budding rock stars and aspiring local musicians hung out for hours, perusing the vast vinyl offerings and picking the brain of the musical Gandalf. Patrons marveled at his photographic memory and were thoroughly entertained by his rapid fire quips and anecdotes. With remarkable recall, Ort could name thousands of record titles and provide all manner of detail – the name of the bass player, the release date, practically anything you wanted to know.

The satisfied look on a customer's face who'd just found a hard sought after record of "The Legendary Stardust Cowboy and his Lost Planet Airmen" was all the reward Ort wanted – along with a few meager dollars.

Hanging around and listening to Ort answer his phone in his usual, very unusual manner was entertainment in itself. "Ort's Oldies and Lemon Meringue Repair Shop," Ort speaking. For the next couple of hours, the phone was not answered *in the same way a single time.* His repartee was about as good as anything you'd hear at The Improv in L.A. "Ort's Earthworm Wake-up Service," Ort speaking. "Hello, Ort's Egg Breaking Institute"…and so it went.

But Ort's tutelage didn't end when the shop closed, it just moved. Keeping pace with the rhythm of the college town, he resumed his continuing education in a random booth at a downtown hangout. Folks followed.

The dean of the downtown music scene was proud to be Athens's amiable number one repository of rock and roll trivia. Old times and old songs were never forgotten at Ort's.

The Last Resort

The Last Resort was one of the *first* choices for superb entertainment. So tonight, Ed and Will met up with friends to hear some great music.

John didn't join them for good reason – his band was booked solid. These days they were in big demand and actually making money. The *starving artists* were starving no longer.

Some terrific entertainers played the always packed, eclectically festooned venue on Clayton Street: Jimmy Buffett, The Randall Bramblett Band, Gamble Rogers, Leon Redbone, Steve Goodman, Towns Van Zandt. And also the zany Steve Martin in his trademark white suit and arrow through his head prop – for his famous "wild and crazy guy" routine.

The headliner tonight was a crowd favorite, the Reverend Pearly Brown. The Reverend had performed several times before, usually to capacity crowds who loved hearing the soulful blind musician from Americus. He played his Martin guitar in the bottleneck blues style that made each plaintive note moan and sigh along with his heartfelt singing of old gospel songs. He told every audience, "I've been blind since birth, but I've seen it all."

And that he had. His career had spanned 40 years. Pearly's main concert hall was the street along with some regular venues from town to town. But now in his golden years, he limited his singing to a few small clubs like The Last Resort and his regular spot back in Macon – the sidewalks of Cherry Street and Broadway.

When he took to the stage, the audience knew they were encountering something raw and authentic. Pearly's leathery brown face grimaced in earnestness as he sang "the old songs" in his raspy baritone voice. A tear often punctuated some of the lines that deeply moved him. His songs carried a message of hope and consolation for those who identified with Pearly's faith in God.

"How well do I remember how Jesus pulled me through.
I prayed and walked the floor a night or two, night or two.
I said, Lord, take and use me: that is all I can do.

*And I gave my heart to Jesus
How about you?"*

His faithful following at the Resort included Will who'd
enjoyed getting to know the musician personally and then
helped promote one of his concerts. (Dr. Andrews also contributed to the effort by sketching a poster to distribute
around town.) Between songs, Pearly smiled and rocked
from side to side recounting one story after another. The
audience was thoroughly charmed by his openness and
child-like wonder.

At 65-years-old, the troubadour, married with two children, was remarkably independent. "I take care of myself
just fine...God knew what he was doin' when he made me
blind...and I don't want people to pity me."

Pearly came by his love of music from his grandmother,
who'd lived to be 100. From childhood, she'd never forgotten the hardships of those who'd come before her. So the
songs she passed on to Pearly weren't merely entertaining
tunes to wile away the time, but songs fraught with meaning. "She taught me the Bible and made sure I'd carry on
the music that comforted her during difficult days."

After his younger years at The Academy for the Blind in
Macon, Pearly returned to his home in Americus. Later, he
was ordained at the Friendship Baptist Church and learned
to play the harmonica and accordion. And so began a career – walking the streets of many Southern cities, singing
gospel music for spare change from passersby.

During a performance at LSU in 1961, a folklorist re-
corded Pearly which led to an extended tour with the
Southern Folk Festival. He traveled up and down the

East coast and in 1966 he even played in a competition at Carnegie Hall where he won a treasured limited edition Martin guitar. Journeying on, he made sure his schedule put him at some of Martin Luther King, Jr's rallies and only wished his grandmother had lived to see "the changes a comin'" from all the hard won advances of the civil rights movement.

But with the end of the '60s, interest in folk music waned, so Pearly took to the streets close to home once again and played at local coffee houses. "I like takin' my music to the street, cause that's where the real people are...all kinds of folks – good, bad, happy, sad. And whoever I meet, I'm gonna try to love 'em."

Rev. Brown was the last of a vanishing breed. At a time when students talked incessantly about "being real" and "finding yourself," folks saw in Pearly a man who actually embodied those qualities. Everyone who knew him admired his simple, honest life. As the Coke ad said, "it's the real thing."

Getting into the groove of winter quarter was tough and for the most part, students had forgotten that the guy behind the attempted assaults hadn't been caught.

Judy stopped looking over her shoulder and worrying about her girls long enough to enjoy Pearly's concert. But next day, she was jolted back to reality when she found a note on her car seat. The message terrified her – she quickly locked the doors and sped off.

In Sue's office, the two looked over the very disturbing scrawl.

Hope you and your freinds had fun. Saw you at last resort. Think your smart. Next time il do it.

"This guy's stalking me!"

The police had a general profile of the offender and even though he was dangerous, his botched attempts meant that they were likely dealing with an amateur. Nothing had turned up from the parking lot search after the last incident, but this week, the case took a step forward. Several students had gotten a good look at a suspicious guy lurking around campus; police had a description.

A composite sketch was now plastered everywhere.

⊷⊶

"What we have here is a failure to communicate."

"Cool Hand Luke"

Ed woke up shivering with a nasty crick in his neck. A cold snap had hit and the blanket wasn't enough for the chilly draft seeping in from the old window. Ed was the kind of guy who enjoyed order and quiet – good for thinking. But this place was a revolving door of free spirits, who came and went at all hours and weren't really into schedules. Yet through his foggy daze, one clear thought emerged. A couple of weeks had gone by. That was plenty of time for Dr. Hall to sign a paper and mail it. At this point Ed had to know what was going on. He got himself together and made a call to the D.C. paper – they checked – still no letter.

Ed was frantic and suspected that there was more to this than an absent minded professor who couldn't manage his inbox. Dr. Hall's iciness towards Ed was unmistakable, yet hard to explain.

He needed help. Maybe Dr. Mac would know what to do.

"Have a seat, Ed. Any word yet?"

"Well, no except for this one hang-up that I can't seem to get past."

Dr. Mac propped his feet on his desk and twirled a pencil in the air. "Yeah, what's that?"

"I got all my stuff in right off, but they keep tellin' me that Dr. Hall's sign-off isn't there yet."

"Well that should be an easy fix, have you asked him about it?"

"Well, yeah. A couple of times. And he knows about the deadline."

Dr. Mac leaned over his desk, looking at Ed. "So what did he say?"

"He *kinda* said he would do it."

"What do you mean, Ed?"

"Well he never seemed really interested and was bothered that I was there."

Dr. Mac went over it again. "Ok, so you took the form to him, explained that it's a Washington Post internship and all you needed was his signature?"

"Yeah."

"And that was weeks ago?"

"Right. I got everything else to them as fast as I could."

"I know you did. But you're sure he hasn't done it?"

"Talked to the Post again this morning, they don't have it. I guess it could be lost in the mail or something."

"OK, Ed. Let me look into this. I'll call my friend up there and talk to Dr. Hall. We'll get this fixed, it would be silly not to. I'll let you know as soon as it's all worked out."

Dr. Mac made the call. Ed was the top candidate but they needed the signed paper to finalize it – or else they'd have to offer it to the next candidate in line.

"Mornin', Mac"

"Hello Peter."

"What's up?"

"I need to talk to you about Ed."

Dr. Hall bristled. "What's he done? Is he causing you trouble?"

"Ed ? Of course not. You know what an outstanding student he is."

"Yeah, but grades don't tell the whole story. Is he blowing off in his column again?"

"I'm not sure exactly what you mean. But here's the thing. He's really close to getting a great internship. Seems all he needs is your signature."

"I remember something about that."

"Well, I'm not sure if you understood how close the deadline is."

Dr. Hall stared into Dr. Mac's eyes.

"You didn't like his column, did you?" Mac asked.

"Well let's just say I don't appreciate journalists who have a platform and fail to advocate for important causes. And his column? Self-righteous blather."

"Peter, what are you doing?"

"Why are you so concerned about this Ed guy?"

"Well, he's almost got himself a great opportunity, for one thing. And I think he deserves it."

"Yeah, he's a solid enough student, but have you stopped to think about who else may be competing for this spot?"

"No, I haven't. That's not my job. But I do know that Ed's *our* student and he's got everything it takes for it, and *that is* my job – and yours – to help him."

"Except for one thing, Mac. You're forgetting the big picture. It's always critical to get the right people in there – those who really understand the world we live in and how things need to change."

"Peter, are you kiddin' me? Is this a political thing to you? Why, Ed's just a student. He may not even know his political views yet. Isn't that what he's supposed to be doing here? Getting an education to help him develop his outlook?"

"But some students are *already there*. You can tell who the right ones are. They're ready to shake things up."

Dr. Mac leaned over the desk, closer to Dr. Hall. "Peter, you and I agree on almost everything. We fight for the same causes. But in this matter, I'm afraid you're leaving out something pretty darned important – *integrity*. And that's something you can't table, no matter how strongly you feel about your beliefs."

Dr. Hall's face turned red as he lept out of his chair and glared at Mac.

Mac stood his ground, coming even closer to his face. "So you find that paper – sign it –and *I'll* mail it *myself*, certified."

175

Dean Drewry

About the time Will himself fell victim to the winter blahs, his instructor announced a guest lecturer for this morning's class and it was none other than Dean Drewry. After devoting 40 years to building UGA's journalism program, the retired dean still came to his office every day in a dapper three piece suit and was happy to lecture when called upon. The man was an institution and had played a big role in establishing the prestigious Peabody Awards for excellence in broadcasting.

Whenever he taught, students always benefited from his wealth of knowledge, but he was especially known for his wit. His humorous anecdotes were unrivaled.

Will knew that today the conditions were just right for the dean's wizardry. Anytime 300 hundred students gathered in a large lecture hall, there's bound to be a contingent who'd succumb to the effects of sleep deprivation. The seasoned professor was well aware of the ravages of the student's late night habits and when he'd notice a few eyes glazing over and heads bobbing, like a good DJ, he'd "vary the playlist" and keep students engaged.

This morning, he stopped in mid-sentence, walked very deliberately to the left exit door, carefully opened it and stared out for a good 10-15 seconds.

Without explanation, the dean returned to the podium and picked up where he'd left off, then stopped abruptly again and repeated his quizzical stare from the right exit door. After a dramatic pause, he took up the podium and his lecture once again. Little did they know, but Dean Drewry had the students right where he wanted them. A few minutes later, he pulled off his glasses and addressed the puzzled group with stone cold seriousness.

In his protracted Southern drawl, he explained: "Ladies and gentlemen, I believe I owe you an explanation for my behavior today. You see, for some time now, I've followed the stories of alien visits to earth with great interest. After much thought, it occurs to me that if they did visit our planet – being the sophisticated, enlightened creatures that they are – they would surely choose one of the world's leading repositories of knowledge and thus they would make our acquaintance at The University of Georgia. And of course, their first stop would be at the esteemed Henry Grady School of Journalism – where clear, cogent communication is exemplified every day.

"So today, during our class period, I felt it incumbent on me, as a leader at this citadel of learning, to monitor each door and extend to them our wonderful Southern hospitality – and perhaps, some sweet tea – to welcome them to our fine institution here in the great state of *Jaw-ga*."

Only a consummate storyteller could engage a lecture hall full of drowsy students with an outlandish tale of an alien visit and bring a wilting class back to life. Great storytelling has long been a delightful tradition in the South and the dean definitely had the touch.

Nothing like a salacious bit of gossip to liven up a Monday.

Ronnie was in love. After a repeated pattern of collecting several lady friends, then tossing them aside, he'd met Stephanie. Suddenly the tables had turned. The guys would've never believed it except they'd heard the story straight from Ronnie who explained to them how it was very much "meant to be" and he was serious. He'd met the girl of his dreams and, as luck would have it, she was on the rebound.

Up until now, Stephanie's life was the stuff of fairy tales. Stephanie and one Preston Sinclair Parker began their enchanted journey as high school sweethearts. The golden couple was destined to a lifetime of happiness. After graduation, the talented quarterback and homecoming queen were off to UGA where they enjoyed many blissful days together and continued their social ascent. Preston pledged one of the top fraternities and Stephanie joined one of the very best sororities. She'd already won her county's beauty pageant and those in the know believed she could possibly become the next Miss Georgia. Preston's future looked bright as he was groomed to take over the family's thriving business.

Things were going great for the anointed couple until one day Preston forgot to read the script and decided "they should date other people."

As devastated as Stephanie was, she hadn't been raised to admit defeat and pine away over lost love. Saving face was far more important than tending to a broken heart and fortunately she was in the hands of experts. A trusted band of sorority sisters rallied around her and formulated a foolproof plan.

And that's where Ronnie came in. With his good looks and party pedigree, he was the go-to guy to ease Stephanie's pain and elicit jealously from an old beau.

But from the start, Ronnie was head over high-heels and had lost complete control of the situation. Before he could deploy his charm, Ronnie was the one helplessly beguiled.

No one could believe the transformation.

Ronnie had met his match. The sophisticated debutante, blessed with extraordinary beauty and poise, was too much for him.

His friends gazed in disbelief as they listened to a love-struck Ronnie wax on tenderly about Stephanie. Gone was the playboy bravado and shark-like grin.

"She's unbelievable. You gotta meet her."

Then he looked at his watch – no one knew the guy even owned a watch.

"Hey, we'll get together soon." And with that, he rushed off to class.

The guys walked away, scratching their heads, wondering who this imposter was.

"It's like a real life version of 'The Invasion of the Body Snatchers.' Way too bizarre," Ed said.

Will was still trying to get a handle on the new Ronnie when Dr. Mac suddenly stopped him in the hallway.

"Will, I gotta tell you this. But I'm sure you already know. Your dad's a really great guy."

"Well, yeah. He is."

"We've been working on this committee together and I've gotten to know him pretty well."

"He mentioned something about that."

"I mean, he's a real gentleman if there ever was one. It's always refreshing to see someone who cares about students."

"Yeah. That's him – always has been."

"What I really like is to get him talking about FDR and all the stuff he's written on diplomacy and foreign affairs – it's fascinating."

"He'll talk about it alright – that's his specialty."

"No one can move mountains in committee, but he sure knows how to handle difficult people. He practices a little diplomacy himself. I admire that."

Normaltown

After another four hour set, John packed up his gear. He was totally tapped out and bone weary from a week of classes, performances and too little sleep.

Suddenly, someone from behind called his name. As much as he liked talking to fans and other music lovers, tonight he just wanted to go home and crash.

The voice called again. "Hey, John." He reluctantly turned around and standing before him was one of his heroes, Charlie Clinton. The singer/songwriter was a local celebrity with a large following and lately he'd been playing with big names in the business.

The Athens music scene had a reputation for launching a lot of talented groups and performers and a bunch of them hung out in a distinct downtown area called Normaltown. Through the years, the heart of Normaltown was Allen's Hamburgers – a favorite hot spot where a steady stream of musicians cut their teeth. And the place had a colorful story of its own. UGA history major, Governor Zell Miller had worked there during his college days for $7 dollars a night.

And when Lewis Grizzard wasn't writing about UGA football or driving around in his beat up VW Beetle, you'd find him there, shooting pool or holding court at a table, spinning a tale or two.

Normaltown got its unusual name from earlier days when a school for women studying education, called "The Normal School," was established. The name stuck and the area was fast becoming much like the Greenwich Village music scene – a hotbed of creativity in a close-knit neighborhood.

Normaltown definitely had a funky feel. The odd mixture of houses and quirky little businesses ran the gamut from near-condemned student rentals to quaint '40s and '50s family homes with an occasional Southern mansion thrown in the mix. The unusual enclave was near Athens General Hospital and the streets surrounding the Naval Supply School campus. Athens may be a lot of things, but it's not exactly a seafaring town. So how does a landlocked city score a naval post? It all came down to politics; influential Georgia senators grabbed huge chunks of military spending for projects in their state.

One pioneering artist, Terry "Mad Dog" Melton, led the way in the town's burgeoning music culture. The Athens High star athlete, hung up his cleats, grabbed a guitar and never looked back. He became "The Man" on the music scene at Allen's and The Last Resort and honed his skills playing six nights a week to cult-like fans at Your Mother's Mustache – just a street up from campus. His 15 minute extended blues rendition of Credence Clearwater Revival's "Suzy Q" would've made BB King want to get up and slap his momma.

Athenians came by their love of music honestly. It was embedded in their souls and soil by the earliest settlers in the South – the Irish, Scots and Welsh.

Wales is known as "The Land of Song." For generations, coalminers, who toiled by day in dark and dangerous mines, emerged to fill the nights with music. These folks were lovers of life – they'd fight for it, sing about it, and generally carouse. The fact that Elvis, Jerry Lee Lewis and Tom Jones descended from the Welsh says it all.

Just look around town. Athens is full of Celtic folk – the McDonalds, McClouds, MacDougalls, McGaritys, McCues, Harris and Howells. (Makes you wanna break out the kilts.)

Clinton smiled. "I heard some of your stuff tonight. You've really got it goin'."

John stood there in disbelief. "Yeah? Well thanks."

"We should talk about playin' together sometime. I mean if you're interested."

"Sure. Of course. That'd be fantastic."

Before he knew it, John and his band were regularly on stage with Clinton. The two became friends and Clinton gave his young friend a behind the scenes look at all the ins and outs of the business.

Even though his full schedule left little time for anything else, John made sure to stop by and see his family now and then. He never knew who'd be there, but usually found Gary off studying in a corner somewhere.

The two brothers had talked more in the last couple of months than they had in a years. John was amazed at how much his reticent younger brother had grownup. Gary wasn't a kid anymore, but a young man with serious goals.

John walked into his brother's room. "Hey man. How's it goin'?"

"Good. Me and some guys got to hear you the other night – not bad," Gary said.

"Thanks. Almost forgot you're about to graduate."

"Yeah, comin' up."

"So what you gonna do?" John asked.

" UGA, what else? Should hear anytime."

"OK. Any ideas on a major?"

"Pre-med. Been thinkin' about it for a while and that's what I wanna do."

"Seriously, dude? You wanna be a doctor?"

"Yeah, That's it."

"Cool. I just didn't know. But I'm tellin' ya, my business courses are tough enough. All that science won't be easy."

"I know. We'll see."

"Well, as long as you're waitin' around to learn your fate, you might as well come out to the club tonight. I'll get you in. The guys'll be there, too. You can hang out with them."

ART AND SOUL

I n a town like Athens, you never really knew what interesting person may be just around the corner. Will always kept
his radar on – and one day, down on Clayton Street, it signaled a high alert when he met an odd, but fascinating man.

Ed Weeks was the common man's poet. Just about everyone knew him from his flowing white hair, irrepressible
smile and charming oratory.

He'd created an unusual job for himself – advertising
for local businesses by lugging around a makeshift sandwich board. The job suited him well – giving the sidewalk
stroller a natural forum for beguiling downtown patrons
with his poetry and bringing in a little money to supple-
ment his small veteran's pension.

Mr. Weeks had been writing poetry since he was 13 and
now drew from a lifetime of remarkable experiences. After
a stint as a B-17 tail gunner in Europe during WWII, he

came to UGA on a track scholarship, but his social life soon got him *off* track and he never graduated. After a divorce, he'd bounced around for years doing odd jobs in various cities to stay afloat. In one final attempt to get his writings published, he embarked on a long walking odyssey from Athens to New York City. But the effort failed. Although he didn't catch a break in any of the literary salons of the big city, he'd later say that the journey wasn't a total waste of time because of all the wonderful people he'd met along the way.

But when it came time to settle down, he decided to return to "the happiest place I've ever known – Athens."

Will did his part to get the word out on the Poet Laureate of the Classic City by writing a long feature on him for The Red and Black.

Mr. Weeks wandered around town, gathering sidewalk audiences and regaling them with stories and poems all delivered with true Shakespearean eloquence. People of all ages and persuasions stopped and listened to his playful, yet poignant verses.

Typically, the master performer got things going with some lively banter – then shook lots of hands, gave a few hugs, and told a string of stories and jokes. After which, he'd clear his throat, compose himself for a minute and, with a flourish of his hand, recite one original poem after another.

"The Playboy"
When I was young my elders warned
'Tis wise to love but one,
But I ignored their sage advice

And sauntered blithely on.
Along life's crooked pathways
I scattered here and there
Some tiny portion of my heart
For many maids to share;
For each one had some special charm
That caught my roving eye,
And each took the bits of love
I squandered passing by.
I never dreamed that day by day
My heart was growing small.
Now each girl has a part of it,
And I have none at all.

The group exchanged thoughtful looks and applauded in approval. Later he'd hold court with small crowds at one of the more trendy eateries and entertain as long as folks listened and contributed money for "beverages to lubricate his vocal cords and stimulate his imagination."

Will didn't rush the interview, but listened long enough to appreciate the many facets of the paradoxical man. They ended the last session at Mr. Weeks's residence – a bleak room in the dilapidated Georgian Hotel. His neighbors were a menagerie of other down and out souls whose lives hadn't worked out exactly as planned.

Will jotted down his final notes and left. Walking into the foyer with its fading Roaring '20s art deco trappings, Mr. Weeks called out. "Be sure to write a good story on me. Make em' laugh about the funny old guy who lives alone in the rundown hotel and takes an 'occasional' drink now and then. You'll do that now, won't you?"

And that's exactly what Will did.

Will returned to class. There was no avoiding taking Interpersonal Communications under his least favorite professor because he was the only guy who taught the course. The prof was considered an expert in the field and had authored "the textbook," used far and wide in every program, but he wasn't a good teacher by any measure.

He came to class looking like he'd slept in his clothes. And his manners were as crude as his mismatched and stained attire. Word was, the professor may have *written* the definitive text on the topic – but he'd never *read* it. His monotone voice droned on like elevator music and he actually seemed to bore himself as much as his students.

Somethings just don't add up. This "learned" windbag with a big title gave his audience so little – while a mile away, an unheralded street poet poured out his heart and embraced life – yet barely had enough money for his next meal.

Will turned in the story on Mr. Weeks late that afternoon and noticed a file cabinet of old articles. The others had left for the day and Will thought it would be fun to hang around and browse through some of them. As he started reading, a loud *thump* startled him. *No,* he told himself, *you know those weird sounds in buildings when it's quiet.* He, along with everyone else, was on edge these days because of the attempted assaults so it was probably just his imagination getting the best of him. But he did worry that someone may have propped open the exit door again. Students were notorious for that sort of thing.

Back to the files. But this time the footsteps were real – and quickly coming towards him. Before he could turn around, a heavy arm wrapped around his neck so tightly that he couldn't move.

Time froze. Then, just as suddenly, he was let go and spun around in the chair. Coming face-to-face with his tormentors, he saw two sports writers dancing around and laughing –congratulating themselves that they'd pulled off a good one.

Will gathered his wits, jumped up and shoved the one nearest him. "That's not funny, with all the stuff goin' on around here!"

"Not funny? Man, you shoulda seen your face! Now *that* was funny!"

"We had ya, dude. And what's that puddle on the floor? You didn't wet your pants, did ya?"

"Yeah, OK, but you blockheads better not pull anything like that on the girls. Hope you have that much sense."

Will composed himself and picked one of the yellowed papers – the story of the old Iron Horse.

Ah, yes – like so many hometown stories, Will had heard bits and pieces about the Iron Horse sculpture for years. Here was a chance to get the real scoop and maybe retell it to a new group of students.

"A horse is a horse of course of course..."

Mr. Ed

The two ton iron sculpture had been making headlines and generating controversy since the day it was unveiled at Reid Hall in 1954. The university had commissioned Chicago sculptor, Abbott Pattison, to do five works on campus, but when he displayed his equestrian masterpiece, the visiting art professor had a tough go of it. Abstract art was not a common thing in Athens at the time and people voiced very strong opinions about the artwork. It was just the kind of hullabaloo that students live for so it didn't take long for them to express their own *commentary* on the sculpture.

First, it became a "horse of a different color" when they splattered it with green paint. Then came the idea to stuff a bunch of hay in its mouth. But the coup de gras of their critique was placing a generous collection of manure strategically under the horse's hind quarters – and later setting the whole thing on fire.

The artist was incensed at the desecration of his work. So much so, that the Atlanta Journal and Time magazine published stories on the horse's travails and the sculptor's outrage.

The art faculty contemplated what to do with the gift. Campus views were divided. After much debate, a horticulture professor offered to take the horse out to his farm so that those who wanted to could drive down Highway 15 and see it.

Although the horse was unceremoniously "put out to pasture," it nevertheless stands regally on a rolling hill in Greene County. (Apparently there's no truth to the rumor that the horse had its backside facing Athens.)

Will thought that amid the current churning of opposing opinions and sharp debates on issues of the day, the struggle to accept other viewpoints was really nothing new at all.

A Beautiful Friendship

The two very different professors had become friends in the most unlikely of settings – during meetings of the curriculum committee. These faculty meetings usually brought out the worst in professors and spawned plenty of jokes. *A committee – where minutes are kept and hours are lost.* And just give a bunch of academics "Robert's Rules of Order" and they're bound to sink in a quagmire of motions, counter motions, citations and amendments and subsequently lose all memory of what they were working on to begin with.

But the push was on – a new dean was hired and he'd already presented a list of lofty goals to department heads and committee chairs. And there'd be no delays or excuses.

The Dean of Arts and Sciences especially had his eye on the curriculum committee. While other faculty committees generally took care of business, unfortunately this particular bunch lived up to the worst stereotypes of ivory tower academics.

Despite his frustrations, Dr. Andrews had continued his research on updating liberal arts courses, vetting new courses and omitting redundancies while the obstructionists resisted any and all new proposals.

But now, Dr. Mac had brought fresh vitality to the pro- ceedings. He'd studied Dr. Andrews work and clearly saw the benefits of a more seamless selection of course offer- ings *across* the curriculum. Dr. Mac strongly endorsed Dr. Andrew's proposals and persuaded the others. The two teamed up and crafted a version that was unanimously accepted. Then Dr. Mac made use of his parliamentarian skills and pushed the measure to a final vote. And it was exactly what the dean had in mind.

An experienced sage and a young blood had made things happen. And – like Bogart said to Claude Raines in "Casablanca" – it was "the beginning of a beautiful friendship."

Dr. Mac had quickly settled into Athens and soon felt right at home. And, except for the Chicago accent, you'd almost think he was a native. He enjoyed mixing it up with longtime locals at the Dogwood Manor.

Miss Crumwell hugged him and seated him at Dr. Andrews's table who smiled in amusement as the matron gushed over the good-looking professor.

"Man, I sure was sorry to hear about Reynolds losing his job. It's hard to fathom. Doesn't make any sense at all," Mac said.

Dr. Andrews sighed. "He's been a friend for a long time and everyone knows what an exceptional teacher he is."

"I know. I'm assuming it's an administrative thing. Trimming the budget or something."

Dr. Andrews put his fork down. "Well, it will have a size- able effect on his pension. Two more years and he would've had full retirement. This cut will hurt him."

"*Really?* Now that's just not right," Mac said.

"No, it's certainly not."

The two gentlemen left it at that since they didn't know the whole story.

But Dr. Hall had made no secret that it was his call to dismiss Reynolds. He saw the seasoned professor as past his prime and pushed to replace him with a much younger man – a personal friend from his grad school days.

The conversation moved from campus politics to the personal. The more Mac learned about Andrew's life and family, the more it piqued his interest. Andrew's early years had been so different from his own – growing up in Chicago's upscale north side then sheltered in the world of academia.

Andrews was actually born in the Belgian Congo – the son of a pioneer linguist who'd worked with a team to translate the exclusively oral language of Baluba into a written one. He may have been too young to remember it all, but Andrews held on to his father's diaries filled with accounts of all the challenges that the family had faced. Mac always prodded him for the next story.

The missionaries' difficulties began as soon as they left port in 1917. Crossing the Atlantic during WW1 was always perilous and danger struck when a German U-boat tailed their ship waiting for the right time to strike. But before they got off a torpedo, a heavy fog rolled in. Shrouded by the thick mist, the ship miraculously slipped away to safety. Some called it a huge stroke of luck, but Reverend Andrews saw it differently and always believed it was the gracious hand of Providence.

The young minister got right to work – overseeing the church, a school and a hospital and in addition being on call 24 hours a day for "counseling"– devoting any leftover time to translation work.

Besides the constant threat of tropical disease and deadly animals, the country was also a hotbed of political turmoil. Another issue emerged that the minister could not ignore. In the lucrative business of stripping rubber from the trees, the Belgian government allowed abusive practices of the Congolese people to run rampant. Living with them day by day, Andrews saw the cruel treatment firsthand and regularly wrote to U.S. officials, urging them to intervene. Other more prominent voices of the day, such as Mark Twain, also called out King Leopold's greed and exploitations and finally, after years of international outrage, the plight of the people gradually improved.

Personal trials also came and weighed heavily on the family who was so far from home. Before Martin's birth, two children had died in infancy. The sparse notation in his father's diary simply read "I've buried my heart in Africa." The birth of Martin and his sister eased their grief for a time, but then they were hit with another devastating blow when Mrs. Andrews contracted near fatal encephalitis – sleeping sickness. Things looked dreadfully grim as she was quickly moved to England for treatment. After months of care at London's renowned hospital for tropical diseases, amazingly, she recovered.

Mac was lost in another world as he listened to Martin's stories. Then he did something he rarely did – talked about his own family. From an early age, Mac's father had groomed his children for success. As one of Chicago's top corporate attorneys, he'd expected Mac to follow suit, just as his older brothers had. But Mac, the youngest and possibly the brightest, took a different path and incurred his father's displeasure at every turn.

It wasn't that he was a defiant son; he'd worked summers at the firm with an open mind. But the tedium and minutia of the law frankly bored him silly. Mac was not a detail guy – he operated in big picture terms – and the young idealist wasn't enticed by a high six figure salary either. Everyone knew what a gifted communicator he was and that his exceptional writing ability would serve him well as an attorney, but the law just wasn't for him.

Into his sophomore year, his emerging self-knowledge collided with his father's expectations. It was inevitable – Mac had to declare a major and tell his dad.

He stood before his father and carefully explained that he'd decided on a career in journalism. Mac had felt the wrath of his autocratic father many times before, but never like this. He screamed out an ultimatum – "You defy me and I guarantee that you'll live to regret it." They both walked away and never spoke again. Mac was more than happy to leave the hurt behind and take a position far away from Chicago.

As he listened to his friend's saga, Dr. Andrews pushed backed tears. The fatherly professor couldn't imagine how Mac's father rejected a son he should have been immensely proud of.

"I'm so sorry" was all he managed to say.

⇥‡ ‡⇤

B&L Warehouse

Will hadn't seen Mr. Weeks out with his sandwich board in several days. He took the hotel elevator to his floor, and as the door opened, that unmistakable musty smell and eerie silence greeted him.

Will was one of the few people the poet allowed to visit his dreary room. He found his friend teetering on the edge of his bed, woozy and half dressed. This was the other side of Mr. Weeks that audiences never saw.

He moved some old newspapers off a chair and sat down. They talked awhile and Mr. Weeks said he'd decided to try again – to break free from the bottle. He accepted Will's offer to drive him to the detox clinic where he'd been treated several times before – maybe this round would take. Stains of dried blood on his shirt really worried Will and made him wonder if time was running out for his friend.

It may have been the best news of his life. Ed read the letter three times, laughed and almost cried. The Post had given him the internship. A celebration was in order and the appointed place was the B&L Warehouse. All the friends came and it was a lot like old times but even better. Ed was headed to the big leagues, John was on stage and even Ronnie had found true love.

Although he was still at odds with Ronnie, Will was ready to have a good time and he wasn't about to let anything spoil it. Besides, there was nothing more amusing than watching

Ronnie gush and dote over Stephanie, all the while being reduced to a silly schoolboy – it was hilarious.

Partygoers went around back and took the long, creaky steps to the entrance of the decrepit building. Even though it was a fire code nightmare, hundreds of students jammed into the cavernous old warehouse on Oconee Street, week after week. John's group was up first. It'd been a while since Will had heard them play and he was amazed. The guy had much more talent than he'd ever realized.

John's fantastic set primed the Friday night crowd in short order, making it easy for The Hampton Grease Band to take the party to the next level. The blues/rock band was famous for their wacky stage antics and they let loose tonight as never before. The crowd got their money's worth, probably because it was their last performance together. Turned out the band was breaking up. They'd had a great run but each guy was ready to do his own thing.

The night was all that it should've been. And for the grandest of the grand finales, both bands took the stage. John's lightning fast fingers on his Stratocaster ripped through a thundering rendition of Marshall Tucker's "Can't You See." The crowd stormed the stage and rocked on for another half hour.

Even though it was late, the downtown streets were alive with revelers, spilling out of everyone's favorite warehouse. And there was another reason to hang around. The news that the stalker had been arrested spread quickly through the crowd.

The tip from the young lady at the dorm led police to the guy they'd been after for weeks. From the outset of the interrogation, the troubled young man, who had a history of run-ins with the law, couldn't keep his story straight. Rattled and distraught, he broke down and confessed within an hour.

Next day, Judy picked up the police report, talked to a couple of sources, and dashed off a story. As she typed the final sentence, she heaved a deep sigh of relief. The yellow brick road was safe once again.

⇒╫⇐

Mac called, eager to nail down his next lunch with Dr. Andrews. He really wanted to talk, something was on his mind.

"Hey Mac, you've got me curious."

"Yeah, I want to get your take on an idea I've been mulling over."

"So what are you up to? You're not staging a coup or anything are you?" Dr. Andrews's eyes twinkled as he ribbed his friend.

Dr. Mac laughed, "No, we liberals aren't always causing trouble."

"Well good. It's a tight afternoon and a regime overthrow would be hard to fit in."

Mac was still smiling, enjoying the banter. "You may not agree with this, but you're a fair minded man."

"Hope so. Could be I'm just getting older and realize that everything's not always black and white."

Mac nodded and fidgeted with his napkin. "Everyone thinks your governor's about to make a run for president. I've looked into it and he's the kind of guy I could really get behind."

"Jimmy Carter? He'll run. And it won't surprise me if he gets the nomination. Carter's positioned himself quite nicely. In '72 he became chair of the Democratic Governor's committee – so he's in with the right people. The man's a strategist for sure."

"What really appeals to me are his domestic policies. I think he's genuinely concerned about racial issues and the poor. I mean a peanut farmer from the South – how much more in touch with the common man can you get?"

"Sounds like you're sold. And your plans?" Dr. Andrews asked.

"I've talked to some of his people and I'm seriously thinking of getting involved. Press strategy, writing releases, that kind of thing."

"OK."

"I think Carter could very well be the next FDR," Mac said. "But I'd love to hear what you think his foreign policy would look like."

"Well, peanut farmer, then governor. I'm not sure that's enough to qualify someone to sit in the Oval Office and take on all that's going on in the world right now. He'd need to get up to speed mighty fast. I understand that he's a detail guy – tends to micro-manage. But it's important in foreign relations to keep the big picture in view. He says the right things especially about human rights, no one argues that, but finessing global politics is the tricky part. I hope he grasps the complexities of it all."

Dr. Andrews paused. "By the way, moving from the global level to the local, Will's excited about taking that old Plymouth down to Mr. Weeks. That car's a sight, but it just keeps on running. He always liked it, though and the old thing served him well. His mom's thrilled with the news, she can't wait to get the monstrosity out of the driveway."

The car wasn't exactly in showroom condition. The '62 Plymouth station wagon had the back half of the roof sawed off and replaced by a used camper top rigged to the frame. The floor board was almost rusted out and various parts were missing or barely hanging on, but it did have a powerful 289 engine with a pushbutton transmission. Will had bought the car a couple of years ago at a yard sale for $25 (oddly enough, from a marriage counselor who was going through a divorce.) Anyway, she just wanted it gone. The car was still good basic transportation which was exactly what Mr. Weeks needed. Now with his driver's license reinstated, he'd be out on the road again. Mr. Weeks joked that he and the car were a work in progress and both needed some serious rehab.

Mr. Weeks smiled. "By the way, I really liked the article."

Will was pleased to hear that. The full page write up had shaped up nicely and had generated more sandwich board business for his friend as well.

"R-E-S-P-E-C-T"

The streets around the B&L Warehouse eventually cleared. But not everyone had gone home – they'd just migrated elsewhere. For the musicians, it was the Five Points's Waffle House – a great place to chow down and unwind after putting their sweat and soul into the night's performance. Pecan waffles drenched in butter and syrup, bacon and hash browns, and a couple of hefty platters of eggs was the ticket for recharging the guys at the starving artist's country club. The jukebox and a collection of characters made the venue the perfect place for late night cuisine and conversation.

Clinton had a lot to teach his eager protégé about the music business. John took it all in and was now proficient at setting up a sound system for large outdoor concerts – like those at Legion Field. He was really into the technical side of things – engineering the maze of wires for all the amps, lights and the mixing board that showcased a band's signature sound. Clinton could tell a good story and as far as John was concerned, he could talk about life in the music scene until the sun came up.

"You know livin' here is great. Just think of all the music this town has. The Jesters came outta your old high school. And I can remember going down to Charlie Williams 'bout every weekend and hearin' 'em play. They did their frat party kinda music – beach, Motown. Man, they were good – good enough to tour with The Platters and Marvin Gaye. We've got everything from psychedelic, funk, disco, country, to alternative. Athens isn't called *The Liverpool of the South* for nothin' – it's like an incubator for talent."

"Yeah, it's pretty cool," John said.

"Here's somethin you oughta do. You know Dirk and Tony from high school, right?"

"Sure"

"Go take in one of their shows."

"Yeah, OK."

"It's not exactly your kinda music, but man, can they fire up a crowd."

The Great Gatsby would've been right at home frequenting the Holiday Inn Lounge on Broad Street.

It was *THE* place to be and *THE* place to be seen. Five nights a week crowds of up to 200 people would be singing along with the band, shagging and hobnobbing until closing time. Dirk Howell, Tony Brown along with other musicians like Tony Pritchett and David Prince made up the core of talented entertainers who enchanted crowds night after night. It wasn't just a job for those guys – it was a way of life.

People especially loved the way Dirk and Tony brought so much showmanship and drive to their Motown and beach music. Dirk's fluid voice – with a little Rod Stewart gravel mixed in – along with Tony's full-throttled crooning made everybody want to jump up and dance.

"Come on ya'll! Get out on the floor. Don't be shy. It's a sorry dog that won't wag his own tail," Tony yelled.

Dirk was a pro at scanning the crowd and picking up on any lulls. He'd nod to the lead trumpet guy signaling him to gear it up.

"Hey ya'll. Do you know what time it is? *Does anybody really care what time it is?*" Precisely on cue, the horns came in flawlessly with Dirk, launching into a great cover of Chicago's "Does Anybody Really Know What Time It Is?"

Folks hit the dance floor. The band followed it up with the Temptation's "We're Havin' a Party" and kicked it up with one terrific song after another.

The devoted fans even developed their own alumni network that stretched throughout the region and beyond. The band knew their patrons well – *and* all their favorite tunes. When they arrived, Dirk would shout out a welcome with a guitar lick and a line or two.

"All right now. Look who just walked in the door and's gonna tear it up. None other than Will 'Get Ready' Andrews!"

A few minutes later, Tony yelled to a regular. "OK, and who's that in the house tonight? – Jill Owens, Miss 'Mustang Sally' herself. When ya'll see her in that '68 Mustang, you better get outta the way! Yeah, she may look like an angel, but the girl's a real demon on the road. And there's Mr. 'Shaggin Shoes' Swindall Evans – my man. I tell you, we got it happenin' tonight!

For those growing up in Athens, opportunities abounded to take in all kinds of entertainment. And every weekend, it was one great band after the other. For years, Dirk and Tony had heard the great Southern soul men like The Tams and The Drifters time and again. It "really got a hold on them" and they'd started their own group in high school and were soon booked to play the best parties around. And for years, the dynamic duo made sure that the soul sounds of Motown continued to echo through the night in this college town.

John sat in the back and soaked in a masterful performance. It was a tour de force. The crowd erupted and the Queen of Soul herself would've given the band plenty of R-E-S-P-E-C-T.

John found Will to tell him about seeing their old friends in action. But before he said a word, he knew something was wrong.

"You OK?"

"I was just at the hospital. It's Mr. Weeks. He's in bad shape."

John sat down.

"I stopped by to check on him and it was awful. He was drenched in sweat and totally out of it. And all pale. I called an ambulance."

John saw the pain on Will's face. "I'm sorry, man. Maybe he'll be OK."

"I dunno. What you been up to?"

John turned to leave. "Tell you later."

Mac had finally gotten things rolling in the stodgy curriculum committee. Optimism had replaced the old dread of sitting through another fruitless meeting. And if the momentum continued, they'd be able to accomplish most of the items on the agenda before year end.

But for some reason, the same old malaise set in. Mac took the floor and tried his best to revive the group but things were going nowhere.

That was it – Mac lost it and screamed at the chairman. "How 'bout getting' off your haunches and doin' some work?" But the chairman didn't budge. He was an old hand at whiling away his tenured years.

Mac came nose-to-nose with him. Suddenly everyone woke up from their dozing and glared at the brash young man.

Mac wasn't giving up; he pounded the table." If you don't want to get things done, at least have the decency to get out of the way of those who do."

Finally, Mac stormed out. "I'm not wasting any more time on this charade. I can't stand watching you squander opportunities!"

The startled teachers defaulted to their favorite solution to any dilemma. They deferred the issue to the next meeting and promptly adjourned. It was a very pompous way of doing nothing.

Dr. Andrews followed after his friend and tried to calm him. "Believe me, I know how frustrated you are."

Mac kicked over a trash can. "I just don't think it'll ever change."

"Who knows? But right now, I'm worried about you. What happened back there?"

"Guess I lost my temper. This kind of stupidity really gets to me."

"Mac, you're one of the bright stars here. If anyone's had an impact on students, it's you and you've got a very promising career ahead. Just don't blow it."

"Yeah, I know. But they just make me crazy with all their political games and posturing."

"Understood. But remember there's one thing they do very well – hold a grudge. Don't let that gray hair and polished speech fool you. They can turn into a brood of vipers in no time."

Mr. Weeks eventually made it home from the hospital and Will tried to stop by whenever he could. But the carefree poet wasn't the same person. Will didn't understand all that was going on, but apparently Mr. Weeks *did*. His liver was shot – and he'd supplied the bullets. They were able to stop the bleeding this time, but at some point, it would all happen again. The doctors told him that long term there was nothing they could do. One day the bleeding would be too severe to control. And now Mr. Weeks realized that any day could be his last.

Mac walked slowly into Martin's office and sat down.

"It's my dad. He's got cancer."

"Mac, no. I'm so sorry."

He took a few minutes to compose himself. "Mom called. He's having surgery this week but they don't know how far it's spread."

"That's really tough."

"Yeah, Mom said she'd let me know as soon as they hear. They'll call when the surgery's over."

"Mac, you've got a lot to think about."

"I know."

"You can call me anytime, you know that. And I'll definitely keep you and your dad in my prayers."

"Thank you, Martin. Means a lot."

"YOU SAY YOU WANT A REVOLUTION..."

Most speakers who lectured on campus came and went without much fanfare. But when Jane Fonda arrived, it was standing room only in the Memorial Hall Ballroom and reactions to her talk reverberated long after she left the podium.

Timing is so important – in life, sports and – war. And in June 1972, a shocking photo that appeared in newspapers worldwide would be forever embedded in the minds of millions. A photographer captured the horrifying image of a 14-year-old South Vietnamese girl screaming and running naked with napalm scorching her skin – napalm dropped from an American bomber. The appalling image caused international outrage.

Ironically, only a month later, another iconic photo taken in Vietnam circled the globe. The picture of well-known actress, Jane Fonda, standing on a tank in Hanoi, extolling the virtues of the People's Republic of North Vietnam infuriated many Americans – especially our soldiers.

Fonda's political evolution stood in stark contrast to her father's highly patriotic movies and traditional John Ford westerns. But Jane and her brother Peter (who'd made his mark playing a drifting hippie in the huge box office hit "Easy Rider") were part of a different generation. An accomplished actress, Jane had come a long way from her film debut in the campy sci-fi movie, "Barbarella." Her provocative dress and stance in the movie caused quite a stir, and now her *militant* stance – posing in combat fatigues with the Viet Cong – shocked the nation.

The controversial actress passionately espoused her views and tried to justify her actions for over an hour. A very conflicted audience listened to her remarks with muted politeness except for a row of vets who stood against the back wall – seething with indignation. One man, in particular, looked like he was about to explode.

Will had known the sergeant and heard his story from vet meetings and bull sessions he'd covered for the paper. The soldier had almost died in Vietnam. A buddy saved his life when he pulled a manure tipped Viet Cong punji stick out of the ground and rammed it into the sergeant's throat as a make-shift trach. It kept him alive until the medics arrived and carried him away. Fonda's views stoked his boiling hot anger. The troubled man's face said a lot more about the lasting effects of America's longest "undeclared war" than hours of classroom lectures and professorial pontifications.

Fonda was one of many celebrities who offered all sorts of views on the complicated conflict.

But early on, most people expressed support for the military. In 1966, the heart-rending and very patriotic "Ballad of the Green Berets" topped the charts. At that time, most of the country was gung ho behind the war effort and the popularity of Sergeant Barry Sadler's moving recitation largely reflected public sentiment: "put silver wings on my son's chest...make him one of America's best." But as the war drug on, public opinion soured and songs echoed a growing disenchantment – songs such as Joe Cocker's "Give Peace a Chance." Protest anthems became more and more the norm.

The country had come together with remarkable unity during World War II. We all loved John Wayne as Sergeant John Stryker storming the Japanese fortified stronghold in "The Sands of Iowa Jima." And who didn't get chills during the stirring reenactment of the three lone Marines raising the American flag on Mt. Suribachi. (The actual soldiers recreated the final dramatic scene in the movie using the very flag from the battle.) Tragically, 7,000 Marines died in the fight to take a volcanic rock island in the middle of nowhere – more than in any other engagement in the history of the Marine Corp – yet the country stood behind them. Admiral Chester W. Nimitz aptly captured the nation's gratitude for the men's tenacity and bravery: "Among the men who fought on Iwo Jima, uncommon valor was a common virtue."

But that was "a popular war."

To revive support for the current war effort, an aging and noticeably plumper John Wayne once again took to the silver screen. He'd invested his own money in filming a flag-waving version of the bestselling book "The Green Berets."

The story line pits a cynical, anti-war reporter against Special Forces Colonel Mike Kirby, played by Wayne. The hero leads his Green Berets, whose motto is "kill 'em all and let God sort 'em out," on a daring mission behind enemy lines to kidnap a top Viet Cong officer.

Much of the filming was done at Ft. Benning – hardly a place of impenetrable jungles and rice fields. And every so often, you'd see random camera pans of tall Georgia pines and a few bewildered looking Columbus citizens in faux paus snippets that had slipped through the editing room. Editing aside, "The Duke" took care of business, as Bachman Turner Overdrive would say – and accomplished the mission in a blaze of glory.

Vietnam was the first war that American families had watched *live* as they ate dinner in their dens. The three national networks covered the combat every night. Death tolls were tallied up like a sports scoreboard "247 Viet Cong killed and 34 American casualties." Even the most disengaged citizen had to wonder... *How can we wipe out so many enemy troops; drop more bombs than we did in WWII and still be in a stalemate after all these years?*

Finally a cease fire treaty was signed in Paris on Jan. 27, 1973 marking the "official" end of the war. Soldiers who left combat zones found themselves adrift among a citizenship who still grappled with the fallout from a wavering foreign policy that'd cost so many American lives. It had been a roller-coaster ride of major escalations, then de-escalations from the fog of erratic, pretzel-shaped policies. Politicians had placed massive constraints on our military that'd been called on to fight a very different kind of enemy. The Viet Cong were ruthless, elusive in guerrilla warfare and backed by Communists superpowers.

Americans grew weary of watching nightly newsreels of our wounded being carried out of bloody jungles. And in the end, the Viet Cong captured Saigon. The country gathered around TV sets as CBS anchor, Walter Cronkite, reported the chaos and desperation of the final hours. His moving commentary described the enemy crashing American jeeps into the Presidential Palace and the last helicopters taking off from the American embassy with frantic people clinging to the copter's landing platforms. A weary Cronkite signed off with: "We have reached the end of the tunnel and find no light there."

Instead of sitting in barracks or ditches anxiously awaiting their next mission, many demoralized souls took their GI bills and now sat in sedate classrooms feeling like they were "Still in Saigon" as Charlie Daniels put it.

The vets had left the country as anxious adolescents and returned as confused young men. Some got solace and help through the campus vet office in Memorial Hall and others took advantage of the free counseling that was offered. But for the most part, they 'just dealt with it" on their own and tried to adjust to the world they'd left behind – burying themselves in their studies or getting a job. Far too many turned to drugs in a desperate attempt to forget.

Although families held touching reunions at major airports across the U.S., unfortunately, the general public and many college students "welcomed" these vets back to their homeland with a collective war-weary yawn.

In previous conflicts we'd always welcomed out troops home with open arms and confettied parades. But this time most turned away in indifference, some in disgust and even a few strident voices called them "murderers" and "baby killers."

Never before had coming home been so devoid of the comfort and healing the veterans so desperately needed. Where was "the thanks of a grateful nation?"

"It's not good, Martin. They got some of it, but it's already spread. So, it's chemo – and that's pretty rough itself. They give him about nine months at best."

Martin shook his head." Mac, I can't even tell you how sorry I am. How are you holding up?"

"I don't really know. I haven't talked to him in so long and now this ..."

"And what about your mom?"

"She's torn up. She wouldn't know what to do without him. He handles everything. On the phone, she can hardly talk, she just cries."

Mac hung his head. "I guess I should go. Go home."

"You have to, Mac and I can guarantee you won't regret it."

"I know. But I'm not even sure he wants to see me. It's strange how some of the simplest decisions in life can be so hard."

Tears of a Clown

One day, when folks around Athens were celebrating the wonders of springtime that mark the renewal of life, death intruded.

Mr. Weeks had died alone in his hotel room. Will found it very hard to wrap his mind around it. The eccentric poet had started out as another story for Will, but he'd also become a real friend.

Will was a lot like most students who clung to the carefree days of college. Knowing it wouldn't last forever, they still went to great lengths not to leave the bubble before they had to. But sometimes harsh reality comes crashing in and deep down Will had known this day would come.

The gifted man had brightened the day of so many with his personality and poetry, but the one person he couldn't seem to get through to was himself. Smokey Robinson's words rang true: *"There's some sad things known to man..., but there's nothing sadder than the tears of a clown when there's no one around."*

Will was not accustomed to grieving. But he allowed himself some time to feel the weight of his sorrow. He drove around awhile, noticing the trees in full bloom, the fresh breezes and the girls in their spring attire. On such a beautiful day like this, Mr. Weeks would have been right in his element – out holding court, entertaining – enjoying people.

Will finally decided to stop in front of the old Georgian
Hotel. He pulled out one of Mr. Week's poems and slowly
read it to himself.

"On Observing Small Turtle with Big Plan"
By Ed Weeks
Small turtle, Sittin' there with your hooded beady eyes
ablinkin,'
Are you thinkin' what I think you're thinkin'?
Perhaps considering a trip across this asphalt strip?
May I strongly recommend you reconsider.
The experience could prove most bitter.
Oh, I can tell
By looking at your shell
That you're a hard case
But let me point out that this aint no rabbit race;
And, Oh yes, I can see
That you like to stick your neck out same as me.
But don't stick it out too far, or some speeding motor car
Just may come hurtlin'
And swiftly end your days of turtling.'
What do men in mean machines
Know of tiny turtles with ridiculous ambitions
Like crossing busy highways
Under extremely hazardous conditions?
No, no, small turtle,
You'll never get across, so I'll just give you a toss
Back in the woods.
That's where you ought to be;
And you leave this rotten road to men in mean machines
And fools like me.

"Cha-cha- Changes..."

David Bowie

No matter what else was going on, you still had to go to class. As usual, all the really great electives had filled up super-fast which left Will stuck with a random sociology class.

The young graduate assistant walked confidently into the classroom with her well prepared handouts and study guides. Today she was lecturing on her favorite topic – gender and culture. It wasn't just part of the course – it was her passion. She'd done her master's thesis on the women's movement and was totally committed to the cause.

The previous lecture on "Maslow's hierarchy of needs" had laid the groundwork for her remarks today. By this time, students could practically recite Maslow in their sleep since the theory was showcased in *any and every* humanities class they'd ever taken. Many freshly minted Ph.Ds. declared it to be the Rosetta stone for understanding the human psyche. (You wondered how mankind had survived all these eons without it.) But now we had it – along with a host of other self-fulfillment mantras that were creeping into the curriculum.

"Good afternoon everyone, you probably know that for the next two weeks we'll be discussing the women's liberation movement and the subsequent changing roles of women in our society.

"I can't wait to get started. I have *so* much information to impart to you, but I really want to get *your* views on this important issue before I get into my lecture. So let's begin.

"Please, just speak out and say whatever comes to your mind. I can't wait to hear your insights...OK. Don't be shy. Let's take some time to share our thoughts.

"Yes, I see your hand there in the back. Go right ahead."

"I think equal pay for equal work makes sense and it should apply across the board for men and women."

"Thank you, now to this gentleman."

"Yeah, it's only fair," said another student, "it's definitely the right thing to do."

"Well...I'll tell you my *views* on women. I'm like these other guys; only they won't say it. I'm all about gettin' the *best views* of all the goodlookin' women I can."

A female student jumped in, "Here we go – the Neanderthal speaks! All you males think about is sex and football!"

Another guy chimed in. "That's not true! We think about other things, too. Cars, beer. You know, to start with."

An agitated female student stood to her feet, "You're nothin' but a bunch of narrow-minded, patriarchal, capitalist pigs!"

"Well, I like what Lewis Grizzard says about women's lib. 'Sure I believe in women's liberation. I've already liberated two of 'em and I lost a lot of money in the process.'"

The comments ricocheted back and forth for the rest of the period. The frazzled instructor had completely lost control of the class but still tried in vain to end the verbal melee. It was no use.

Will wasn't much into sociology but decided to keep an open mind. *Isn't that the whole point of higher education? Considering all points of view?* At least, the class fit his schedule and gave him a needed elective. He took it all in and left thinking that, even in his short life, things had changed radically in the way men and women acted towards each other.

Everyone had friends who'd take a circuitous journey to "find themselves." Case in point, Will stopped by Athens's premier incense-enhanced hippie emporium, The Purple Onion, the other day. He had to look twice because he hadn't seen Teresa Randolph in years. The little girl at Barrow School had become famous when she won a national competition and became "Little Miss Sunbeam." She was exactly who they were looking for – an innocent, All –American girl with golden pigtails. From then on, her picture adorned the packaging for all Sunbeam bread.

But she'd grown up, thrown off the marketing image and discovered her own identity. Little Miss Sunbeam now made her statement in tie-dyed shirts, long flowing blonde hair and bell bottoms. Young women were changing and charting their own course.

Roles and relationships got kind of crazy and confusing. Some women identified with Tammy Wynette's "Stand by Your Man" but then there was the *new* mantra, "I Am Woman… Hear Me Roar!" with Helen Reddy. The gals in the South weren't exactly burning their bras en masse just yet, but neither were they content to be a perpetually, perky, 1960s Donna Reed housewife either.

Women had choices but once you made one, you might be locked into a rigid role or "typecast." Decked out in a dark androgynous pantsuit, ready for battle in the male-dominated corporate world, the career woman had to be tough enough to take on men, who hardly welcomed her into their ranks. Or she could drop out of the rat race for an artsy lifestyle. (Bohemian clothes are surely more comfortable and yoga's quite relaxing.) A few were still happy just to get their "MRS degree," but most were simply trying to navigate huge cultural changes and doing the best they could to be themselves.

Most progressives and traditionalists did agree on a few things – like addressing longstanding inequalities such as equal pay and career opportunities. Women had woefully few legal rights when it came to divorce settlements and, for many, even getting a credit card without a co-signer was difficult.

Jane Fonda wasn't the only influential woman making waves these days. Awhile back, Gloria Steinman commanded attention when she gave her "new lifestyles" talk at UGA's Conference on American Women.

A capacity crowd listened intently as the nationally-known feminist talked about her life and odyssey in becoming a women's rights advocate. In the early '60s, she'd gone undercover as a Playboy bunny and written a scathing expose on Hugh Hefner's enterprise. Later, she launched a national publication, MS, the first magazine owned and operated solely by women and exclusively devoted to women's issues. Audiences enjoyed hearing her tongue-in-cheek comments about males, "Women need men like a fish needs a bicycle." And "A woman's place is in the house – The Speaker of the House."

Then there was Helen Gurley Brown, the acclaimed editor of Cosmopolitan magazine. With her national bestseller, "Sex and the Single Girl," she'd become the Pied Piper of female promiscuity. Brown proclaimed that a woman could and should "have it all" – scintillating relationships, upwardly mobile careers supported by a progressive, understanding husband *and* a fabulous family – you didn't have to choose love over work or vice versa.

But there was one person who seemed impervious to change – Miss Ruby. Now Miss Ruby was a fine Southern lady and an outstanding teacher in her time, but the spinster's day had passed awhile back – at the end of Calvin Coolidge's administration. Still, she insisted on substituting.

With paramedics on standby, she'd come to the high school in her flowing black dress that swept the dust on the floor when she moved. It was probably the height of fashion back in 1901 but now it just made the female version of Ichabod Crane look even odder.

After lamenting not having one of the good looking education majors filling in, the guys went on to have a field day with the partially blind, mostly deaf sub. Anticipating an afternoon algebra class with Miss Ruby, they messed around at lunch till the consequences of *tardy* flashed in their minds. The situation was especially dire for Will who simply didn't have enough logic chips in the left side of his brain to solve *anything* for X and Y. (Even if he'd been tutored by Euclid or Pythagoras, it wouldn't have helped.)

They devised a foolproof plan (or more like a plan that only a *fool* would try to *prove*). While they smeared ketchup generously over Will's leg, his friends concocted a story about a reckless driver hitting Will as he "burned rubber" in the parking lot.

The guys breathlessly hauled Will into class with his arms draped over their shoulders, dragging his injured leg. Miss Ruby was shocked by the "excessive bleeding," but was so impressed with the part about Will *insisting* on coming to class and delaying medical attention that she launched into a mini sermon.

"Students, as you know, I've dedicated my entire life to education and its days like this that make it all worth the effort." Then something about Will being a shining example of a young person valuing his education at any cost. She directed the guys to take Will to the school nurse, assuring him that she'd give him a copy of her personal notes and see that "he didn't miss a thing."

During UGA's early years, females had a tough go of it. First, they had to continually fight just to get enrolled. Finally the day came on Sept.18, 1918 when Miss Witcher Walker entered President David C. Barrow's office and signed her name to the registrar's roll as an undergraduate student. (A few women had been admitted as graduate students in select fields before this date.)

Although Georgians didn't exactly rush headlong into this revolution, steps towards progress turned a corner when Walter B. Hill, a strong advocate for admitting women to the university, became president and immediately made plans to build a female residence. He proposed removing the graves in the old cemetery on Jackson Street to another location, and using the land for a women's division.

Longtime University Registrar, Tom Reed, noted in his journal that it was a wet, cold day when the president surveyed the land. By the time he got home, his feet were soaked and he was chilled all over. He fell quite ill and died of pneumonia within a few days. The friend who accompanied him on that walk remarked that "Hill literally gave his life for the cause of coeducation."

The small group of beleaguered ladies that set foot on campus that year was snubbed, for the most part, by their male classmates. Undeterred, the women formed their own student government association, elected a president and excelled in the classroom, all the while pushing against stringent and peculiar rules imposed on them for campus conduct.

Athens native, Mary Lyndon, broke through a barrier and became the first woman to earn a master's degree in 1912. Later as Dean of Women, she made sure that UGA ladies adhered to proper decorum which meant wearing skirts and stockings on campus, bloomers for P.E. and donning hats and gloves when venturing downtown.

In a 1926 report by the Dean of Women, Anne Brumby, noted that a male faculty member was aghast at the widespread practice of women powdering their noses in public. The dean promptly admonished women to powder their noses in private "and take your chances of it staying powdered." Even up until the late '60s section 2, item 1 of the student handbook said: "Pedal pushers and Bermuda shorts may be worn in designated areas of the university residences but not in public living rooms or parlors." And still, it wasn't until May, 1965 that women were allowed to wear shorts or slacks on campus. Not only had dress codes changed dramatically, but women went on to play the rough and tumble game of rugby as a club sport.

Fast forwarding to the early '70s, women now outnumbered men on campus. Of course, guys were happy with the opportunities those numbers afforded them while women were justifiably proud of their academic achievements even though the statistical odds for romance were stacked against them.

Changing times also brought the demise of one of Athens's longstanding institutions. Effie's had been in business as a house of ill-repute (in various forms) for 70 odd years. After surviving numerous protests and police raids through the years, it ceased operations in 1974. Shifting cultural mores and "free market competition" had apparently diminished the client base, so the city bought the property on Elm Street and burned down the houses as a practice drill for the fire department. In an act of historic preservation and entrepreneurship, a retired postal worker got permission to retrieve 1,082 bricks from the site. He shellacked them twice and affixed a gold inscription of authenticity to each one, and sold them for $15 each.

Long time Dean of Women, Louise McBee, had been a tireless advocate for women's issues, but admitted that progress moved at a turtle's pace, in academics, campus athletics and the work place.

But elsewhere in the culture, the advertising tag for Virginia Slim cigarettes, "You've Come a Long Way Baby!" was certainly apropos. Nowadays, at the first hint of spring it was tank tops, mini-skirts and cut-offs. From an archaic dress code to sunning themselves, in the most limited attire, around dorms and sorority houses – and on "Brumby Beach." And nobody worried anymore about "women powdering their noses in public."

Mac couldn't sleep. He'd wrestled for hours about what to do. The stark realities of his dad's illness left him numb and confused. The chemo treatments were rapidly taking their toll and had brought the hard-driving man, who'd achieved about anything he'd ever wanted, to his knees. Mac never imagined seeing him so weak.

His dad hadn't said much about the past. But as he held on to Mac's arm, he asked him not to go. His pleadings made it hard for Mac to leave to catch his plane. He finally told Mac that he loved him and was very proud of the man he'd become. Mac could hardly speak.

Saying goodbye to his mom was just as hard. Heartbroken and child-like, she desperately needed help.

Mac didn't like living so far away now.

Of course, faculty positions were set for fall. But a last minute vacancy opened up at nearby Northwestern University and it was a perfect fit. Mac certainly didn't want to leave Georgia in a bind, but he knew there was a ready pool of folks eager to snap up the job at a moment's notice.

He'd sent everything in and Northwestern called to set up an interview.

Mac explained his decision to Martin.

"As hard as it'll be to see you go," Martin said, "you're doing the right thing."

"Yeah, I feel like's it's the only choice I have now. But I still don't know how to deal with the whole relationship thing. I mean, he's dying. What do I do?"

"Well, you may have to find a way to forgive him. I'm not saying it's easy."

"Honestly, I don't know how to do that."

"Maybe a good place to start is just to try to understand your dad. What shaped him. Understanding someone is not the same as excusing them – but it may give you a measure of sympathy. It opens the path to forgiveness."

"Well I do know that his dad was stern and distant. He grew up poor and was determined never to go without again."

"I'm close to your dad's age. And at this stage of life you do a lot of looking back and soul searching. I imagine your dad's doing the same, especially as he's facing his final days."

"I'm surprised how much he's mellowed already."

"You two should keep talking. You never know where it may lead."

Express yourself

Spring was in full bloom. You couldn't get out of those classrooms fast enough and into the honeysuckled air that fueled spring fever. Students enjoyed chilling out between classes at Memorial Hall plaza which was also the designated free speech area.

It was a beehive of activity and a place where, each and every day, our cherished First Amendment rights were thoroughly exercised. The university's true diversity was on display as passionate individuals extolled all manner of beliefs, causes and political platforms. And hanging out there was also cheap entertainment. The clash of cultures rivaled any scripted comedy routine. It was especially fun to listen in on conversations between good ole boys and hippies.

Of course, the relevant youth of the day were always regulars, continuing onward in a very sincere search for Truth and Justice. Others gathered because they'd always gathered – the old professional hippies who did a little ranting and pontificating but mainly sat cross-legged and waited for "the answer blowin' in the wind" (after they'd been blowin' on some inspirational cannabis).

Will listened to a few impassioned remarks by a group of shaggy-harried orators on how to run the country and conserve energy, but after a while the speaker's own energy level abated and it was back to the bongo drummin' and misty-eyed, James Taylor guitar strumin.' Eventually, they got tired of grousing about the oppressive power structure and felt the need for some "munchies" and granola and perhaps a meditation/siesta time between sessions. That way, they'd be ready to find another happenin' place to party later on.

For several years the shorn heads of the Hare Krishna's had become a standard feature on the plaza. "Hare...Hare...Krishna...Krishna"...for hours on end – without end. (Down South, we believe in benedictions and amen means *amen*.)

An eager young marketing student offered them some creative recruiting ideas – think of it – game day robes in red and black. And chanting "Hare Dawgs!" and maybe clang their cymbals in time to the Redcoat band. Might be just the thing to attract a few more followers.

One group's devotees sold their glossy magazines and pamphlets on campus, in malls and at the Atlanta Airport to raise money for their cause. To the casual observer, it seemed that the general idea was the more magazines you sold – the faster you'd ascend to Nirvana.

The Moonies, followers of Sun Yung Moon, trumpeted their beliefs – and threw in the added bonus of an arranged marriage with hundreds of other couples as well. (Might be tricky getting all the cousins over to Seoul for the ceremony, observed a local bystander).

Another group, ready to tell you their views of a better life, was the Transcendental Meditation folks. (But one thing left out in the mound of literature they offered were pictures of Maharishi Yogi and his fleet of Rolls Royces – it did eventually make "60 Minutes" though.)

A fellow from South Georgia strolled by them, shaking his head, and shared his two cents about becoming "one with nature."

"Yeah, I can tell you 'bout communin' with nature – it ain't all it's cracked up to be. After bustin' your butt in the fields from sun up to sundown, you don't always feel so spiritual. And you'd better watch your comtemplatin' or your foot'll end up in a cow pie." His buddy turned down a brochure. "I ain't in no way interested in *transdental anything*. Already had my wisdom teeth out and that was bad enough."

On many campuses, a classical symbol for higher education marks the nexus for students congregating. Perhaps a replica of Rodin's famous sculpture, "The Thinker." But for UGA it was none other than a small bronze Bulldog presiding over the campus hub. And some days you'd glance over at him and swear you'd see him smiling and shaking his head at all the goings on.

Actually, free speech wasn't anything new on campus. UGA's two oldest student groups were literary societies who'd hosted spirited debates on the issues of the day. Phi Kappa and the Demosthenian Society had gone head to head over evolution, slavery, women's rights, and alcohol.

But one student orator emerged who was too much for the faculty to handle. They'd reached their limit with his rowdiness and the famous Georgian, Robert Toombs, got himself kicked out on his ear in his junior year.

Legend has it that the defiant young Toombs returned on commencement day and delivered his *own* stirring oration near the Chapel. The renegade enticed students out of their seats mid-ceremony until there were more people gathered around him on the lawn than inside.

Toombs went on to serve as a senator and ironically was a big backer of higher education at UGA. The university that had rebuked him later offered him an honorary degree, which he refused time and again. And supposedly, in an odd quirk of fate, on the day he died, lighting struck the large oak where he'd delivered his spellbinding speech on that graduation day.

Will sat awhile at the plaza and enjoyed looking over the crowd. It was clear that this was an age of *hair.*

You could pretty much gauge someone's political views by their "do." For the guys, the longer and shaggier their hair, the more radical their outlook. Fuzzy, out-of-control sideburns were all the rage. Sheers were used sparingly and barbershops felt the pinch.

And for a really cool look, you had the big, blown-out Afro – like Bob Dylan or Jimi Hendrix.

The ladies went for long, flowing hair – over the shoulders or down the back, often scented by Herbal Essence shampoo. Some liked it more earthy, letting it shape up as nature would have it – Janis Joplin and Joni Mitchell inspired. Others styled it in long layers – a look later made famous by Farrah Fawcett.

Hair was a big deal, so much so that a hit musical – "Hair" celebrated it on the Broadway stage. And in the spirit of the times, the cast performed completely in the buff.

The tennis courts beckoned and Will was just in time to make a fourth player for a doubles match and facing him across the net was Ronnie. Will had almost forgotten their high school tennis days, but seeing him on the court brought it all back. Another instance of Ronnie's singular ability to use his friends and blow opportunities. Ronnie had raw talent. And to help out the team, Will spent a lot of his court time doing drills geared to sharpen Ronnie's skills. It paid off. The team won another regional title and Ronnie went on to make alternate on a community college team. But true to form, his grades torpedoed the deal – and that was that.

Will's serve. He crushed it – straight to Ronnie. "Man, I've never seen you hit it so hard!"

The match was neck in neck; both of them were making great shots.

Next serve – another rocket – aimed right at Ronnie.

Ronnie dodged it. "Dude, you're on fire, but you don't have to slam it down my throat! How come you're playin' so all out? C'mon man, it's just a pickup game."

After a long pause, Will answered. "I just feel like it."

SPRING FEVER

"*A nd Mr. Manuel Diaz, playing in the Number 1 position wins the final game to make it a perfect love set 6- 0 and another win for the Bulldawgs...*"

Love sets weren't just the pairing off of starry-eyed students with a bout of spring romance – but something UGA's championship tennis team had become famous for as they chalked up win after win.

Situated on a hill near the Coliseum and the baseball field, UGA's tennis complex was home to a tennis dynasty in the making. Thanks to Coach Dan Magill, the renowned tennis program had won its share of SEC titles since he took the helm in 1955.

The sport had come into its own when more and more fans were drawn to the game from watching high profile players like Jimmy Connors and Chris Evert battling it out in big time TV matches. Besides their skill, finesse and laser-like shots, Connors and Evert charmed the sport's world and became celebrities in their own right. And with the advent of better courts and powerful, lightweight rackets (which made playing easier and a lot more fun), more and more week-end warriors took up the game.

Then Billie Jean King struck a resounding victory for women on the courts. The 29-year-old Wimbledon champion and staunch women's rights supporter challenged Bobby Riggs to a match to prove that women could excel in professional sports just like men. Fifty million Americans tuned in to witness the much hyped, televised "The Battle of the Sexes" in the Houston Astrodome.

With Riggs's big mouth and flagrant male chauvinism, he was just the kind of opponent she'd love to beat. The overconfident Riggs expected to waltz in and win. But while he gambled and partied and gained 15 pounds, Billie Jean conditioned and worked hard on her game.

Before the match, Billie Jean gave her rival a squealing piglet, made a few comments to the press touting the athletic prowess of women, and then let her racket do the rest of the talking. Billie Jean easily beat the noticeably winded and out of shape former champ and won the $100,000 along with unquestioned bragging rights.

Athens was at the forefront of the tennis action. UGA's facility was one of the largest in the country, seating 5,000, and regularly hosted the NCAA tournament. Students enjoyed sunning themselves in the stands surrounded by a beautiful Southern landscape of Azaleas and Dogwoods, many of which, Magill had planted himself.

With Magill's formidable coaching and promotional skills and a fine collection of great players, some of the largest tennis crowds in the country filled the venue week after week. We had hometown hero, Danny Birchmore – the guy who had it all: honors student, team captain and UGA's first All-American tennis player. (At age 18, he defeated none other than Jimmy Connors to become US Clay court champion in 1969.)

Coach Magill was such a blue-blooded UGA fan, that he was known as "Mr. Bulldog." He'd come by the title honestly, taking his first fulltime university job in 1949 for $100 a week. Before coaching the tennis team, he promoted UGA athletics by tirelessly crisscrossing the state and organizing Bulldog clubs in every county. He regaled football fans with thrilling moments from past games during his radio spot during halftimes. The names he bestowed upon players sealed their place among the greats. Peter Rijeka, UGA's first soccer style kicker from Germany, became "The Bootin' Teuton." Jimmy Poulos, "The Greek Streak," Francis Marion, "The Swamp Fox," (a great player and later a NFL defensive coach). And Charlie Trippi, "Georgia's Italian Stallion." And who can forget the terrific kicker, Bobby Etter, "The Big Toe from Cairo."

As the tournament began, the crowd quieted down and the only sound you heard was the rhythmic bouncing of the ball right before the server unleashed a 100 mph rocket. Then the match was on. Fans broke their brief silence and whooped and hollered with each dramatic shot. You would've thought it was a football crowd. The genteel decorum and hushed whispers that marked the refined traditions of other top tournaments like Wimbledon and the U.S. Open had no place in Bulldawg country because when it comes to sports – Dawgs will be Dawgs. Fans were certainly respectful of visiting teams, but opponents always knew they were in for a *long* day when they set foot on UGA's courts.

Between official play, the courts were open at select times to faculty and former high school players. Will kept a close eye on the schedule and had great fun playing among the regulars. Just being on the courts where Georgia's elite won match after match, was inspiring enough, plus you never knew what interesting people you'd meet for a pickup game.

The university had its own eclectic group of tennis enthusiasts – faculty, coaches and towns people. Defensive coach, Erk Russell loved the game and hustled for every point – offering up a slew of colorful quips between volleys. Folks wouldn't expect to brush up on Milton or Shakespeare during a match, but if Dr. West, head of the English department, was playing, he'd make terrific shots accompanied by eloquent literary allusions. Other players admired math professor Dr. Ball's blistering backhand which he delivered with calculated precision. Dr. Blackstone was also a regular. The former Duke football player turned philosophy professor took his wins and losses "in a larger existential context." You'd be hard pressed to find a more intriguing assortment of people to enjoy the game with.

Looking down from the sprawling tennis courts stood the Coliseum. Over the years young folks had danced by the hundreds on the arena floor to the Tams, James Brown, The Four Tops, Temptations and other groups long before officials got all concerned about crowd control and security.

Sometimes the high school tennis team practiced on the UGA courts to *loud* sound checks of touring rock bands setting up. And when the band ran through their biggest hits, it turned into a free mini concert for anyone within a three block radius.

"Man, the best was Iron Butterfly goin' over and over the opening chords for 'In a Gadda da Vida baby.' You could feel the ground quake," John said.

The lyrics weren't exactly akin to Shakespearean sonnets, and who knew what some of the bizarre phrases in rock songs actually meant, but what did it matter – as long as the amps were turned up and the beat kept you movin.'

"Remember sneakin' in to see Grand Funk Railroad? We hid in that equipment cart and just rolled on in," Ed said.

They all laughed.

"Yeah, had to wait a good three hours for the show to start, but it was still pretty cool," John said.

"What wasn't cool was being there in our all-white tennis clothes. But hey, it was free," Ed said.

The guys reminisced about their wacky stunts, awkward moments and good times way back to Barrow Elementary School. Perched on a hill directly across the street from the UGA Athletic Complex, Barrow and the university campus were practically kissing cousins. Back then, girls wore dresses to school and standard attire for the boys were heavy-duty denim jeans mainly because the playground was harder than titanium and full of rocks. (Only eight hearty blades of grass sprouted from the barren dirt.) The lush university turf beckoned and the kids crossed the street anytime they could to watch the varsity football and track teams practice and the Redcoat Marching Band rehearsing. (This *was* definitely a case where the grass was truly greener on the other side.)

The old school building hadn't changed much since it opened in 1923 – Georgia pine hallways and original chalk boards. Cast iron steam heaters sizzled on frosty winter mornings and there was no air conditioning during those sultry weeks that book-ended the school year. The whole building was like a museum of Norman Rockwell Americana. Moms carpooling in station wagons lined up and down the street in the mornings and afternoons to transport their young ones. Each school day started with reciting "The Pledge of Allegiance," and on some days, "The Barrow School Song" was also sung with great gusto:

"I love to go to Barrow School
The best ole school I know
For five days out of every week to Barrow school I go
Oh to Barrow I love to go
Oh to Barrow I love to go
The best ole school I know"

"And now days, you'd have to drug their Kool-Aid to get kids to sing somethin' like that," John said.

Everyone respected the teachers, many of whom looked like they'd been there since the cornerstone was placed in 1923. There were no real discipline problems to speak of because if you stepped out of line, you got walloped. The teachers held high standards. No monkey business. Lots of math and grammar drills and reciting key events and dates from history and poems – all by memory.

On days when the rain poured – everyone wore those thick, heavy yellow raincoats and galoshes better suited for North Atlantic fishermen – and hung them on pegs in the cloak room next door to dry out. The girls actually listened to the teacher while the boys endlessly fidgeted and squirmed in their seats.

Like kids everywhere, the students lived for recess. One day, on the playground, Will made a remarkable discovery when he looked up and noticed Susan Echols. It'd never occurred to him how beautiful she was. But now with the sun light shining through her hair, he was smitten. *Maybe this is what all the dragon-slaying and mushy love songs are about.* For a moment, kickball took a backseat, but then the sharp pain of the ball hitting him in the stomach brought him back just in time to incur the wrath of his teammates for dropping the ball.

"C'mon, Will, you idiot, what's the matter with you! Can't you catch the ball? How 'bout it!"

It just wasn't a good day for kickball. Later a booming kick sent the ball flying into the old lady's yard next to the school. She was a weird old lady who apparently had nothing better to do to then spend all day peeping through her Venetian blinds. Anytime an errant ball landed on her property, she'd dash out like the Wicked Witch of the West and confiscate it with fiendish delight. *No one* was brave enough to retrieve it – not even the class bully who cringed at the suggestion.

When February came around, you got another shot at young love. The kids mustered up the courage to give each other those miniature candy hearts, carefully selecting the *special* ones for the right person. Decorated shoeboxes served as their "mailboxes" for receiving Valentine cards. They "addressed" 30 or so of those red and white penny cards, one for each classmate. Here was a chance to push the boundaries of your affection beyond the usual taunting, teasing and ponytail pulling.

When the UGA basketball coliseum was being built in 1963 all the Barrow kids eagerly monitored the weekly progress as the massive concrete supports were poured. And one day, it sprouted up from the ground like a giant concrete prehistoric creature. On a dare, Athens's native and All-American safety, Jake Scott, fearlessly road his motorcycle over the concrete arch from one side to the other. (And that's when Coach Dooley banned football players from having motorcycles.)

Hometown boys prized their fine collection of sports memorabilia. One of Will's favorites was a UGA game ball autographed by All-American Fran Tarkington. Will guarded it like Jason with his Golden Fleece. From time to time, athletes from Dr. Andrews's classes invited them to the Sunday buffet at the McWhorther athletic dorm. It was great mingling with some of the stars up close. Will couldn't believe the voracious appetites of the Woolly Mammoth size linemen who kept piling steaks on overflowing plates and still went back to graze on the bountiful buffet.

McWhorter Hall was named for Athens's legend – Bob McWhorther. UGA's first football All-American played from 1937-1947 and scored 61 touchdowns. The debonair, dashing halfback was the embodiment of a scholar/athlete and Southern gentlemen. McWhorter was captain of both the football and baseball teams, but turned down a pro baseball contract to return to his hometown to practice and teach law. The University of Virginia educated lawyer then served as mayor of Athens for four consecutive terms. Moms and dads, with their young boys in tow, always pointed him out as a role model of "a great player who *also* studied and *did extremely well in school.*"

Years of wonderful memories centered around the Coliseum and those fields. Will learned to drive in a 1960 Rambler in the Stegemen parking lot. Ramblers were lousy lemons of a car with a top speed of 51 mph *if* you were going downhill on Lumpkin and had a strong wind behind you. The cheap foam padding exploded through the bench seats within the first few months of ownership. The ugly behemoth steered like a Sherman tank. No AC. Ford *did* have "a better idea" with the cool Mustang.

The best times of all were marked by the sweat the guys left on the turf of the UGA practice fields. They'd play pick-up games until they couldn't move or the setting sun shut 'em down – it just didn't get any better than that.

Spring Game

Spring was at its peak and everyone was back from the beach, sporting tans around campus that affirmed they'd done it – gotten in on the Spring break action at Daytona Beach, Ft. Lauderdale or, everyone's favorite, the Redneck Riviera – Panama City.

No beach trip for Will, he'd sworn off them after being traumatized a couple years ago when he and Bob cruised down to Ft. Lauderdale in Bob's new Mustang. It worked out fine for Bob. The handsome halfback attracted lots of ladies while Will got sunburned, found a few shells and bought a surfer T-shirt. The only women Will attracted were two very talkative, older factory workers from Ohio staying next door in the motel. No, they all can't be "California girls," but Will had hoped for someone other than the 3rd shift bowling champ. Regardless of what you see in the movies, great romances don't always blossom from random rendezvouses on the white sand.

But back on campus, plenty was going on – officially and unofficially. April was a fitting month to celebrate Earth Day and this year, it was sure to be bigger than ever as more and more people were really into protecting the environment. Dr. Eugene Odum's pioneering work had made UGA's Ecology department one of the best in the nation and students jumped on board. Dr. Odum had become a nationally recognized environmental advocate and the man who'd made the term "ecosystem" a household word.

Activism in the burgeoning movement was paying off on a larger scale as well. The Environmental Protection Agency had been established and Congress had recently passed the Clean Air Act and the Clean Water Act.

With a lot of focus on Earth Day, another event was also grabbing attention on campus, and to no surprise, it involved football. Cleaner water may have been springing forth nationally, but for football fans, "hope springs eternal" when they get their first look at next fall's team.

The spring game came – and so did Sonny, standing proudly on the sidelines in Sanford Stadium when the red and black squads faced off to show their stuff. As always, Coach Dooley and his staff had spent the last few months working around the clock preparing for the game and it was show time.

Now let's be clear – there are really only *three* seasons in Athens – football season, recruiting season and the spring game. So today, the crowd was big, the excitement unquenchable and the countdown was on.

They looked good. Studying the lineup, it was certain that wide receiver Gene Washington and tight end Richard Appleby (a Clarke Central grad) would be hauling in long passes. And the dangerous duo of Horace King (another Clarke Central star) and "Glidin" Glynn Harrison guaranteed they'd be lighting up the scoreboard with plenty of runs into the end zone.

Come fall, Erk Russell's tough defense was sure to strike fear into the hearts of many SEC quarterbacks. Erk was a class act – a master motivator and a coach that his players simply loved. Will had enjoyed watching UGA coaches at work during open practices since he was a kid. Seeing Erk in action – the way he drilled and fired up his troops – it was no wonder that his players were ready to go out and wreak havoc. It's hard to know how a coach can extract so much from players. Why they'll push beyond their limits for him. But anyone who knew Erk, realized that it wasn't just his methods that propelled his players to win, but also Erk, the man. The list of stars that he'd developed were a Who's Who of Georgia greats – Bill Stanfield, the Miami Dolphins all-pro, the great Jake Scott (16 interceptions in a season – a

UGA record), "General" George Patton, Jiggy Smaha, the outstanding mauler from Macon, Ben Zambesi... The coach had his stars, but what really made the difference was the way Erk molded his players into a fierce fighting unit.

He was a superb communicator. No mistaking his thoughts on a subject. His "calendars" were priceless with humorous reminders carefully placed alongside the demanding summer workout routines, including instructions such as: "Run three miles, hate Georgia Tech four times."

He asked no more of his players than he himself was willing to give. Undoubtedly, the most lasting impression that players and fans remembered were the times Erk rammed his bald head into a helmeted player to celebrate a great play – leaving his forehead dripping with blood. (He truly left everything on the field as the cliché goes.)

Throughout his long career, his players always learned a lot more than X's and O's and defensive formations. Erk took pups and made them into tenacious Bulldawgs.

Even though Sonny's voice was hoarse from shouting at the top of his lungs, he kept talking. "This is it, Will. It's our year to be number one. What we just saw today, before our very eyes – is a championship team. I'm tellin' ya, Dooley's done it."

"They look good. No doubt about it," Will said.

A couple of other boosters joined Sonny and they discussed promotion ideas and tactics to get more media coverage for the program. And after dissecting every last aspect of the team's performance, the conversation shifted to business.

Sonny pulled the boosters in for a closer huddle. "Guys, I'm gonna let you in on somethin'. You wouldn't believe the returns Jack Marshall's gettin' me. The guy's on fire."

"He's got his own outfit, right?"

"Yeah, Marshall Wealth Management."

"That's it and if he keeps makin' money for us the way he's been doin', we're all gonna be richer than we've ever dreamed. I mean it's amazin'. And think of what it could mean for the program," Sonny said.

The talk of big money got their attention. The two men quickly found Jack who was over buying a couple of Cokes from a concession boy still making post-game rounds.

They waited.

Marshall fumed. "Can't you see how watered down these drinks are? I mean *really*." The flustered server tried to steady the tray of drinks while Marshall yelled and cursed at him." What about some quality? You can't sell junk like that in *this* stadium!"

The poor guy just stood there, speechless. It'd been a huge crowd – a hot day and ice melts.

Marshall shook his head."Geeezzz"...Then he turned to the boosters and immediately changed gears. Passing out business cards, he started in on a hard sell of his investment strategy.

"I mean anybody can give you the same old returns with the same old methods. But I spice it up – its more than basic stock and bond trading. I add some long-short positioning, options, commodities, and a little currency trading. Since we're not bound by the stodgy ways of a big firm, we've got the freedom to make a tremendous amount of money. "

The men listened intently.

"Sure there's a little more risk, but you wouldn't believe the upside. It'll change your life," Marshall said.

Ronnie came up to Will and put out his hand. "It's been a while."

Will reluctantly shook it. *Guess it's time to let it go.* He thought. *The whole thing was Amy's scheme anyway.*

The two chatted, and then Ronnie paused and looked him in the eye, "Will, we've been friends a long time so I want you to be one of the first to know."

"Yeah?"

"I'm thinkin' of poppin' the question. You need to get to know Stephanie. There's nobody like her."

"Congratulations, man."

Will was sort of happy for his friend, a bit envious and mainly surprised. *But just how did Stephanie tame this reckless party animal?*

Streaking

Will hurried to Sue's office. She said it was urgent.

"Ok, Will, we've got to get out there and cover this mass streaking thing. Word is, it's happenin' tonight."

"What?"

"You know. Clemson just raised the stakes on the contest."

"A contest?"

"Haven't you heard? Clemson broke the record when 500 students streaked through campus – big groups of 'em ran in the buff through lecture halls, dining halls, all over. It's getting national coverage and that's about all it takes to rev up somethin' like this."

Will laughed. Now he got it. *This is* something a Bulldawg can really get behind.

The streaking phenomenon had become a huge craze on college campuses and locally most folks had witnessed at least a dash or two. And now the mania had taken on a life of its own. Good ole boy Ray Stevens's song, "The Streak," had climbed up the charts to number one. Someone was even selling a wrist watch that displayed a streaking Richard Nixon.

Here at home, some imaginative UGA coeds climbed on top of the Krystal hamburger store on Baxter and danced around for a while as several guys kept them supplied with burgers and fries. Eventually, police told them they'd been dining a bit too long and sent them on their way.

Later Athens's police used tear gas to disperse a crowd before they completely stripped down to streak. But now with a record at stake, a student government officer appealed to the administration for the OK to unleash the crowd and go for the title. The two sides struck an agreement. Police, on stand-by, would refrain from stopping them as long as the students didn't get *too* out of hand. Both sides accepted the terms – and it apparently had something to do with "turning the other cheek."

On a beautiful evening, spring fever morphed into spring streaking to surpass Clemson's numbers and claim the crown. Of course, in the past, UGA had produced an impressive number of Rhodes scholars, but that sort of achievement takes time and this can be done in a night, weather permitting and if enough clothes come off.

Will set out to cover or *uncover* the story and he'd never seen anything like it. Music blasted out of stereos perched on dorm windows and it looked like the entire student body had packed the quad. Wild-eyed instigators popped up on the steps of Memorial Hall and delivered rally cries to the runners – "Break the Record!"   "Go Dawgs!" The mob roared and was ready to go.

And so it began. The crowd cheered each streaker who zipped past onlookers lining the long path that snaked through the quad to their final destination at the Sanford Bridge.

More and more students came out and cheered them on. Bystanders caught the fever and threw caution (and their clothes) to the wind – running the gauntlet to the finish line and the record book. Some folks ran as couples. One creative young woman (possibly a descendant of Lady Godiva) appeared on horseback and trotted around for a bit accompanied by loud cheers and long looks.

Streakers seemed to be everywhere – one even fell from the sky when he parachuted from a small plane onto the intramural fields. You had to hand it to the guy – he'd taken streaking to new heights and brought it back down again – enduring some serious crosswinds in the process. Stephanie had watched the whole thing from a respectable distance and found the parachuting streaker particularly amusing – until she realized it was her very own Ronnie. And later when the news made it to her hometown, few were laughing. Some said the stunt was daring, even clever – others said it was just plain dumb. But when Will saw his old friend untangling himself from the chute – he had his answer.

Finally, victory was declared. 1,543 proud UGA streakers proved to the world that they would not be out done in this matter and now Georgia triumphantly held the national streaking record. (That was never to be broken.)

Some may ask – why do students do such a thing? Well, there are young students, particularly males, who won't pass up an opportunity to do something spontaneous and stupid if the conditions are right – and this event definitely fit the bill for spontaneous and stupid.

And a generation that embraced disco for a time may not have had the greatest number of brain cells firing properly on that balmy spring night, especially if they'd been fueling up on Ole Milwaukee and Red Ripple before changing into " their uniforms."

"Group think" certainly took over. It wasn't exactly an activist group championing a cause – but just more or less something to keep students from studying.

Will filed his story and, remarkably, no one was hurt or arrested. The victory was definitely a point of pride for the participants, yet certainly not something you'd be seeing in the university's recruiting brochure.

Of course, things can look different in hindsight – or *hinniesight* – as the case may be – and one day these leading citizens may have had some second thoughts about the merits of being part of this "happenin'." But then again; it was springtime – in Athens.

Idlewild South

After running around as a Bulldawg in the buff, John searched through the bushes and found his tie-dyed shirt and bell bottoms, got dressed and left for, what turned out to be, the road trip of a lifetime.

They hurried off in Clinton's van with little time for explanation. Clinton had been away for weeks on tour with the Allman Brothers so they just threw in their gear and hit the road. John was floored when he heard that their destination was Gregg Allman's cabin near Macon. He'd never asked, but hoped that one day he'd at least score some good tickets from his friend's connections, but *this* was beyond anything he'd ever dreamed.

The Georgia grown, Southern rock band loved their secluded spot just outside their hometown. The quiet woods was a refuge for them – a retreat for recharging after living out of a tour bus. Far away from the crowds that packed out their performances, the musicians came home to their cabin, chilled out and ended up creating some amazing music. And now, John tagged along in a state of half disbelief and half awe.

Maybe it was the gentle breeze in the tall pines that shaded Idlewild South or just the break from the grueling tour schedule. But deep in those Georgia woods, the creativity flowed. A bunch of talented musicians – jammin', talking, improvising, rehearsing and partying – and it went on round the clock.

All kinds of folks roamed in and out and John stumbled on one fascinating story after another from various roadies and musicians.

One guy pulled up a chair and described the magic of this hideaway. "It was kinda like a birthplace" where the band connected in a way that forged their own style of music. He described the night around the fire when the guys got a clear vision of their future and pledged their all to the band. A breakout album fittingly titled "Idlewild South" came next. They had come a long way from scraping by and surviving on Mama Jean's generosity. The kindhearted woman had taken the long-haired boys under her wing and kept them fed during their lean times at her "kitchen" on Cotton Avenue.

Others joined in the conversation and got to reminiscing about the biggest outdoor concert since Woodstock, which, of all things, took place in an obscure town in middle Georgia. The famed "Southern Fried Woodstock." It happened a while back one Fourth of July and "it was totally unreal."

"Man, that Independence Day would have blown the minds of the old Founding Fathers. It was us, Hendrix, B.B. King, Grand Funk Railroad – imagine it, three whole days of 'round the clock music, 30 acts all together, and 300,000 fans. I mean no fireworks *anywhere* could top the fireworks those rockers launched that 4th – it was outta sight."

Big time Atlanta rock promoter, Alex Cooley, had put together a phenomenal lineup for the long weekend of non-stop music in the small town of Byron. He'd found the perfect spot at The Middle Georgia Raceway – plenty of open land and right off the interstate. Fans braved bumper to bumper traffic and scorching 100 degree, Sahara-like heat radiating off of I-75 as they crawled along the highway. A three day pass was only $14, but on the first day, thousands who hadn't bothered with tickets stormed the main gate and all of a sudden it became a "free concert."

Folks in Byron lived quietly to themselves. The little hamlet actually had more cows than people, so when hordes of rockers rolled in and invaded their land, it was a shock. The town buzzed with both curiosity and trepidation – most folks concluding that "it's gonna bring all them hippies from all over creation for some kinda rock and roll shindig…and who knows what'll happen then."

The guys telling the story bent over laughing describing locals' reactions to the onslaught. "Why, it has to be the most outlandish thing I've ever seen in my life." Then one fella jabbered on about the town not seeing so many outsiders "since Sherman marched through on his way to Savannah."

Once the swarm of fans piled in and covered every acre of farmland with tents and blankets and sweaty bodies, the Allman Brothers opened the show. The party rocked on day and night. Then on the last night, a helicopter swooped in and delivered Jimi Hendrix to center stage. At the stroke of midnight, July 4, with enough amps to wake the dead, he thrilled the crowd with his electrified version of "The Star Spangled Banner." It went down as one of the most memorable yet controversial versions of our national anthem to date.

Tragically, less than a year after the Byron blowout, Jimi Hendrix died of a drug overdose and Duane Allman was killed in a motorcycle accident near his home in Macon.

John didn't want to sleep any more than he had to. Fascinating for sure – but it also gave him an unfiltered look behind the scenes. He couldn't wait to tell anyone and everyone about the unbelievable weekend.

⇥⇤

Gary looked up and there was John – about as wired as the mellow musician ever got off stage.

"It was something else. We packed out Charlie's VW van. You've seen it around – with that Pink Floyd 'dark side of the moon motif' on one side and the western sunrise with the Eagles's vibe on the other."

Gary laughed. "It stands out, all right."

"Well, when we drove up, some of the guys in the band looked it over and went on about how cool it was. Somethin' about a ying/yang kinda thing."

"Yeah."

"I was sittin' right next to Dickie Betts. He's like a force of nature or something. The way he coaxes that awesome sound outta his red guitar."

Gary just stared at him, eager to hear more.

"Each guy brings their own special thing to the group. It's so cool to watch – they have this like really unbelievable sense of how the music flows. You oughta see them weave in and out of their solos. Man, they're good."

"Awesome."

"And we got into the Macon music scene. Stopped by Mama Jean's Restaurant for lunch – they still love that place, best soul food anywhere – it's near the Capricorn Record's studio.

A little further down Cotton Avenue was Macon's culinary claim to fame, Nu Way Weiner's. The neon sign had been a beacon for food aficionados since 1937 and nobody made a big deal about the misspelling of *wieners*. Started by a Greek immigrant, Hames Mullis, in 1916, his hot dog stand/restaurant was the second oldest in America and "People would go a long way for a Nu Way" as their little jingle said.

"Didn't some other big guys come outta Macon, too?" Gary asked.

"Oh yeah. Little Richard, Otis Redding. A couple of DJ's really believed in their music and got 'em noticed. Hamp Swain at WIIB and "Satellite Papa" Brown kept playin' 'em all the time."

Gary could hardly believe that his own brother had spent that much with the Allman Brothers. *That's about as cool as it get.*

Then John noticed a large mailer with a UGA logo on the bed.

"What's that?"

Gary roused himself out of his star struck stupor. "Oh, yeah, I was goin' to tell you."

He opened the packet and pulled out his acceptance letter into the honor's program along with a nice scholarship package. John was blown away when he looked at the papers. He'd never realized that Gary had one of the highest SAT scores in his class and was graduating near the top.

John slapped him on the back. "That's awesome. Congratulations."

He left feeling very proud of his brother and knew that it was a good start but all the education Gary had in mind would be very expensive. He had no idea where he'd get the money.

Mac settled into a pleasant calm, believing that things were falling into place. He returned from his interview at Northwestern certain he had the job.

The young prof knew how to read these things. The interview had gone well and he'd really connected with the department head. It looked like a perfect match and they were under the gun to fill the position.

Then a surprising call came, Northwestern had chosen another candidate – they were sorry.

What happened? What could have possibly come up in the past few days to change the outcome? As astute as Mac was, he just couldn't figure this one out.

"Any news?" Martin asked.

Mac sat down in his friend's office. "It's a no go. They've hired someone else."

"But you were pretty sure you had it."

"Yes, I was. It's really strange. They all but said it outright. And I'm sure I was the last one interviewed. So I dunno."

Martin was confused too. "It's hard to know. These things can take some strange turns, but it's odd for them to change their minds so abruptly when they're up against a hard deadline."

They both sat thinking, then Martin had an idea. "You know I have a former student up there and I heard he was just promoted to head of the history department. He's been there a long time and knows everybody. Why don't I give him a call?"

"Won't hurt. I'm curious now, as much as anything else," Mac said.

"I was his major professor during his graduate school days and we got to be pretty close. A good man, but near the end of his dissertation, he had a rough go of it when his twins were born prematurely. I had to fight some hard-nosed bureaucrats to get his deadline extended."

How do you top a streaking story? Well, you don't. And that's the answer to a feature writer's dilemma. Or is it? But perhaps besides the sensational, there are always interesting stories out there – colorful, authentic and right under your nose. And Will had a feel for them.

For starters, one of his favorites was his unusual friend in the unusual house on Yonah Street. Even though Will knew most of Conway Prentiss's stories, he visited him again to check some facts before writing it up. But with Conway, who was delightfully prone to embellishment, the *facts* could be an elusive thing.

True to form, Will found the old man rocking on his front porch dressed in his tobacco stained brown corduroy suit that he wore year round (smoking a pipe secured in his toothless mouth by a mound of rubber bands). The two rocked awhile and talked while Conway waved to everyone who passed by. He'd never met a stranger.

A cast of characters resided in Conway's large but run-down turn of the century house that hadn't seen a broom or dust cloth in ages. But this was his idea of *home*. The big-hearted man often loaned money to "near-do-wells" and transient tenants who never paid him back, but he didn't care.

Will watched a menagerie of strange looking folks come and go and he knew that it wasn't from lack of means that

Conway lived in this curious manner but from choice. He was well educated and "from a good family with money" and easily bankrolled his eccentric lifestyle.

But the gentleman did have one loyal companion who was always at his side. His flea-bitten but faithful old hound dog was the only one who seemed to really care for him.

Conway continued talking as he surveyed his front yard full of junk that resembled the set of "Sanford and Son." His favorite stories were from WWI and all variations of a standard theme. They all began the same way. Conway was attending to some menial task when a high ranking officer urgently summoned him. "Prentiss, you ever led a platoon through artillery fire? We got men trapped near the lines and I need you to get 'em outta there." From the mundane to the heroic, that's how it went. Maybe a little wobbly on certain "details," but delightful stories, nonetheless.

Whatever made Conway tick, he exuded a peace of mind and contentment that escaped most people and, after spending time with him, Will always felt better.

On Saturday, Will stopped in to see his parents and grab his camping gear from the shed. It was the time of year to get back to the mountains.

Under the oak tree in the front yard, his mom chatted with Mary Hanes who looked as relaxed as Will had ever seen her. With a broad smile, she announced that she'd be retiring this June. It was a year earlier than planned, but all the pieces had fallen right into place.

The president of the university was stepping down and taking a consulting position with the state's Board of Regents. She'd worked hand in glove with the man for years and was not about to "break in" a new president and unfortunately, her sister needed more care now. But thanks to some investment wizardry by Mr. Marshall, her nest egg had grown substantially and nicely complimented her university pension, setting the stage for comfortable living.

The Andrews were overjoyed for Mary Hanes. No one deserved it more or had worked harder.

"And speaking of Mr. Marshall, we'll be rock climbing together this weekend," Will said.

Will hadn't meant to let *rock climbing* slip out; he'd meant to call it a *camping trip*.

Mrs. Andrews moved to the edge of her seat, but before she could launch into her litany of motherly cautions and warnings, Mary Hanes jumped in. "I'm sure you'll have a great time. Jack's a firecracker at everything he does. I'm just glad he was kind enough to take on a small client like me. I really don't know what I'd done without him."

"Yeah, he's one of a kind, for sure and must be some kinda genius with money," Will said.

Mary Hanes started laughing. "Will, that piece on Conway was delightful. We read it out loud in the office and everyone got a kick out of it."

"Thanks."

"Will, I think you've met about every eccentric in town. But you know – you don't really need to leave campus to find quirky characters. They're everywhere," Mary Hanes said. "I bet you've heard the story on that old ice cream truck you see around."

A couple of resourceful students had bought a 1956 Ford Good Humor truck complete with bells and annoying music jingles and set out to make money and meet women.

They actually attracted a lot of business as they drove the noisy contraption around town merrily hawking their treats.

"I never thought they'd get all the permits they needed, but they did and they're making a go of it," said Mary Hanes. "But, I'll tell you, a lot of things I've seen in the past few years are beyond my wildest imagination."

Mary Hanes had more to say. "Have you ever thought about how much alike some of those *non-conformist* students look? I'd say they end up doing a lot of *conforming* as they mimic the real radicals."

She continued. "But there's one student who certainly marches to the beat of a different drum. You know him, Will."

"Who's that?"

"That 'Jeremiah Johnson' guy who built himself a cabin on the Oconee River."

"Oh yeah, I've met him – Jim DiGennaro, captain of the wrestling team. He does a lot of canoeing and one day he spotted an old run-down cabin he thought would be a fun place to live. He tracked down the owner who agreed to let him fix it up and live in it," Will explained.

"My word," said Mrs. Andrews.

"You wouldn't believe all the work they put into it. You have to respect their ingenuity. He and his roommate sawed down 20 trees and fitted the rough logs together to refurbish it. Then, they invited the whole wrestling team down for the fun part and had a blast making a mud pit and slinging gobs of ooze at the cabin to make it waterproof," Will said.

"That *is* impressive."

Mary Hanes patted her friend on the knee. "And Jim and his dog moved in and's as happy as can be even with no running water or electricity. He cooks on a wood stove and dines in the most serene setting anywhere."

"And guess how he gets to campus?" Will added, "in his canoe."

"Will, I can guarantee that you'll never run out of people to write about in this town," Mary Hanes concluded.

She looked at Mrs. Andrews. "Almira, have you seen the old Episcopal church downtown lately? You won't believe what they've done to it."

Mrs. Andrews gasped. "Martin told me all about it, but I can't bring myself to go by and see such desecration."

The old church had been transformed into makeshift apartments and was now the site of bohemian student living at its best. It was a happening place but not in a way that any bishop might sanction.

Will chimed in. "Now, Mom, it's just a building. Things change. You gotta admit, it's certainly creative and probably not sacrilegious."

"Will! How can you say such a thing? I'm just glad that Edna and Mrs. Cullison aren't hearing this. After all their efforts they put into your youth group. You'd think you'd know better."

And the good ladies at the church had indeed been longsuffering in corralling youngsters onto the right path. As a little kid, Will had many a blissful Sunday morning snooze on those gold velvet cushions that covered the pews. The service went on around him at a steady hum, no passionate admonitions from the pulpit to disturb his slumber. By this time, the influence of seminaries and university religion departments had a major effect on mainline denominations and many settled into a more ala carte approach

– take what you like and don't upset people. Such uncon-
ventional beliefs as the "God is Dead" theory out of Emory
University (which made the cover of Time magazine near
Easter, 1966) had caused quite a stir.

When the guys reached their teens, they migrated to
the balcony, as far away as possible from the watchful eye
of the minister. They sat as a unit, more like gang members
than worshipers. Alarms really went off one "youth" Sunday
when Will and his buddies were tasked with collecting the
offering and marched reverently down the center aisle with
apparently *empty* collection plates. The guys, in truth, had
collected the morning offering, but met in the lobby and
quickly hid it all under the maroon velvet pad lining the
ornate silver plates. Mr. Wilson, one of the venerable but
humorless pillars of the church, received the apparently
empty plates red-face and uttering a four letter word under
his breath – and it wasn't *love*. The matter was adjudicated
but Mr. Wilson still kept a wary eye on the prodigals.

After all, many of these teens had been raised by parents who'd read Dr. Benjamin Spock and implemented his
permissive principles to child rearing. The book had been a
landmark bestseller and Dr. Spock's viewpoint found its way
to institutions. Many churches adopted a *"keep 'em fed and
entertained…and maybe they'll stay out of trouble"* philosophy for
"reaching the youth." Often well-intended, there were times
it looked more like "the inmates were running the asylum."

But the times made for a great youth room. In the spirit
of the flower children, it was fixed up like a faux hippie
coffee house and decorated with psychedelic posters, black
lights and weird stuff hanging here and there – plus the
timeless pool table.

If you stopped and thought about it, their playbook on discipleship was more of a product of the culture and not so much the way Matthew, Mark, Luke or John had laid it out.

"You university and Athens people are Chihuahuas for God and Bulldawgs for sin!"

street preacher on UGA campus

≈+≈

Mac found Martin working at his desk.

"Heard anything?"

"Yes, and close the door. I hate to tell you this," Martin said grimly.

"What?"

"It's Peter. He threw you under the bus, Mac."

"What?"

"He told Northwestern that he couldn't 'in good conscience' recommend you. Some nonsense about you being a loose cannon with a hot temper."

Mac fumed, "Are you kiddin' me! How could he just flat out lie like that?"

Martin stood up and moved near his friend. "We both know he can't be trusted. But I can't believe he'd stoop this low either."

"Martin, this is downright wrong – almost criminal. And he knows about my dad. How can anybody be that petty?"

"Apparently *he* can. Mac, you'd better take some time to cool off before you say or do anything."

"He lied to my face. That jerk looked me right in the eye and said he was behind me all the way. And what did it matter to him if I got the job there? I'd be gone and out of his life."

"There's no explaining it. It's diabolical."

"What about ethical standards? The university upholds those, right? I'll bring him up on violations."

"Sure, but proving something like this is difficult. I've seen it before. It's usually just one long, drawn out mess and, in the end, nothing's accomplished. And you don't have the time. All you need to be thinking about now is your family. You can't change a man like Peter Hall."

BETWEEN A ROCK AND A
HARD PLACE

S tanding precariously on the edge of the rock Will yelled
"Belay on?"

"Belay on!" Marshall called back.

With the go ahead signal that Marshall had checked and
secured the rappelling rope, Will slowly let some slack out
of the rope until his legs were at a 90 degree angle with the
ledge. Then he pushed off the hard surface with both feet,
let out more rope with his brake hand behind his back and
hopped five to 10 feet at a time down the cliff. After a few
more hops, he steadied himself and took in the spectacular
view all around him.

Marshall had made good on a weekend of rock climbing
and rappelling and knew just the place – the mountains of
Pisgah National Forest, NC.

They'd gotten off to a late start the day before. On Friday afternoon, Tom and Will had waited outside Marshall's office, packed and ready to go. The plan was to leave right after lunch and arrive in time to leisurely set up camp before dark.

As they waited, voices behind the door became louder. Finally a man stormed out. Marshall appeared soon after, snatched up last minute items and threw them in the car with the rest of the gear and luggage. He didn't say much – just barked out a few clipped instructions and slammed the trunk.

Out on the highway, Marshall talked incessantly about his demanding clients and their unrealistic expectations and the more he complained, the faster he drove.

"Whatta they expect? Miracles? This is one tough market and they all think they're gonna get rich overnight."

Tom eventually interrupted. "Dad, slow it down some. We've got plenty of time."

Marshall snapped back. "You came for an adventure, didn't ya? Surely you guys can take a little speed."

Will steadied himself enough on the outcropping to look up and see Tom way above him making cat-like moves rappelling down the craggy cliff toward the ledge that Will stood on. Tom glided over the contours of the rock face knowing better than to try to out muscle it. Will remembered Tom's words from the night before. "You gotta work with the features you're given, don't try to attack the cliff – flow with it."

Finally, Mr. Marshall carefully leaned back, hopped off the ledge and gradually made it down the daunting surface.

Their legs twitched uncontrollably as they paused on a narrow outcropping. It felt good to take in a few deep breathes and relax tense muscles, but they didn't dare let their guard down.

The precarious perch provided a stunning panoramic view of three states – Georgia, Tennessee and North Carolina. They savored the invigorating mountain air and drank in the expansive scenery as slivers of misty clouds rolled by.

Will tried not to look down or think about why the Cherokee Indians had named this huge granite overhang Devil's Courthouse.

Yesterday they'd practiced climbing and rappelling techniques on small surfaces and saved the biggest challenge for last.

Marshall was in a totally different mood today – almost giddy. Yet even he was careful to check his emotions as he methodically navigated his way down. He knew if anything required full concentration, it was hanging on the side of a sheer rock face. Will watched him closely, relieved that Marshall respected the danger involved.

"Man! Can you believe it? Look up there – that was quite a feat, guys – coming down that thing!" Marshall yelled out.

They all shared the same feeling of conquest. After a lunch of tuna sandwiches and trail mix, they got a second wind and decided to tackle one more cliff.

The three put every other thought aside as they meticulously inspected their equipment, looking for any knots or signs of fraying in the rope. Tom checked and double checked everything – he was exactly the kind of guy you'd want around when your life was hanging by one third of an inch of spun nylon.

After 45 minutes of rigorous effort, they arrived safely back at the landing area near the trail that took them back to Marshall's Jeep right off the Blue Ridge Parkway.

Spent but elated, they cleaned up in a nearby creek, relaxed around the fire and talked non-stop as they basked in their camaraderie.

Marshall leaned back in his camp chair and sipped hot coffee. "You know what? Dangling off the mountain was almost the same rush as driving that supercharged 442 around the Daytona 500 track. I never thought anything would ever match that.

Will, my man, you're a good one to tackle a mountain with. I'll take you on my team anytime."

Will smiled. "Looks like I can trust you with my life too."

"That's exactly what we did today, gentlemen, so Will, you can drop the Mr. Marshall. It's Jack. And remember, guys – a real friend always has your back – like we did out on that cliff today."

It was late but before calling it a night, Mr. Marshall talked a little more.

"Here's an important take-away from today. Don't let anyone tell you that something can't be done.

"You gotta believe in yourself. A lot of people tried to talk me out of starting my own firm. Man, am I glad I didn't listen to those cowards. It always pays to be bold."

Will and Tom sat by the glowing embers for another couple of hours recounting the day's exploits.

"I sure hope Dad can sleep. He stays so wound up. At home, it takes a couple of stiff drinks and listening to Schubert for him to even close his eyes."

"He doesn't strike me as a Schubert kinda guy."

"Oh, yeah, he loves classical music. The more melancholy the better. It's the only time he slows down."

Will got to know Tom better on this trip and gained a new respect for him, but he still didn't understand how the father and son could be so different. With a dad like Marshall, Tom could get about anything he wanted, but he just wasn't into extravagant living and not really the hang loose hippie type either. He was just Tom – a solid guy with a sense of purpose.

Mac was furious and kept thinking about all the things he wanted to say to Peter. But in the end, he had enough restraint to realize he'd better cool down and think through his response. And he'd been around enough to know that he wasn't dealing with a reasonable person.

After a few days, he decided that nothing would be gained by confronting someone as petty as Peter Hall. And he didn't have time. His family needed him.

Mac kept looking around and finally found a position at a small college near home. It was one of those catch-all type jobs that small schools are forced to invent – a hodgepodge of advising students, overseeing a small student newspaper and doing grant writing. Mac, who was more than qualified, was quickly offered the position. He accepted it without hesitation knowing he could easily pick up his career again – after the inevitable.

Ed was biding his time. With D.C. constantly on his mind, he counted the days until he'd be right in the seat of government, which, for a policy wonk like Ed, would be "hog heaven." Then right here in Athens an extraordinary opportunity presented itself.

Like any university, UGA courted noted Georgians who'd retired from significant posts and offered them teaching positions – and they'd gotten a real gem in Dean Rusk, the former Secretary of State, and he was speaking today.

For eight years Rusk had served two presidents and now, in his golden years, the Georgia native maintained an office on campus for writing and teaching select classes in international law.

Rusk delved into the complexities of the Vietnam conflict, lessons learned from the Bay of Pigs and, of course, the Cuban Missile crisis. As the nation held its breath, the two super powers, armed to the teeth with nuclear weapons, countered each other's chess moves in a showdown that lasted 14 anxious days.

"Kennedy's mission was clear – to find the safest and surest way to prevent the Soviet Union from installing nuclear missiles on Cuban soil, only 90 miles from Key West, Fla."

At one point, Rusk had to explain to his wife why so many security personnel were camping out in *their* basement. The answer: preparing for a worst case scenario – if the nation's capitol was shut down, the government still had to function and maintain communications – even from neighborhood basements. And in the event of an actual strike on D.C., doomsday plans were in place to evacuate top government officials to stocked bunkers in deep recesses of the nearby West Virginia mountains.

After deftly dodging Armageddon, the press latched onto Rusk's summation of the crisis, "we've been eyeball to eyeball and the other fellow just blinked."

Rusk was born in rural Cherokee County, but had lived most of his childhood years in the family home on Whitehall Street in West End, a suburb of Atlanta. The Rhodes Scholar later served in WWII as a distinguished colonel in the Burma-China-India theater.

The secretary was frequently asked to speak about the tremendous weight he bore during the missile crisis and often referred to a pivotal moment when he was riding through the streets of D.C., back to the White House for the latest briefing. Rusk told of strengthening his resolve by recalling the first sentence of The Westminster Catechism that he'd memorized as a young boy in Sunday School:

"What is the chief end of man?"

"Man's chief end is to glorify God and enjoy Him forever."

Ed was thrilled to learn from the man who'd worked right beside the president during such perilous times. The fascinating presentation was inspiring, but then things quickly went downhill when the Q&A began.

Anyone who'd spent *any* time at a university knew the script all too well. Before thoughtful questioners spoke, up jumped the "usual suspects." First up was "Mr. Nit Pick," the cantankerous, nerdy sort, who never seems to see the forest for the trees. "Great talk, Mr. Secretary, but I believe the Soviet warship, the Sverdlous's 5.9 inch main gun batteries were outmatched by our 8 inch gun cruiser. Was that a factor?"

Dean Rusk looked incredulously at the young man. "Son, the main thing is, after intricate military maneuvering and extensive negotiations...disaster was averted."

Then he quickly called on another student with his hand raised, only to find "Mr. Nit Pick's" cousin, "The Young Arrogant Know It All." He's the one who poses a question not to get an answer, but mainly to impress others with his knowledge.

"Mr. Secretary, I'm an honor grad student in political science and have spent considerable time researching the options for resolving the crisis – for my Master's thesis. Now the air strike option..."

"President Kennedy weighed all options and his final directive was to implement the blockade. It worked," said Rusk.

"Next."

Then "The Sharer" jumped to his feet. "Your talk reminds me of that book...I read it... 'The Guns of August'... and I can see how it really influenced the president's thinking. I mean, he said so himself...that's pretty cool... especially the part about..."

By that time, Ed was fighting off a wave of nausea when "Mr. Inconsiderate" popped up. True to form, his question *only* pertained to himself but took up the time of the other 299 people in the audience. "Can you tell me why no one in the State Department has replied to my application for assistant to the Under Secretary of the Oversight Committee for economic development of the indigenous peoples of Patagonia?"

But hold on... there's one more. "The Bonafide Kook" – who's a least good for some comic relief. You know it's coming when she nervously whispers into the mic, "Mr. Rusk, thank you for your brilliant part in protecting our nation. But I must tell you about another looming danger that *really* worries me and threatens the survival of Western Civilization. During a dramatic pause, the young lady carefully scans the room for people "who may be watching."

"Most people aren't aware that *all of us* are getting massive doses of ultrasonic waves from low-flying communist satellites. There's hundreds of 'em up there and they're already compromising our immune systems and when you combine that with how fluoridated water is destroying our cell structure, it's no wonder we're on the verge of The Apocalypse. It's just a matter of time, *UNLESS we* act now! "

So what do you do about people who turn a valuable educational experience into an exasperating marathon of absurdities?

Now – that's a GOOD question.

Tanyard Creek

"Come on – before somebody sees us!" Will motioned the guys forward towards the tunnel.

It was a fitting way to mark the end of their junior year and something they'd planned for a long time. Everyone had hoped that Ronnie would make it, but they couldn't wait any longer – Ed was leaving soon and tonight the bright full moon was perfect for their quest.

For years the guys had heard about the inviting concrete culvert that ran beneath the football field. Sanford Stadium was built by convict labor in 1929 right on top of Tanyard

Creek which runs the length of the field. It's rather strange, but that's the way it was designed. The guys were pretty sure if they ventured through the tunnel, they'd have the stadium all to themselves. It'd been done, so they'd heard.

Outside the stadium, a heavy growth of weeds and kudzu covered the ravine. The English have their ivy, Napa Valley has their premier grape vines but here in the South we have kudzu – and lots of it. UGA has a tangential claim to be an Ivy League school because of its roots winding back to Yale. But there's no need to press the point. With the peculiar vine creeping all around, Georgia easily outshined the Ivy League moniker with its own prestigious distinction as a "Kudzu League College." The fast traveling, fertile plant practically grew right before your eyes – and in no time completely covered parked cars, people lounging on park benches and slower moving senior citizens.

But UGA came up with its own an eco-friendly solution by employing a rapid response unit of small goats to "nip it in the bud." The Chew Chew Crew snacked their way across campus to their favorite dining destination on the lush banks of Tanyard Creek. And it was a perfectly reciprocal arrangement – they grazed all day, never showed up late or hungover and did a great job *eating their greens* and kept the kudzu in check along the creek's steep banks and ditches.

Ed scanned the periphery. "Keep moving. Remember cops patrol the lot every couple of hours." Armed with flashlights, they proceeded down the ravine.

When they started through the tunnel, John cautioned the guys to "watch their step" about the same time he slid on a rock and fell into the cool water.

"Ouch!"

"What'd ya do now?" Will asked.

They waited for John who did an awkward little dance trying to maintain his footing only to slip again and bump his head. "These rocks are impossible."

"C'mon, man, watch where you're goin'. This isn't a Three Stooges act and we've only got about 30 more yards to go," Will advised.

John moved cautiously, making sure to be last. "Whatdaya think lives down here?"

Will laughed. "Oh nothin' much. The usual critters we always see near the creeks – moccasins, rats, salamanders."

"But it's – like – *real* dark, and creepy. I heard when people get tired of those Boas and baby gators, they bring 'em here and let 'em loose."

"No way, dude. Older guys used to tell us that stuff just to scare us," Ed said.

"Yeah, and grown-ups let us believe it to keep us outta here. Along with stories about crazy hobos hidin' out," Will added.

Ed stopped. "That's all legend stuff. Your imagination's outta control."

Will chimed in. "I mean use your head, dude. The only thing that can live here in the dark is that albino blob sort of thing that hangs on the wall and jumps you outta nowhere."

"Yeah, heard about that, too. I'm gettin' outta here!" John turned on his heels – ready to bolt.

Will doubled over, laughing – leaving Ed to get the mission back on track. "OK you two knock it off. John, get it together, man. We're close now."

Will may have been laughing, but that didn't mean he liked being down in this tight, dank place either. The eerie silence was occasionally broken by their voices echoing off the concrete tube and the tinkling sound of water dripping. Will didn't worry about fanciful creatures lurking around but he *was* worried about the flashlight. *How old were those batteries anyway?* A little late to be asking that question.

But the batteries held out and, in a few minutes, they finally arrived at a drainage outlet inside the revered Sanford Stadium. They popped up like gophers and sprinted over the manicured turf, straight to the 50 yard line.

"Man, this is awesome!"

They looked around at the dew glistening on the grass.

"This is totally worth it," Will said.

They paused a minute and soaked in the view of the immense stadium, bathed in moonlight. The exhilaration of having the UGA field all to themselves overtook them and they frolicked like schoolboys at recess.

Ed yelled. "Go long, Will!"

Will cut and weaved like he once did on the old sandlot field, turning around at the 35 with John close on his heels for the stop. Ed threw the air pass. More runs, more pass routes, then they all fell down on the turf, laughing and reliving their glory days. It was fun of the purist sort.

They caught their breath and talked about the great games they'd seen here – something Athens's folk never tired of.

"I was just a kid, but can still remember seeing that famous flea flicker play to beat Bama in the last few seconds. Unbelievable," Ed said.

Will laughed. "And remember Coach Dooley running down the sidelines, trying to keep up with Kent Lawrence or Buzzy Rosenberg running in for a touchdown?"

Will suddenly got serious and spoke in a ceremonial tone. "Ed, I believe it's time."

Ed pulled out three fat Cubans to commemorate the special night as they contemplated heading into their senior year and realized that their college days were about to end – the end of the yellow brick road.

They puffed on the cigars and talked more about the old days – and the future.

"Yeah, pretty soon, we'll have to be all respectable and responsible," said John, "wear suits and all that. No more stunts like this."

"We don't want tonight to be *too* memorable. Better get outta here before we're arrested," Ed warned.

They jumped to their feet and took one last lingering look.

"What ya doing, John?"

"Leavin' my cigar on the field – a little something for Coach Russell."

The guys left. The wind blew a small puff of smoke from the upright cigar planted like a flag dead center on the 50 yard line.

As much as Will didn't like to borrow things, he kept thinking about that Swiss camping stove. Jack made sure he had the latest and the best equipment and that sleek little device would sure come in handy on the trail. It weighed only two pounds and when it came to loading up a backpack, only a couple of things mattered: what do you *really need* to survive and how much weight are you were willing to carry. The back and forth deliberation made a hiker downright per-snickety about his choices.

But Jack had convinced Will to take the stove along and it was ready for pickup. As he walked into his friend's office, there was Mary Hanes, about the last person he'd expect to see there. "Hey, Will, Jack was kind enough to give me a few minutes on my lunch hour."

"You mean you get lunch? I thought ya'll just ran on fumes."

Mary Hanes laughed. "Well, true and usually it's a working lunch – that's what the boss likes to call it. But occasionally we break and go out like normal people."

Jack heard the chit-chat and ushered Will over to his desk to check out the stove.

"Have a seat, Will. It's been awhile. What ya been up to?"

"Not much."

"So you know Mary Hanes?

"Yeah, we've been neighbors for most of my life. She's one sharp lady. Isn't she?"

"The best," Jack lowered his voice, "I sure could use a go-getter like her around here. We'd rock the world."

"Bet so. But I only pictured your clients as cigar-smoking rich guys," Will said.

Jack laughed. "Yeah, there's a few of them, but in a place the size of Athens, you have to throw the net out wide. And I like to help the average hard-working person – makes you feel good. Besides just dealing with wealthy people will drive you crazy. They're a demanding bunch."

"So I guess you're following this Watergate thing?" Marshal asked.

"Yeah, we talk about it all the time in class."

"And what's your take?"

"It's a sad state of affairs. To think the people with the most power are that corrupt," Will said.

Jack's expression completely changed and, for a moment, he looked like any other middle-aged man staring vacantly from behind a desk.

He spoke softly – his words tinged with sadness. "Everyone has their price. I've known two, maybe three honorable men in my life. Guys who'd do the right thing at any cost. But that's about it."

Jack's pensive look told Will that the hard-charging man had let his guard down, but only for a few minutes, then he snapped back to his usual bravado.

Will quickly skirted past the awkward moment. "There's a lot of talk about the economy in the news, too. What do you think?"

"There's good chance we're slipping into a recession. Behind all the talk, real numbers are pointing in that direction," Jack said.

"Sounds like we could all be in for some tough times."

"Yeah. I even thought about cutting back a little myself. Maybe sellin' the Jag. But that's a loser mentality. Know what I did instead?

I went out and bought myself a vintage Austin Healy. You can't just cower in a corner. You've gotta be bold, look fate right in the eye and spit in her face."

Will said nothing.

Jack looked back at the papers on his desk. "And no hurry on the stove – I'm not goin' anywhere."

"Can't Hurry Love"

Will took off to the mountains for the weekend with two of his best camping budies, but before lacing up their hiking boots they indulged in one last bountiful meal at "The Hungry Owl." The establishment was about as far away from the five star dining list as cornbread is to caviar and unless you had a strong endorsement from a trusted friend you'd never set foot in the rustic, rundown joint with its rickety screen door and torn vinyl booths. But fellow hikers and locals (who were certifiable sober) all gave the place rave reviews.

To say it was a hole in the wall is an insult to *holes in the walls*. First, you had to look hard to even find the shack – tucked away on a side road and perched on a gully-riddled piece of mountain land. But the food was fantastic – the best fried chicken anywhere, just picked green beans, creamed corn, home-grown tomatoes and biscuits smothered in local honey. The business was a family affair with everyone pitching in. For the finishing touch, the grandmother brought in her luscious blueberry cobbler straight from her kitchen where she'd spent a lifetime perfecting the recipe.

It was invigorating to breathe the mountain air again. Days walking through the forest and nights at camp got Will thinking about life and the future – and *still*, something very important was missing. His college years were passing, relationships hadn't panned out – and he really wanted to find *her – the girl, his girl*.

He didn't know exactly what to do. You'd think it would be easier. Why couldn't women have a special mood ring that flashed a clear response to your charming overtures? Maybe if he dusted off the Magic Eight Ball it could answer a few romance questions. You shake the black orb and watch a cryptic answer emerge from the murky blue dye. He'd really like to see: "Outlook Good," "You May Rely on it," but he seemed perpetually stuck in: "Reply Hazy, Try Again." And he definitely didn't want the "Don't Count on it" to pop up.

The whole *guy/girl* thing was mind-boggling anyway. Females possessed an amazing maternal instinct but they also had a very unpredictable *infernal* instinct which made them subject to volcanic-like eruptions even when they appeared in their most angelic state. To be honest, these unpredictable actions and outbursts were usually triggered by an insensitive act of stupidity by a male. And guys, well aware of their predisposition to stupidity, were often at risk of stepping on emotional landmines.

You'd think that a huge blockbuster on the big screen, "Love Story," would shed light on this mystery. Hollywood cast the gorgeous Ali McGraw and Ryan O'Neil as two star-crossed lovers presenting the notion that "love means never having to say you're sorry." The very sentimental, tragic romance may have softened the prematurely cynical, but guys *knew* that if you wanted to get anywhere in a relationship, you'd better spend a good bit of time "saying you were sorry," even if you didn't exactly understand why.

Painful memories of past heartbreaks just added to the misery index and served as yet another confidence killer. Male or female, the first heartbreak hits you like the iron anvil falling on the Roadrunner. You're devastated. Crushed. Maybe that's why it's called "having a crush." During those early years, you can't imagine ever getting over it. *How can I go on?*

Piling on more angst during the teen years was the maturity gap, although the *maturity* part of it didn't bother guys much. They seemed blissfully unaware that the functioning part of their brain was about the size of an English pea until they were 25. But it did explain their inane aura of invincibility and magnetic compulsion to perform crazy stunts. Adding insult to injury, young women were so poised, full of charm and social graces and at the height of their flowering beauty at the very same time that most guys were painfully awkward, socially inept and clueless. And now in college, males acknowledged the fact that female students were often the high achievers. It was humbling to know that Greek women consistently had one of the highest GPA's on campus.

For Will, love songs on the radio kept hope alive. In his younger days, he'd spent late nights listening to the syrupy ballads on WQXI, "Quixie in Dixie," on his red transistor radio hidden under his pillow after "lights out." It kept him believing that his girl was out there somewhere although those songs can skew your understanding of romance.

But he always knew that things would look up when fall arrived. Like the swallows returning to Capistrano every year, hundreds of lovely ladies descended upon Athens for Rush. Even though most were way out of your league, every guy – Greek, freak, or geek – relished the annual beautification of Athens.

When the ladies strolled by, it hit you like a one, two, three Mohammad Ali lightening combination. And they knew *exactly* what they were doing. First, you were dazzled by their beauty, then overwhelmed by a coy smile or that flirtatious flip of the hair. The final blow was being left in a cloud of perfume as they walked away – overwhelmed and defenseless.

With "sorority row" only blocks from the high school, Will and the guys got quite a schooling in the allure of the opposite sex.

But it was eye-opening to see the flip side of the equation. A few of the girls were not as they appeared. You'd witness them hug and gush over "a friend" one minute, then systematically rip her apart after she'd walked away. Chilling. *Imagine what they'd do to a hapless male?*

In the end, it was the cool guys and athletes who ended up with the ladies –understandable and thus it has always been. Even back in ancient Athens, the great warriors like Achilles, Hector and Hercules won the ladies while the rest of the bunch did the best they could.

But figuring it all out was complicated, especially when the music fueled raw emotions, and despite some good effort, everything you'd been taught about the ideals and wonders of true love faded fast. The timeless Southern virtues of chivalry and enduring love were nowhere to be found in the infectious tunes of Elvis and Mick Jagger when that thundering, intoxicating beat got a hold of you. And that's exactly what lured Will and his high school friends out of their bedroom windows on many a fall or spring night – to answer the call of the music from Milledge.

A cool breeze floated through the screen and held you in its spell. Then in the distance you heard it – soulful melodies, soaring harmonies – and then the horns came in – Memphis horns!

You had to get out the window and in on the action. The pulsating beat drove you to the frat house lawns – running to "Naa, Na, Na, Na, Naa" of "The Land of a Thousand Dances" along with a couple of rounds of "Hey Baby" – until you finally made it to the bandstand and rendezvoused with your friends cause it was "another Saturday night" and "if you ain't got nobody," maybe you'd find somebody.

Music lit up your teenage soul. The infectious rhythm got your motor running and, for the moment, it sure felt like the very essence of life. For the girls, it was just the spark to ignite their spontaneity and they'd dance – like nobody's business. The utter joy of it all unchained them from their worries. And *POOF!* Troubles faded as they became one with the music.

Everywhere you turned, the mores of the Bible Belt clashed with the party scene. One day you're dreaming of settling down with a sweet girl like Mary Ann from Gilligan's Island. Next minute, the smoldering Ginger sure looked good. So what'll it be? "Devil with a Blue Dress" or "Venus in Blue Jeans"?

MASTER STORYTELLERS

By now, Will had covered several well-known speakers. Some had something to say, some didn't. But the Student Union had saved the best for last – tonight was Truman Capote and next month was Tom Wolfe.

Sitting in an elaborate, white Rattan chair bathed in a pink spotlight, Truman Capote, held hundreds of students in the palm of his hand as he read one of his famous short stories.

Who'd have thought that blasé "supercool" college students would sit like kindergarten children during story time listening to an eccentric little man as he read "A Christmas Memory" out on the quad on a warm April night – for almost an *hour!* Dressed in a black suit and Fedora, he looked more like "The Godfather" than America's most famous novelist.

But the transfixed students hung on Capote's every word as he told the touching story of a lonely six-year-old boy and his enduring friendship with his eccentric aunt. The story was based on his own childhood in rural Alabama.

Buddy lovingly describes the wonderful times he had visiting his quirky Aunt Sook who had no choice but to live with straight-laced relatives who had little use for her child-like imagination.

All year long, the two saved their pennies to make special fruitcakes flavored with generous portions of whiskey – which they frequently sampled. Then they'd give them as Christmas gifts to all sorts of unusual people they'd befriended.

And each year it was the same. They'd make new kites for each other and fly them together on Christmas morning. Aunt Sook gleefully described the kites as "two souls blissfully frolicking in heaven."

Away at boarding school, Buddy and his aunt send a steady stream of letters to each other, but the story takes a sad turn when Aunt Sook dies and Buddy realizes that it was their last Christmas together.

You could've heard the proverbial pin drop as Capote slowly described a heartbroken Buddy pondering his friend's' death:

"And when that happens, I know it. A message saying so merely confirms a piece of news some secret vein had already received, severing me from an irreplaceable part of myself, letting it loose like a kite on a broken string. That is why, walking across a school campus on this particular December morning, I keep searching the sky. As if I expected to see, rather like hearts, a lost pair of kites hurrying towards heaven."

After thunderous applause, Capote answered a few questions from the audience. Most of the queries were about his popular bestseller, "In Cold Blood," which recounts the grisly murder of a Kansas farm family by two deranged men in the mid '50s.

"I wrote 'In Cold Blood' as a literary experiment. I was trying to synthesize my skills as a novelist and a journalist. I spent over six years doing research. Much of the time was taken up with interviews and conversations with the murderers."

He said he tries to write "four or five hours a day, but I mess around about two or three hours wasting time. I am one of the world's great pencil sharpeners."

Then he talked about traveling with the Rolling Stones on their U.S. concert tour in 1972. "It was interesting, but after you've heard 19 Rolling Stones concerts it does something to your ears."

What's gonna happen when these masterful storytellers like Capote and Lewis Grizzard, and Dean Tate and countless unsung old men and women telling tales on porches and courthouse squares are gone? Who will take their place?

Ed and Will were big fans of the insightful, provocative author, Tom Wolfe, whose unique approach to journalism and edgy ideas made great fodder for journalism classes.

New Journalism was a hot topic. Writers like Wolfe wrote from a first-hand experience point of view, often embedding themselves in the group or situation they sought to portray. They worked from an extremely subjective perspective and employed various literary techniques more commonly found in fiction. Seeking the essence of "truth" in an article was more important to them than merely presenting cold "facts" and by immersing themselves in the story they believed they'd find "The Truth."

Wolfe's book "The Electric Kool-Aid Acid Test" gave readers a close up look at the current drug culture. Written as a personal account of the "Merry Pranksters" and their protracted, communal acid trip, he chronicled their cross country journey in their painted-up psychedelic school bus. Wolfe intimately depicted their use of LSD and other drugs in a search for the *ultimate* mind-blowing experience.

Then in "Radical Chic," he pulled back the curtains on New York's cultural elite and exposed their pretensions. Beneath all the glitz, glamour and moral posturing, a number of them adopted radical causes mainly because it was the fashionable thing to do.

Added to these successes, was Hunter Thompson's bizarre stream-of-consciousness, drugged- filled account of American politics "In Fear and Loathing in Las Vegas."

Wolfe then compiled a collection of articles in a recently released book fittingly titled, "The New Journalism,"which included works by himself, Thompson, Joan Didion, Gay Talese, Truman Capote, Norman Mailer and others.

Journalists debated the dramatic tilt towards such subjective reporting. Critics claimed that these writers acted more like psychoanalysts and they threw aside objective standards. But despite the controversy, all of the books were bestsellers.

Will read through the program several times and found a quote that summed up Wolfe's impact:

"Wolfe possesses an invaluable asset: he can spot a phony or pretentious trend before most of his colleagues, and have the courage (or effrontery) to say out loud what others are unwilling to say at all."

Reviews

Finally, the author walked to the lectern to loud applause in his trademark three piece white suit. The audience rolled with his erudite critique of social issues laced with his acerbic wit. He called this uncanny knack for discovering underlying trends a "social X- ray." Wolfe had coined numerous terms and turns of phrases but his description of the current crop of young people as the "Me Generation" had gained the greatest traction with the media and intellectuals.

Afterwards, students had a lot to discuss. The guys talked awhile with Ed's friends from his sociology class and that's when it happened. Will "saw her standing there" – a brown-eyed beauty with a warm smile and long, lovely hair cascading over her petite shoulders. But it was more than just her looks – there was something special about her – he'd been watching her and she really seemed genuine and kind. Will knew he had to say something no matter how inane or awkward – he couldn't let her get away so he made his move. And the more they talked, the more Will's attraction grew. Finally he blurted out, "You hungry? How 'bout goin' to the Varsity for a bite to eat."

Ginny looked bemused and laughed but was apparently intrigued enough with this fellow to say "Yes."

Ed took a couple of steps in their direction but Will quickly waved him off, "See ya later." And the two turned and walked away.

Chili dawgs and frosted orange drinks don't usually produce life-changing conversation, but time flew by as they spent hours talking and laughing and getting to know each other. Will never imagined that going to a speech on New Journalism would be an avenue for a new romance. He asked her out for Friday night. She smiled and accepted. Will was ecstatic.

Over the next weeks, thoughts of Ginny filled all of Will's waking hours as deadlines and headlines took a backseat. He could barely think about anything else.

Van Morrison sang about the "Brown-eyed Girl"... and Will had found his own brown-eyed girl – one that he absolutely adored.

One Last Sweet Tea

Dr. Mac sealed the last box as a torrent of mixed emotions flooded his mind. Looking around his apartment at everything disassembled and packed up, he fought back tears. Part of him didn't want to leave Athens and so many good friends – and, in a few minutes, he was about to say one of the hardest goodbyes of all.

As much as he wanted one more lunch at the Dogwood Manor, Mac wondered if he could hold it together. A grown man, a professional man crying in Miss Crumwell's establishment just wouldn't be right.

But he took the risk and the tears came – but it was Miss Crumwell who sobbed inconsolably as she gave Mac one last embarrassing hug. Finally, she composed herself long enough to serve the men their sweet tea. Mac savored every sip knowing for sure he'd find none of that in Chicago – about as likely as finding a Moon Pie on the Magnificent Mile.

Athens felt like home. As many times as he'd heard, "Ya ain't from 'round here, r ya?" he nonetheless had been embraced by some of the warmest people he'd ever known. He looked over the crowd wistfully. *It just doesn't get any better than this – a lively college community thriving in a delightful Southern town* and he'd miss the students – scores of students he'd taught and mentored.

Martin was his closest friend and had become almost like a father to him. And it went both ways. The young idealist had come into Martin's life and rekindled his love of teaching during his last lap before retirement.

For the moment, Martin put aside the sadness of seeing Mac go and tuned into his friend. "You holding up, Mac?"

"Yeah, it's coming together pretty well. Pullin' out on Thursday."

Martin's eyes moistened. "It's been quite a year and one of the highlights for me has been getting to know you, Mac."

"You're one of my closest friends, Martin. And, man, what a year. It's certainly been challenging, to say the least."

Mac looked out the window, reflecting on all the twists and turns he'd recently navigated. "I've learned some things. For one, every liberal's not a saint and every conservative's not a demon. There's a lot more to friendship than ideology – I'll take heart and integrity any time."

"Well said, Mac. And I've learned some things too. We needn't be so suspicious of change. Sometimes it's a good thing," he smiled. "You'd think I'd know that after studying so much history.

And, I must tell you that I'm very happy to pass the baton on to a man like you."

They lingered longer than planned, trying to cover all they wanted to say. The visit ended with a heartfelt hug.

"By the way Mac, do you have a *first* name?"

"Felix Olsen. It's a family name.

"Of course, Mac …has to be."

Dean Tate

It's usually just the parents who'll sit through long, drawn out graduation ceremonies, but John was feeling rather proud of his brother and arrived early to get a good seat. He had great hopes for Gary's future but also had to make some decisions of his own.

John hadn't said much, but Clinton made him a fantastic offer to tour with his group. Professionally, it would give him a good shot at the next level. But Clinton had been straight with him. "There are no guarantees, still I can name groups who've gotten big breaks on this circuit. Course, some didn't. It's kinda like minor league ball, doesn't pay much, but gets you noticed."

John had mulled it over for days and even though it seemed like what he'd always dreamed of – something just didn't feel right about it.

He settled into his seat and braced himself for the onslaught of boring platitudes – *seize the day, reach for the stars, etc.* But that wouldn't be the case today – Dean Tate was the commencement speaker.

Tate came to the university in 1920 as a student and ended up serving more than 50 years as a teacher and administrator. As Dean of Students, he never lost the common touch – his heart beat with the pulse of the student body. It was no wonder that he was one of the most beloved men in town and throughout the state.

Legendary UGA sports announcer, Loran Smith, said it best. "Georgians should love their university as he did. He was the embodiment of the spirit of the university. He wanted the football team to win, but he was just as happy when the debate team won."

The dean took time to mingle with students. He'd carefully listen to what they had to say then dispense sage counsel.

Tate had helped hundreds of young men and women stay on the right path, but that didn't mean he'd put up with nonsense. "Working with a sorry boy is like goin' huntin' and havin' to tote the birddog. Some of the rascals 'round this campus believe when choosing between two evils, you choose the one you haven't tried before!"

You never knew when or where he'd appear offering advice and encouragement. He'd ask who your daddy was, where you were from and what you wanted to do. He was equally enthused if you said you wanted to run a barbeque joint or become governor. "That's just splendid, splendid my boy... a noble ambition."

During a lifetime of service to UGA, he'd seen and done just about everything. Back in the days of hand written, hand delivered forms, registration each quarter was a slow motion rigmarole. But when Dean Tate showed up, often wearing his red suspenders and beanie cap from his own college days, he calmed long lines of panic-stricken students and patiently guided them through the maze of paperwork.

The man who everyone counted on to uphold tradition was also on the cutting edge of advancement. In 1961, a new day dawned at the university with the arrival of Charlyane Hunter (later Hunter-Gault). The journalist paved the way for African Americans to attend the university and later became a national correspondent for the Public Broadcasting System and CNN. Dean Tate worked hard to alleviate friction surrounding the event and helped to enfold the newcomer into the student body. With his kind, yet commanding demeanor, he led the way into a new era.

The consummate mentor, he had the ability to shape the will without crushing the spirit. "Everybody needs a kick in the rear and a pat on the back. You just have to know *when to do which.*"

The dean always drew on his faith and love of people and peppered his remarks with homespun Southern proverbs and UGA lore. He especially liked the plain but profound common sense of old men who congregated around the old courthouse squares in small towns.

The audience welcomed him with warm applause as he took the podium and entertained them with humorous stories from his many years at the university.

"You know that I came to this great institution on a track scholarship. Now, I know, you're looking up here at my enlarged girth and thinking *that's hard to believe.* But there was a time I was quite fleet of foot. And I'm gonna give you one of the great lessons I learned from our coach: 'life is a marathon not a sprint.'"

After another 20 minutes full of stories and witticisms, he gave his final charge to the graduates.

"Do you know what the founders of our esteemed institution said was the purpose of this place?

'To inquire into the nature of things.' So, yes be inquisitive, try new things. Be bold in your academic endeavors but don't *major* in extracurricular activities and don't be foolhardy or else you'll end up in real trouble. I can tell you – if you're hell-bent on running with the hound dogs on Saturday nights you're gonna get fleas.

I know that young Dawgs are full of vim and vigor – and in addition to cultivating a lifelong love for learning, you're gonna make some mistakes. And you just might end up in the Dawghouse every now and then. BUT keep putting one foot in front of the other no matter how heavy your legs may be – finish the race."

Ronnie was a totally different person with big plans of settling down with Stephanie.

And he'd finally connected the dots. He'd need a good career which meant buckling down and getting his degree. No more working in a class here and there around his social schedule. The guy was focused and actually doing pretty well.

But one day, when he thought life couldn't get any better, Stephanie dropped a bombshell. She broke up with him, and even worse, went back to Preston.

It was all so predictable and everyone saw it coming – except Ronnie.

Preston had his fun, but he'd also kept a wary eye on this Ronnie guy. As the new man about town, Preston had played the field, all right, but he didn't let it go so far as to let Stephanie slip away. He stepped in before Ronnie gained any serious ground and declared that dating around *only* served to remove any doubt that Stephanie was *the one*. Preston had played his hand quite deftly and won.

Ronnie was devastated. His dreams were shattered. Hopelessly despondent, he moved back home and dropped out of sight. No one could help him. His parents tried everything but to no avail – and he wouldn't talk to anybody.

When he skipped finals altogether, Ronnie sealed his fate. His college career was over.

SUMMERTIME AND THE LIVIN' AIN'T EASY

College towns have a nice seasonal rhythm. In Athens, fall is fantastic. Winter easily tolerable. And Spring fever is downright contagious. During the summer lull, the student population drops dramatically. Townsfolk cheerfully exchanged the hectic pace of their college town for welcomed traffic relief on the narrow streets – streets that had been designed for a much smaller Athens, not the ever expanding city of today.

Now in the languid days of July, summer poked along uneventfully, just the way Southerners like it. And that's when Sonny found a golden opportunity. A firecracker of a sale exploded on the market – a large tract of land only a few miles from campus that was the perfect location for an apartment complex. The seller needed the money and, hoping to unload it quickly, listed it an unbelievably low price. The student body's rapid growth and a tight housing market fed a growing demand for more apartments, especially newer and more upscale units.

Sonny knew that as soon as word got out, there'd be a swarm of eager buyers so he jumped on it. His brother agreed. With a credit line in place and plenty of cash available, snagging the land should be easy. But there was no time to waste.

To get the ball rolling, he met with Jack to withdraw cash for the sizeable down payment.

He burst into Jack's office with a self-assurance that even surpassed his usual hubris. "Man, you won't believe this land. A deal like this doesn't come along every day."

Jack hardly looked up.

Sonny ignored his friend's indifference and went on, "It's a steal. We're talkin' prime property and when we get ahold of it, we're gonna kick it straight through the goalpost. The right apartments in that location will be a gold mine."

Jack, who usually lit up at the prospect of any client making big money, seemed distracted. Sonny may have been outlandish in his football predictions, but his calls on real estate development were spot on. And Jack knew it.

"OK, let me see what I can do. Keep in mind we have to time this thing right," Jack said.

His tepid response irritated Sonny. "Yeah, but make it quick. I gotta nail this deal soon or it'll be gone."

"Yeah, I know, just give me a little time."

One student who hadn't left town for summer was Ginny – and Will was thrilled. He couldn't imagine not being with her. They both worked summer jobs, and even though they'd spent as much time together as possible it never seemed to be enough.

During their evening walks in the Botanical Gardens and day trips to the cooler North Georgia mountains, they really got to know each other. And beyond the first stirrings of attraction and affection, their relationship became something much deeper. In the unhurried days of summer, their souls melded together into a beautiful intimacy that neither of them had ever known before.

The next day everything seemed squarely in place for Sonny. First he stopped by the bank to pick up the check from the wire transfer. While the banker fiddled for several minutes, Sonny wondered what was taking so long. "Look, man, we're about to ink an important deal. Think you can get goin' here?"

Sonny sighed and huffed and finally pounded the counter with his large fist. The startled man looked up and informed him that the funds weren't available. "Should be here by now," he explained, "maybe some kind of transmission delay, but that doesn't usually happen. I've gone through everything on my end. Better check with Jack."

"Hey man, thought you'd call or something. You made the transfer, right?"

"Not just yet. I've got a lot goin' on, Sonny, just like you. You get that, I'm sure," Jack answered.

"Get what? All I need for you to do is pull out my money and send it over. It doesn't get more straightforward than that. "

"You know how it is; nothin's as simple as it looks."

"C'mon, Jack, this is a huge for us. I just need my money. So let's make it happen."

Jack fidgeted and nervously shuffled his papers. "OK, you'll get it tomorrow."

Ginny's job at the summer camp was working out well for her – she earned a little money and it also counted as a practicum for her social work degree. As in many towns the size of Athens, diverse neighborhoods bump up against each other and on one side of the university, a government project provided low-cost housing to those who needed assistance. But the need didn't end there – especially among the children. And summer camps were a great way to help out. It was impressive coming together – civic groups, churches, retirees and a host of UGA students. Playful and energetic college students and a gaggle of kids with open hearts, yearning for attention, made a perfect match.

Mr. Reynolds had taken on the job of coordinating the tutoring services this year. His "free time" may have been due to the underhanded dealings of Peter Hall, but still, he had *no time* for self-pity and he'd developed an innovative program that thoroughly covered the basics and also offered all sorts of fun activities as well.

Herman was involved too – organizing book clubs where kids received small but treasured prizes for meeting their reading goals. He was delighted when the youngsters came up with the idea to put on mini plays of their favorite stories – complete with props fashioned at craft time where they made magic with cardboard boxes, paper towel rolls and whatever else was handy.

On field trip days, the staff loaded up buses and off they went to UGA Ag sites, where kids who'd never held a baby chick or milked a dairy cow were awestruck. They topped it off with the best ice cream they'd ever tasted at UGA's creamery – hand-dipped and straight from the cow. Ag students had operated the creamery since 1941. For the staff, the squeals of ecstatic kids more than made up for all the nerve-wracking head counts and the constant challenge of wrangling in stragglers.

Boy Scout Oath
"On my honor, I will do my best
to do my duty to God and my country and to obey the Scout Law;
To help other people at all times;
to keep myself physically strong, mentally alert and morally straight."

The blistering Southern sun was turning afternoons into an absolute sauna. The peak of summer heat is one of the "charming" aspects of the South that even Southerners can do without.

If you'd heard it once you'd heard it a thousand times – particularly when you talked to a *transplant* from another part of the country as you stood there soaked in sweat from walking only a city block. It went like this: "Yeah…this heat is really something isn't it? You could fry an egg on the sidewalk…then the standard metrological cliché: "And you know it's *not the heat but the humidity* that really gets you."

To cool off his overheated body, Will reclined on a bench under the shade of a Magnolia beside Park Hall, closed his eyes and let his thoughts drift to a cooler time, recalling a snowbound camping trip a couple of years ago.

One November, Will and a couple of ole scouting buddies, did what they loved to do – stopped at a convenience store, stuffed a few random food items in their backpacks and set out to the North Carolina mountains for a weekend of hiking. When the guys embarked on a new trail they'd never hiked before, they realized that the most important thing they'd forgotten was to check the weather.

They hadn't gone far in their jeans and light weight shirts when a fierce wind kicked up and they felt the temperature dropping with every step they took. It started snowing big time. Not just a few fluffy flakes but a Vermont-like winter wonderland snowfall soon blanketed everything – including the trail. Red Appalachian Trail markings on trees and an occasional mileage sign were the only things that kept them from wandering off into oblivion. Freezing and near exhaustion from a hike that was far more rigorous than they'd bargained for, the guys finally came across one of the three-sided wooden AT camping shelters. After several attempts, they got a small fire going, gobbled down Rice Crispy Treats and Spam and wearily crawled into their sleeping bags. A long night of shivering in the cold gave them plenty of time to contemplate how they'd violated nearly all the principles they'd learned in Scouts – and defied common sense. Fortunately, the weather improved dramatically the next morning so the guys hightailed it down the trail and back towards civilization, stopping just long enough to enjoy some superb sledding on pieces of cardboard they'd found in the shelter.

But bungling a few life-saving lessons from Scouts never diminished their love of the outdoors. Part of the fun was using all kinds of cool gear and suspending hygiene standards – you got dirty, stayed dirty and no one objected. Back then, almost every scout troop was sponsored by a church – Troop 1, 1st Methodist; Troop 22; Milledge Ave Baptist; and Will's Troop 19, St. James Methodist.

Quite a few UGA students assisted the troop leaders countering the stereotype of irresponsible, self-absorbed college guys. Most of them were former Scouts who simply wanted to give back a little, help shepherd the next crop of Tenderfoots and enjoy tromping around the woods again.

Scouts taught you to be "one with nature" way before the hippies "were down with it" and, most importantly, how to *survive* as you "communed." And long before it was "a movement," young scouts learned respect for the environment. It only took *one time* of getting totally drenched and freeze in a wet sleeping bag all night to learn *the right way* to put up a tent.

Will's troop tackled lots of the AT trails in Georgia and the Carolinas and earned special patches for each historical trail hiked – patches which became valuable enough to trade like baseball cards.

Lord Baden Powell, the famous British officer, who founded the Boy Scouts, had lots of pithy sayings that still guided the worldwide program he'd started.

"A week of camp life is worth six months of theoretical teaching in the meeting room."

"We never fail when we try to do our duty. We always fail when we neglect to do it."

"Be prepared. Be Prepared For what? Why? Any old thing?"

"Leave it better than you found it" (That meant cleaning up your campsite before you left – young scouts diligently followed this maxim in conserving the great outdoors, but it somehow never translated to cleaning their own rooms.)

Troop 19 started their first overnight camping trip to Jekyll Island, Ga. with a late night "ghost walk." Moonlight flickered through the ancient gnarled oaks covered with Spanish moss forming an eerie canopy over the sandy road as the scoutmaster told ghost stories and legends about the island. Will kept his Swiss army knife handy just in case any pirates ambushed them from limbs overhanging the spooky road. The troop slept under the stars and dreamed of Spanish galleons, gold and miscellaneous marauders.

When morning came, the Tenderfoots were anxious to pass their knot tying requirements for a promotion to the next level. They'd practiced the knots for weeks. After much effort, Will finally mastered the tricky bowline knot. He was so elated that he rushed over to tell the senior patrol leaders about his big accomplishment.

"Hey look guys. I did it! Check out my bowline knot!"

"Scram, kid...get outta here." The teenagers practically *threw* Will out of their tent.

Will was crestfallen. *What was the big deal?* The guys just sat there huddled in a circle, examining something – probably from the Boy Scout manual.

But before Will was summarily ejected, he realized that what was holding the older guys undivided attention was a magazine featuring a "Miss July." He left scratching his head, but gained a full understanding in a couple of years.

It was always great to get out of the suburbs and explore the outdoors. One of the troop's favorite overnight adventures was canoeing the Okefenokee Swamp. Seven hundred square miles of mysterious cypress trees, sinister-looking black water (from the tannic acid of decaying plants) full of strange creatures and bizarre birds and, of course, loads of alligators. The gators weren't shy about coming right alongside your canoe. They were mostly submerged except for their beady eyes peering up at you just over the water line. Their message was clear: *You're in our backyard.* Talk about intimidating.

The troop always camped a couple of nights on Billy's Island, the site of a once thriving community of loggers and moonshiners in the '20s. Now the only thing that remained was a hodge-podge of abandoned buildings, railroad tracks, rusting cars and skunks who circled the tents on nightly commando raids. (When you got back home, it took tons of Tide to eventually rid yourself of the awful, pungent odor.)

Another memorable smell from Scout days was the smell of liquor from an afternoon of ushering rowdy football fans to their seats. Except for the risk of being baptized by various libations, it was great community service and a free ticket that put you right in the middle of the action. In Athens, even tee-totaling moms understood why their youngsters came home smelling like a Jack Daniels distillery.

But the best thing about Troop 19 was its legendary leader and consummate adventurer – Fred Birchmore. Besides his day job in the Athens's real estate market, Birchmore was mainly known as the guy who traveled the world on the most amazing exploits.

The stories he told were hard to believe unless you'd seen the pictures and knew of the family's impeccable integrity. The bike that he'd ridden around the world back in his 20s was on display at none other than the Smithsonian Institute. (He'd named it Bucephalus, after Alexander the Great's horse.) You're still likely to see Birchmore jogging on UGA's track at dawn, staying in shape for his next quest.

After a full day of rigorous hiking, the Scouts were rewarded by sitting around a roaring campfire as Birchmore told tales. From being waylaid by bandits in the mountains of Afghanistan or battling hunger on a desolate trail in the Andes Mountains, the dirty-faced boys hung on his every word as they clutched their sticks loaded with toasted marshmallows. And closer to home, he told stories about his 2,000 mile hike of the Appalachian Trail in tennis shoes, which he'd done on three different occasions (at last count).

To wind things down, Birchmore showed the boys samples from his gigantic arrowhead collection, then led spirited singing of old camping and gospel songs. He'd finally wrap up the day with a profound thought to ponder from a homespun parable or Bible story.

Sonny's brother had reluctantly agreed to give the wire transfer another day and then he called the bank – still no funds. The delay with such a significant deal pending made no sense.

Sonny charged into Jack's office.

"What the heck's goin' on, Jack? Where's my money?"

"There's been a small problem, just a technical thing."

"What'd ya mean? You're not makin *any* sense, man. What's wrong? Somethin's gotta to be wrong."

Beads of sweat formed on Jack's forehead. Sonny had never seen him this nervous.

Jack began to ramble. "No, everything's fine. C'mon you can give me a little more time. It'll all work out. Always docs for you and me. Right?"

Sonny and his brother couldn't figure out what was holding things up. In a meeting with their lawyer later in the afternoon, they explained the situation. The attorney leaned in and listened carefully. "Yeah, but this is really strange. Get this: "I have another client who just had the same problem with Marshall."

Will didn't work far from the camp and dropped by whenever he could. Being a kid at heart, he naturally jumped right into whatever football or basketball game was going on and enjoyed the fun every bit as much as his pint-sized teammates. Ginny smiled at his boyish enthusiasm and especially noticed how kind and patient Will was with the kids.

Ginny did a little bit of everything – mainly administrative stuff, but she also had opportunities to use her training. Even in the fun days of summer, the bleak side of the children's lives often surfaced during her screenings. Ginny wasn't at all prepared for how deeply their needs tore at her heart.

She wanted so much to help the children yet she wondered what she was actually accomplishing with the clerical stuff eating up big chunks of her day.

It was hard for Will to watch her struggle. "I know you want to change the world. But it may not be like you think it'll be," Will said.

Ginny rested her chin in her hands. "Well thanks. Great way to encourage me after a hard day."

Will reached out for her hand and held it gently. "What I mean is you may not see big and dramatic results. You have to take it one day at a time and one kid at a time. And sometimes, you may never know who you're getting through to."

She gave it some thought. "Yeah, maybe I haven't been so realistic."

He put his arm around her. "I know. But those kids can't help but see how much you care and that means more to them than you can imagine."

She rested her head on Will's shoulder and felt a little better.

Characters and Kelly

Fall quarter had begun and was as vibrant as ever, especially for one Will Andrews who had everything going for him. He was a senior now, and with Ginny by his side, the future looked bright. Will had hit the ground running by getting an early start on his internship at the Athens Banner Herald.

The ideas for features kept coming and he was writing better and faster by the day. Readers enjoyed his punchy pieces and in-depth stories about the town's more color-ful citizens. Unlike some of the bigger cities, Athenians embraced their "unusual" citizens rather than ostracizing them. These folks were just as much a part of the town as the Dogwood Manor, the Varsity or Sanford Stadium.

As a hometown boy, Will had a virtual vault of material to work with. He'd known these people for most of his life. In the last couple of weeks, Will had written about some of the most notable eccentrics, starting with "The Mayor of Five Points" – or so he called himself. The mayor faithfully patrolled a patch of land he'd claimed near Hodgson's. From a rusted 1950's porch chair, set among his collection of junk, he presided over his domain at Athens's busiest intersection.

But the *finest* collection of junk was found at The Trade Shop. Down Park Avenue, past Easy Street sat a hodge-podge of old sheds cobbled to, what appeared to be, a former chicken coop. Stepping through the portal of this odd emporium, you peered over such an enormous accumulation of odds and ends that it looked like a bomb had gone off in a flea market. You knew at once that you'd need a Daniel Boone to even begin to wade through the stuff and that's where Mr. Paschal came in. He'd worked in the store for most of his life and knew every inch of it like the back of his hand. Through the years, Will couldn't resist taking home such treasures as Studebaker hubcaps, Australian hunting knives and an Evil Knievel banana seat for his Spyder bike.

And readers wanted to know the real story behind the Vine Lady's porch. At one time or the other, everyone had passed the house down near the train trestle and slowed down to stare at the gobs of brightly painted ivy adorning her dilapidated porch. The Vine Lady's idea of home improvement was to paint the leaves of her abundant vines different colors according to the season – or her whims.

Essie Mae Ash was a friendly soul who'd eagerly talk to anyone who wondered about her artistic creations. She explained to Will that people are "powerful curious" and ask how she has the time and patience to keep the growing ivy leaves painted. "I tell 'em when you get to be 81 years old, all you got is time and patience."

Most people knew James who'd claimed a choice spot for his panhandling around the Arch where he spent the day collecting "just a little spare change for a cup of coffee." His life story was a little hazy – about like he was most of the time. Folks said he'd been a cab driver for 20 years or so until one day a hit and run driver struck James on Broad Street. Ever since the accident, he walked his "beat" with a crutch and moved a little slower, but from a face of deep wrinkles, his eyes peered out as bright ever. "Yeah, I've had a hard life, but the Lord keeps His eye on me and I'm thankful for that."

But the story that topped them all was the anniversary article on Cobern Kelly. Kelly wasn't a town character, but he was undoubtedly the man in town with the greatest *character.*

He'd devoted his life to shaping the young men of Athens as director of the YMCA. For 23 years, generations of boys revered Kelly as their coach and teacher and father figure. He did just about everything – from playing the ukulele to botanist to refereeing squabbles. He was a true servant/leader who worked tirelessly and would do anything for his boys.

The Y boys just called him Kelly. No one seemed to know much about his past, except that he ended up in Athens after serving in the Navy. The story goes that his devotion to mentoring impressionable youths came from some kind of dramatic encounter with Japanese soldiers in WWII. Kelly sent up a fast prayer for survival, pledging to dedicate the rest of his life to the welfare of the young.

The lifelong bachelor taught the fundamentals of every sport imaginable. But according to former Y boys, like football greats, Fran Tarkington, Andy Johnson and Jake Scott and hundreds of other ordinary guys, he taught them something even more important – about life and hard work.

At summer Y camps, the guys explored the wonders of nature, caught critters all morning, played football in the afternoon, and boxed after supper. Kelly then capped off a full day of activities with an insightful Bible study at night.

Kelly never took vacations, but when he did travel, he had a herd of boys in tow. During summer months, he loaded up an old International Harvester bus with 30 to 40 kids and ventured out West. After a brief break, he turned around and set out with another busload for Canada. Forty kids on an old bus with no air conditioning and only one man driving – and nobody stepped out of line.

The Athens's Y was the second oldest in the nation and always had close ties to the university. (In earlier years, UGA's basketball team played on the Y courts before Georgia had its own gym.) Later the Y grew beyond anything Kelly had envisioned and kept pace with the times. You have to wonder what Kelly would've thought about an Egyptian woman teaching a weekly belly dancing class. But with his adventuresome spirit (after he'd dropped his ukulele and scratched his head), he'd probably have tried a couple of moves himself. Even though the ladies said it was excellent exercise, some Y founders may have frowned upon the course, believing that dancing *abdominal* was *abominable*. But as Bob Dylan told us, "the times they are a changin'."

In the same way that everyone recalled where they were when President Kennedy was assassinated, every Y boy knew exactly where he was when he got the news that Kelly had died suddenly on April 11, 1968. The principal at Alps Middle School held a special assembly and called on student council president, Doc Eldridge, to make the sad announcement.

All of Athens went into mourning. The Athens Banner Herald dedicated its entire front page to his memory. The paper recounted stories from men who'd credited Kelly with changing their lives. With a lump in his throat, one prominent citizen admitted, "I always carry his picture in my wallet."

Men still visit his grave at the Y grounds on Hawthorne Avenue – like it was the Lincoln Memorial or the Washington Monument – and break down and cry when they speak of him.

Mr. Reynolds enjoyed watching the romance blossom between his favorite camp worker and his favorite student. Finally one day he abandoned his reserve and blurted out, "You've got yourself a great guy and you've got yourself a great gal. So let's get on with it."

Ginny blushed and laughed, then got right back to the pile of papers before her. She was good at details and very meticulous – but sometimes she got lost in it. Will, on the other hand, was more of a big picture guy who was apt to lose his car keys. Opposites do attract and everyone could tell that the two were a good match.

Will stopped by mid-day for a couple of hours and as soon as they heard the car door open, three kids wrapped themselves around his ankles and practically dragged him to the playground. Ginny labored over forms and schedules, coordinating the final two weeks. After Will and the kids played a rousing game of dodge ball, the couple slipped away for lunch.

Ginny didn't say much. Finally, Will broke the silence. "I wish you wouldn't worry about dotting every *i* and crossing every *t*. You'll get it right. I'd hate for you to miss out on the fun."

"Gosh, I know. I haven't spent as much time as I wanted to with the kids and it's almost over."

Will smiled at her, feeling tender and protective. "They love havin' you around, just playin with 'em."

"Yeah, I see that."

Ginny was slowly getting used to having someone really care about her, even about the little things in her life. It was nice and new for her. Her family was one of those that looks OK on the outside, but has problems – nothing really disturbing, yet her Mom and Dad were too bogged down in their own issues to nurture kids. At 17, Ginny went off to college. Her Mom pulled up to the curb, unceremoniously let her out and said goodbye. Ginny carried her bags to the imposing dorm alone, working her way through a crowd of tearful parents and boisterous students as her Mom drove away.

But college had given her a fresh start. She'd found her place in a wonderful sisterhood of friends and her sorority became her adopted family. And now there was Will.

Five Points

"All new news is old news happening to new people."

Malcolm Muggeridge

Even though the Banner Herald assigned Will feature stories, he was still obliged to pay his dues just like anyone else. That meant getting lots of cups of coffee, fact-checking for reporters, writing obituaries and civic club notices – whatever needed to be done. Reporters took turns contributing to a popular column called "Ask Athens's Answer Man." Readers wrote in seeking information about anything on their minds – like how to get a pothole fixed, property tax questions, mail order scams, or anything they were wondering about. The questions and answers ran in Saturday's edition.

Someone wrote in to get the story behind the unusual plaque at Five Points. Will also wanted to know – he'd noticed it as a little kid when he walked with his mother to the neighborhood beauty parlor and later cruising around on his Spyder bike.

The burnished bronze plaque was bolted to the curb on Lumpkin Street and bore the sad words:

"Martin Reynolds Smith, the son of Mr. and Mrs. J. Warren Smith, was instantly killed here by a speeding auto truck on Nov. 15th, 1922.

May 22, 1916 – Nov 15 1922"

Years passed and the curious marker was still there, ignominiously located a few feet from a city trash can.

This has got to be a parent's worst nightmare – losing a young child in "a senseless tragedy."

But the inscription didn't tell the whole story and Will's inquisitive nature prompted him to do a little research.

Curiosity is a curious thing. Even though it was only a story about a day in the life of a small boy from a small town, it still raised a lot of questions.

Who was the 6-years-old boy? What happened? There couldn't have been more than a dozen cars in the whole city in 1922. A "speeding truck" at that time probably was going about 30 mph tops. Did the poor boy just dart out in the street? Did the driver go to jail? How did the family handle this tragic death?

After poking through the old files in the storage room, he found a clipping dated Jan. 18, 1923.

Turns out that Martin Smith's father was president of the Georgia National Bank and the family lived on Milledge Circle, just a couple of blocks away from Will's home.

The boy was riding his bike when he was struck by John Miner, a driver for a local delivery company. According to the truck driver, the boy was "snaking" – riding his bike from side to side on the street. Yet some eyewitnesses said the driver was speeding. Martin was killed instantly. In the first case of vehicular homicide in Clarke County, Milner pleaded guilty and was convicted of involuntary manslaughter. He was given the minimum sentence of one year on the chain gang.

And now Will knew the story, the reader knew it and so do the many others who've simply wondered as they've passed by the sad memorial.

There's always a story somewhere – you just have to open your eyes and do a little digging.

The Sage of Phi Kappa Hall

Dr. E. Merton Coulter had left a note in Dr. Andrews's box for Will "to come by and pick up an early graduation gift."

Since he was a boy, Will had really enjoyed hearing stories from the old professor who'd been enlightening students since 1919. The colorful North Carolina native from a small rural community shattered the stereotype of the boring history teacher and made the past come alive. Dr. Coulter had been retired for years, but still came to his office in the historic Phi Kappa Hall *seven* days a week to work on yet another article or book.

The man loved his books and when space got tight (which was always the case), the spry bachelor just stacked them on the floor, table tops – anyplace he could find. His filing system was the same at home with the added benefit of storing them on the racks in his oven.

During his prime, the professor taught his intro to American history in the Chapel. He'd get so wrapped up in what he was saying that he'd pace closer and closer to the stage footlights and come precariously near the edge of the stage. (Students had running bets on when he'd fall off.) Everyone enjoyed his wry sense of humor. When someone asked about his recent research trip to Paris he quipped, "Very profitable, but what can one really do in Paris after the library closes?"

The Southern historian had lectured far and wide during his career and had built a national reputation. As a founding member of the Southern Historical Association, he'd served as its first president in 1934 and had edited the *Georgia Historical Quarterly* for 50 years. But despite the steady lure from prestigious institutions, UGA held on to their beloved professor and Coulter was happy to call UGA *home.* His Georgia history books served as the standard high school textbook for years – shaping generations of students.

But the professor wasn't all work and no play, sometimes with his friend, Dr. Calvin Brown (an accomplished scholar whose roots also ran deep in the rural South), he'd frequent many of the social events in Athens (sometimes sporting a kilt). When the two weren't hiking mountain trails together, Dr. Brown was busy developing a comparative literature program used across the country. Another good friend on the faculty was Dr. Albert Saye, a noted political science scholar who'd written civic books used statewide. The Harvard educated farm boy endured constant pain from a severe congenital back condition that made it impossible for him to stand up straight. But when time came to emphasis "the extraordinary, potent and powerful writings" of the founding fathers and expound on vast portions of the Constitution from memory, he'd still stand on his desk, practically bent over in half.

When Will ventured into the professor's hobbit hole office he heard the rustling of papers before he actually spotted Dr. Coulter's bald head hidden among the clutter.

Coulter looked up from his work. "Will, good to see you. How time as flown. Seems like yesterday you were banging away on your dad's old typewriter, your feet dangling off the chair."

"Yes, sir."

The historian congratulated Will on his upcoming graduation and handed him an autographed copy of his bestselling book "College Life in the Old South." The two chatted, then Dr. Coulter launched into a story about old Dr. Church and how his portrait ended up spending years in a seedy saloon in Columbus, Ga.

Of all the portraits of past UGA presidents hanging in the Administration Building none had a more unusual history than the framed likeness of the university's longest serving president, Dr. Alonzo Church (1839-1859).

The senior class of 1854 had presented the portrait, mounted in an elegant gilded frame and inscribed with the names of all class members to the school in an official ceremony near graduation. Church later retired in 1860 and moved to his country home just outside of Athens and, with Northern troops marching through Georgia, residents clamored to hide family heirlooms or ship them away to distant relatives for safe-keeping.

The portrait was sent off and, amid the confusion of the war, was lost. Years later, Church's a son-in-law was tracking down a witness and made a shocking discovery in a run-down dive in Columbus.

Above the bar, hung a painting of a distinguished gentleman that seemed totally out of place. To his astonishment, the lawyer recognized it as the missing portrait of Dr. Church.

After protracted negotiations, he was able to rescue the vintage portrait from its shady surroundings – and like Odysseus of Greek lore, who endured a long and perilous journey home – the picture was reunited with the portraits of fellow presidents that grace the lobby of the Administration Building. (They say if you get up close, you can still smell a trace of beer and cigarettes emanating from the worn walnut frame.)

Sports Legends

Anxiety gripped the town. Losing the first game of the season was a blow and even worse – the Dawgs weren't looking so good. To boost the sagging spirits of fans, Will wrote a feature highlighting past UGA greats.

A look at the university's rich sport's history would surely take their minds off of their worries. After all, Georgia fans hadn't come by their devotion overnight.

It all started way back in 1892 on a spot of land near the quad and behind the chapel known as Herty Field. But in truth, it was more dirt and rocks than "field."

The football program hadn't been going long when a terrible event almost shut it down. A star player, Von Gammon, sustained a horrible injury that left him unconscious on the field. Tragically, he later died from head trauma. It shook the state and beyond. The press and stunned university officials wanted to disband football on the grounds that the game was just too dangerous. But right before the final decision, Von Gammon's mother sent a letter to UGA officials imploring them to keep the program going. The grief-stricken mother said she knew her son would want students to keep playing the game he loved so much.

Football recovered and the program continued to grow. Then in 1942, UGA's spectacular running back, Frankie Sinkwich, brought home the first Heisman Trophy. That year in the Orange Bowl, Sinkwich showed the kind of grit that heroes are made of when he wore a specially designed helmet to protect his broken jaw and ran and passed for 335 yards, leading the team to a victory over TCU.

In his three years at Georgia, "Flat Foot Frankie" gained more than 2,200 yards and scored 60 touchdowns – 30 rushing and 30 passing. The Associated Press named Sinkwich the "Number One Athlete" for 1942.

And the next year, another remarkable running back, Charlie Trippi capped off his fabulous freshman season with a superb showing in Georgia's Rose Bowl win over UCLA before 93,000 fans – a win that elevated Georgia football to the national scene.

It was a fairytale week for the young players who were wined and dined in Hollywood and hobnobbed with the stars. Yet Trippi never forgot how UGA had changed his life.

"I came to Georgia a poor boy. My first year in Athens I wore Coca-Cola work pants and a t-shirt all the time. That's all I had. But Georgia completely turned my life around and gave me a chance to excel at football and I was able to have a successful career in professional football."

Trippi's rousing locker room speech during the 1947 Sugar Bowl rivaled George Washington's rallying cry to the discouraged troops at Valley Forge.

Georgia was behind 10-0 at halftime. Trippi took matters into his own hands and asked Coach Wally Butts if he could speak to the team alone.

After pacing the locker room awhile, he hopped up on a bench and said:

"We have waited all year for an undefeated, untied season. We are not going to blow it all now. Those of you who do not want to give 100 percent, take off your uniform and get in the shower now. Those who want to give it everything they've got, let's go get'em and go out like champions."

The inspired Dawgs scored 21 points and kept North Carolina out of the end zone for the second half. Trippi was named captain of the All-American Football Board and was selected for top honors on every post season team. Not bad for a poor boy from Pennsylvania coal country who didn't have enough money to buy his own football cleats in high school...

Theron Sapp is forever revered in Bulldawg lore as the man "that broke the drought with Georgia Tech." During a windy, sub-freezing afternoon in Atlanta in 1957, the stout fullback recovered a crucial fumble at midfield in the fourth quarter. After some tremendous passes by Charlie Britt to Jimmy Orr, Sapp ran the ball *six* times in a row and got the Dawgs to the Tech one yard line. Britt made a hand-off to Sapp yet again who plowed through the Tech defense and scored the first touchdown against Yellow Jackets since 1953 – a touchdown that broke the nine year losing streak against their arch rival. The lone TD was enough for a win and enough to signal that the Dawgs were back and had thrown the miserable Tech monkey off their back.

Anthony Joseph "Zippy" Morocco, the son of Italian immigrants, started out shining shoes as a boy to help with family's meager finances and then became a two sport star in football and basketball at UGA. Using his massive 5'10" and 165 pound body, he dashed and darted all over the field, hauled in long passes and wowed fans with electrifying punt returns. He's still in the record books as one of Georgia's great punt-returners.

When basketball season rolled around, Morocco tore up the courts with his elusive dribbling and proved his worth as a scoring machine in UGA's antiquated basketball arena, Woodruff Hall. The old structure was actually more of a barn than an arena and was called out by Hall of Fame Kentucky coach, Adolph Rupp as: "The only SEC basketball facility where *wind* was a factor."

UGA's basketball team also holds the record for the most lopsided win in NCAA history. Alfred Scott, a 6'8" chemistry major from Macon, scored 62 points in leading the team to a 122 -2 win over Southeastern Christian College in 1922. And off-court, Scott was equally impressive. He went on to earn a Ph.D. in chemistry from Princeton and served as department chair at Georgia from 1927-1962.

Will always remembered watching the famous 1965 UGA – Bama game from prime seats with his dad. Georgia shocked the football world when they defeated the mighty Crimson Tide that year despite Bama's ultra-cool QB, Joe Namath. In a last minute trick play, ever since immortalized as "the flea flicker," quarterback Kirby Moore zipped a short pass to Pat Hodgson who tossed a perfectly timed lateral to Bob Taylor who then miraculously raced 74 yards into the end zone with the last few seconds ticking away in the fourth quarter and the Dawgs trailing by one point. Dooley decided to gamble and go for a win instead of kicking the extra point, Kirby fired a pass to Hodgson to win the game 18-17. The stunning upset was a turning point in Vince Dooley's career.

All of these heroic tales were repeated again and again by the town's elders to motivate the young, impressionable sprouts of Athens to: eat your broccoli, be nice to your sister, study, and mind your elders. The animated story tellers savored every detail in telling the tales – no matter how many times a young person had heard it. The mythic Greek warriors had nothing on these legendary warriors of UGA…

And Will had his own tale that he knew one day he'd pass on to his grandkids. He was there in the stands on Thanksgiving night, 1971 to cheer hometown hero, Andy Johnson as he single-handedly led the Dawgs to a stunning fourth quarter comeback against Georgia Tech. It was the first time the famous rivalry was nationally televised and the All-SEC quarterback delivered a breath-taking performance. With California surfer good-looks, Andy was also a terrific baseball player and one of the most humble guys you'd ever want to meet. Seemed like a story straight out of a Hollywood script – except it was all true.

Jasmine and Generals
Near the end of the day, Mr. Beck summoned Will to his office. The editor was a hard-boiled newspaper guy in his 50s, the no nonsense type who ripped through a story in no time and still found the smallest flaw. His office was a mess and he certainly didn't have an eye for fashion, which may have had as much to do with his meager editor's salary as anything.

Mr. Beck swiveled in his chair, closely eyeing the intern. "Will, for a young whippersnapper, you're OK."

Will let out a sigh of relief.

"You've certainly got an eye for the offbeat and unusual slice-of-life stories. We're gettin' a lot of good feedback from folks in town about some of your pieces. And that's great 'cause we have to crank this stuff out and keep ad revenues comin' in – *that's* how we get a paycheck."

"Yes sir."

"But don't start thinkin' you're settin' the world on fire. No need to get a big head. This business'll grind you down. About the time you think you're hittin' it outta the park, you'll get a call from somebody who says you're a complete idiot 'cause you misspelled some third cousin's name in yesterday's obituary."

Will nodded.

"Then you'll go to lunch and the sewer commissioner will get in your face like a pit bull 'cause you got the budget numbers all wrong on his new project.

"You'll need the patience of Job and the hide of a rhino to survive. And remember, you're paid to be accurate and interesting, but we're not talkin' about sittin' by a babbling brook and comin' up with flowery things to say. And if you miss deadlines and screw up stories, your job and the paper's credibility are on the line. You hear what I'm sayin'?"

"Yes sir. I understand."

Even though it was an unusual place for a date, it became one of their favorite spots. It took Ginny awhile to warm up to the old cemetery as a good picnic site – and it was certainly not one she'd want to mention to anybody. But it was beautiful.

Will drove them down the long winding East Campus Road, across the tracks and in full view of Sanford Stadium sat 100 acres of bucolic bliss – the Oconee Cemetery.

The more Ginny visited, the more she appreciated this picturesque acreage with its rolling hills and century old

trees. Some say to learn the history of a place, visit its cemetery and this site was loaded with Georgia history. Here was
the final resting place of university presidents, prominent
judges, a bunch of congressmen, veterans of all wars, and
two governors. But about the time Will got to the fourth
and final general, Ginny was battle-weary herself and *very*
hungry.

As they finished lunch, Will went on about other notable residents – Dr. Crawford Long, a pioneer in using
anesthesia – and his UGA roommate, Alexander Stephens,
a renowned constitutional scholar along with Dr. Lorenzo
Moss, who'd developed some kind of system for classifying
blood.

They wandered over to a section designated as "Bulldog
Haven" where Coach Wally Butts, the two-time nation-
al championship winner, was interred along with other
Bulldawg stars.

The couple strolled hand in hand, taking in deep
breaths of jasmine as they listened to the gentle mur-
muring of the river and talked about shaping their own
legacy – together.

Will liked the fast pace of newspaper work and he especially enjoyed the people he met and telling their stories. It
was the kind of work he was wired for. The past few weeks of
real world experience gave him confidence that out there
somewhere was a job for him which could bring in enough
money to support himself – and maybe someone else.

A serious career talk with Mr. Reynolds had given Will
more direction and insights into the job market – where to
start looking, what to expect and how to get your foot in the
door.

"Will, if you keep this up, I feel sure you'll get picked up by a good paper – maybe a mid-size outfit and then shoot for the AJC. Remember, as much as you need a job, they also need talent. But don't forget the old 99 percent perspiration thing," Reynolds advised. "Good writing is a gift, but one that *you* have to develop."

With things on the upswing, Will got up the nerve to mention his plans to Ginny.

"So, how would you feel about living in Savannah?"

"I dunno, why?"

"I'm thinkin' about the Savannah Morning News. It's a reach for a rookie, but it'd be a great first job."

"It's a bigger paper, right? Think you've got a chance?"

"Well, I'm on a pretty good roll and Mr. Reynolds knows the managing editor there. He says to go for it. And any feature writer would love to be in a historic town with colorful people around every corner. There's no end to 'em in that city."

"I love Savannah – artsy, quaint and has a very cool vibe. And near the beach."

A TOWN TURNED UPSIDE DOWN

As more and more clients witnessed Jack Marshall's bizarre behavior, their suspicions ballooned. There were enough red flags to prompt an investigation by federal regulators who poured over Jack's books going back several months. Nothing added up and they came to an alarming conclusion.

Jack had started out using legitimate investment strategies that paid off handsomely, but he kept raising the stakes. He believed that more risk always meant higher returns.

Then one day, he rolled the dice with a huge chunk of his clients' money. He lost it all, but would never be able to admit making such a reckless move. Volatility was one thing, but creating a massive loss was unthinkable. And if this got out, clients would leave in droves.

But Jack didn't worry; he'd fix it one way or the other. He'd tweak the statements just this once and buy himself more time. Sure it was hazardous, deceitful and downright illegal – but if you can't take the heat, get out of the kitchen. Besides, no one was looking and in the end, it would all work out – nothing more than a bump in the road.

By now, he'd spent enough time on damage control and it was time to get on with the money making. Set back or not, Marshall knew he had *the touch*, so he climbed out even further on the limb.

Wrong again. The stock market plummeted and he lost a truckload this go round. Things were spiraling out of control and the business Marshall had built from the ground up was now in serious jeopardy. But he couldn't let clients know the truth, so month after month he falsified statements to show big returns on money that simply wasn't there and, before he knew it, he'd jumped into full Ponzi mode.

When the time came for Sonny to withdraw his funds, the well was dry.

The Feds promptly shut down Marshall Wealth Management, froze his accounts and indicted Jack on multiple counts of fraud. The number of counts filed against him added up to a very serious charge.

At first, Will was horrified and wondered if it was for real. But as the afternoon wore on, more information came into the news desk and dispelled any hope that the initial report had been a rumor. Stunned clients anxiously waited for word about their accounts while authorities kept busy unraveling Marshall's records.

Mr. Beck called Will into his office.

"Close the door and listen up.

"We've got this thing brewing about Jack Marshall. He's just been indicted by the Feds. This thing's gonna rock the town – he's a high profile guy with a very long client list. This is huge and I'm afraid it could be devastating to a lot of people. We're puttin' together a team to cover every angle of it. Our senior guy's gonna head it up and you'll report directly to him, so follow his lead. I want you in that courtroom every day gettin' the facts as this thing unfolds. No cute stuff. Just the basic nuts and bolts of the deliberations. And I'm banking on your hometown connections to get some side stories.

"Think you can handle that?"

"Well…"

"Well, what?"

"Well, I'm really a feature writer."

"So I'll let you in on something. Here in the real world, you're whatever kind of writer I say you are. Features are fluff and fillers – this is a *news*paper. Do you really think people want to read about a little old lady's garden when a crime of this magnitude's shaking the town?"

Will got the message.

"OK, I'm glad you're up for it. Grab your stuff and sign in with the court clerk and get up to speed on this case."

The Trial

Will had passed by the large, columned building for years but never gave it much thought. He'd probably heard somewhere along the way that it was the federal courthouse – one of those innocuous, official looking structures where some sort of government business occurs – likely the site of necessary, yet uninspiring nine to five drudgery. But that was hardly the case today at the Federal Building on East Hancock as the trial of one of Athens's most well-known citizens began.

As he entered the imposing granite building, Will wondered what on earth he was doing in a place like this. The capacity crowd clustered close together in the section reserved for the public. Everyone quieted down when the judge emerged in a black robe, took his place behind the high bench and went over the rules for the proceedings. The 12 jurors were ordinary folk, a good cross section of the populace – one was a plumber – a middle school teacher, a homemaker, and an insurance agent – about the kind of mix you'd expect.

The judge gaveled the United States District Court into session. Will couldn't resist glancing at a hunched over Jack Marshall in the defendant's chair. But what Marshall may have lost in swagger, his attorney had in spades.

Marshall had secured the services of a high-powered defense lawyer from Atlanta. Tanner Culverson was an old style Southern lawyer given to the gift of gab with high flown rhetoric that flowed as smoothly as a lava lamp. He'd represented a number of dubious characters in his 30 years and still loved legal maneuvering and out-foxing the other guy as much as ever.

Then Culverson met *Miss* Katherine Overstreet – the petite, young prosecutor assigned to the case. *This is who they're putting up against me?* He laughed to himself and mentally chalked up an easy win. His assistant smiled when Culverson whispered that the "the *girl* looks like someone my daughter would bring home from cheerleading camp" and certainly not like a serious contender in the courtroom. *This should be a breeze.* Besides, part of his genius was sizing up prosecutors and jurors. His take on Overstreet was that she'd watched a lot of "Perry Mason" as a kid, stumbled into law school and filled an affirmative action slot for the feds.

But the defense didn't realize they were up against a formidable adversary. Overstreet was relentless in pursuing the truth. Still, Culverson couldn't believe that a prosecutor, whose most prominent feature was her long stylish hair, would be a threat at all. What he failed to see was her sharp intellect and unquenchable sense of justice. And it didn't take him long to realize that Overstreet wasn't bamboozled by defense attorneys who tried to schmooze a jury or bury their opponents in technicalities. She cut through specious arguments like a brand new Veg-Matic. Culverson soon understood how she'd earned the nickname "Genghis Kate."

After the judge completed his instructions, the prosecution and defense gave their opening statements and the two attorneys ripped into each other like a couple of bantam roasters in an illegal cock fight.

"Now, I'll suggest to Katherine – or is it *Kate* – that she needs to step back and look at this in its full context. You all know very well with the multitude of state and federal regulations and convoluted rules that it's all too easy to get *carried away* with the daunting task of complying to every little jot and tittle of complicated accounting methods. There's always going to be *occasional* minor inconsistences in recording financial transactions even under the best of circumstances," Culverson claimed.

"Oh, I hardly think Jack Marshall *got carried* away at all with accurate accounting, the problem here is that he did get *carried away* with *carrying away* the life savings of so many citizens of Clarke County who trusted this Pied Piper! But I do appreciate Mr. Culverson's use of such an apt term. And the only thing that is possibly *convoluted* is his blatant patronizing defense of the man who maliciously swindled innocent citizens. He was not 'occasionally inconsistent in recording financial transactions' but just plain lied and outright stole their hard earned money that he'd supposedly invested. I mean *really*, has the defense not reviewed the evidence? His skyrocketing returns looked like something NASA launched into orbit. They were totally preposterous and he *knew* full well how much these good people stood to lose because of his unconscionable actions," Overstreet argued.

Then they grilled the prosecution's first witness and incited him with so many leading remarks that the judge had a hard time keeping up, but eventually reined in both attorneys with repeated warnings and much gavel pounding.

The judge finally called a recess. Will had never endured anything so intense. As he hurried out of the courtroom with the others, he thought he was done for the day. But he wasn't.

As soon as Will reached the sidewalk, a woman he'd never met, grabbed him. Through heavy sobs, she pleaded.

"I know you're just a reporter, but *you've got to* explain what really happened. How many people he's hurt. We've lost everything. "

Will's heart sank.

As the days went on, the prosecution produced an abundance of witnesses and it was very hard for everyone to hear their tragic stories.

The forensic accountant's work was "a cinch," he said. It was clearly a case of falsified client statements and empty accounts. Almost all of the money was gone. Marshall's statements were a total sham.

Culverson didn't have a lot to work with in defending his client. His main argument was the standard "buyers beware" warning along with the responsibility to "weigh the risk of any investment. Returns are never guaranteed." Not much to go on, so he fluffed it up with his very best song and dance routine, slathering on as much charm as he could muster as he strode from judge to jury and returned to a beleaguered Jack Marshall, all in a manner worthy of F. Lee Bailey. He inwardly hoped for a "Hail Mary," possibly from digging up an obscure legal loophole or using Jack's old cronies to pull some backroom shenanigans.

It had been a long time since the citizens of Athens had been this upset about a trial. They were shocked that one of their own had committed such egregious crimes against friends and neighbors. Everyone had strong opinions on the Marshall case and no one was holding back. But deciphering *what* people thought and *why* proved to be futile. Will couldn't understand why he hardly met anyone who still had an open mind. No one wanted to consider the evidence – they'd already decided on a verdict and that was that.

Small town charm is real. "Green Acres" and "The Waltons" captured the decency of everyday people. But when a crisis comes, it's like Marvin Gaye's "I Heard it Through the Grapevine" – rumors run rampant. You can see how the old West tales of "skip the trial and just hang 'em" really happened. And there were a number of people right here in Athens who were ready to forego due process and erect the gallows.

Everywhere Will went, he was besieged with various disgruntled people. Most, of course, were outraged at Marshall and simply wanted justice carried out – the guilty punished and wrongs righted – they pressed Will to "hit him hard."

But a few were wary of the young reporter's relationship to the accused and questioned his objectivity. Besides, what kind of person would hang around with a guy like Jack Marshall? More and more people recognized him as one of the reporters for the paper and Will never knew when an offhand remark would turn confrontational.

The stares from the guys at the lunch counter cut through him so he hurried to finish his sandwich and get out of there. But before he made it to the door, he was cornered.

"So, go ahead and tell us just how in the world you can be fair when you're the guy's friend."

"I hardly knew him and if he did half the things they say he did, I hope he goes to jail. Guess we'll see what happens," Will said.

When evening came, Will retreated to his apartment. At least, he'd be out of the crossfire for a while. He called Ginny and explained that he wasn't much in a mood to go out – he hoped she didn't mind. She brought over his favorite pizza from Steverinoe's but Will only ate a few bites.

"Tough day, huh?" Ginny asked.

"Yeah and I didn't want this assignment in the first place."

"It's gotta be weird – I mean since you know him and all."

"That's an understatement. Sure he was over the top, but I never thought he'd do something like this," Will said.

"It's gotta blow your mind."

"Yeah and it's pretty disgusting. To think he acted like nothing was happening while he was robbing people blind. That's about as cold as it gets."

"Nobody can really explain something like this," she said.

Will realized that all he'd done lately was dump his problems on Ginny and now he was pretty embarrassed that he'd leaned on her so much. But when he looked into her soft, brown eyes, he saw nothing but a sweet concern. *She really is a kind soul,* he thought.

Will composed himself. "Well enough about that." They flipped on a mindless sit-com and enjoyed a quiet evening together.

August Jam

Finally, Saturday came. Hanging out with John was a welcomed relief from the stress of the trial. It'd been a while since Will had seen his friend, maybe because they were frightfully close to all that grown-up responsibility they'd joked about.

Will really wanted to hear about August Jam. On a steamy August weekend, the Charlotte Motor Speedway in

North Carolina overflowed with rock stars instead of racing cars and John was right in the middle of the action. With his growing reputation as a go-to guy for technical set-ups, John worked behind the scenes, rubbing elbows with the likes of The Allman Brothers and The Marshall Tucker Band – and some of the biggest names in rock. Working with the production crew, his team had pushed the limits in pulling off the massive, two day outdoor concert.

"Man it was outta sight. You shoulda seen all the equipment Emerson, Lake and Palmer brought in. Somebody said it was 36 tons." John shook his head and laughed. "It was all kinds of lights, oscillators and lifts. Stuff I'd never seen before. Those guys are cybernetic crazy, but when it came together, it was totally awesome.

It was pure chaos out there. Nobody cared if they had tickets – the crowd just stampeded in. They tore down fences and rushed the infield. Then it poured and turned the place into a giant mud pit. But, man, they just kept rockin'."

"Wow, bet you'll never forget it," Will said.

"And I got to work with the coolest gear. I'm talkin' quality stuff that you don't think about. It'll blow your mind."

John had worked 14 hours days, coordinating the power to amps and lights and the sound system from bunches of cable feeds from the grid and others from generators hauled in on trucks. He'd trekked through mud and mobs of partiers to get the job done and stretched himself to the max. And when it came off without a glitch, John was one happy guy.

Will asked, "So what you gonna do now?"

John settled into a chair. "Well, I told you about Clinton's offer."

"Yeah. Pretty cool."

"I've thought it about it a lot, and I don't think I'm gonna tour with him, at least for now."

"You're kiddin' me?"

"I'd just be at the bottom of the heap, one of the fill-in guys tryin' to get somewhere," John said.

"But that's what you've always wanted."

"Yeah, but things change. I figure if I stay here, I can make good steady money doin' tech stuff. Plenty of bands need that kinda thing. And I'm really into it."

"Makes sense, but what about your music?"

"I'll still play. And it might keep it fun if I'm not tryin' to make a livin' at it."

"I keep thinkin' about Gary. Man, he's gonna need all the help he can get. The kid's gonna go somewhere but he won't have much of a chance without enough money. You oughta see him – he works like crazy, studyin' all the time and still baggin' groceries at Bell's."

"That's cool, John. Gotta hand it to ya, you're really steppin' up."

"Will, its Ed, called to see how you're doin'. Sounds like you've got a front row seat for the drama down there."

"Hey man, great to hear your voice. Yeah it's wild – for Athens. We're not use to this sort of thing."

"I've been following the trial. Dad calls and sends me clippings of your articles. It's weird that you actually knew the guy," Ed said.

"Yeah, and I was totally shocked, man. I mean I had absolutely *no* idea what he was up to. Guess nobody else did either – that's the problem. How's it goin' in the big city?"

"It's great, man. But you wouldn't believe the pace. It never stops and you're never finished. A lot to learn. Big stories are always goin' down and you may never find out all you need to know. You just have to sort out what you have and write it up fast. I'm still here at the desk, finishing up before I head home," Ed said.

Will looked at the clock – 9 pm.

"I hear ya. The trial's nothing like stuff up there, but it's still pretty intense."

"Yeah, things get magnified in a smaller place," Ed said.

"I'm startin' to wonder if this thing'll ever end," Will said.

Ed paused. "Well, the thing is, for some folks, it won't."

"And that's the terrible truth. I see 'em every day and it really gets to you."

"You'll get through it, man. Just hang tough. Hey, last week, I was in the main news room when Woodward briefed the staff on the Watergate trials. Nixon may be gone but John Mitchell and Halderman are about to see some justice. It was very cool and you know there's record enrollment in J schools now. People wanna do what you're doing."

Even though President Nixon had resigned in August, the national soap opera continued with no foreseeable end. The TV monitors in the J School and the student center showed breaking news and developments on Watergate and profs used the latest reports to promote lively discussions in the classroom.

The congressional hearing directed by the unflappable trial judge John J. Sirica and members of a Senate investigating committee finally got to the bottom of the tangled web of deceit that spun out of the President's inner circle. The hours of tape recordings from the botched spying efforts were disturbing. And on top of that nobody had heard a President sound so "earthy" and "non-presidential" and, in some instances, downright petty and paranoid. The tapes revealed Nixon's inner most thoughts and explained his Machiavellian schemes – schemes carried out by blindly loyal aides.

The scandal had been going on since May 1972 when surrogates from Nixon's Committee to Re-Elect the President (sarcastically referred to as CREEP) broke into the Democratic National Committee's Watergate offices and stole copies of secret documents, then bugged the phones.

The Watergate travesty intensified the already cynical view of the country's political leadership. Finally, in response to the cover up, Nixon's Press Secretary, Ron Ziglar, issued an obtuse statement smothered in government-speak that captured the essence of the whole sad affair: "This is now the operative statement, all previous statements are inoperative."

⟩⟨⟩

The trial was a slow to slog to who knows where. It's one thing to study "due process" in a civics class, but sitting through the daily courtroom grind was as numbing as listening to elevator music.

The prosecution had built a very strong case. And all Culverson could do was continue his empty, blustery talk that he hoped would beguile and confuse the jury. And then, from under some rock somewhere, he'd dredged up a character witness or two, but their testimony didn't amount to much.

Court adjourned until next morning. Will felt like a lightning rod and couldn't figure out why people wanted to unload on him.

The guy marching towards him was one of Marshall's closest friends. They'd worked together in their early years after college. Lucky for this guy – he handled his own investments and had kept his assets safely out of Marshall's reach. To him, Marshall was the fun guy, the party guy. And that's the image he held on to. The man was convinced of Marshall's innocence and had concocted a theory that he'd been "set up" by people who were jealous of his friend's success – a scapegoat of some nameless, faceless entity.

He got right in Will's face. "Who do you think you are trashing a man like Marshall? You better remember one thing. If you don't back off, I'll see to it that you never get a job in this state.

"You journalists are all alike; you tear people down and just make up things to suit yourself.

"Why don't you think about the years he was on the Chamber and how he worked with United Way?

"But you don't care. The National Inquirer's about all you're good for."

Even though Marshall only had a handful of supporters, they were the ones who were nasty and the most aggressive.

Whenever Will was out, he'd come to expect tearful out-pourings or a searing remark or two.

Even Mr. Duncan at the Five Points bakery, a man Will had known all his life, spouted off when he picked up some donuts for the newsroom. Marshall had been a loyal customer and the baker refused to consider the possibility that he was anything but "a really nice guy who bought my donuts, asked about my family and tipped generously."

But the victims were the most troubling thing about the whole the situation. He'd heard too many stories of devastating losses – people losing their kid's college fund or money saved for old age. All because of a man they trusted but who turned out to be nothing more than a common thief and a con.

It was ironic that Will Andrews was caught up in the town turbulence. He'd never been one to stir things up. There were of plenty crusading martyr-types around to do that. But not Will. He was more of a people pleaser and sometimes just a plain coward. He'd much rather make folks laugh than make waves. It baffled him that people didn't understand that he was only a low-level intern *reporting* the news, not *making* it.

At this point, he was simply sick of the whole mess. But he reminded himself over and over that conveying the victims pitiful plight to readers did, in fact, serve justice in some small measure. It was the least he could do.

The South's Oldest Football Rivalry
The streets of Athens overflowed with people as Will walked into the Banner Herald office. He was so immersed in his work that he didn't even realize it was game day. That was

bad enough but then he saw folks in orange and blue. *The Auburn game. I'm missing the Auburn game.*

He stared at the stack of notes compiled from the week's testimonies. Sifting through the papers would yield his next article but the information also stirred up troubling images. On Wednesday, Mary Hanes was sworn in. She sobbed as she told the court how her losses had left her life in shambles. She explained the rapid progression of her sister's disease which substantially added to their expenses – expenses she thought she'd prepared for now mounted up as debt. Will hardly recognized the frail woman she'd become.

He summarized the awful revelations from the Federal Building that had come to light. He finished the article, picked up some food and headed home in time for the kick-off. Today, it'd just be him and a radio and Munson. Even if someone handed him tickets to the game, he just wanted to be alone.

Senior year. How did things get so serious? Wasn't it supposed to be the best year of all?

He turned on WRFC and tried to forget the trial for a couple of hours.

Munson's voice was almost as soothing as hearing his Mom's when he was a boy.

"Dawg fans, we're gonna have a real nail-biter of a game today! Those tenacious Tigers from Auburn are going up against our beloved battling Bulldawgs in the South's oldest rivalry – it goes all the way back to 1892 when they played in Piedmont Park in Atlanta – and today, we have another memory maker taking place right here Between the Hedges... Fans, get the picture. Look at your radio dial – to the right are our Bulldawgs lined up in their silver britches ready to receive the ball from the Tigers who are on the left of your dial... They won the coin toss and have elected to kick the ball to us...

"We've got to come out of the gate like Secretariat on Derby day and keep that breakneck pace going on offense by hittin' 'em with everything we've got ... *IF* we let up – they're gonna pounce on us and we'll be checking into "Heartbreak Hotel"... Whatdaya got, Loran?"

"Larry, I'm down here on the sidelines and the coaches are ready and the players are pumped up...Coach Dooley just told the players the story of the first Auburn – Georgia game when the Tigers mauled Georgia. You'll also remember that we were beaten so badly, they decided to get rid of the mascot which, in those days, was a goat. Larry, you know how the legend goes – they say they even barbequed the poor creature and finished him off at dinner that night. And after the history lesson, the Coach told the boys we just can't let up today. We have to play like true Bulldawgs."

It didn't take long for Will to get into the game, but the Dawgs struggled early on which didn't help his sagging spirits. The team was down at the half and he doubted he'd be hearing the chapel bell tonight. Will thought back to the care-free days of lining up with other freshmen and ringing the bell all night after a win.

Even though the Dawgs lost, fans milled around downtown, pointing out various sights and reminiscing about days gone by. The defeat may have dropped the party mode down a notch or two, but for most alums, just being back on campus was more than enough reason to celebrate. "That sweet soul music" and Southern rock flowed from all quarters and went on well into the night. Trial or no trial – it was still fall in Athens.

LIFE GOES ON

Will rounded the courthouse block for the *fourth* time desperately hoping for a prized parking spot. Finally, the seas parted and he landed one on Clayton Street right in front of the imposing double-barreled cannon. Will laughed and allowed himself a momentary diversion as he thought about the bizarre artillery piece.

The cannon was one of a kind and preserved more as a whimsical tribute to a failed weapon of mass destruction. Its inventors got an A for effort but an F for execution. The problem was that the cannon barrels weren't properly synchronized. (Where were those Georgia Tech engineers when we needed them?) The cannon balls were chained together, but when the cannon fired, they never left the barrels at the same time. Needless to say, this created more danger for the soldiers shooting it than for the enemy. Years later, the cannon, which was forged at the Athens foundry, was donated to the city and given a prominent resting place as an odd remembrance of the Civil War. The ominous looking cannon was strategically placed on a grassy mound of dirt, in front of city hall – pointed due North – ready to greet any "invaders" who may have had a notion of venturing into Clarke County.

For a brief moment, Will thought of re-telling the old cannon story to a new audience, but then realized it would have to wait. The only thing to write about now was the trial. Athens was under siege itself and nothing else seemed to matter yet story ideas still popped into Will's head.

Just yesterday, he'd seen the Newton sisters out shopping at Bell's. "Preparing for their garden club meeting." They told Will they'd be serving ambrosia, finger sandwiches and, of course, home-made cheese straws. The ladies looked like they'd stepped straight out of a Jane Austen novel and ever remained the model of old-fashioned propriety. The two sisters were among the first female graduates of UGA, and now in their 70s, were as lively as ever and always busy with their community work. The aging spinsters still lived in their old Victorian house on Prince Avenue where time stood still and everything was perpetually prim and proper. They always addressed each other formally, Miss Catherine laid out the club's agenda for the meeting as Sister Emily nodded in agreement. Since Will was backed up against a bin of cabbages, with no polite means of escape, he was forced to hear every detail.

Another good story, worthy of a fresh re-write. But it was just not the time.

━━━╬━━━

Another week of long days in court had come and gone and Will had missed yet another football game. But he still enjoyed the old fall ritual – walking among devoted fans after another hard fought battle. He also took solace in the two tickets he had for the big Tech game.

Among the alums and students, Will caught a glimpse of a familiar figure in the crowd. He wasn't sure, but it looked a lot like Ronnie and it suddenly occurred to him that he hadn't seen the guy in months.

Will was astonished as he moved closer and saw how rough his old friend looked. Ronnie had been one of the coolest guys on campus, always out and about in his polished Weejin loafers and pressed Oxford shirt. But now he looked like he'd just rolled out of bed and struggled to steady himself as he tottered down the sidewalk.

In any college town, it was all too easy to fall into the "eternal sophomore" trap – aimless guys stringing their lives together with one party after the other, trying desperately to hang on to a world that's passed them by.

Sortin' It Out

The trial was moving along at a snail's pace. Surely, it would end soon, but today was a particularly somber day and the misty gray morning mirrored Will's frame of mind. Even so, it was welcomed relief from a night of fitful dreams. Crazy things like: Marshall laughing at him as he fell off a cliff or friends living in squalor. Writing about the mechanics of the trial wasn't so difficult, but all the fallout had wormed its way into his psyche.

Throughout the proceedings Marshall sat with his head down or stared straight ahead. Once in a while, he turned and looked around the room. The few times their eyes met, a chill ran down Will's spine.

Tonight, he didn't even want to see Ginny. Will knew he'd asked too much of her in recent weeks and the last thing he wanted to do was bring her down again. She'd amazed Will with her unwavering support and displayed a logic and perspective well beyond her years. He'd never forget how she'd weathered this difficult time right by his side.

Ginny hated to think of him all alone and insisted on dropping by with take-out and hoped Will would talk, hash out some things. It would be good for him. But after a while, they realized they were only going in circles. There were just no easy answers to this dismal state of affairs and they were left hoping they'd at least figure out how to deal with the part that touched their lives.

Ginny was sympathetic – sympathetic enough not to let Will sink into discouragement. They both knew that it's a lot easier to avoid a rut than to climb out of it once you're sucked in.

She sat down, in front of Will, eye to eye. "Remember Will – 'We walk by faith and not by sight.' I know you know that."

"Yeah, I do."

She spoke in a gentle but no nonsense tone.

"Okay then. You need to pull yourself together and get going on whatever it is you should be doing now."

She stood up, kissed him and left.

Will was taken back. He wanted to be coddled, but got a kick in the pants instead. He thought about Ginny's good advice and shook it off. She'd given it to him straight and Will reluctantly admitted that that's exactly what he needed.

＝≼╂╀≽＝

Sonny and Jack had been big buddies in chasing big money, but even Sonny couldn't believe what Jack had done. He'd seen his friend cut a few corners now and then – who didn't? But outright fraud? And now it was personal – Sonny was ruined.

The guy he'd trusted to manage his hard-earned wealth had lost it all. Those ridiculous numbers showing up on his statements month after month were nothing but smoke and mirrors. At first, it only looked like a business setback, a missed opportunity, but when his accountant tallied up his assets against what he owed suppliers and the bank, the losses were staggering.

Soon the creditors came. They took the business, and then his house. And as everything was swept away, his wife walked out with the kids. His brother's predicament wasn't much better and he doubted he could ever forgive Sonny for getting them mixed up with Jack Marshall in the first place.

It was hard to believe, but Sonny Butler was back to pounding nails as a day laborer. With his meager wages he found a small house to rent on the outskirts of town – the kind of house he would have once leveled in a heartbeat.

Mary Hanes had always had a keen sense of justice and, day and night, she fiercely hoped that Jack Marshall would get a strong dose of it. Partly, she blamed herself for trusting a guy like him. She should have known better. He was simply too good to be true. Mary Hanes had always been wary of those types, but now when it really mattered, she'd fallen for a scam. *Couldn't he at least have chosen his victims better?* She asked herself these questions over and over as she closely followed the trial in the newspaper.

Will had to go see her. He needed to explain things face to face, like his friendship with Marshall and, most of all, to tell her how very sorry he was.

He walked into the small house, shaky, still searching for the right words. Mary Hanes sat limp and subdued on the sofa. "So how do you think the trial's going? I've read the printed version – now tell me what's *really* going on."

"It's moving along. The prosecution's strong and definitely convincing the jury."

Will swallowed hard, "I'm so sorry. I had no idea he was the kind of person who'd do such terrible things to people."

Mary Hanes stroked the terrier. "Oh, I know, Will. You're certainly not the only one he fooled."

He had no glib words of comfort for her; nothing he could say would make Mary Hanes feel any better.

Her sister called from the bedroom, she needed help getting up. Will left.

Words of Wisdom
When Will made his way through the crowd out front for another day of testimony, he came across Dean Tate.

"Tough going, Will. There's nothing much harder than being betrayed by a friend," Tate said.

"It's pretty awful. He seemed like a nice enough guy and I can't even begin to understand it all," Will said.

"Well, there are some real Jekyll and Hydes out there. You have to keep your eyes open," Tate said.

"And somehow I'm way closer to the whole sordid thing than I want to be," Will said.

"Oh, I know. Believe me. I'm very familiar with being in the middle of a firestorm."

Will shook his head. All he'd ever seen before was the good-natured dean, but now it dawned on him that the man had dealt with more than his share of problems. It must have been hard to shoulder all the responsibility as Dean of Students through the years. Will knew of times he'd taken a stand on tough issues and had to battle it out with some very difficult people.

"Want some advice?

"Sure."

"Keep your perspective. Remember it's not about you. Don't let what people think get to you. Sure it's no fun, but the newspaper has a big part in the work of justice. And your job is to inform people. *Anyone* who learns *anything* from this mess will undoubtedly be better off. And it's a comfort to the victims to know that people care. So stand tall and stick to the big picture, my boy."

Dean Tate's words were even more deliberate now. No jokes, homespun anecdotes or delightful ramblings. He was deadly serious as he looked Will in the eye.

"I'll tell you, Will, what I do know for certain. This world is full of a vast amount of good and beauty, but evil's always on the prowl. And there'll be troubles along the way. Things we can't explain. But know this – it's all under the control of the Almighty."

Tom

About the only person in town that Will hadn't talked to these past weeks was Tom – and he was about the *last* person he wanted to see. Not that he thought any less of Tom Marshall but he just didn't know what to say.

He walked up to the courthouse and there they were, face to face, on the front steps.

Tom put out his hand. "Hey, Will."

For a moment, Will was speechless.

"I know. No one knows what to say," Tom said.

Will groped for words. "I'm sorry, Tom. I'm sorry about the whole awful thing. And I never wanted to write about it….."

Tom interrupted. "You had to, man, it's your job. Dad's the one who screwed up – big time. He put us all in this mess. I still can't believe it. And I'm sure I'll never forget all the people he's hurt. I just wish I could do something to help."

It had been excruciating for Tom to sit through the trial. But he'd done it. Will had watched him from a distance with profound sympathy.

"It's been a real nightmare. And I dunno what to do. One minute it's all I can do not to write him off; the next minute I feel sorry for him. Have you seen him? He's pitiful. But he's still my dad. I don't think I can just turn my back on him."

Tom's searing pain poured out as he talked, yet Will knew that neither he nor anyone else could truly understand the depths of his agony and how he'd begin to cope.

"Yeah, I have to remind myself a hundred times a day that I'm not my dad. I certainly didn't steal anybody's money and I had absolutely no clue what was going on."

Even with all the finger pointing, *no one* blamed Tom. Most folks felt sorry for the young man who was caught up in his dad's prolonged public humiliation.

And by now, everyone knew Tom's story. In truth, he was nothing like his father. And if anyone had the inner strength to weather a thing like this, it was Tom Marshall.

Despite his dad's bluster about Tom joining Marshall Wealth Management and growing the firm even bigger, Tom was on a different path. He'd gone to Georgia as a privileged kid, pledged a top fraternity yet was acutely aware of a gnawing dissatisfaction in his soul. He was drawn to many of the late night bull sessions in the frat house and that's where he found a couple of guys who actually had something worthwhile to say. After a number of heavy discussions, Tom had what most would call a spiritual awakening. So much so, that he was never the same. Will identified.

"I don't know how you do it. I couldn't hold up under something like this," Will said.

"It's crazy. Some days, it's all I can do to just get outta bed. I've done a ton of thinkin' – had to. I couldn't have made it without my friends. They stuck around and made sure I kept my sanity. My pastor's also been there for me. We've talked for hours and he's given me really good advice."

"So whatda ya think you'll do now?"

"Well, I'm sure I'll be tryin' to figure this thing out for a long time. But first, I need to take care of Mom."

"Yeah."

"There's so much to sort out. She's lost the house, so I'm movin' her up to Atlanta to live with my sister – she needs to get outta Athens anyway."

The Mural

Even though senior panic lurked in the back of Will's mind – it had to stay there. There was simply no time for it. He had to keep his head down and ride this thing out. But soon he'd graduate and need a job and a clear career path. And until that was nailed down, what did he have to offer Ginny?

Despite what the Rolling Stones claimed, time was not on Will's side. Journalism jobs were few and far between and the pay was low – scratch that – downright pathetic. Plus, even to get your foot in the door, you had to know somebody. And you'd better be willing to go above and beyond and have a solid internship and a sack full of impressive clippings. These days, Will had no way to gauge his work at the paper. Reader opinion ran the gamut.

After another long session, it was time to blow off some steam. The first hint of fall was in the air so he jogged over to his old stomping grounds – the North campus quad.

He strolled around for a while and wandered into Brooks Hall – a place on campus he'd often returned to since he was a boy and for good reason. He looked up at the old mural that covered the wall. His father had painted it back in the '40s as his Master's thesis for an art degree and it told the story of "The First Amendment." Even though a great many things had changed – his dad shifted to history, the journalism department moved and the expanding business school took over Brooks Hall – the mural remained as a tribute to the power of the pen.

The men and events portrayed on the walls had shaped and protected our democracy's freedom of speech and freedom of the press. Jefferson, Benjamin Franklin, Pulitzer and others.

Will recalled their words:

"If I had to make the choice between having a free government vs a free press, I would choose a free press." Thomas Jefferson.

"No government ought to be without censors; and where the press is free no one ever will." Thomas Jefferson.

"Put it to them *truthfully* so they will be guided by the light, *clearly* so they can understand it, and *picturesquely* so they will remember it." Joseph Pulitzer.

The individuals memorialized on the mural had paid a high price for "speaking truth to power." But he wondered: *Are their words just dusty platitudes from history, stuff you learn in classrooms – or are they true in the real world?*

After all, Will's struggle was, in fact, pretty puny. He certainly wasn't out to be the next Woodward or Bernstein. All he was doing was covering a local trial and trying to handle it like a grown-up.

The image of the Arch in the upper corner of the mural caught his eye and he noticed another quote, inscribed at the top. Displayed in a half circle were the words from the Bible: "You shall know the truth and the truth will set you free."

He paused. His answer was right before him.

The Verdict

It was finally going to be over. The judge's gavel would come down one last time and a verdict would be rendered.

Will knew life would go on but then again he wasn't exactly sure what *going on* meant for himself or for the town – how they'd recover and deal with the lingering scars.

The closing arguments were succinct and had gone as expected. No last minute surprises. Kathleen summed up the very damning evidence crisply and methodically laid out the facts of Marshall's devious plan to defraud his investors.

Culverson merely rehashed the same threadbare arguments he'd presented throughout the trial. He fervently insisted that his client was innocent using his most flamboyant flourishes to sway the jury. Yet his endless talk of "accounting errors and lapses in judgment" rang hollow. No amount of suspender snapping, colorful metaphors and dramatic antics could outweigh the overwhelming facts.

Remarkably, the jury had only taken an afternoon to deliberate and this morning they'd reconvene. The tension in the room was palpable as the judge asked if they'd reached a verdict.

"We have your Honor. We, the jury, unanimously find the defendant, John Stephen Marshall guilty." The jury foreman then answered the same to every count of fraud.

Boisterous cheers erupted in the courtroom as Marshall hung his head and sighed.

The judge gaveled the court to order and sentenced Marshall to serve time and mandated that restitution be made, which in reality wouldn't amount to much.

Court was adjourned. Will jumped from his seat and hurried to the back hallway he'd been using to slip out of the building and avoid conversation.

He turned a corner and right before him stood Jack Marshall, handcuffed and guarded by a deputy. The prisoner stood at an elevator that would take him down to a sheriff's van, waiting to transport him to the Federal Penitentiary in East Atlanta.

Will froze as their eyes locked. With his cockiness stripped away, the feeble man mustered one last gasp of defiance. Will watched an eerie smirk come over his face. "Hey Will, a friend always has your back. Guess you forgot that."

If there was a playbook on how to recover from a collective kick in the gut like this scandal, no one in Athens had found it yet.

But slowly, the healing began. Townsfolk gradually picked up their lives, and as Dean Tate used to say, "Put one foot in front of the other."

After a while, conversations in the community didn't focus on the trial anymore. And even though it was a lackluster season, it didn't take long for football to take center stage again.

Will went back to his feature writing. And for a nice change of pace, he'd done a piece on Mr. Reynolds and his summer tutoring program that readers really enjoyed. The story profiled several young students who'd made big improvements. The community efforts had paid off. Finally, something uplifting to write about.

Will realized that his future plans, or anyone else's for that matter, weren't a sure thing. But he did his part by working hard and worrying less.

It was time to salvage what was left of his senior year and Ginny made that very easy to do. He introduced her to more of his friends and stood back and watched them fall in love with her just as he had.

It was great having Ed home over Thanksgiving and he'd come up with a practical idea for the guys to help each other sort through their accumulated junk. A good move before graduation. "Get a jump start," Ed said.

The project turned into more of an archeological dig as they uncovered layer after layer of *stuff* – items they'd written off as long gone now surfaced in a friend's pile. Like Will's old tennis shoes from Mrvos's class (which explained the mystery of the foul smell). Then they unearthed John's glow-in-the-dark Frisbee from freshman orientation and his faded "Never Trust the Man" T-shirt. Near the bottom, the guys discovered one of Ed's old prom pictures and had a good laugh at the gangly kid sporting an iridescent blue carnation – a blue not found anywhere in nature but dyed to match the color of his date's dress.

They even went so far as to pare down their huge record collections. Vinyl records were being replaced by eight track tapes and Ort would pay a fair price for them. No one remembers whose idea it was, but the guys decided to give the money to Gary. Another quarter's expenses were coming up and the cash from their combined efforts would get him off to a good start.

It was fun going through the albums and reminiscing about the past few years – some titles even went back to their early "Hut" days.

Who could forget seeing James Brown "feelin' good" with the Fabulous Flames – and that killer horn section on "I Feel Good?"

John pulled out a Three Dog Night album. "Wish I had a dollar for every time I've heard 'Joy to the World.'"

"Still haven't figured out the 'Jeremiah was a bullfrog' thing yet," Ed said. "But I'm sure one day some squirrely professor will do a paper on it."

They brought out one record after the other – taking time to enjoy it all.

The poignant "Keep On Smilin'" by Capricorn artist Wet Willie from Macon. "Running on Empty" by Jackson Brown and The Who's "We Don't Get Fooled Again," Joni Mitchell's "I've Looked at Clouds from Both Sides Now," The Guess Who and a collection of smooth ballads from Atlanta boys, The Classics Four.

"And remember Janis Joplin gettin' all philosophical with that great line from 'Me and Bobby McKee'? – 'Freedom's just another word for nothing left to lose.'"

They ended up hauling four full boxes of records down to Ort's, laid them out on his counter and watched Ort's eyes light up as he surveyed the offerings. No doubt the vinyl would sell well – they were all big hits and in great condition. The guys felt really good about helping Gary.

Will Andrews had been thrown into the deep end of the journalism business and survived. And when the dust settled, it was apparent to all that he'd actually done a pretty good job of covering the trial. What's more, he had some solid experience under his belt and the job front looked more promising. A couple of editors had taken note of Will's work and set up interviews.

One Last Big Game

One more big game then the Dawgs were bowl bound! When the fun of football pleasantly mingles with the joy of the holidays, it's icing on the cake for the citizens of Athens.

No matter how disappointing the season had been, Will and Ginny hit a big pre-game party with other fans who all embraced an unwavering belief that the Dawgs would still triumph in the end. The finest Dawg fans, with the longest and strongest UGA lineage, gathered.

The age-old stories of big games and big plays took on mythic proportions as they were passed from generation to generation. Just as the ancient Athenians passed on their Homeric tales, the youngsters of Athens, Ga. had heard the heralded feats of UGA stars *again and again* – retold by countless coaches, teachers, preachers – really anywhere three or more old codgers gathered to rehash, and inevitably embellish, the tales of old. They savored every detail and spared no superlatives and all it took was the most obscure reference to UGA's past to trigger the storytelling.

"Funny you should mention that, I'll never forget...." is the way it would start and you practically had to get a Vaudevillian stagehand with one of those giant hooks to drag the bard from the spotlight. These pre-game rituals were great entertainment in themselves. The most reserved, accountant-like citizen went through a total transformation. He'd start re-enacting the play – gesticulating expansively – and then commandeer whatever household object was handy to use as the game ball. Bystanders came in as half-backs, somebody blocked and bankers *went long* in packed living rooms while women frantically pulled their children to safety, dogs howled and perfectly good lamps were demolished.

And the menfolk weren't the only fanatics. Athens's most esteemed matriarchs threw off restraint and cheered with the best of 'em. They'd carry on in the loveliest of aristocratic Southern drawls – "Go Jaw-ga! Go! ... Go! Jaw-ga Go!" and with each sip of their "special punch" the roars only got louder.

During the week, these ladies were the very picture of respectability – decorum reigned from start to finish – but at the first sound of Larry Munson's voice, they changed into fire breathing fiends. Don't be asking for any recipes or inquire about the cousins over in Fulton County until the game was over. And when post-game analysis started, nobody was surprised when the ladies rattled off as many arcane sports stats and team trivia as the male "experts" lounging in their Lazy Boys.

Will and Ginny were most happy to follow in the footsteps of these diehard Dawgs fans.

BEYOND THE YELLOW
BRICK ROAD

"What gorgeous flowers. How'd you find this place?" Ginny asked. "Looks historic."

The couple ambled along through the exquisitely groomed and manicured gardens.

"Yeah, I thought you'd like it here. That small building over there honors the first garden club in America. It started right here in Athens. Pretty cool isn't it? I think there's something like 300 different kinds of plants and flowers on this little plot of land."

"It's really beautiful," Ginny said.

"Just like you."

Will threw a blanket on the ground and pulled out two Varsity takeout boxes. It was a perfect day for a picnic.

"Don't know how I've missed this? I walk the quad all the time – but it's kind of tucked away," Ginny said.

"Do you know what today is?" Will asked as he took her hand.

"Sure, it's Thursday – why?"

"It's our anniversary. We met five months ago today and had our first date at the Varsity. Remember?

Ginny smiled. "Yeah, I guess it is."

"I was going to get you some flowers but here's a whole garden, just for you."

"How sweet."

"OK, choose the ones you like best and I'll pick 'em and bring 'em over."

"Will, you can't do that!"

"OK, guess not. But check out that rose over there," Will said.

"It's really spectacular."

"I think you should go over and take a closer look."

Ginny shook her head. "Will, you're actin' kinda strange, even for you."

"Stop and smell the roses, right? So go ahead. You won't believe the scent."

Ginny walked over. "OK, if you insist. But that looks like a bee or something."

"Better not be a Yellow Jacket," Will said.

Ginny took a closer look and screamed. "Will! It's a ring!"

Will jumped to his feet. "I know and I love you! I really love you. Will you marry me?"

The seconds seemed like hours as Will waited for her answer. He watched her giggle and flutter around and finally she said "Yes!"

The lunches were long forgotten (but enjoyed by marauding ants) as the young couple cuddled and kissed on the blanket, oblivious to anyone passing by.

After a while, they floated through the quad, practically waltzing to the Arch where they paused for another long embrace. Blissfully unaware of anything or anyone around them, a bewildered young guy finally got their attention. "Uh, excuse me, but I lost my tour group. The guide said if we got separated, just to wait by some kind of steel arch or something. Is this it?"

Will grinned at the awkward young fellow. "Yeah, just turn around. That's it right there."

All evening, Will and Ginny talked endlessly and completely lost track of time. Neither wanted the day to end and it was very late by the time Will finally took her home.

As he drove away, he replayed the scene over and over in his mind – and each time he still couldn't believe it – *she said yes!*

Everything was a delightful blur as he thought about the past few months and then imagined the years they'd have together. And most of all, he thought about the girl he absolutely adored.

He flipped on the radio and a familiar tune broke into his thoughts.

"...so goodbye yellow brick road."

Yeah, that's it, he thought, *four years of "the yellow brick road"...and it's almost over.*

Then Elton sang it: *"I've finally decided my future lies beyond the yellow brick road."*

Will smiled.

EPILOGUE

The Athenian Oath

The Athenian Oath was recited by the citizens of Athens, Greece over 2,000 years ago. It is frequently referenced by civic leaders in modern times as a timeless code of civic responsibility. Athenian youth took this oath when they turned seventeen. This stirring admonition is on a Greek statue of Athena placed downtown at the Banner Herald plaza in 1996 when Athens was one of the venues for the Olympics.

"We will never bring disgrace on this our City by an act of dishonesty or cowardice. We will fight for the ideals and Sacred Things of the City both alone and with many. We will revere and obey the City's laws, and will do our best to incite a like reverence and respect in those above us who are prone to annul them or set them at naught. We will strive unceasingly to quicken the public's sense of civic duty. Thus, in all these ways, we will transmit this City not only, not less, but greater and more beautiful than it was transmitted to us."

ABOUT THE AUTHORS

Doug Vinson was born and raised in Athens, Ga.and earned an undergraduate and Master's degree from the University of Georgia (making him a double Dawg).

In addition to teaching college journalism courses at The University of West Georgia and Radford University among other schools, he's also worked more than 30 years in public relations for colleges and corporate organizations.

Doug and June have been happily married for 38 years and have collaborated on a number of writing projects including a well-received play, "A Redneck Opera." Their most enduring collaboration was raising their two children, Jess and Mark.

The Vinsons now live in the south Atlanta area.

www.facebook.com/1collegetown